Forgetful

By
Nick Mann

Strategic Book Publishing and Rights Co.

Strategic Book Publishing and Rights Co.
12620 FM 1960, Suite A4-507
Houston TX 77065
www.sbpra.com

ISBN: 978-1-62516-857-3

To Ruth

Table of Contents

Table of Contents

Table of Contents

Prelude

Seminar Incident

August 1999: Dr. Benjamin Parks walked into Douglass Hall and thought, *I don't know if I'll ever do this again. But I'm going to remember and cherish this summer. This has been quite a ride.*

"Good morning, Dr. Parks," Ben heard as he crested the steps up to the second floor. Delia Menendez and Xia Liang stood at the door to the seminar room as if waiting for him to arrive.

"Good morning, young ladies," he replied. "Isn't the classroom open?"

Ben was distracted by these young ladies and something he'd observed on more than one occasion during the summer. They were both drop-dead gorgeous. Ben fought to keep the lecherous old man thoughts from showing visibly on his face. This effort, he found, was made much easier because Addie had been so exceedingly nice to him the night before. He realized that Delia was speaking.

"It's open," she said. "Xia just wanted to say something to you before we went in."

Ben slowed his walk forward, stopped in front of them, and waited.

Xia spoke hesitantly.

"Dr. Parks, sir. I have made a comment in my journal. I showed it to Delia and told her that I wanted to discuss it with you in private. She said 'no.' She said that it should be public so everyone can hear."

Xia looked over to Delia for encouragement. Delia nodded.

Ben asked, "What would help you, Xia?"

"I am an undergrad, Dr. Parks. Everyone else is a grad student. They are all very smart and very confident. They have strong

9

opinions. I want to say something, but then I wait my turn. My turn never comes."

Another guilty thought, *I'm obviously not monitoring and doing a great job of gatekeeping. I should have seen that Xia wanted to say something. I should have let her in.*

Ben was having a hard time staying focused this morning. He hoped that didn't continue because he knew that the most important skill required in facilitating a seminar like this was the ability to stay present and in the moment as the process twisted and turned in unexpected directions.

Xia continued, "Dr. Parks, I want to practice. I want to share with the students. But I am a little shy. Will you help me?"

"Of course, I will. How shall I help you, Xia?"

"Call on me, Dr. Parks. Just call on me. Okay?"

How elegantly simple was this request.

"I will, Xia. And thank you for asking."

***

Gillian on the Porch

May 2006: Ben Parks sat on the enclosed porch with his mom as she sipped lemonade from a straw. Ben's dad Richard Parks had dropped her off so he could run some errands. Gillian Parks couldn't be left alone because she wandered into things, got confused, and had been known to have accidents. Penelope Parks Tompkins, Ben's younger sister, now lived with their parents, but she'd gone out of town for the weekend to visit her own grandkids . . . leaving Dad alone to watch Gillian.

Gillian, at one time, had been a fabulous cook. She'd majored in home economics at that Alabama HBCU so long ago. In those days, "Home Ec" was considered one of the only sensible majors for a black woman if she really wanted to get a job. To this day, she loved cooking shows, so Ben had turned the satellite TV on the porch to "The Iron Chef" program. Gillian stared at the fifty-inch Samsung flat screen and seemed to recognize something. Ben wasn't sure. But with her occupied and safe for the moment, Ben went to the kitchen to refresh her lemonade. Suddenly, from the porch, he heard his ninety-one-year-old mom's voice, "E, I, C;" then, "A, C, I;" then, "I, A, G, I, C, E." Gillian had gone into another zone, calling out "nonsense"

10

letters Ben thought . . . many random letters, signifying nothing . . . and he had very mixed emotions.

Part One:
The Beginning

Chapter 1
The Alley Incident

A Friday afternoon in August 1999: Loud voices from back in the alley caught the attention of Benjamin Parks as he walked his slow, end-of-the-day–and-I'm-really-tired walk between the Green Line Metro station near Howard U. and his home on Elm Street, NW, just past 5th. Fifty-five-year-old Ben Parks' light gray linen suit was wrinkled, and the light gray short sleeved Pronto-Uomo crew neck he wore was probably a bit musty . . . "*but not terribly so,*" he'd mused as he put it on for a second day's wearing this morning. He wore his small JanSport combination backpack and roller bag with toilet articles, sleeping shorts, and a couple more duplicate Pronto-Uomo shirts, one white and one black. On his shoulder was his cloth briefcase with lightweight Toshiba NB205 computer, pens, and assorted paper files. And on the other side, in his hand, was the eco-friendly Casio power point projector he carried for the sort of two and a half day job he had just finished. It had been the kind of assignment he loved more than anything else: extended work with small leadership or decision making groups, or other sorts of teams. Ben felt the sweat on his face and back and now thought that tomorrow morning, he'd definitely need a fresh shirt. Tomorrow's challenge would be in an entirely different world of focus.

Ben's feet were hurting. His feet almost always hurt . . . flat as they were. In warm weather, he liked wearing sandals, fortified with his special orthotics . . . but only sandals that he could shine. None of those rough leather, earth-shoe looking clogs. He liked highly-shined shoes. Currently, he wore a brown pair of Rockport Coastal Creek Slides and he looked down to see a single scuff caused by that misstep he'd made stepping up from street to sidewalk just a moment ago. Ben could be clumsy. It wasn't unusual for him to get his feet crossed or trip when walking. He also dropped things. That was one of the little patterns that really got on his nerves—dropping things. Well, he thought ruefully, he liked shining shoes. So, the little blemish on his sandals would give him an excuse for shoe shining—one quiet and relaxing task this evening.

But the biggest task for the evening was the prep work for tomorrow's seminar, which might not be easy going. This teaching gig with the local university consortium was in some ways a labor of love. Certainly, it didn't put a whole lot of food on the table. To earn money, Ben was a consultant. He worked with federal agencies and a few big corporations, as well as with some select non-profits at a much-reduced rate, mainly helping them to deal with needed changes on the inside or undesired changes imposed from the outside.

It was a pleasant evening, probably in the upper seventies. This was one of the good days for Washington during those funny weather times in the late autumn. Ben listened to the incongruity between the noises that had stopped him in his tracks and the chirping of birds and scurrying of squirrels completing their end-of-day digging—wherever they could find a tree-box to dig in here in the LeDroit Park section of town. He stopped and listened at the entrance to an alley. There definitely was trouble brewing, and this was his neighborhood. He was two blocks from his home. If it were later and completely dark, he might not have ventured back there. He might have listened for a while, and if he became too alarmed at the noises, called 911 from his cell phone. But with enough light left in the day so that he could at least see clearly ahead and all around him, he moved quietly toward the voices that were getting louder with every step.

"Wha-da-fuck was u eyeballing her foh?" said one gravely male voice for perhaps the tenth time.

"Man, I wasn't paying no tention to that skank," said another voice . . . at which point there was the audible noise of a punch and a deep grunt just as Ben rounded the turn in the alley. Stooped over on one-knee, the victim of the confrontation was dressed in wrinkled Wrangler jeans with an obviously hand-me-down and loose fitting athletic shirt inscribed with the number seventeen and the name "Doug Williams." His short nappy hair was uncombed and matted as if no grooming of any sort had been done in a while. He was trying to catch his breath.

Three young men were all dressed in the standard uniform of the hood at that time: white or black A-form undershirts (they called them wife beaters) with blue or black jeans from The Mad Skills Store on Georgia Avenue, and no belts. The jeans all dropped mid-way down their asses. The one in front had a large gold watch chain tied from one of the belt loops and flowing down and back up into his right front pocket. One of the young men behind the lead instigator wore locks tied up with a black bandana. The other was shaved headed—what the young folks called, "the cue ball." The leader's hair was in an elaborate and well-kept corn row design. The three attackers wore fancy black Nike sneakers, with not a mark or scuff anywhere to be seen.

"Who-da-fuck you callin' skank, you piece-shit? I beatchu 'til yesday cum back."

The three street-uniformed young men, probably in their late teens or early twenties, stood around the fourth man, who might have been eighteen or nineteen. He was coughing and holding his gut. But Ben couldn't see any blood. Just then, one of the other three tapped the puncher on the shoulder. He turned and looked at Ben.

Smiling, Ben asked, "You dudes won't mind a witness, will you?"

His eyes on the puncher, he kept the other two standing men in his peripherals as he forced his expression to stay even. He clutched his computer bag over his right shoulder, and felt the tug of the back pack. Now realizing that his left hand was occupied with his power point projector, Ben thought he was really unprepared with this load for a situation that might require some quick defensive movement.

One of the men behind the puncher screamed, "Ol man, u betta get yo ass outta here. Wha-da-fuck's wrong wichu?"

"Nothing's wrong with me, but thanks for asking" said Ben. "You know, it's the end of the day. I've been working all day and, you know, man, I could use a beer at the end of the day. I just got off the Metro."

The young men were starting to look at each other and a smile was coming into Cue Ball's face. The young man on the ground started to stand, but was kind of wobbly. Ben took one step forward, dropped the projector bag and helped the man regain his feet as he continued.

"I'm trying to get home to kick off my shoes, pee, put on some

Miles, and suck down a beer . . . when I hear this noise back here in the alley in our peaceful neighborhood."

Though his buddies were unfreezing, the puncher was still glaring.

"Dis punk yoh frien? Maybe, I needa fuck u up, too."

Ben paused, an extended silence. Then, "I really hope you don't do that, son. You know I'm sceered ah you." (Ben tried to copy the vernacular speech his sons used so frequently around the house. He knew he wasn't good at it, but he tried anyway.) "I mean who wouldn't be, as ripped as you are. You work out, don't you?"

The man looked hesitant and, for the first time, relaxed the scowl.

"I hope you won't kick my ass. I don't even think it's necessary." Ben paused. "But," he continued, "If you do, I guess I'll just have to try to remember as much as I can about you. Does that make sense to you?"

Having regained his composure, the young man who had been struck started stumbling past Ben toward the street, and Ben picked up his projector and stepped over as he passed to place his body between the three tough guys and the retreating man. After he was out of sight, Ben asked, "Well, is there anything else we need to talk about, young men?"

"U Tony's ol man ain'tcha?" asked one of the three.

"Oh, you know my boy. Have you guys been to my house?"

The puncher shrugged his shoulders and raised his hands to the sides in a gesture of exasperation. He looked back at his boys, and they were both grinning at Ben. Now, he stared at them with a serious expression.

Ben had started to feel that drip and then the tingling in the back of his throat just a moment ago. Why, at the most inconvenient times did he have to deal with this particular one of his many ailments? Now the tingling was starting. Abruptly came the coughing . . .

"Argh, argh, argh, argh, argh, argh, argh."

Ben was now stooped over. The nasty looking phlegm from his chronic bronchitis came out as he spit to the side. The boys were watching, as he reached with his right hand into his pocket and took out his Albuterol inhaler . . . exhale, squeeze, and inhale . . . two quick puffs of mist. Cue Ball and Black Bandanna had actually stepped forward with looks of concern on their faces. Lead Guy just stood with a look of disbelief.

"You okay, Ol Man?" said Black Bandanna.

"Yeah, 'cept I just blew any tough guy image I wuz workin'. Thanks, son!"

Things settled and he stood and composed himself.

"It's been nice talking to you fine young men."

Ben backed out for about ten steps, and then turned his back and walked the rest of the two blocks to his home.

Chapter 2
Home Cooking

That night Ben put three place settings at the table. He had come in and cooked some whole wheat spaghetti with turkey meat sauce that swam with mushrooms and tomato pieces. He placed a bowl of mustard greens from the Sista Chef, heated on the stove straight out of the can except for the slices of bacon he'd added, on a coaster on the dining room table. Ben and the boys loved almost anything made by Sista Chef. His younger son, Rico, was upstairs . . . probably drawing, as usual.

"Rico! Wash up and come on down for dinner," he yelled up the stairs.

As the eighteen-year-old Rico plodded down the steps, Ben's twenty-five-year old son Tony came through the front door sporting his heavily wrapped left hand, his short cast showing up past his wrist. Tony had sprained his hand on a heavy bag and had been lucky not to break it. He had broken it once before in his fifth amateur boxing match several years earlier. Nonetheless, Tony came in with his usual whirlwind of energy, smiles, confusion, and mischief.

"Sup, Pop? What's for dinner?" asked Tony. That was how Tony always came home. Ben was already serving Rico's plate, and Tony could see that it was spaghetti. Ben didn't answer, but smiled.

That's my son . . . Tony, he thought. *Just likes to hear himself talk.*

Soon thereafter, Addie, Ben's wife, came in. She'd been to some kind of teacher in-service training that happened each year before schools started up again in September. Ben stepped toward the front door to greet her. She paused. "B," she said quietly.

"Hey, A, how was your day?" he asked.

"Fine and yours?" responded Addie, as she moved quickly past him up the stairs.

Ben looked after the retreating figure of his wife. He always liked to watch her from behind. She wore a 50 percent cotton and 50 percent silk, olive green, two-piece pants outfit made in India and imported by a trendy boutique shop over in Takoma Park, Maryland, a suburb of DC. The outfit fit her form loosely, as was usually her preference unless she was wearing jeans. In her ears, Addie wore her customary small diamonds that were the everyday jewelry on display when she didn't want to bring out the heavy artillery. She had nothing at the neck other than the lanyard with her Montgomery County Public School System ID badge and assorted classroom keys. Her outfit was completed by comfortably fitting and understated sandals. But especially from the rear, Addie's nicely put together figure always enticed Ben.

"I know what you're doing Benjamin" said Addie without turning or slowing her step.

"You know I love you, A," called Ben loudly because now she was upstairs out of sight. Ben returned to the dining room.

"Pop, you're an *old* dog, but you're still a dog," teased Tony. Rico chuckled softly.

"Mind your bee's wax, youngin,'" said Ben, re-taking his seat.

The father and two sons sat at the dinner table. Mostly Tony needled Rico about all manner of things that black teenage boys thought about those days. Pac couldn't out spit Biggie. Biggie was the bomb. The Football Team (Addie and Ben forbade anyone in the house to say the full name of the Washington professional football team) were going to beat the Texas team twice this season—home and away.

Addie laughed loudly from upstairs. Ben heard her ending one of her nightly calls. It was some quick rehash of an incident at school today with one of her co-workers. Then she hung up and came back down to the kitchen. By now, she was dressed down into more comfortable at-home clothes—one of Ben's oversized Howard University sweatshirts, a relaxed set of cut-off jeans, and bare feet. She was arranging her meal on a TV tray when Rico got reinforcements. The doorbell rang, and Sammy (alias "Sniff" because of his asthma and his nose, which was often runny . . . though not today) and Derek (or "Dirk" as all Rico's friends called him) piled through the front door and into the dining room.

Sniff would later that year be the first of either of his two son's friends to succumb to the violence of the DC streets. He would be mowed down randomly in a drive-by shortly after graduating from Harris Multicultural High School. Graduating together from the Washington High School for the Arts, Dirk and Rico would then go on to collaborate for years in their budding professional music career . . . after Rico shifted his focus completely away from the visual arts. They would never forget Sniff, and several of Dirk and Rico's lyrics would be remembrances of their lost friend. The boys grabbed chairs and Ben quickly said, "You can't eat at my table without washing your hands."

Both young men barely missed running into Addie with her TV tray as they reluctantly stepped back to the first-floor bathroom. "'Scuse us, Ms. Parks," said Sniff.

"Don't run in the house," answered Addie with her big, public school teacher voice.

Then Ben heard the water running. Did they wash their hands? Ben didn't know, but at least they went through the motions of humoring him. They grabbed their own place settings and helped themselves.

For the rest of the pleasant dinner, the arguments were more even. Tony could hold-forth in just about any verbal contest, but Rico, Sniff, and Dirk all had their views and they stuck them in whenever Tony took a breath. In one exchange, Sniff sniffled. Tony said, "Boy, you got another cold. Every time you come in here, you got a cold: summer, fall, winter, or spring."

Sniff said, "It's not a cold and you know it. It's asthma."

"Asthma. What the hell is asthma? You clog up and your nose runs, it's a cold. You cough, you got a cold. You got the chills, you got a cold. That bronamasaurus thang Pops is always talkin' bout, ain't nothing but a cold . . . and while I'm at it, the other day, I heard one of those TV doctors talking about that pneumonia thang. He was saying that a lot of people say they have a cold when they have pneumonia. And then he said, you can't catch a cold just from going out in the cold. I tell you every time I don't dress right in this funny weather, I catch a cold. If you got pneumonia, as far as I'm concerned, you got a cold."

Ben wasn't much of a small talker, but he just laughed out loud at this. Even Addie heard this soliloquy from upstairs where she was talking on the phone with her sister, Sue Ann, who still lived back in Newcastle, PA where Addie grew up. Addie called down yelling, "Tony, you're one crazy boy. And, yuns (whenever she talked to her sister, she slipped back into the Western PA lingo) need to keep down the noise in this house."

Ben laughed but didn't comment. His son had taken a liking to kinesiology in school and now was becoming a personal trainer, and Ben knew that he could differentiate between asthma, a cold, bronchitis, and pneumonia. But he knew that Tony just had to have something to say and the more he could get under Sniff's skin (all in fun), the more he liked it. Ben, in his more sarcastic moods, used to say, "Anyone with too much to say has to be lying, because there's not that much truth in the world."

Ben Parks didn't enjoy chit chat, but he liked listening as long as his sons didn't try to draw him in. And, they didn't.

Your children know you better than anyone else in life, thought Ben.

When through the years, Ben had tried to chit chat, invariably he either quickly bored himself to tears, ran out of ideas, forgot what he was saying, or his mouth got out of sync with his brain and Ben said something patently stupid. None of those felt good. So here, he ate, listened, and smiled. He loved to listen. He loved these young men. Of course, he loved Tony and Rico. He loved Sniff and Dirk, too, though they weren't his.

Tony had all kinds of friends from all over the city. A lot were from the neighborhood and a lot were his former classmates from the Harris Multicultural and Vocational High School where Sniff was now in school, located over in the Columbia Heights section of the District. But Tony's contacts extended into many corners of DC, and traveling through the city with him was like witnessing Mr. Network himself.

"Sup, Tony?" "Hey, T!" "Sappnin' Big Man."

Those were some of the variations of the greetings he got . . . all returned with some sort of hip response that Ben thought he should write down . . . but by the time he'd found a piece of paper, he'd forgotten that particular exchange and three more had occurred in the meanwhile. Ben was a lover of language, and he appreciated the rich and colorful banter of the young urban scene.

Rico, who if he wasn't drawing in the house, was always trying to get over to "uncle" Levi's in-home recording studio. Ben's high school best friend had become an international music force. He often gigged in the Apple or on the West Coast, but Levi Chance also directed the choir at church, and he taught Rico the ins and outs of his thirty-six-track recording board whenever Ben's younger son could sneak over there to his pretend "uncle" Levi for a lesson. Rico was quieter than Tony and had fewer apparent friends. But the ones that he had were as thick as thieves. They went to school together, hung with each other, and they all seemed to love Ben's cooking . . . whether it was spaghetti, chili, fried chicken, smothered chicken, barbecued shrimp, grilled steaks, layered ground beef lasagna with small pieces of sausage and mushroom slices, or his all-time most famous dish—fried fish (it might be catfish, tilapia, whiting, croakers, or a combination on any given day) cooked with canola oil out in the backyard in one of Ben's huge black skillets.

On the weekends, Ben's big southern breakfast spreads were the talk around the neighborhood kids (Rico's friends all called him Pop): bacon, sausages, salmon cakes, fried oysters, grits, home fries smothered in onions (with a small side plate of potatoes free of onions for Tony—who could spot an onion on the dining room table all the way from his bedroom upstairs). There were all manner of eggs with or without the yokes, biscuits, the fluffiest pancakes anyone could remember having, whole wheat cheese toast, cinnamon-raisin French toast, and buttermilk with a side-plate stacked with individually wrapped Lactaid pills for anyone who needed them. And there were those New Orleans styled beignets— Ben had been perfecting them since he'd gotten hooked at the little diner place down on 18th Street in Adams Morgan—along with decaf coffee, decaf teas, and all manner of juices.

Saturday morning breakfast at the Parks' house ran from about 9:00 a.m. until 1:00 p.m. This was the mission of Chef Ben. But for Sniff and Dirk, there was no waiting for the weekends. They showed up almost anytime, especially around meal time.

"Hey, Pop!" said Sniff.

"What's happening, Pop?" asked Dirk.

"Fellows, what a pleasant surprise," came the usual cryptic joke from Ben.

All of these neighborhood kids' parents knew Ben, and he knew them. He had been in the neighborhood for several years before Addie and Adam (Ben's step son) had moved in after the marriage.

Neighbors were generally cordial, but most probably couldn't have been called friends . . . even the men who stopped by the backyard in warm weather for dominos (muggins AKA "add fives" was the only game allowed), high and low bid whist with or without jokers, double-deck pinochle, tonk, or Ben's favorite small stakes gambling game—Bouree (street spelling: Boo Ray).

Ben also had a lot of colleagues, clients, and professional associates. But he didn't make many new friendships of the sort that he had with Levi, Davita, Lou, Clyde, Tracy, Gerald, and a few others from the old Michigan Park neighborhood where he'd grown up back in the day. What Ben had were neighbors, colleagues, clients and students, old friends with an emphasis on the "old," dance partners, and family—plenty of family. In fact, the size of Ben's family was almost matched by the size of Addie's—who were mostly back in Western Pennsylvania, but some also in New Jersey.

In the parental routine of today, however, all the LeDroit Park neighborhood parents seemed to appreciate anything the others would do to ensure their kids were safely engaged and away from the danger that potentially loomed around every corner in the streets. Gone were the days of the fist fight. Ben knew he probably wouldn't survive in his sons' streets. He'd been too hot tempered. He'd rejoiced at his younger son's quiet even-keel, but Tony had always worried him greatly. He thought that, perhaps Tony's saving grace from the sudden MAC-10, TEC-9, or Glock induced tragedy, was that everybody knew him and everybody seemed to like him. Ben always worried, nonetheless.

There were LeDroit Park neighborhood parents who drove kids. There were parents who went bowling with kids or took kids to ball games. There were parents who pretended to shop at the mall, though their real purpose was to just be there because that's where their kids hung out. There were parents who were sticklers about homework and could get kids (theirs or those friends of theirs to whom they had access) to open their books after school and at least pretend to study.

Ben could cook. That was his contribution. He enjoyed cooking and seeing young black men eat. He never had daughters and very few young neighborhood girls came by. Not until they were older and had girlfriends, did Tony or Rico ever bring any "females" as they were called to the house. A couple of incidents along the way had immediately brought Addie from downstairs, and she would watch those young girls who dared to enter like a hawk. News probably traveled fast around the neighborhood.

Ben enjoyed the boys' frivolity and their colorful, though usually coarse language. Mostly, he really enjoyed the deep friendship that they obviously had for each other. As this particular meal wrapped up, the boys started up the stairs to Rico's room.

"I know you're not going to stuff yourselves and then leave me with all those dishes" said Ben.

Dirk blushed and rushed back down and into the kitchen. Rico and Sniff followed less enthusiastically. But the deed, eventually, was done by the three of them. Ben didn't watch . . . he didn't want to.

Chapter 3
The Trainer

Tony grabbed a gym bag that he had dropped when he came in the house. "Come on, Pop," he said, "let's go out to the porch?"

Quizzically, Ben moved toward the front of the house.

"Not the den-porch Pop; the back porch."

Ben wheeled around to his son. He was mostly a serious guy, but they'd put him in a good mood. "In the back is 'outside.' The porch is on the side."

"Pop" said Tony. "You and A fixed that two years ago. It used to be a side porch. Now, it's all enclosed and frrresh. It's a den."

"Son, let me break it down. The next owners of this house can call it a den if they want. They won't know any better because they won't have ever seen it as a side porch. If we die and you inherit the house, you can call it a den. For me and my wife, it used to be a porch and it's a porch now. It's just a really, really nice porch now. You got that!"

Amused and for once lost for words, Tony had stopped dead in his tracks. Finally, he said, "Furious! My man!"

This was a moniker that one of Tony's friends had put on Ben some years back, when the movie "Boyz in the Hood" was out. Tony gave his Pop some dap as they walked "outside." On the way through the back door, Tony reached into the gym bag and retrieved an assortment of what looked like colored flags. He turned to his dad with his hand out and smiled.

"Go ahead, Pop. Take them."

As he felt the gifts, Ben realized they weren't flags. Their feel was rubberish. There was a red one, a yellow one, and blue one. Ben saw a logo on the red one that read, "Stretcha-band."

Tony watched his dad realize what they were. Reaching out, Tony felt beside Ben's neck on the left side.

"How are those traps feeling?" he asked. "Maybe they're getting a little better? Are you back swimming yet?"

"Nope" said Ben. "I'm scared of hurting myself even more."

Ben knew his frequent spasms in various parts of his body had nothing to do with his swimming. He knew they were mostly caused by his long stretches sitting at the computer when he was in his home-office in the basement, as well as by the long days in front of client groups where he seldom sat, and where he often took notes on boards in front of the room for hours at a time while group members discussed whatever issue that had stumped them. Their being stumped was why they employed the services of an organization development (OD) consultant in the first place.

Ben's spasm pain, whenever it cropped up, usually stopped him from swimming. It also stopped him from moving around effortlessly in rooms with small to large groups wrestling with this planning issue, that productivity problem, or the other problems of folks not sharing information or wanting to work together. The pain stopped Ben from dancing, which was one of his socializing routines. In the late years, he hadn't danced as often as he once did. But he tried to swim three times per week whenever he was home in DC. He didn't have access to swimming in New York, where he spent at least one week per month on client assignments. Dancing was aerobic and fun, but swimming was for everything: body, mind, and spirit . . . the whole package. And after coming out of the pool and showering, his ten or fifteen minutes in the dry sauna were like heaven. This time relaxed him—as long as he hydrated well to stave off a bout of coughing.

But now Tony had grabbed the red band from his Pop's hand and expertly tied it on the metal banister of the steps that led down onto a small patio and garden. The knot was in the middle of the four and one-half foot band, and Tony demonstrated while he instructed.

"What you're going to do is hold each end back here."

He took a step back from the place where the knot in the center connected with the banister pole.

"Then, you're going to pull back evenly and slowly on both sides, keeping your elbows into your side. As you pull back, you're going to close your scapula."

Tony stopped. "Those are those big bones on your back, Pop."

"I know what the hell scapula are, you wise-ass!" said Ben. Tony just grinned.

Continuing, Tony said, "With your scapula as close to touching as you can manage, you're going to count slowly to ten and then release back to the front slowly. You're going to do five or six reps of that, twice every day."

Ben grabbed the band ends from his son and executed the movement. Awkward at first, he picked it up on the third rep, with plenty of unwanted coaching, which felt like needling, from his offspring.

"Is that it?" Ben asked his son.

"Nope! Just one more thing" said Tony. He took the yellow band and tied it in a loop around the lowest part of the same banister pole.

"You say you've been having trouble with your free-style kick. Here's what you're going to do twice a day for the next week, along with the one I just showed you. In a week, you're going to try to get back in the pool."

Getting past the issue that his son was being quite authoritative in telling his father what to do, Ben was interested and amused. Tony stuck his Jordan-clad right foot through the loop that was lying on the floor. He braced himself with his left hand against the opposite railing, lifted the foot that was inside the loop, and slowly began to kick out until the band was stretched taut. When he was there, Tony counted aloud, "One, two, three, four, five, six, seven, eight, nine, and ten."

Then he slowly let the tension out of the band back to his starting position.

"See that, Pop. You're also going to do that twice a day along with the other one. I'll have you cut like me in no time. Those old ladies at the pool won't be able to keep their eyes off you."

Before Ben could say anything, Tony said, "Now, I gotta run."

Tony paused and then said, "Before I split, Pop, word on the street is that you had a run-in with a dude who calls himself Chaos."

Ben was surprised. His expression registered confusion.

"Don't play me, Pop! Just this afternoon, you were in an alley with Chaos and a couple of his boys."

Now the scene and the dude with the fancy corn rows came to Ben.

"Damn! Word travels fast."

Ben looked at his son with amazement. Then a thought hit him and he instantly worried.

"Don't say anything to Addie!"

"Pop" said Tony. "I'm not going to say anything to your wife 'cause she'll say it was dumb for your old-ass going back and mixin' with those wanna-be-toughs. So, I'll say it. That was dumb, Pop!"

Silence . . . then he said, "Yeah, it probably was dumb."

More silence. . . .

"There's something obvious that you oughta be saying now Pop," said Tony.

Still more silence . . . Ben understood.

"No, I can't really say what would happen if that situation came up again. You want me to say I wouldn't do it again. And maybe I wouldn't. And maybe I would. I don't know, T."

"Pop, you used to always talk to us about consequences . . . intended consequences and unintended consequences. Remember?"

Ben nodded, worried about where his son was going. Tony continued, "You know if something foul had gone down, I'd have to act."

Suddenly, Ben was terrified. "Shit, shit, shit!!" was the only thing he could say.

Actions have ripples, he thought.

"Tony, I made an on-the-spot calculation it would be okay . . . and it was okay. But if it hadn't been, that would have been my bad and my responsibility . . . not yours."

Tony smiled an odd smile—part love, part sympathy, and part street wisdom. Then, after more silence, he said, "Pop, it don't work that way. Just know that. Now, I gotta run."

Chapter 4
Fights

Tony and Ben went back in and through the house to the front door. Tony was in the lead and he'd slammed the door before Ben could catch it. Ben, with a heavy heart from the conversation he'd just finished, slowed to inspect the job done by Sniff, Dirk, and Rico on the dishes in the kitchen. He was having a hard time focusing.

When, he thought, *did life become so freakin' convoluted and so damn difficult?*

He refocused on the kitchen.

Not bad, thought Ben. *Not great, but not bad.*

The job probably wouldn't be good enough for Addie . . . but Ben would take the grief if any was coming.

"You be safe, Pop," said Tony waving as he hurried out to his old junker of a car—hoopdie as the kids called it—a 1985 green and black Toyota Cressida with about one hundred and fifty thousand miles on it. Before sliding in behind the wheel, one more look from Tony. "Please be safe, Pop!"

Ben waved. Tony pulled off.

"Too loud . . . that car needs a muffler . . . used to be top-of-the line in the Toyota family" Ben thought as he watched Tony drive away—seat pushed way back in a way that always made Ben wonder how his son could even see the road.

Tony's baby-mama (Coral Peterson) went to night school, and Tony was expected to take the precocious kid (AR for Ashton Robert Peterson) to his apartment, make him do his homework, and otherwise occupy him until about 10:00 p.m. when Coral would retrieve Ben's grandson for the rest of the night. The routine would have been unconventional in Ben's generation, but was fairly common with the young DC parents of today. Ben listened as he walked back inside. He could barely hear the boys upstairs in Rico's bedroom.

That's good, he thought to himself. He didn't want them to be loud. This was Addie's quiet time.

Ben thought again about Tony as he went out back to indulge himself in one of his rituals. He knew the sun would set soon. He'd poured himself three fingers of that single malt Irish whiskey from the liquor cabinet, dropped in a few cubes, and stepped out back to commune with nature. Down the steps from where Tony had just given him this new workout routine, he sat on the patio in one of his two blue painted metal chairs with the cushions made of waterproof material; and stared out across the small yard to the break in the opposite houses where, as luck would have it, some architect of long ago had arranged for him to be able to see the sun as it went down in the late summer and fall every year. How prescient that architect must have been.

Anthony Richard Parks, Ben's first born. After high school and with his girlfriend pregnant, Tony had worked construction. He'd also started doing security, even before he turned twenty-one, at local clubs. Not the kind of clubs that his Pop went to. DC had a bustling night scene, and there were clubs catering to all clienteles. The clubs where Tony worked were for the twenty- to thirty-year old, Go Go and Hip Hop set. Mostly it was black kids from the city. But that scene also drew in college kids from the local universities, and the cameo appearances by local college athletes were always something to be reported when Tony saw his Pop.

Tony was good with his hands, and once he had turned twenty-one, he was a much sought-after bouncer. But a mixed martial artist, enamored of the power of Tony's overhand right, convinced Tony to start going into the gym to learn serious boxing. That started his brief amateur boxing career. Working out at the boxing gym off Thomas Circle, he developed the right into a devastating knockout punch. Trinidad Foster, the martial artist, worked on Tony's right and taught him how to slip punches to set it up. He taught him how to time the other fighter in order to conserve the right until just the right moment. And Tony learned to bob. Overall, Tony became a thinker's fighter with a devastating right and slippery defensive moves whenever he needed them under the tutelage of Trini Foster.

Tony and Trini moved around from various boxing gyms in DC

and then Maryland and eventually settled out in Southeast Washington at Knockout as their preferred sparring gym. Tony had started out as a standup fighter which worked okay for him because he could take a punch like a brick wall. But Trini worked for months on the bob; the move that had made Joe Frazier famous. Tony eventually liked it and became skilled at ducking under and popping back up with the right hand.

His first fight was a draw. Then he reeled off four straight wins in about three months. Ben had bought Tony a collection of videotapes of Joe Frazier's fights. He watched them and developed an obsession that may have caused his downfall. By now, he could bob like Frazier, but that wasn't enough.

"Pop, could he really put 'em down like that with the left hook?"

"Absolutely!" would be Ben's response.

"That's the dopest punch I've ever seen," Tony would say.

Tony shadow boxed, ungloved, in the basement of the LeDroit Park house and one night Ben saw a problem. He remembered telling Tony to firm up the fist on his left hand, the same as he naturally did with the right hand.

"Left hooks are different than left jab or even crosses," said Ben.

"If you're ever going to start throwing left hooks, you'd better be able to stand the force in your fist. On your right hand you're hard and your thumb is tucked just right . . . out of the way . . . look at that left hand Tony . . . firm it up."

Tony would do so immediately in the safety of the LeDroit Park basement.

One of the worst arguments between Addie and Ben came when Ben had, at the last minute, extended a trip up in Manhattan. He'd stayed over at the client's request to attend a meeting that turned out to be forty-five-minutes long and somewhat inconsequential. But in doing so, he'd forgotten that Tony's first amateur fight was that night. Tony had acquitted himself well in the draw fight with a much more experienced fighter.

Addie had called him, and texted him from the gym. Rico was there and he'd picked up AR and brought him along. Tony's mom, Yvette, was there and AR went to sit with her when she came in. Big step-brother Adam was there, without his family, but he was there sitting with Addie. Ben wasn't there. He'd forgotten. Tony never mentioned it to his dad, but Ben sure got an earful from Addie and later from Yvette.

"Your son, Benjamin Parks!" screamed Addie on the telephone to Ben when he returned her call from his walk-up apartment on Hamilton Terrace in Harlem.

"Tony had a fight tonight! You were supposed to come home!"

"Shit!" muttered Ben, suddenly remembering and feeling like a weight had swung hard into his mid-section.

"No shit, you asshole" screamed Addie. "You were supposed to come home this afternoon. You can't forget stuff like this. That's your son. All you think about is yourself and your work. Tony needed you tonight and you weren't there. And by the way, you never told me you were staying an extra night. When you go to New York, you just drop out of touch for days at a time."

Ben blathered into the telephone as Addie continued her tirade. He had no excuse. Of course, he could have begged off on the last minute meeting the client had called for the next morning. He'd just forgotten all about the fight.

"Tony looked good, Benjamin," said Addie. "He didn't win, but he didn't lose, either. I don't like to watch that stuff, but I was there. And everybody else was there except you. Tony's face was sad after the fight when he should have been feeling proud of his first official fight. You were supposed to be there!"

The phone clicked loudly as Addie hung up. Ben had caught all the rest of Tony's fights, even if he had to fly back from the city and back up the next morning.

The fifth amateur fight, at the DC Armory, was a thing of beauty and a tragedy at the same time. Tony had promised his pop a surprise. In the first round he covered up and took punches. The other fighter jabbed with his left incessantly . . . once, twice, sometimes four or five times in a row. When he followed with a straight right, it was always just a single shot. They looked like hard punches, but Tony either took them off his gloves or shoulders; or sometimes he bobbed and came up with combinations in twos and fours. Ben could see that he was mainly timing.

Between rounds, Tony looked over at Rico sitting next to Ben and popped his gloves together twice. This was the signal. He'd told Rico to start shooting the camera when he popped his gloves together twice. He'd told Ben it was going to be pretty. Trini, in the corner, squirted the water bottle in Tony's mouth and slapped him in the face to pull him back to focus just as the bell rung for the second round. The other fighter came straight ahead. Tony bobbed and didn't throw a punch. He backed and circled to his left. The other fighter followed until the two of them were squarely in front of Ben and Rico and the rest of the family, sitting in the 3rd row; the perfect shot. Tony popped his gloves two times. Rico started shooting on speed setting.

As Tony had predicted, the fighter started with his jabs. After the second double left, Tony knew the single right was coming. He bobbed, and as he came up his right hand pushed the other fighter's missed right up higher so he had a clear shot with the left hook. Ben saw the whole thing unfold, just like slow motion. Then, incredibly, he realized that Tony had missed.

Ben told Rico to stop shooting.

Now Tony was throwing combinations; twos, fours, and even some sixes. The other fighter retreated and Tony pursued. They circled until, low and behold, Ben realized that Tony had walked his opponent right back to the same camera shot. Tony popped his gloves two times. This time Rico didn't need prompting. The camera whirred.

Tony had stopped throwing combinations and the other fighter momentarily looked confused. Then he went right back into his pattern: Double jab, triple jab, double jab and right. But this time Tony came closer as the right started, pushed it up past his bobbing head, and came up with the prettiest left hook.

Two things happened simultaneously: the other fighter dropped like a sack of potatoes . . . out cold. And Tony screamed in agony. Ben was thinking that, except for the soft left hand inside his glove, Joe Frazier would have been proud.

Rico got the whole thing in frames. Tony had broken his left hand . . . end of boxing career, beginning of career as a personal trainer. Tony bounced back with a vengeance and flew through the trainer certification process. He developed a unique style of personal training that the young legal, marketing, lobbying, IT, policy, and banking professionals on K Street just flocked to. It was personal training, with a boxing twist. For a young man his age who hadn't been to college, Tony was doing all right for himself. Now

"Tough Gym," his newly opened place that was very near Balance, where his boxing career had started, was maxed out with nearly four hundred monthly members.

As for Ben and Addie: If it wasn't about Tony, they always seemed to be able to find something else to spar about.

Chapter 5
The Birds and the Benches

Something about birds thought Addie.

She was in their bedroom lying on the bed, resting from her day at school. She worked hard, and the kids at school wrung every last thing out of her during the day. Her thoughts couldn't get off of the little boy, Dante. All her little first graders had been out on the plaza that Friday afternoon working on a task: to find out how many more benches would need to be on the plaza for all the students from both first grade classes to be able to sit comfortably. There were four benches on the plaza. Each wrought iron bench was 3½ feet wide and eighteen inches deep, with a two-foot high back rest. There were seventeen kids in Addie's class and fifteen in the other first grade teacher's class.

"Move over!" screamed one of the agitated little girls.

Three kids had fit themselves comfortably onto one bench and were counting together on their fingers to solve the current four-bench capacity question before trying to answer the harder question of how many more were needed. But across the plaza, five kids had managed to squeeze themselves onto a similar bench. The agitated little girl, looking across the plaza, was convinced that her three classmates weren't maximizing the capacity of this particular bench. Similar dramas and different dramas were occurring around the other two benches and still other kids were standing in the middle of the plaza with clip boards, talking and making whatever marks they were making. Addie was watchfully standing at the edge of the plaza just at the entrance back into the building. Though totally professional, she couldn't help enjoying all the variations in learning styles and interaction styles that came out whenever her kids tackled this kind of math problem. But then there was Dante standing alone. Eventually, she had approached him.

"Dante," she said in a moderate tone.

No response. Dante was looking up in the sky. A little louder Addie had repeated, "Dante."

Still no response. Addie circled so she could face the little seven-year old.

"How are you working on the problem Dante?"

Dante continued to stare upwards.

Now: "Dante, Ms. Parks is speaking to you. You have an assignment and your time will be up in another fifteen minutes."

Finally, Dante spoke, "The benches are dirty."

Addie hadn't been sure she heard what he had said.

"What was that Dante?

Now the little boy spun around in a circle, still looking upward.

"The benches are dirty . . . there's bird poopy . . . the birds are up there."

At first Addie's impulse was to check the benches. But she caught herself because she'd checked the benches beforehand, and because she knew that Axel, one of the school custodians, was always diligent about keeping the plaza clean and scrubbing the benches when needed.

"Dante, the benches are not dirty. And you aren't doing your assignment. When we go back inside and you don't have an answer, you're going to get a check mark for today's work."

Staring back blankly, Dante finally said, "I want to sit on a bench all by myself."

Addie bent low and got real close to Dante's face. Now she spoke in a low tone looking directly into his eyes.

"Dante, do you see where Cicely and Jose are?"

The little boy lowered his eyes from the sky. He had to move to the side to see around Addie. He found his two classmates.

"Yes, Ms. Parks."

"Ms. Parks wants you join them and see how they are solving the problem. If they have an answer, see if you understand it. If they don't have an answer, try to help them. Do you understand?"

Dante started to cry. Addie took the little boy by the hand. She led him back toward the door where they stood together watching the other kids until she blew the whistle. Back in the classroom, there had been many answers from the various groups of kids: four more benches, five more benches, eight more benches, and nine more benches. In each case, Addie's focus was on their explanation of why. Dante had been quiet during the whole process.

But now, this evening, there needed to be a telephone call to Dante's mom. Addie knew that she was a young mom, probably twenty-five or twenty-six at best, and that she had three other kids: ten, nine, Dante at seven, and one at six. Addie hadn't seen evidence of a dad. How would she tell the mom that Dante wasn't present . . . that he was somewhere else . . . that he was always somewhere else? What did she expect the mom to be able to do about it?

What am I going to do with Dante? worried Addie.

She tried to rest, but her mind was on the phone call she would need to make before the evening got too late. But she had a theory.

Dante has had some kind of incident involving benches and birds, she thought. *If Dante's mom can tell me about what happened, then maybe we can figure out how to get him past it. And maybe she can work with me on a solution . . . and see me as an ally. That's what I'm hoping.*

Addie reached out for the phone, paused, and then sleepiness overtook her. She set the clock to go off in another thirty-five minutes. When the alarm sounded, she popped up and made a call to Dante's mom that helped her to understand this little boy's strange behavior at school. Addie then finished off a lesson plan for next week and fell back asleep.

Chapter 6
Addie's Blues

Addie always needed time when she came home to just be alone and relax, at least at first. Sometimes, she recovered and could engage with her husband. Sometimes, she even engaged with Rico. Sometimes, she could chat with girl friends for most of the night, or with her sister, or with her son, Adam. And sometimes she couldn't.

Ben smiled as he thought about his wife, Addie Sherrie Parks, Master Teacher. He thought about the three plaques on the wall of the smallest bedroom on the second floor of the LeDroit Park house. This was the bedroom Addie had converted to her study. Spanning about a ten-year period, the plaques hung next to her undergraduate degree from Middle State and her graduate degree from Trinity in Washington, DC. The first time back in 1991, it had been a celebration.

"B!" said Addie as she had opened the package in that day's mail. "Look!" "Look!" All she could say was "Look!"

Who's Who: The Top Teachers in America

July 14, 1991

Honoree

Dear Addie:

We are pleased to confirm that your biography will be published in the second edition of Who's Who: The Top Teachers in America.... Your principal will be duly notified, along with a request that this administrator notify parents, local government, and/or media as is seen fit. Your principal will be told that you have not lobbied for or applied for this award, and that no money has been paid to us by you or on your behalf.

This honor only comes to teachers across the country in one way. Unsolicited by us, former parents and former students nominate teachers and must write letters of justification for the award.

So, it is with our greatest admiration that we commend you, Addie Sherrie Parks. Thank you for your service to the young students of our Nation.

Respectfully yours,

(Publisher's signature and name)

Ben had kissed his wife with pride.

"You're so awesome, A," he had said. "Some of your kids even realize it."

Addie half-smiled and half-frowned.

"No, really! This shows it. You have a treat coming," said Ben.

Then they had gone to dinner at Arigatou Sushi. That night, the occasion of her first award, Addie had been amorous when they got home from dinner and they had made love. Since then, Addie was also in the fourth and the seventh editions of the *Who's Who?* Now, there were two more plaques, worded slightly differently each time, but all with the same thematic message. The last two times there had not been a celebration. Nothing much had been said. Each time, Ben had discovered the plaques on the wall after Addie had already hung them.

Addie needed refuge. One of her saving graces was Victoria, her good friend and fellow teacher. Another was Han Bonefant, the Korean next-door neighbor. Addie took Han on as a project and her English coaching helped Han tremendously. The women gardened together in their adjoining backyards. Addie, Han, and Han's husband Lou had become thick as thieves.

Ben knew Addie needed peace and quiet after a day of teaching. The boys knew it, too, and were respectful.

Chapter 7
30th Street Station

Early June 1985: The cab had just deposited Ben at the 30th Street Station in Philadelphia, PA. He and Ted had been conducting a workshop at a diversity conference on the campus of Temple University. Ted had headed to the airport to catch a flight to Buenos Aires for another one of his international development assignments. Ben was headed home to DC for some time off. But he sort of wished he were going straight into another assignment.

The breakup with Yvette had happened almost two years ago. But Ben hadn't really found his stride emotionally or socially, and he'd spent most of his non-Daddy time being consumed in work—one job after another, after another. Without too much contention, Yvette and Ben had agreed to joint custody and pretty much equal time with the boys. But Yvette had still wanted child support, and Ben's willingness to go along had probably greased the skids to getting a reasonably amicable deal done.

The boys were with Yvette whenever Ben was out-of-town, and generally they were with him whenever he was home. So now, as soon as he hit Union Station in DC, he'd liberate his car from the rooftop of the Union Station garage, and then before heading back to the new home on Elm Street, he'd drive over to pick up Tony from elementary school; then double back to get Rico from daycare. It was after Memorial Day, and Tony was learning to swim at the Recreation Department's newly opened pool up at Coolidge High School. Ben's weekend would be mostly hanging out around Coolidge with Tony, while keeping an eye on Rico playing on the jungle gyms and in the dirt, grass, and sand.

At 30th Street Station, Ben located his train on the large roll-up display system in the middle of the mammoth waiting area. He had about forty minutes to kill. He started over toward the food court area. But stopped . . .

I know this person, he thought.

She had deposited herself right in his path. Ben stepped to his right but she moved to stay in front of him. About five-foot-four with short reddish-grayish locks, she was quite striking. Actually, she might not have caught Ben's attention if she hadn't been parked three feet in front of him staring at him intently—not quite with a smile . . . more with the question. "How long will it take for you remember?"

Ben tried to focus. He stared back at the woman but didn't speak. Finally, she said, "Well, I have a train to catch and I'm guessing you do too. So you'd better hurry up and recognize me Benjamin Xavier Parks."

It had been more than fifteen years. The then young girl had blossomed into a full blown woman and the look was quite different. But the voice was the same. It was Addie. When she saw recognition come over his face, Addie dropped her one tote bag, stepped forward, and moved herself up against Ben. Reflexively his arms went around her and she felt like home. This was Addie, his college sweet heart from Middle State.

What the hell is she doing here? he thought. Then, *I don't care. I needed this. This feels so good.*

Now, just as abruptly, Addie was backing away, much too soon. Ben hadn't held a woman—not this way, not with anything more than lustfulness—since his breakup with Yvette. He heard Addie saying, "Check your jacket pocket Benjamin!"

He fumbled into his right pocket and there was nothing. Then he checked his left pocket and found the slip of paper she'd slipped there while he held her. A phone number and the words. "You almost made me late for my train. Now, you have twenty-four hours to call me. Then we'll catch up. I have to run. Bye for now. Love, A."

That was all of the exchange there was. Addie was gone. Ben looked to see which train she was catching. It was the same line he was catching, but she was headed northbound instead of southbound. Three more years after their chance encounter at the train station, and after a whirlwind reunion of college sweethearts, Addie and Ben had married, and she and her son Adam had moved from New York to DC and into the LeDroit Park house on Elm Street. She had immediately become the Queen of the place. Adam had just graduated high school before leaving New York, and within a few months he was off to enter college at Penn State.

The good news: Addie filled a spot that Ben needed filled. Addie was his companion. Addie brought passion back into Ben's life. The bad news: Addie was a Queen. She had a take-charge way about her that was unyielding. Sometimes, Ben didn't mind yielding. And sometimes, it was torture. For instance, Addie hated his taste in furniture and especially in art. She proceeded to remake the Elm Street place to suit her feminine tastes (doilies, tablecloths, curtains instead of blinds, and such), and these were the first of the series of married-folk fights they started to have.

Eventually, Ben had relented. She'd heard him say one-day to Tony when his son couldn't have been more than eleven or twelve years old.

"The walls can go bare for all I care. All my shit is coming down and if Addie wants to buy some art, that's on her. And she can put the couch wherever the fuck she wants it."

That caused another fight between them later that night. How dare he talk about her like that to one of the kids?

Chapter 8
The Neighbors

Benjamin Xavier Parks had grown up over in Northeast Washington in a section called Michigan Park. Most of his lifelong friends as well as a number of his relatives were from the same section of town. Lou Bonefant, Han's husband, was one of the homeboys who'd grown up with Ben and was now his neighbor in LeDroit Park. Ben's high school buddy, Lou had bought his red brick row house in this neighborhood before Ben, and when Yvette and Ben had split, Lou had tipped Ben to the white brick vacant home with tan trim that was right next door. It was a solid house, with a round turret-styled façade containing three attractive windows and a set of six wrought iron steps leading up to an ornate, solid wood front door. But inside, the house had needed plenty of work . . . and Lou, Ben's contractor of preference, was immediately hired to finish the basement that would become Ben's office away from Parks Freer Associates (PFA) in the Dupont Circle section of town.

"I can do basements, kitchens, and additions," said Lou. "I can paint your house inside or out. I can do your plumbing. I can do your electric. I can build you a deck or patio. I'm the best in the business," he sometimes said.

"In fact, I could do office buildings and apartment buildings and sports complexes just as well as Carr or Donnelly or any of those big cats."

Ben knew that Lou usually made decent money. He also knew that Lou's aspirations and talent were much bigger than the small jobs that kept him busy. He always listened with empathy and without comment when his friend ranted about the big construction firms. What he never said to his friend was that playing at that level was not very much about talent or skill. A lot of people including Lou had the talent or skill. But those kinds of jobs were mostly about financing.

Yes, Ben thought. *Lou could build anything—from a basement renovation to a multi-story office building—if given a chance. That he'd probably never get to play at that level was just another example of the phoniness of the meritocracy principle in our dear old capitalist system.*

As for the house in LeDroit Park, Ben probably was never going to move from this cherished home, although Addie thought he could afford, and she deserved, a much nicer place in a nicer neighborhood. But Ben actually liked this neighborhood, and Howard University, his last alma mater and occasional place of side-employment, was right up the street. And he hated moving. He traveled so much; there was a certain kind of stability in coming back to the same house, in the same neighborhood, trip after trip, month after month, year after year. Besides, he had said to her many times. "I've seen too many of my boys go house poor. It just isn't worth it."

But Ben wasn't up to the multitude of upkeep tasks on an older house.

Addie knew that Ben and Yvette had owned a home over by the Big Chair landmark across the Anacostia River in Southeast DC. But when they'd split, and Ben had moved out, Ben had bought the place in LeDroit Park. Then came that scene in the Philadelphia 30th Street train station.

Chapter 9
Rico and the Boys

An August Friday evening in 1999: Ben knew what the boys were doing. But around 7:00 p.m., he tapped on the closed bed room door anyway.

"Ba-dum-pum-pum," was his usual rap.

Sniff opened the door. "Sup, Mr. Parks?"

Ben stayed at the door taking in the scene. Ricardo Benjamin Parks had been working on another one of his hand drawn comic books. There were super hero comic books, rap star comic books, cops and robbers comic books, and probably some others that Ben didn't know about.

Dirk was lying face down across Rico's bed. Sniff left the doorway and sprawled back on the bed next to Dirk. Rico was squat on the floor below them and around him on the floor were the latest panels he'd been sketching.

"C'mon, Dirk" said Sniff. "Finish!"

Rico's two friends high-fived each other. Rico's latest super-hero character was named "Bryan" for some reason. His prologue read:

> In another Galaxy, a benevolent force loads a power giving gemstone onto an unpiloted space ship and launches the ship towards Earth. The ship finds its way to Washington, DC and finally to a remote section of Rock Creek Park. Five homeless African Americans live together there in a series of small tents . . .

"So, now Bryan is the only one of the guys who doesn't run when that thing crashes in the park," said Dirk.

"Why doesn't he run?" asked Rico.

"Cause he sees a gleam coming from the wreck and he's curious," said Dirk.

"Okay, he's curious," chimed in Sniff . . . "but he's also kind of stupid. I know I wouldn't want to go near something like that."

"That's why you'll never be a super hero," said Dirk.

Now Rico and Dirk high fived. They continued with Rico mostly listening; spinning out their different versions of Bryan's story. Nobody paid any attention to the old man smiling and standing in the doorway.

Ben knew that after Dirk and Sniff left that night, Rico would be up until early in the morning. He'd be writing in words under the panels he liked, drawing new panels, and weaving together the tales based on the fanciful imaginations of Sniff and Dirk, mixed with his own sense of what would be exciting or interesting.

As the story line developed, Bryan, who was one of the homeless men, would be somehow changed by his encounter with the alien gem stone—taking on some amazing super powers. The Bryan story was now at twenty-one pages, with anywhere from five to eight panels per page. The carefully bound pages of Rico's previous comic books (inserted into plastic sheets and kept in a three-ring binder) were an extreme source of pride for Rico . . . for Tony and Adam Quarles (the step-brother) . . . for Addie and Ben. . . and for Rico's mom (Yvette Parks). And Ben figured they'd soon be source material for a college application portfolio. This kind of thing would improve Rico's chances of getting into a good art school like Kansas City, Rochester or Columbia in Chicago.

Ben had never steered Rico to draw. Neither did Yvette when the boys stayed with her. Both of Ben's sons were average (C to C+) students, just like Ben had been at that age. But Ben's parents had tried to steer him more, and Ben had rebelled. Ben's determination was to try to pick up on signs from his boys that his parents had missed with him, and to flow with whatever direction emerged—so long as it was goal-oriented and legal. Tony had wanted to box, and Ben had supported that even though he'd always been fearful watching his older son in the ring. Eventually, Tony turned his interest to fitness. Drawing was what Rico liked to do, and Ben thought that was great.

Rico was going into his last year at Washington High School for the Arts in September. He wanted to finish this comic book before school started back up. So Ben let him regulate his own hours and spend as much time as he wanted. Rico was working part-time six days per week in the afternoons as a creative drawing instructor at the Upshur Recreation Center over on 13th Street, Northwest. Saturday would be a busy day. But Rico would draw until he fell asleep and then get up around 11:00 a.m. or so. He'd still be able to shower, eat, and get to work.

Chapter 10
Citronella Candle

It was almost 8:00 p.m. that same Friday evening, and Ben sat upstairs in the guest bedroom. He finished polishing his sandals to perfection. This is where all his clothes were hung. In the master bedroom next door, all the closets and chests were full with Addie's things. The houses in this section of DC, vintage 1930s, had one thing in common: small closets. To supplement, Addie kept most of her things upstairs in the attic's oversized cedar closet that Ben had had installed before she'd moved in.

After finishing his sandals, Ben positioned them near where his clothes were laid out for tomorrow. He liked to prep this way because he was a little bit color-blind, and if he got up rushing in the morning, he might pick some weird combination that he'd only realize when Addie or even worse, some student, made a comment. This way he could take his time.

Ben went downstairs and out again to the back porch, after pouring himself a stiff Irish whiskey and pulling a Rock Creek ginger ale out of the fridge for a chaser. He'd intended to light one of his citronella candles but didn't have a match. He re-entered the house through the back door and into the kitchen just as the Blackberry on his hip buzzed with an email message. He glanced quickly and decided that he didn't want to read the message from Ted (his partner) right now because it was certainly about business and he wasn't in the mood. Holstering the Blackberry, he paused confused. Then he went over to the faucet and ran some tap water until it ran hot. Retrieving an oversized cup from the cabinet, he filled it with hot water to take out and sip . . . one of his many routines for dealing with his chronic bronchitis. But he knew this wasn't what he'd come back in the house for.

"What was it? Damn Blackberry!" At times like this he felt helpless . . . stupid . . . old . . . and more and more, scared.

"Tick, tick, tick." Ben heard the irritating wall clock sound as time slowed.

Shit! If it's important, it'll come back to me . . . I hope, he thought.

Ben returned outside and stared down to the patio at his blue chairs with the small table in between. There were the unlit citronella candles.

Bingo! he thought.

Back in the kitchen, Ben opened a drawer and retrieved a half-used book of Giant-brand wood matches. As he turned back toward the back door, he dropped the matches on the kitchen floor.

Damn! he thought, *You're losing your mind AND you're clumsy, too!*

Fumbling on the floor, he got a grip on the match box, and with it firmly in hand he headed back outside. After lighting the candles, he was finally able to relax down on his flagstone patio.

Chapter 11
Ben at Work

As the sun half disappeared over the roofs of a line of row houses several streets away, a scene came to mind from the just completed retreat with the five top execs at the city government's public health agency. Ben worked as an organization development consultant. His assignments ranged from facilitating large scale change processes; working with senior executives in a coaching role; stimulating creative approaches to solving organizational problems; working with various small groups like the one at DHS; conducting various types of assessments, and other miscellaneous assignments such as helping competing factions dialog when they needed to work together.

OD-type people like Ben, as a profession, weren't well known outside certain circles. But among corporate types and increasingly in government agencies, OD trained consultants had been relied upon for a long time for things like coaching executives through difficult organizational transitions, facilitating various types of planning, and especially for helping groups work together more effectively—playing nicely in the sand box as it was sometimes called. OD was Ben's line of work.

The focus for his clients this week had been teenage obesity. The huge percentage of overweight teens in DC was a priority health and political issue in the city, and this agency that was a client system for Ben had the lead role on a major initiative to reduce its prevalence, morbidity, and mortality. The setting had been so perfect.

At the Mansion on J Street in Northwest Washington, DC, five row buildings had long ago been fused together into one somewhat opulent, somewhat funky historical preservation site, party spot, and bed and breakfast-cum-conference center. Seventy or more rooms were splayed through the facility at odd angles, with step-up and step-down passages on all five floors. Probably twenty-five of the rooms were made up as guest rooms with various themes based on historical figures. Ben Parks had over-nighted in the Sojourner Truth bedroom.

The conference room in which Ben and the group of five had held their meeting was located on the third floor. They entered through an anteroom where the host staff placed coffee, tea, juices, and finger foods throughout the day. In the meeting room were three overstuffed couches and several chairs around a large glass table. Oversized and ornately treated windows overlooked J Street. Around the walls were all manner of artistic hangings, curios, and knick-knacks such as an autographed picture of Walter Johnson (the Washington Senators baseball player from the 1920s), another famous portrait of Marian Anderson singing on the steps of the Lincoln Memorial, as well as a rare photo of both Franklin and Eleanor Roosevelt—who were not often known to appear together—seated together on a love seat sized couch. A large, ornate harp sat in one corner next to a small upright piano. Wall hangings included a couple of Yoruba masks, a Mayan robe, a set of crossed swords, an old trombone (probably played by somebody famous), a framed front page newspaper article from 1929 on the crash of the stock market, and another framed op-ed article on the opening of the John F. Kennedy Center for the Performing arts. The author's opinion had been that it was in the wrong place and should have been built on a large parking lot that eventually became the site of the Ronald Reagan Building. Some things, but not all, in the room had small price tags hanging off them.

Adjacent to the one chair that Ben occupied was a screen on which he projected images from his projector situated on the glass table. Whenever the appropriate time came in the meeting for a concept, illustration, definition, discussion question, cartoon tension-reliever, or theoretical framework relevant to the conversation at-hand, Ben would find the right slide and show it on the screen. He could also use his laptop computer to take simultaneous notes that projected on the screen so folks could see what he was tracking and whether he was accurately representing or had mischaracterized any of their comments. If Ben didn't note something they thought was important, someone would inevitably give him an eye signal or even say, "Ben, that's something we want to capture."

***

In the scene that came to mind as the last little bit of sun disappeared from his backyard reverie, there was Doris Smith, M.D., the gorgeous double-dark Johns Hopkins educated medical chief of the agency, a black woman who by sight might have been guessed to be thirty-five, or forty-five, or fifty-five—give or take a few years—though she openly talked of grandkids. Doris had had an insight.

"Well," she said, "I started to explain myself and then thought about what Ben had said about how unsatisfying it probably would be to do so. So, I won't go there."

Heads nodded.

Previously, Ben had interrupted an exchange between Antoine, the graying coffee-colored, DC-homegrown chief of staff from Southeast DC who'd been a couple years behind Ben at Middle State undergrad, and Blanca, one of the two community outreach managers (one had responsibility for programs in Northwest and Southwest, and the other covered Northeast and Southeast DC). Antoine, had said, "Blanca, I want to know why you took it upon yourself to let one of your staff use those unvetted obesity statistics at a public meeting, when . . ."

Blanca, across the room on an opposite-facing couch perked up and was about to go into visible counter-attack mode just as Ben interrupted. Ben's comment, "Thanks Antoine for such a wonderful teachable moment. Can I just break in here?"

The thing about these kinds of clients (the senior staff of the District of Columbia Public Health Agency and certain others of Ben's regular clients) was that they were typical of the most rewarding kinds of small groups with whom to work. Ben loved to work with small groups whose missions were noble and interesting. The senior execs at the public health agency were all smart and opinionated. But over time they had come to understand that they pulled against one another in grossly unproductive ways, precisely at the worst times when programmatic crises were at hand, resource choices needed to be made, or other strategic or political judgments with much at stake were being discussed. The strong opinions and presumption of their own individual knowledge, correctness, power, stature, and their innate competitiveness made it hard for them to collaborate at exactly the times when the enterprise most needed them to be working together.

Fortunately, this group and those like them had had an epiphany at some point and had come to realize their need to rely on outside help in the form of the consulting firm Ben co-owned (Parks Freer Associates) to steer them through these high-stakes moments. And when a group like theirs found someone who could really help in the toughest of moments, they tended to cede to that person enormous credibility and trust, and to use them over and over as current events required. That's why these DC public health execs had booked Ben to sit with them through this particular childhood obesity off-site planning retreat at the J Street Mansion.

Silence had settled until Ben spoke again.

"Antoine, you obviously think Blanca shouldn't have done that, correct?" Antoine nodded.

"And yet you asked her why," observed Ben . . . another nod from Antoine. His expression had been akin to a kid getting his hand caught in a cookie jar. The funny look distracted Ben for a minute. Then, he'd lost his point.

More silence . . . unfortunately more than seemed appropriate for simple rhetorical effect. Antoine fidgeted. Blanca glowered. Doris looked amused; probably because she knew that whatever Ben was going to say, she wasn't part of this little drama.

Ben searched inside his mind for what he'd been saying and why he'd brought it up. Signs of recognition from the group . . . they'd worked with Dr. Benjamin Parks long enough to have seen this before. Sonja Clement, the law school trained, Jewish forty-something-year-old agency director smiled and softly said in her always formal way, "Another senior moment, eh, Dr. Parks?"

As always, they were indulgent. An itch at the back of Ben's neck,

Was there a fly in the room? Ben thought.

He scratched. No fly; just a phantom itch. Then suddenly, he had his train of thought back. Turning to the group Ben in a quiet voice said, "Right! But here it is. The point I wanted to make is that there's that sneaky 'why question' entering the room."

He paused. "I guess I haven't told you-all about 'why questions' before! Did you see Blanca perk up Antoine? Blanca, you looked ready to give him chapter-and-verse on why you did it."

Blanca, a Mexican-American pharmacist by training, but long since a converted and highly respected community organizer, didn't reply. She continued looking resolute; now at Ben and then back over to Antoine. Sonja and Arthur, Blanca's bearded, long-haired white co-lead on agency outreach programs (he'd been a labor union organizer before coming to the DC government) sat looking partly amused and partly glad they weren't in this particular one of Ben's interventions.

Ben continued, "You see, 'why questions' under certain circumstances, aren't really questions at all. And this is a case in point. As soon as Blanca heard your 'why?' she immediately geared up to respond to the statement behind your question . . . which was your judgment that she shouldn't have done it. If I hadn't interrupted, Blanca would have launched into her reasons that would have been in the verbiage of explanation but the tone of righteous justification. And does anybody in this room think Blanca's reasons would have satisfied Antoine?" . . . another pause.

"No! Most probably" continued Ben "he would have countered with rebuttals to Blanca's reasons, which would have set off even more vehement justifications from Blanca. At some point, both would have realized the futility, and both would have been very unsatisfied with the exchange . . . probably thinking that the other person was again being unreasonable. But neither would have wanted to back down at this point. What do you think? Am I off base here?"

As it became clear where Ben was going, Sonja and Doris had started smiling in obvious delight. Antoine's sheepish smile was more subtle, but nonetheless his expression was a cop to the truth of the observation. Blanca was still somewhat agitated, but sat back in the overstuffed couch pillow and breathed a sigh to relax.

"You read us again, Dr. Parks! Where do you get this stuff from?" said Sonja, smiling.

"Maybe I've personally made every communication mistake known to mankind, Ms. Clement" said Ben, returning the formality by using her last name.

"So I make connections when I'm learning these principles . . . and I try to remember them so I don't get in trouble again."

Now, everyone laughed and the tension had gone out of the room. What followed was yet another one of their evocative and generative reflections together that were often the product of Ben's interventions. This time it was about their communication patterns and how they sometimes were insidiously unhelpful. These conversations never happened in this group without Ben's presence and sometimes subtle, other times confrontational nudging.

Now, in total darkness on the patio except for the flickering citronella candle, Ben thought of Doris finishing her retrospective:

"No, I just won't go there. And I won't get trapped by 'why questions' anymore. If you don't agree with something I've done, don't ask me why unless you're really interested in understanding my reasoning. Otherwise, just tell me you don't agree."

She chuckled, "I almost started to explain myself until I remembered what Ben had said about how unsatisfying it would probably be to do so. So (repeating more emphatically), I won't go there!"

Doris, who came from a very wealthy family and didn't really have to work to support herself, often felt in this group that, with the exception of Sonja, she was the only one among these senior managers who understood the medical and public policy ramifications of some of the public health considerations that were made in this agency. So she sometimes felt under attack and had actually come to the retreat a bit apprehensive that it would turn out to be a beat-up-the-medical-program fest. To her relief, it hadn't turned out that way, and she'd relaxed by the first afternoon. But in checking out at the end of the retreat she'd expressed appreciation that Ben's presence was comforting and allowed her to have input that she could feel good about, and "not go there" if it was going to be unsatisfying.

***

The retreat had ended several hours before Ben encountered the three tough guys in the alley back in LeDroit Park. But thinking back on it, Ben knew that this had been one of the every-so-often experiences that reminded him that what he did made an impact on people in very out-of-the-limelight ways that were nonetheless profound. He felt blessed to have stumbled into this line of work twenty-some years ago, and then later that he had trained at Howard University in night school so he could do it even better. And he'd even managed not to cough very much during the whole two and a half day retreat . . . except at night as he fitfully slept and coughed throughout the night in the Sojourner Truth bedroom.

Chapter 12
Dr. Prescott

Now, after 9:00 p.m., Ben was back upstairs looking around the unmade guest bedroom. He picked up a few dirty clothes from his clothes hamper, tucked them under his arms, and went down two flights to his basement office. Dropping off the laundry next door in the appropriate basket, he stepped into the office, settled into his specially-measured Healthy Back Store office chair behind his desk, and began to read.

This consortium teaching gig that he'd be going to in the morning was more work in a two-day seminar once per month than two or three OD consulting assignments that earned him real money. The idea to pull Ben into this thing was the brain child of one of the respected Deans at Howard University (nicknamed by the students, 'The Mecca'). It had started at a diversity conference in 1995 in Denver, Colorado where Dr. Ralph Prescott had seen Ben and his consulting firm partner presenting at a conference. Prescott had become intrigued with Ben, after seeing him work back and forth with Ted Freer, a handsome gay man who spoke six languages, and who had written extensively and consulted internationally on the discipline of project management. Ted also was a noted author on issues of gays in the third world.

After their presentation, Prescott had approached as Ben climbed down from the stage of the Convention Center and walked with him back over to the Embassy Suites Hotel nearby. He offered his hand, saying, "I'm Ralph Prescott from . . ."

Ben interrupted, "Dean Prescott from Howard University. Of course, I know who you are. What brings you out here two thousand miles from the Mecca?"

"Frankly, I didn't know why I signed up to attend this conference, but now I'm feeling like something led me here. Let me get right to the point. You and Ted Freer are the first credible pair of intellectuals that I've come across to deal directly and believably on integrating sexual orientation into the mainstream diversity narrative."

Ben flushed and mumbled, "Thanks!"

Ralph Prescott was well known and respected in both the academic community as well as a community activist and frequent expert commentator on the DC talk shows. Prescott continued, "Lesbians and gays like Ted are usually on their own when holding forth about sexual orientation . . . oh, excuse me. I remember Dr. Freer saying that gays are frequently not having sex, and that a more apt term would be 'attraction orientation.' But I digress. The uniqueness here was you, Dr. Parks . . . a black straight male like you so publicly attaching himself to this topic; that was a thing of courage."

Ben had this urge to deflect. But he stayed quiet.

"Yes, Dr. Parks" Prescott had said. "That was out-of-the-box . . . quite out-of-the-box!"

Ben wasn't really thinking of it that way, but took the compliment. That set him up for the pitch.

"I've had this idea of a seminar on culture for grad students at Howard that would pull in select students from other Universities in the CWMAU," said Prescott.

Ben had smiled and thought almost mockingly, *Who the hell comes up with these acronyms?* But he'd actually heard of the Consortium of Washington Metropolitan Area Universities. He'd just never worked with them.

"You'd be a great fit to take the lead," said Prescott.

Ben's first thought was that he was busy and this would be a distraction.

"I'm really honored that you'd think of me Dean. But, no thanks" Ben had said. "I have a pretty full plate. Besides, I don't do what you just saw without Ted."

"What I just saw was erudite and respectful on a very difficult subject matter," said Prescott. "But it's not what I have in mind, exactly. Our black and other POC students at Howard are actually pretty progressive on the issue of attraction orientation . . . it's race in particular and culture in the broader sense that they stumble on.

And many of the mostly White students at all the other local Universities mirror the confusion. But there aren't venues for talking and learning across these cultural divides. At least, there aren't guided scholarly venues like someone such as you could lead."

Ben was flattered, but said "No" again.

***

But back from the conference, Prescott contacted Ben and continued to press the case.

"I'm sorry Dr. Prescott, but I'm just not feeling it," said Ben on the telephone one evening.

"Ever seen The Matrix?" asked Prescott.

Ben had no idea where this new line of attack was coming from, but he marveled at Prescott's craftiness.

"Yes I have," he responded warily.

"You know, it took Neo a long time to come to accept that he was 'the one.' You remember that?"

"So, Dr. Prescott, why am I the one?" challenged Ben.

"I thought you'd never ask, Dr. Parks. You're the one for three reasons. First, you're smart."

"Well, Dr. Prescott, you're starting off on very shaky ground. I'm not particularly smart. My dad is smart. One of the characteristics I inherited from my dad is that I work pretty hard. People who work hard, through their persistence, can come off as appearing to be intelligent to others."

"Dr. Parks, that's just remarkable. Let's say that I'm buying your argument—which by the way, I don't—this first reason is really the least important. There are a lot of smart people walking around on the face of the earth who are just plain stupid!"

Ben couldn't hold it. He burst out laughing and the laughter continued for an embarrassingly long while. Finally, he stopped and Prescott asked, "You all right? Are you ready for number two?"

"Go ahead, sir," choked Ben.

"The second reason is you hold a set of values that are frankly very similar to mine; and they are the kind of values that I believe are needed if we ever are to get better at cross-cultural understanding. Remember Dr. King's idea about how if there's ever going to be peace in the world, we have to get away from focusing so much on our tribes and become more ecumenical. That's what I believe, and I think you do, too. And before you attempt to parry this one, remember that I saw you in Denver and that your values were very much on display in that setting."

Ben remained silent.

"So, here's the clincher for me, Dr. Parks. This one wouldn't be very potent if you didn't have the first two qualities. But the first two wouldn't be enough by themselves to make you the one."

Suddenly, Ralph Prescott reminded Ben Parks of himself. Ben had done a fair amount of studying in the areas of rhetoric and persuasion. He could be pretty good at it in certain situations and needed these skills when dealing with certain kinds of clients. This was like listening to an even more skilled version of himself. Ben was completely hooked to hear the third and final reason.

"Vulnerability, Dr. Parks. You've got vulnerability. If I had that quality, I'd do this seminar myself."

Prescott paused for effect.

"I'm too arrogant. I know I'm smart. When I go into a room, as far as I'm concerned I'm the smartest guy in the room. That just won't do for this seminar. As soon as I showed up and presented that vibe, for the rest of the seminar folks would be looking for the kinks in my veneer. With you, there's no need to do that. You're vulnerable and don't seem to mind it. You're going to imagine this seminar in ways that I couldn't because you're going to be willing to take risks that I would never take. You're very rare. You're the one."

That night's call concluded. Although the perfuse praise heaped by Ralph Prescott caused Ben enormous anxiety and even larger doses of fear and humble pie, eventually Prescott's persistence and the intriguing idea of the seminar wore Ben down.

***

So tonight, until he tired, Ben would prep for tomorrow's Saturday seminar.

Chapter 13
What Riots? What about Hondo?

Summer 1959: At the crack of the bat, the smallish rookie shortstop from Venezuela, Zoillo Versalles was off to his right. Diving horizontally, he simultaneously hit the ground as his outstretched glove made contact with the seeing-eye grounder that had momentarily been a surefire hit to bring in the tying run.

Versalles acrobatically rolled over and from his knees threw a rope to Billy Consolo, the covering second baseman for the forced third out. This preserved the one-run lead for the home team in the ninth inning. The exploding crowd, first silent and unbelieving, was jubilant at the rare win for the Washington Senators.

Fourteen-year-old Benjamin Parks cheered right along with the crowd. His dad, a compact, serious-faced young PhD candidate at Howard University, had taken time off from his studies and the two part-time jobs he held to feed the family. Griffith Stadium, named for the cursed owner who in 1960 "stole" this team away to "lighter" pastures, sat at the corners of 7th and Georgia Avenue; and was never full for Senators baseball. You practically had to go back to the days of Walter Johnson or to the Homestead Grays (a Negro team that DC had shared with Pittsburg) to find strong support in DC for a good major league baseball team. These Senators were not a good baseball team, and so Ben's dad had been able to walk up at the last minute and purchase two bleacher seats, having somehow found time in his busy schedule. That was how Richard Parks entertained and fellowshipped with his son . . . whenever he could. Mostly, Ben and his sister Penny were raised by their mother, Gillian Parks.

A surprise trip to a baseball game with his dad was one of the joys of Ben's young life.

***

March 3, 2006: Talking on the telephone with his dad, Ben asked, "What's going to happen with Soriano?"

Without a pause, Richard Parks replied, "He's going to play left field. He might not know it yet. But he's messing with an old time manager who isn't going to have players trying to dictate where they will or won't play."

"Have you ever seen Soriano play second base, Dad? It's not a pretty sight!" said Ben, agreeing with his dad's sentiment.

"Frank Robinson was a gold glover. He's not going to have that mess in his infield."

The father and son chuckled together on this, one of their many baseball commiserations over the years. There were a lot of things that Ben and Richard Parks couldn't, or didn't dare talk about. They were from different generations with very different views in many ways. But beginning when Ben was a very young boy, Richard Parks had transferred to his son a passion for baseball. The national pastime had become a kind of glue in their relationship that had lasted and never failed.

Hanging up the phone, Ben reflected on the complicated relationships and complicated loyalties in his life. The first example was his relationship with his dad, Dr. Richard Parks, "the smartest man in the world," college-aged Ben had often said when talking about his dad. Ben remembered back thirty-eight years to a May evening in 1968, a knock on the door of his dorm room at Middle State.

***

"Dat, da, da, dah! Smart-Man on the phone for BP" teased one of his hall mates. "Better get your dumb-ass out the bed and talk to your daddy."

Ben had immediately tensed. Riots had torn up his home town just after Dr. King was gunned down in Memphis. The unrest had permeated the scene at Middle State also, but not to the extent of the torn up buildings and streets back in DC. Coming out of his room in a robe and running down the hallway, Ben expected bad news. He picked up the phone dangling against the wall at the end of the hallway. Several hall mates observed his conversation from a few feet away in the hall with concern on their faces.

"What's wrong, Dad?" blurted Ben.

His dad's reply was, "Hondo just hit his tenth home run in seven days."

Completely caught off guard, Ben was speechless. After more silence on the line, his dad had softly said, "Just wanted you to know the news isn't all bad back here. Are you studying, Son?"

"Yessir," said Ben . . . then, "Oh, Hondo . . . the Senators . . . he did what?"

"Ten home runs in twenty ABs," said his dad. "Get back to the books, Ben."

That was the whole conversation; a call to his college student son from Richard Parks to share Frank Howard exploits on Ben's beloved last-place Senators baseball team. And a similar call happened a few months later as Ben stayed in summer school to finish the last class he needed for graduation. This time Ron Hansen, the Senator's shortstop, had pulled off an unassisted triple play.

***

Thirty-eight years later, thinking back on this episode, something struck Ben as funny for the first time and he said, "In neither call did I even bother to ask Dad if the Senators won or lost the game."

Ben admired and marveled at the way his dad had always been big on reading instructions. If Ben's father had a set of instructions, he could work through anything. If there weren't instructions, Dr. Richard (as some of Ben's friends called him) would go into intense research mode. He'd draw a little insight from this book . . . some more from this article . . . some more yet from this conversation with one of his mentors or peers . . . and the next thing you know he'd have figured it out. Even if Richard Parks had done something twenty times—he'd still read the instructions before the twenty-first time in order to make sure he did it perfectly.

Dr. Richard Parks, the former Tuskegee airman, turned historian specializing in the lives of African and African Diaspora warriors of any sort; turned President of Baltimore State College (a rival HBCU to Howard U. the Mecca that was forty-five miles up the road from DC) had a loving but complicated relationship with his son. Ben absorbed many things from Richard. He developed an intense love for history and philosophy and became a buff, especially on the Revolutionary War, and the life, challenges, paradoxes, and individual and collective thinking of the Constitutional founders.

But from Ben's childhood he mostly remembered the baseball games at Griffith Stadium. The Senators were awful. They and other local sports teams were the second example of Ben's complicated relationships and loyalties.

Chapter 14
Sports Odyssey

Of course, DC hadn't had a baseball team in decades. So Ben had tried to morph himself. He first decided that he was a basketball fan. Over in Baltimore, the Bullets had been really good once. And after moving to Washington, they'd even rolled over the Seattle Supersonics and won the championship in 1978. That team, with Elvin Hayes, Wes Unseld, Tommy Henderson, Kevin Grevey, CJ (Charles Johnson), Phil Chenier, Mitch Kupchak, and Ben's favorite—Bobby Dandridge—had been exciting. The later versions, known as the Wizards, were never even interesting to watch.

Next Ben had tried football . . . that should have worked since the town was nuts about the Washington Football Team. But Ben knew he wasn't a real fan.

One night, at the Soldiers Legion Post on Capitol Hill where Ben was a member, he had knocked down several Jack and Gingers and was pontificating with some of his Post brothers.

"It's easy to be a fan of the hometown team when they're winning. If you're a real fan, you want your team to win, of course. But you're still with them when they lose; and you NEVER boo the home team. It doesn't matter how bad they lose. If you can't say somethin' nice, don't say nothin' at all."

When Washington's football team lost over and over again, Ben didn't boo. He ceased to care. Besides, when it comes to complications, he never could be a total fan of a team with such an offensive nickname. Ben just seemed to get into sports conversations at Legion Post.

Anyway, when that Washington Football Team had gotten bad, Ben lost interest; even more than Richard Parks. The same had happened with the Wizards. By 2006, the Nats were in the second year in town and were pretty bad. But Ben and Richard would once watch them from the third base side at RFK. Sitting alone in the stands, one of Ben's memorable games was when Ben got to cheer the left fielder, Alfonso Soriano, when he tore up second base for a personal souvenir after stealing his fortieth base, having already hit forty homers that year. Ben also tube-watched probably another twenty televised games from his porch in LeDroit Park.

He was a true fan, and he suffered the Nats losing in silence. He didn't boo from the stands. And at his various watering hole haunts, he stuck up for the new ownership of the Nats when the team looked lousy. He kept hope that they wouldn't try the kind of quick fixes of that other hometown sports owner . . . the guy that tried to resurrect Bruce Smith, Deion Sanders, Mark Brunell, and Adam Archuleta. The list went on-and-on of quick fixes that never worked out.

Ben knew that he was patient and he was a real baseball fan. So for many years, there had been an open spot in Ben's heart that he just couldn't fill. The Orioles weren't his team. He listened to radio broadcasts of them sometimes, and even knew most of their players' names. But they never were his team, and even though he commuted to Baltimore almost every day for nearly forty years, the Orioles never were his dad's team.

Baseball was on the good side of the Richard and Ben Parks relationship. But the relationship Ben had with his father wasn't all rosy. He was actually quite put off by Dr. Richard about some things . . . and vice-versa. Richard Parks, though he bragged to friends about his son's success in business, had never approved of Ben's handling of money—like having no retirement plan for instance. And Ben harbored downright hurt feelings from way back about some decisions Richard had made for him. Dad was 'old school,' sometimes in the best of ways, and sometimes in the worst of ways from Ben's point of view.

For instance, before Ben was five years old, his parents had decided that Ben needed to learn to play the piano. They did the same thing later with Penny, Ben's younger sister. Penny took to it, but though Ben learned quickly, he never particularly enjoyed playing the instrument . . . or more specifically, the classical music that he was forced to play on it.

At some point around ten or twelve years of age, on a late night jazz station Ben had heard John Coltrane . . . and he fell in love with the saxophone. That's what he wanted to play. Mom didn't much care for the idea, but Dad was adamant against it. He'd said, "If you don't want to play the piano anymore, then just stop. But the saxophone is low-class, and you won't be bringing one of those into this house."

Later his dad had suggested that he try the violin, and Ben did. He quickly figured out that he didn't like playing that, either, but nevertheless Ben suffered with his lessons for a few years. He actually became rather proficient and earned some spending money by playing at weddings and community affairs.

But by high school age, Ben's focus was on do wop singing, running track, and chasing girls. The violin didn't fit, and Ben stopped playing. He never again played any instrument well, though as an adult he'd tried to pick up guitar, electric bass, trombone, percussion, and even his first desire—the sax. He was terrible with all of them. So the Richard and Ben Parks relationship had been a lifelong drama of mutual admiration tinged with dissonant chords of disapproval, if not out-and-out clashes of values or perspective.

Chapter 15
Let There be Peace

The complicated relationships in Ben Park's life didn't end with his dad or with sports teams. Addie and Ben's relationship had always been intense. Sometimes, their intensity was as two people closely connected, almost joined at the hip. Other times, what showed up between Ben and Addie was the palpable intensity of disconnection.

Ben and Addie argued. Ben didn't like to argue. Addie debated almost everything. Sometimes, it seemed as if when he turned right, she'd turn left just to get something stirred up with him. If he said "up," she'd automatically ask, "Why up?" . . . or, "How do you know it's up? Why not sideways?"

"I'm around confusion, turmoil, and strife almost every day in my professional career," said Ben to Addie in one of their more fierce conversations.

"I'm dealing with department heads that won't collaborate, retired military commanders who don't understand how to manage civilian employees, and transplanted corporate executive-types who want to run federal agencies like businesses."

Addie showed by her stoic countenance that she wasn't impressed. That only made Ben want to make his point more strongly.

"You've never shown any interest in the work I did with the cops and the crews in Northeast for instance."

Crews were the way DC kids referred to what in other cities would be called 'street gangs.' You know what happened the last time I was down at the church on 6th Street?"

"Okay, I'm interested. Please tell me what happened Benjamin."

Ben thought, "Of course, you don't know because you're really not interested." Then he said, "I think he was called Big Ugly. This gold toothed dude . . . acted like the crew leader . . . flashed this big grin in the middle of a rap when I was trying to see why his boys kept cutting the police off. He said, 'Hey do-gooder man! Ya know you pro'ly the only one here ain't packin'.'"

"Packin'?" was Addie's question with very little affect.

"It means armed, Addie . . . and the crazy thing was that it actually hadn't occurred to me. I remember suddenly looking around at the policemen whose guns were visible. And I thought 'Had these bangers really come packing to a meeting with the police?'"

"Did the police search the crew members?"

"Nope! Nobody moved. Everybody just looked around. The bangers had these shit eating grins on their faces. The police were trying to look unconcerned. Because of the delicate nature of the meeting, I guessed that it wasn't in the cops' best interest to make a big deal by starting a search. The meeting just continued with a somewhat flustered facilitator: me. I remember catching myself several times trying to imagine where the crew members had their guns."

"What's this have to do with you and me Benjamin?"

"What I'm trying to say A, is that conflict and arguments are very familiar me. But when I come home, the hyper-stimulation of all this drama between you and me is a drag."

Ben craved calm and a predictable routine with his wife. Addie didn't want to be careful with what she said or how she said it. She felt that Ben was too sensitive, and that if she knuckled to Ben's desire for calm, she wouldn't be true to herself. She wanted to be free to say and do whatever she wanted. Ben sometimes wished that Addie could see him work so she would know how tough he could be and that he really wasn't hypersensitive by nature; that his reactions to her weren't out of either wanting to control her or of being afraid of her.

When they first married, Addie and Ben argued about mundane things like how to arrange the living room or bedroom furniture. They never could agree on art pieces. She didn't seem to like any of the pieces he had on the walls when she moved in. Eventually, he'd taken most of them down. But, as much as she liked to shop, Addie didn't buy any art that she liked . . . so, many of the walls in the house stayed bare. Ben didn't like bare walls, but tolerating them kept some semblance of peace.

Ben had sulked as the master bedroom had increasingly become Addie's sanctuary, causing him to feel more and more uncomfortable in there.

"You talk on the telephone from the bedroom. You check school papers in the bedroom. You do your nails in the bedroom. Other than the bed, there's never a place to sit in the bedroom because your school work's piled on all the chairs," Ben complained.

Addie had a study for her computer and files. But, the bedroom was where she most wanted to be. Ben had once said, "The bedroom is for one of two things ... sleeping and you and me getting together. We have the whole rest of the house available for everything else."

Addie sucked her tongue and glared for a long time. Later, she'd come back to it, saying, "You're crazy Benjamin Parks and I'll do what I want in my bedroom. And you and me having sex; that's on lock down."

On the other-hand, Ben wasn't good with money. It wasn't that he couldn't be and his dad had certainly been a great example of frugality. It's just that Ben didn't think much about money. An entrepreneur, he usually made plenty of money, but he didn't have a pension plan or 401(k). His health insurance had been covered by his first wife, Yvette. When they split, though Ben rarely went to the doctor, any expenses he incurred were paid for out of pocket. Yvette had still covered the boys. Then when Addie and Ben married, he went onto her plan.

Ben's firm, Parks Freer Associates, had purchased several properties, basically in the places where he and Ted Freer did a lot of work and needed long-term stay over space, but these weren't liquid assets. Recently though, the firm had sold all but the two-bedroom walk-up in Harlem, near 138th Street and Convent Avenue. Ben also co-managed some of his dad's rental properties in DC. But generally, if the revenue stream from Parks Freer Associates dried up for over three months, Ben started to sweat.

As Ben understood it, Addie believed she was a good money manager. She lobbied to assume control of the family finances. But Ben often joked in his mind that Addie never saw a store she didn't like. Her spending he felt; especially in places like San Francisco, New York, or the Caribbean Islands; could be impulsive and lavish.

Ben was a more modest spender (though Addie didn't seem to agree with this view), except for when it came to cars. He liked nice cars, as their garage outside the solid but smallish LeDroit Park house could attest. The house was in constant need of repair for this or that. Addie and Ben had never been able to see money the same way, and they'd basically put a lid on (not solved) their differences by keeping their financial affairs essentially separate . . . that is, except for Ben's dependence on Addie's health plan.

Despite all the agitation, just as was the case with Ben's feelings for his father, Ben fiercely loved his wife, Addie Parks. He knew he loved her just as well as he knew that sometimes he couldn't stand her. And it didn't help Ben's confidence much that Addie was masterful at veiling how she felt about all kinds of things—including how she felt about Ben. Such was the drama that was the ongoing life between Ben and Addie Parks.

Chapter 16
Flashback: Addie before Ben

Addie Sherrie Isles was the youngest of four kids raised by parents who lived in Western Pennsylvania. Those people were of hardy stock. Addie had grown up in Newcastle: hunting country, auto worker country, steel mill country, coal mine country, high school wrestling country, tough guy and gal country. This was God-fearing people country, Joe Namath country, and Steelers country . . . not necessarily in that order.

Her dad didn't work the mines, but both her older brothers (Dave and Emmett) did—at least for a while. Her dad did construction work. Emmett eventually escaped to a professional life, but Dave stayed in the mines for over thirty-five years. Addie's older sister (Sue Ann) was a teacher, just like her younger sister.

As a kid, Addie was good at everything she tried: music (the piano, the organ, the clarinet, and the saxophone); sports (track and field, even girl's tackle football); board games of all sorts; roller skating; and most of all—her studies in school. Cute and slim, she was the apple of her dad's eye, and he spoiled her in every way he could . . . not monetarily so much as with his deep affection and with the small things he'd do to surprise her. Actually, the whole family spoiled Addie.

For them to spoil me that much, Addie recalled, *means they really, really loved me.*

Now Ben spoiled her. She didn't tell him that. But inside her, she knew it was true. They had met during her freshman, his senior, year at Middle State University just a ways over the state border from where Addie grew up.

But Ben also exasperated Addie and vice-versa. Ben had left her back in college when he graduated, and he'd never called or written again from the moment he left campus. Addie would have transferred anywhere to be close to wherever Ben was. As close as they'd been, Addie had been deeply hurt by his lack of contact . . . until finally she'd moved on with her life.

Anyway, through the grapevine she'd heard snatches of Ben's life. She knew that he had gone off to the army. Graduated from Middle State and married by now with her young son Adam, Addie got wind of when Ben came home from overseas and that he was back in DC working in some kind of community program. She knew that he'd become a "player," a term that made her sad.

Actually, the rumor was sort of true. There had been about a ten month stretch between Ben's graduation from college and him getting drafted. Ben's friend Levi had been drafted just two months before Ben. But during the eight months when the two old friends had hooked back up in DC, they had a contest they'd called "the book of the month club." A "book" wasn't something you read. It was tapping a new piece of ass. The quota was at least one per month, and though the friends never checked the veracity of each other's claims, Ben knew that he'd kept up with the quota. Levi claimed to meet the quota the first two months. Then he'd said that he bagged two or three new books every month until they rode him up to Fort Holabird in Baltimore for induction.

Though Addie knew that Ben had been drafted and had gone overseas, only years later would she learn that he hadn't been in Vietnam. Though he didn't talk to her about it, in some ways, Ben acted as if he'd been deeply touched by that war and his friends, Lou, Levi, Gerald, and Tracy. And she knew that he'd lost close friends in the war. After both of their first marriages had ended badly, they'd come back together, starting with that fateful meeting at 30th Street Station.

Much older now, and with Addie's one son Adam and Ben's two, Tony and Rico, they'd blended the families. By 1999, they'd been together now for over ten years. But Addie knew that they'd kept themselves apart in many ways, and for reasons neither of them would probably ever fully understand.

She admired Ben's tenacity when he tackled something. He was methodical, purposeful, and tough as nails in his professional life, and soft in his heart for his family including Addie and Adam. Sometimes, the spark of her love for her husband was so strong that she could hardly stand it . . . much less express it to him. At night in bed, he'd sometimes whisper, "I love you, A."

Her response was usually, "Thank you."

She knew he couldn't multi-task. She got so frustrated with him when she wanted him to do something and he was in this zone or that zone. On the other hand, she knew without admitting it, that she was somewhat the same way. The most recent amazing feat had been his sailing through his PhD program. He'd done the master's on the GI bill back in the 1970s. Then, in September 1985, with no warning, he'd come in one day and announced that he'd been late that evening because he was in class.

"What class?" she'd asked.

"I started my PhD program up on The Hill tonight. I just walked up on campus after work. That's why my car was in the garage."

Addie hadn't even known that he was applying for a PhD program—much less that he'd been accepted. She was furious.

"Your GI bill isn't going to cover this. Hasn't that run out by now? What are you going to do to pay for this PhD program? I told Lou I wanted him to start enclosing the porch this summer. That's going to be a $20,000 job."

"It's directly related to the business, so the firm will cover my tuition."

"So you'll draw out less in salary."

"No. We're actually doing pretty well."

The firm that Ben co-owned with Ted Freer had hit $3,000,000 in revenue for the first time that past year. Ben flew through his classes at a breakneck clip of three or four per semester, although he never cut back on his consulting work. In the last year of his PhD program, Ben had rolled out of bed, without an alarm, every morning at 3:00 a.m. He plodded downstairs and wrote sections of his dissertation until 6:00 a.m., then showered, got dressed and went to work consulting with some federal agency client. He did this six days per week for eleven months.

When Ben defended the dissertation in the spring of 1989, Addie had been pretty amazed and proud. She knew that Ben didn't really need this degree. But she also knew that Ben had wanted to please Dr. Richard and that was a big reason he was doing it. Ben could be clumsy, scattered, and inconsiderate. But when he was on top of his game, he was so capable ... not smart ... but capable ... scary-capable at times. Now the framed degrees hung side by side in Dr. Richard's study up in the Carter Baron neighborhood in DC. On the left, the translation from the Latin started out reading:

> The President and Trustees of Howard University in the District of Columbia award this degree of doctor of philosophy to Richard Roscoe Parks ... on this 12th Day of May, 1960 in this, the 94th year of the university.

On the right hand side on the wall, also in Latin in a frame that matched as closely as possible the framing of his dad's degree, hung Ben's degree.

> The President and Trustees of the Howard University in the District of Columbia award this degree of doctor of philosophy to Benjamin Xavier Parks ... on this 13th Day of May, 1989 in this, the 122nd year of the university.

Addie had thought about getting her degree too. But she wasn't going to do it the way her husband did it. If she went back to school, she was going to quit work and do it full-time. But she didn't want to hear Ben's mouth about her not working. And she didn't have a firm to cover her costs. There were loans and there was Ben. She had been through the loan payback thing for undergrad and for her master's degree. She didn't want that again. She decided to bide her time ... maybe one day.

Chapter 17
The Conversation

April 1999: Now, Addie looked at Ben and saw all his frailties and weaknesses, and felt deep antipathy. She wasn't going to make anything easy for him. She wasn't on his side. *Let him sweat,* she thought. Then, clearing her throat, Addie gave a little expression. It wasn't a smile. It wasn't a frown. It was a little turn of the mouth and lifting of the eyes to the side. Ben had seen it many times in the years of marriage. It usually meant that there was a difference of perspective, a difference of opinion, and that he was about to hear all about it. Addie challenged him about most things, small and large. That was just her way.

Finally, sitting on the other end of the couch in the living room from Ben, Addie spoke, "I think we have a relationship that takes a lot of work. I think that I'm busy and you're busy. I think that you're a workaholic and I'm a workaholic. I'm busy at school with my kids. I'm on a mission to do things in the house. We have repairs to make in the upstairs bathroom, and I can't stand the floors in this house. I'd like a new kitchen. I'm trying to save money to get things done. I have a lot of things on my mind, and you do too. That's what I think. It's nothing different."

Now, she drifted off into a reverie about this man to whom she'd been connected by marriage, and even for years before marriage, all the way back to their time together as college sweethearts. When they were younger, their relationship was fiery. Fiery hot and sensual at times . . . and fiery-hot-nasty with conflict at other times . . . never in the middle . . . never calm . . . never relaxed.

Even in the best of times, there was always a tension and a pull of opposition just under the surface. Yet, there was something about Ben that she wanted around . . . just not too close. Now, she stared at him. He was kind of tall . . . around 6 feet. She liked looking up at him when they stood close. She liked the way they looked together when they got dressed up and went out on the town. He didn't really like to dress up, but she did, and she thought he looked good when he did. As a matter of fact, she could get him to go along with almost anything... maybe not at first... maybe not even the second time. But, she could always wear him down. If needled in just the right way, he had a fiery temper but he couldn't sustain it. Basically, he liked peace and calm and eventually he would usually give her what she wanted if he could.

Ben took in Addie's observations with a nod.

"Yes!" he said. "Yes, I like how you said that. Our relationship takes a lot of work. But, do you think we're putting in the work? That's what I want to know. If the relationship requires work to make it work and we want it to work, do you think we're on top of it?"

"The other part of what I said is that we're busy," said Addie. "Did you hear that part?"

Thrust, parry, thrust, parry. That's what so many of their conversations felt like. Slowly Ben said, "Yes, I heard that part." He stopped and thought about where to go from here.

"You know," said Addie. "I'm tired of talking with you right now. I want to go upstairs and get ready for bed. I have a meeting with a parent before school starts and I want to be out early in the morning. Is there any reason why we should go on right now?"

With resignation, Ben had said, "No, I guess not."

Addie got up quickly and she was gone.

Ben quietly clicked on the boom box. He popped in a CD— Pavarotti's 'Nessum Dorma.' For some reason, that's what he wanted to hear right now.

Around midnight, Ben quietly walked up to the bedroom. The TV and lights were on. A mystery novel was on his side of the bed, and Ben put it on Addie's night stand. Flipping off the TV and turning off the lights, Ben slid in beside Addie, careful not to disturb her sleep. He whispered a little prayer in her direction. Then he rolled over facing away from her. He closed his eyes and drifted into semi consciousness. His mind seemed wide awake ... for the first time, he was conscious of racing repetitive thoughts.

I just, can't... I just can't... I just can't... I just can't... I just can't..

. I just can't... I just, can't... I just can't... I just can't... I just can't...
I just can't... I just can't... I just, can't... I just can't... I just can't...
I just can't... I just can't... I just can't...

How the hell long had he done this? The emphasis was on the 'just.' Over and over, the same phrase—with no ending—running through Ben's mind like a rhythmic choo-choo train . . . first chugging slowly on an uphill grade, then reaching the top and picking up speed for the downhill.

I just, can't... I just can't... I just can't... I just can't... I just
can't ... I just can't... I just, can't... I just can't... I just can't... I just
can't... I just can't... I just can't... I just, can't... I just can't... I just
can't... I just can't... I just can't... I just can't...

This single, repeating phrase continued in his head for pretty much the whole night. The next thing he knew, there was light coming through the curtains and Addie had gone to school.

Chapter 18
The Night Before the Seminar

On that August 1999 Friday night after his experience in the alley with the neighborhood tough guys, Addie and Ben had done their separate things until about 11:00 p.m. Addie had soaked in the tub, Ben had dealt with the feeding of the family, chilled and watched the sunset in the backyard, monitored the creative forces of Rico and company from a safe a respectful parental distance, prepped for his weekend seminar, and laid out clothes for tomorrow.

Then, for an unexpected change, around 11:45 when Ben joined Addie in bed she seemed to have been waiting for him. He had poked his head through the door before entering, as was his custom. Addie was already in bed. She wasn't on the telephone. She wasn't reading or checking school papers. She wasn't even doing one of her Sudoku puzzles.

The television wasn't on. Instead she'd put on the bedroom CD player, and when she saw Ben at the door, without smiling or saying anything, she just slid over to make room. This was to be one of their good evenings. Their intensity that night, that every-so-often happening when just the right vibe somehow materialized, was of the connected variety. At that point, "You Are Too Beautiful" by Johnny Hartman and John Coltrane was playing on the CD player.

Addie scooted forward and Ben positioned himself behind her. They started slowly. With Ben's back against the headboard, Addie sat back between his legs and rested against his chest. He just held her for a while until she moved one of his hands over to her breast. Now, drawing circles around the erect nipple, he smelled her and kissed the back of her neck. The CD changer made its move, found the right cut randomly, and now there was Marva Hicks.

You came and puzzled me so, I can't think. Am I in love with you or is this just another thing? Oh, I just surrender when you call. I am giving up, I'm giving all, and here I go again . . .

After the saxophone solo toward the end of this cut, the chorus reentered and vamped in crescendo,

. . . and here I go again, maybe I'll win but who really knows in this game. Oh here I go again, but who really knows . . .

Eventually, as she pressed back against him, Addie's low sound coincided with her moving Ben's hand lower on her body as she opened one of her legs over and to the outside of his. She placed his hand in just the right place, and Ben enjoyed the feeling of the warm place that had already turned moist as a local DC crooner group sang, *Whatever it takes, I'm going to make you love me . . .*

Addie moved on Ben's probing hand as he found her pleasure button and gently caressed it. Keeping with the lower body action, Addie turned her face to Ben's, and they kissed and played with each other's tongues and lips. They stayed with that as another CD change happened automatically to Gloria Lynn's *I Wish You Bluebirds*.

Addie suddenly spun around to face Ben and pulled him over on top of her. He entered her and they danced their special horizontal dance through another several cuts on the CD changer. Three or four times Ben used the Kegel technique to slow himself down, and then there was Dexter Redding, sounding quite a bit like his more famous dad, on the CD changer.

You gave promise to my life, with your lovely ways you made my love song worth singing. So let me thank you in my song for the joy you bring, the little things that give our love meaning.

Mark Lockett took over for Dexter on the chorus:

Oh, would you write this song with me. Help me phrase the melody. You are what I want this song to be. You inspire me. Lady, be my love song tonight . . .

Addie began to arch her back and seemed somehow to lift and spread herself even further under Ben's thrusting weight, as Dexter and Mark traded the lead back-and-forth . . . then the song eventually modulated:

Oh, you are my life's harmony; ever beautiful, never ending. Let me know you'll always be around. Lady, be my love song tonight. And forever, forever will the song be right. Oh, lady, be my love song

tonight and I'll sing you 'til the end . . . Oh, lady, lady, lady, lady be my love song tonight and I'll sing you 'til the end of time . . .

Addie exploded. Now Ben stopped his Kegel and allowed himself to follow.

Afterwards, he rolled to the side and held his wife until her soft purr let him know she had dozed off. Then he arose to putter, delight in the lovemaking, shut down the music, and finally, smiling, he returned to bed. It was after 1:00 a.m. For a while he lightly cupped that favorite behind place of Addie's in his hands—that wonderful anatomical part, most typically, but not exclusively, on display on the back side of sisters from certain of-color ethnicities, until he, too, was asleep.

Saturday morning Ben awoke around 7:00 a.m. feeling great. But soon, thoughts of his class up at Howard University replaced memories of the last evening. The seminar would start at 9:00 a.m. This would be the last weekend, and Ben's plans were to make it an appropriate finale.

Addie was sleeping in and Ben went downstairs to make his "I'm not cooking for anyone else today and probably need to eat healthy" meal: iron-rich Cream of Wheat, for his anemia, with dried cherries, soy milk, and that butter-like product that's advertised to be good for cholesterol.

Ben would finish off his breakfast with two of the sweetest peaches in recent memory, bought at the roadside Norman Farms locally grown vegetable and fruit stand, just outside DC at the intersection of East-West Highway and Beach Drive. He heated the water for his herbal organic lemon Echinacea tea; and when all was ready he took his seat out back at the small table where he had watched the sunset last evening. It was warm but not hot yet that morning, and Ben enjoyed the solitude before what would probably be a day of emotional fireworks between students in his seminar; hopefully coupled with stimulation, stretching, and enlightenment for at least some of them.

Today and Sunday would be the culmination of Ralph Prescott's academic vision: a summer seminar on race and culture for students drawn from the consortium of local universities. The graduate school dean had pulled in Howard students as well as some from Georgetown, George Washington, the University of Maryland, The American University, George Mason, Trinity,

Marymount, and Catholic University.

He unlocked his Lehman's-12 Centurion bicycle, which was always at the ready on the back porch under the covered awning. Lifting the lightweight vehicle down the steps into the backyard, he tied his satchel into place, mounted, and started peddling through the alley toward Georgia Avenue. On serious workouts, he went straight up 4th Street toward Howard, but he didn't want to sweat that much and the Georgia Avenue route wasn't quite so vicious. The morning air was fresh and exhilarating and Ben's mind moved back and forth between the ecstasy of last evening with Addie and the anticipation of the culmination of an amazing seminar journey that, earlier in the summer, had begun a new career adventure for him.

Chapter 19
Flashback: The
Seminar Starts

The June 1999 (Saturday) Session: In June, the first session of the weekend seminar had been informal, with a lot of introductions, tone-setting, and ice breaking happening on Saturday morning. Students from the various universities and disciplines got to put themselves and their needs out before the group.

A month earlier, Ben had sent out a syllabus and reading list with instructions that students should select a reading that was from a cultural, religious, political, or philosophical tradition other than their own. Ben's loose design idea was to stimulate student reflection about themselves, their cultures, and the culture of others. Then he intended to promote dialogs. Some would be planned and some would happen spontaneously. Perhaps the craziest of Ben's ideas was that he would draw heavily on metaphor and even fantasy. When he thought of the idea, he couldn't help thinking about Rico and his comic books. If Rico knew what his Pop was up to, he'd laugh himself silly; and then he'd feed Ben all kinds of ideas. Maybe Ben would even use some.

Thirty-eight students appeared that first Saturday morning in June at Frederick Douglass Hall on the campus of Howard University. Douglass Hall sat between 6th Street and the Quadrangle (Quad), which was the central grassy park where Howard's traditions like graduation and the annual Greek celebrations, with Stepping on Homecoming weekend, all happened. On the southern end of the Quad was Founder's Library, with its stately clock Tower. On the northern end was the Arts Building where the likes of Donald Byrd, Toni Morrison, Debbie Allen, Roberta Flack, and Donny Hathaway had all taught or studied. Between these two bookends on the east and west were the buildings of various departments, with Douglas Hall the most prominent one on the west-side.

In the southeast corner classroom with large windows and plenty of light on the second floor, Ben had arrived early in order to welcome students as they arrived. Fourteen were from Howard, the host University. All of these HU students were Of Color with nine being African American, two Afro Caribbean, one Nigerian, and two of East Indian decent.

Additional POCs were from the University of Maryland, Trinity College, Catholic University, and GW. Maryland had sent four African Americans and three European Americans. Trinity had sent two African American students. Marymount had sent three European American students, GW had sent three European Americans and one African American; and two each of the European Americans were from George Mason and the American University. Catholic University had sent one Latin American student, one Asian American student, and two European American students. One of the George Mason students identified himself as Republican, as did the two European American students from Catholic University, and one of the European Americans from Maryland. All the rest of the students identified as either Democratic or Independent.

All but two of the African American students identified themselves as either Protestant or Catholic, as did the Caribbean and Latin American students. The Nigerian student from Howard, one of the HU African American students, and one of the U of Maryland African American students were Muslim. One Indian student said she was Catholic and the other, Hindu. Among the European American students, seven identified themselves as Jewish, and the rest as Protestant or Catholic.

An expectant classroom of top students from the various consortium universities had assembled on the campus of Howard University for this highly selective seminar. Some of them were interested in culture in order to go on to careers in international relations. Some were law students or theology students at their various universities. Still others were interested in culture at the community activist level. Finally, there were some who in their papers—written as a pre-requirement to compete for a slot in the seminar—had indicated that they were headed for a career more like Ben's: working within organizational or community settings on issues of leadership, diversity, and change.

"Good morning," Ben had said in opening the session.

One or two students answered back. After Ben had waited perhaps five or six seconds, he slowly panned the room smiling and then said, "Well, I'd be very generous if I called that a D-minus."

He smiled again and several students laughed shyly. Ben went on, "I need you to know that I have some superstitions. One of them is that I believe I can tell a lot about how well an undertaking like this will turn out by whether people speak back to me when I first speak to them."

He paused again, taking time to be deliberate in opening up the session. Now quite a few of the students were grinning back at him.

"Would you like to have another chance?" asked Ben.

Nods and 'yeses' came back at him.

"Well, good morning!" he said again.

Immediately the room responded and predictably overdid it with their cacophony of 'Good mornings' or 'Good morning Dr. Parks' (from the students who remembered Ben's name from the syllabus they'd received in the mail).

"Thank you," said Ben. "I feel a lot better going forward now. Welcome to the first ever Consortium of Washington Metropolitan Area Universities Summer Seminar on Cross-Cultural Relationships" Ben had said in opening up that first session. "I'm . . ."

"What's our grade now?" interrupted Paul Domenici, one of the white students from the Political Science master's program at Marymount University.

Ben paused and pretended to contemplate.

"Well, I don't know. It's not very usual to jump from a D-minus all the way to an A. Do y'all think that's what just happened?"

Ben was careful to drop in a little Southern dialect.

Paul looked like he'd been caught off guard. Ahmad Muhammad, one of the African American students studying for his master's in Intercultural Communication at Howard jumped in, "No, but it's a good solid B now."

Ben was beginning to engage them right from the start. That was the whole point of this little drama he'd orchestrated.

"Really?" said Ben. "A good solid B. What do others think?"

Ben turned his thumbs up in a gesture soliciting their approval, "Let's hear it for a good solid B."

The room erupted with verbal affirmations as well as applause. Ben smiled back. Then to Paul, who'd asked the original question:

"I guess it's now a good solid B. Okay?"

Paul smiled back, saying, "Okay!"

Now Ben moved as he spoke, "Some of you seem to know that my name is Ben Parks and that according to your syllabus and my bio, I'm a PhD. All of that is true. And, I'll offer that you may call me Dr. Parks if you so choose, but I'm just as happy to be called Ben; but not Benjamin. Also, because you have my bio in front of you, I won't bore you with details from my educational and professional background. I will offer that and if at any point in this seminar you have questions about me, you may ask them, and I will try to answer them. Okay so far?"

Heads nodded and there were some sarcastic "Yes, Ben" comments from the students.

"But there is some additional introduction that I'll do that's relevant to the course content, which is culture and communication. I do this because I know that you will wonder many things about me and that some of you may become preoccupied trying to figure them out. So, I'll just tell you some things on the personal side of Ben Parks. And let me be clear. It is not my intention to make any of my cultural identifiers central in this seminar."

"That being said" continued Ben. "I'm a fifty-six year old black man born in the Deep South who grew up here in the nation's capital. I was raised in the African Methodist Episcopal church. My political affiliation is democratic, and I can remember only twice in my lifetime crossing over and voting for a republican candidate. I don't like political descriptors like liberal and conservative because I believe that people are amalgamations depending on what's being talked about; but when pressed I say that I'm progressive."

Ben took a breath and noted the rapt expressions on the faces of the students. Then again, "In terms of attraction orientation, I'm straight and I've been married more than once. My children are grown, and I have grandchildren. That's obviously not a full exposition, but those are the main areas of identity that I can think of at the moment."

Some heads nodded, and for the most part now people

answered with some variation on 'Okay, Ben' or 'Thank you, Ben' or 'Yes, Sir, Dr. Ben.' Ben didn't think he'd heard anyone calling him Dr. Parks at this point, but eventually that was the form of address that most of the students reverted to.

After more opening rituals, which included everyone introducing themselves and saying why they had wanted to be in this seminar, Ben informed students that after lunch they would not be dismissed, but that for three hours in the afternoon, they would be on their own to pull together a one-page paper and talk about insights from their readings. They could work in the class room, in the library, or anywhere else on campus they chose.

"This will be your opportunity to put something on the table that comes from your thinking and from your insights about some striking theme from another cultural perspective. At three p.m., we'll reconvene for probably about thirty minutes to not more than one hour. We'll just check in with you on how productive your afternoon was . . . and we'll organize ourselves for tomorrow which will be a full day of exploring your discoveries, questions, and concerns. And since we've already had the issue of grading come up . . ."

Ben paused and smiled and some students laughed, remembering the introduction on grades.

"Your grades are going to work sort of like they did earlier where I asked you what you thought you deserved. This time it's going to be based primarily on your assessment of the degree to which students' participation supported the learning of other students. That's all I'll say about that for now, but it'll become clear as we go along how the process works."

Ben had offered the disclaimer that he was not expert in all or even any of the cultural traditions that would come under focus. He suggested that some of the students would inevitably know more about certain traditions than he. He indicated that his role would be that of a facilitator and that his objective was to promote dialogs that might illuminate themes that he believed—or rather hoped— would be pertinent to all the traditions under focus.

"So, the six themes that will be at the center of our explorations on culture are tolerance, judgment, knowing, ambiguity, belief, and ideology. My hope is that through exploration and reflection on these themes, we'll all make some discoveries about our own cultures, and that we'll also get some insights about how cross-cultural understanding and cross-cultural communication could work better than it does now in our lives. I hope that makes sense, and I hope this all works. And if it doesn't, you can grade me down at the end of the summer for wasting your time. And I probably won't get invited back next summer to do this again."

Ben had paused and then finished, "I hope that sounds fair."

By this time, it was about 10:00 a.m. Ben then plunged into the main text for the seminar, which was Myron Lustig and Joelene Koester's "*Intercultural Competence*." Ben had chosen this text because these authors went beyond academic analysis to actually offer ideas, strategies, and skills whose use might lead to better cross-cultural communication and understanding. He asked students to form study groups of five or six and to find in their texts anything that spoke to any of the six seminar themes. By about 11:00 a.m., the study groups had a lot to report on, and Ben listened carefully to report outs which lasted for the balance of the morning.

At the end of the morning session, Ben had thought about riding the Centurion home for lunch. It was only a few blocks, but he decided to follow the same instructions as he'd given the students—stay on campus. He'd brought a bag lunch, so he went out on the quad, found a bench, and after eating, he started flipping through some journals he had collected that explicated various religions.

"Excuse me, Dr. Parks" came the soft voice from about five feet away.

Ben had looked up and then looked at his watch. It was 2:35, and he realized that he should get back into Douglass Hall to welcome students as they came back in. He looked again at the source of the voice. Sulukshana Shrivastava stood at a distance with an expression of deep concern. Ben placed his open journal face down on the bench beside him. He knew the face.

What's the name? What's the name, he thought anxiously.

Ben had read over the names of the registered students probably ten times over the past week. He'd particularly paid attention to foreign and unusual names and had even practiced pronouncing them out loud. And now he was blank.

Ben stood. "That's all right, Ms. . . ." suddenly the name tumbled out "Shrivastava" he said. Ben was returning the formality of her address to him. "Are you all right?"

He sub-vocalized a "Thank you, God" for the miraculous appearance of the right name just as he needed it.

"Dr. Parks, I cannot go through this seminar alone," she said.

Ben immediately intuited her meaning. He thought about what he should, or could say.

"You could be such a resource in the class," he finally said.

The young woman, a master's degree student in the College of Allied Health Sciences at Howard, had seemed to appreciate that Ben hadn't played dumb with some kind of lame 'what do you mean?' response; which would have caused her to go down a path of torturous elaboration. Even worse, Ben could have done the 'Huh?' or 'What?' or 'Excuse me?' gambit just to give himself time to react; which would have required her to restate what had been somewhat awkward and painful to state the first time. She seemed to relax at his understanding.

"Perhaps I could, Dr. Parks, but probably not. As I listened to them this morning, I increasingly was overcome by a sense of dread. I realized that they are not concerned with a lone Hindu woman among them. I'm not even saying that they should be, even though there are probably about one billion of us on this planet. And we're not just one belief system. We're actually many faiths under one umbrella name. But here in this country, I'm understanding that I and we are just not on their radar screens."

The young woman seemed so wise. Ben had thought of a way that he might try to persuade her to stay. Just as quickly, he decided, out of respect, against making his argument. Among the thirty-eight students registered in the class, there were Christians, and Jews, and Muslims, and then there was Sulukshana. Ben reached for his pen. Sulukshana opened a folder and took out a withdrawal slip. Ben had signed in silence.

Now there are thirty-seven, he thought.

"Thank you, Dr. Parks, for not making this more difficult than it had to be. I appreciate you respecting my decision and I assure you that I thought intensely on it for the last couple of hours."

"I know you did, Ms. Shrivastava."

"Do you have an office on campus? Is there a way that I could stay in touch with you?" she asked.

"No, I'm adjunct here at Howard." Ben offered her his business card.

"But if you ever want to speak with me about anything, please don't hesitate to call or email me. It would be my honor to help you or just to learn from you. If it's okay with you, I will make your apologies to the rest of the students. There's a lesson that I want them to receive."

"Thank you" was all she said. And then she was gone.

He pondered the notion of Karma, which he understood to show up in Eastern religious traditions such as Sulukshana's and wondered, *If this incident is cause, what will be the effect?* Then back in Douglass Hall, he had begun that afternoon's final session explaining that it could be difficult for anyone from any cultural grouping to be one-of-a-kind.

"Even so," Ben said. "I want to offer another sharpening of intent for this seminar."

This was the argument he had thought to make to Sulukshana.

"Unless the situation in the moment dictates differently, my idea is that this seminar will be constructed as a culture general as opposed to a culture specific conversation."

Ben paused before continuing. He looked through the faces in the rows of chairs and knew that he must elaborate.

"What's the difference?" he asked for effect and then walked to one side of the front.

"When you have a culture general conversation, you're likely to get more comfortable with differences . . . to get a deeper understanding of issues of prejudice, sexism and other isms, to appreciate how communication needs to be different in an intercultural environment versus a homogeneous environment."

Now, Ben took seven or eight steps to his left and was on the other side of the front of the classroom.

"On the other hand, when you have a culture specific discussion, you're looking to drill down in your understanding for instance of women's issues, issues of immigrants, or why and how particular cultural groups may clash . . . such as blacks and whites; Cubans and Dominicans; gays and straights; Catholics and Protestants; etc. Is that distinction clear and do you agree with aiming for a cultural general frame?"

"Not rilly, Dr. Ben!" one student finally spoke up.

It was Damien Brockington, a Howard student who was a

budding playwright working on his master's in the College of Fine Arts at Howard. Ben shifted his gaze back to Damien on the back row, and waited.

"Da black and white thang's da reason I wanted to be up in dis jon' Doc. Ya feelin' me?" he paused. "I'm jus saying . . ." he paused again.

Some smiled at his street delivery, and some looked totally confused. Damien gestured both hands out to the side and dipped his body and face to say 'that's all.'

Ben loved the code switching that had just happened. He looked at Damien and thought of Tony and Rico who also were bi-dialectical in the way that Damien had just demonstrated. He thought that Damien probably didn't know that on invitation from a friend and fellow professor, Ben had dropped in on a rehearsal at Ira Aldrich Theater on campus about a year ago. Damien was directing a play that he'd written. The friend had known that Ben would be interested in the subject matter. As a director, Damien spoke roughly but with eloquence, though with the same passion as in his more Ebonic delivery style. Now Damien was speaking as one of the characters in his play.

"I'm feeling you, Mr. Brockington ,and here's the deal I'll offer. We're going to aim for culture general, but if the situation in the moment seems like we need to shift, we'll shift. Will that work for you?"

Nodding and shrugging his face into agreement. "Now I'm down," said Damien.

Then Ben expressed his regret that Ms. Shrivastava wouldn't be going through the summer with them. The students had seemed to sense his sadness and most seemed to meet him in that emotional space.

"I will track her down here on campus and get to know her," said Ana Choudhury.

Ana was the other East Indian student from Howard. She was a marketing major in an MBA program over at the School of Business.

"Maybe I'll talk a little with her about the culture general versus culture specific distinction. Maybe she'll even come back."

"That would be very nice Ana," said Ben. "Thank you. I'd only ask you not to push her. I sense that she has deliberated quite a bit and I want us to honor each others' decisions."

"I understand, Dr. Parks," came Ana's reply.

Other students had turned toward Ana and their faces showed appreciation. Then, after arranging a presentation order for Sunday, Ben had said goodbye, and the students quickly had cleared out.

Chapter 20
The Sunday Session

Flashback Continued: The Sunday session had been a full day's exposé of thoughts about the six themes in relationship to the pre-work readings. The first two students to share their thoughts both made comments on the theme of judging others, but were rather careful and circumspect in their comments and no other student reacted once they had finished. Ben tried to tease more out of these presentations, but eventually moved on.

Then the third student was Joseph Dele Akinamoto. He was a Nigerian medical student at Howard and a Muslim. Joseph, who in this seminar wanted to be called JD, had read from Rabbi Hayim Halevy Donin's *To Be a Jew: A Guide to Jewish Observance in Contemporary Life.*

"The Rabbi quotes from the book of Exodus in the Bible," said JD.

"The Biblical passage reads 'You shall not oppress a stranger for you know the feelings of a stranger, having yourself been a stranger in the Land of Egypt' and then the author goes on to suggest that mistreating strangers in your land is a transgression."

JD, seated in the third row back on the left side of the room, looked up from his notes.

"It strikes me, Dr. Parks that your themes, judgment and ambiguity could be thought of as opposites. As I read about 'oppression, mistreatment, and transgressions' in these passages, I somehow connected them with the theme of judgment. Maybe that's a stretch but I think not. Harsh judgment of another, it seems to me, will lead to mistreatment. And consistent mistreatment over time can become oppression. So the Jew apparently is taught that doing these things makes him guilty of serious transgressions.

Later, the Rabbi specifically uses the word 'judge' saying that the Jew is supposed to judge on merit and give others the benefit of the doubt. Frankly I would have expected Jewish writings to be less tempered . . . more righteous when it comes to Jews judging others. I'm not a scholar of my own Muslim faith, so I was curious about whether I could find similar tempered guidance in the Koran when it comes to the judgment of others."

Adam Fierstein from the MBA program at GW spoke up from the very last row in the classroom.

"Ben, I'd like to speak to that. Jewish people . . ."

Ben cut him off. "Thank you, Adam, we really want to hear what you have to say. And this is a seminar on cross-cultural communication and understanding. So we might as well take advantage of the opportunity to model an approach. Would you come to the front please?"

Adam shrugged, seemed to think about whether he wanted to be a guinea pig, but then rose from his chair and slowly walked to the front where Ben was positioning two chairs.

"And, Mr. Akinamoto, would you join him in the other chair please?"

JD complied and sat stiffly across from Adam. The chairs were a comfortable three feet apart. JD pushed back to about five feet.

"Other than the introductions yesterday, have the two of you met?" asked Ben.

Both shook their heads. One could hear a pin drop in the rest of the room. The air was suddenly electric. Ben's total attention was on Adam and JD.

"Why don't you introduce yourselves to each other?"

JD made the first move.

"I'm JD Akinamoto, and I've just finished my first year in the medical school here at Howard. I'm from Nigeria, and my ancestors were Ibo." JD reached his hand forward.

Adam appeared to be having second thoughts about his decision to jump up and comment on JD's presentation. But he was here now. Briefly and gingerly shaking JD's hand, he said, "I'm Adam Fierstein and I'm studying Leadership and Management in the MBA program at GW. I hope to finish next spring."

Then after a pause, "Oh and my ancestors were from the tribe of the Israelites."

Both men were still stiff and neither had smiled, though a few chuckles about the ancestor comments were heard at this point from the viewers. Ben held up his hand and asked that folks not kibitz.

Ben said, "Now Adam, you wanted to respond to JD's comment. We really want to hear your response. But first I'd like you to tell us what you heard JD say."

Taking in the instruction, Adam's face strained and he closed his eyes. A slight grin appeared in the corner of JD's mouth, and then he was expressionless again.

"Well," started Adam gazing out at the rows of fellow students. "JD pointed to a couple of passages from a Rabbi's book about Jewish beliefs. He was commenting on the theme of judgment."

Ben, now hovering in the gap space between the two men, but just a little behind them leaned in to interrupt.

"I apologize, Adam. I said you should tell us. What I really want is for you to speak to JD."

Adam stopped and his throat showed a glottal movement. He took several deep breaths and then turned toward JD, who reciprocated by turning toward Adam. Then Adam blurted, "I heard you question whether we Jews were able to withhold judgment. I took your inference to be about Jewish relationships with the Arab world and the religion of Islam."

Adam paused. "There, I've said it. I probably would have said it differently before. But that's basically what I'm reacting to."

Ben started to interject, but stopped himself as JD started to speak.

"The only thing I'd change, Adam, is the words about questioning whether Jews were able. I don't remember exactly how I said it, but that was not my intent. What was surprising to me in the reading was the teaching, not the ability. I'm familiar with the Old Testament passage about an eye for an eye and a tooth for a tooth. It struck me that the Rabbi's comment about giving others the benefit of the doubt was suggesting tolerance rather than harsh judgments like taking eyes and teeth."

Adam's listening observably had become more relaxed and focused.

JD, a thin and wiry man of under six feet, continued in a quiet baritone voice, "I'm aware that my religion, Islam, is criticized as not being very tolerant. Since I value tolerance, it actually hurts a little to know that people feel that way."

Now JD was starting to fidget in his seat.

Ben interrupted, "So, JD, you've clarified and very shortly we want to hear where Adam is. So finish up your thought."

JD responded, "It's just that, growing up in Nigeria, I never heard about this concept of benefit of the doubt. I first heard the term when I came to the US. And then I looked for it in the Koran and couldn't find it. After I re-read the Rabbi's passage yesterday, I looked in the Koran to see if I could find a similar teaching. Here's the closest that I could find."

He opened his notes again and read, "If you shun the great sins on which you are forbidden, we will do away with your small sins."

Ben and the students who were watching had all shifted their gaze to Adam Fierstein. Adam was a much larger man than JD. And his hands were the first thing that Ben had noticed when he walked into the classroom yesterday. They were absolutely huge, having the feel of a catcher's mitt over Ben's when the two had shook hands. He had noticed the same thing when Adam's hand had engulfed JD's in their earlier hand shake.

Adam said, "Well, this has gone in a whole different direction than what I was reacting to. I have to admit that first. And the things that I might have said would have been pretty off the mark."

Adam paused and wrung those huge hands of his for six or seven seconds, and then continued, "JD, I think your comments are much more about your faith than mine. It just took something you read about Jewish beliefs to trigger your reflections."

Adam paused again.

"And I also am thinking that I want to read the book that you read and think about this idea of giving others the benefit of the doubt. I know that I don't give others the benefit of the doubt very often. I don't think Jews and Muslims give each other the benefit of the doubt. I think we're very judgmental of one another as people . . . and for good reason in many cases. But I admire the fact that you

97

went searching in the Koran after you read the Rabbi's book. I don't know if you're interpreting the passage you found correctly and I'm guessing you're not sure, either. But ..."

Adam ran out of steam. "I guess that's all I want to say," he concluded.

This time, Adam reached out his hand to JD ... and JD took it. Their handshake wasn't brief or formal this time. The students in the class erupted in applause. And for the rest of the afternoon, Ben coaxed the class to debrief what had taken place between JD and Adam. He suspended the process and the order of presentations because, as students talked about JD and Adam, they interjected insights from their own readings. But the conversation flowed more organically with the relaxing of the structure. Ben used newsprint to note insights people had about the cross-cultural communication that had just taken place.

Chapter 21
Life Interrupts

On Wednesday night of the week leading up to the second monthly sessions of the Seminar on Cross-Cultural Communication at Howard University, Ben got a call from his sister Penny around 7:00 p.m. This had been a week with no travel and a light client schedule: just a planning meeting with an energy conservation non-profit exec on Monday, paperwork at home on Tuesday, and a couple of executive coaching sessions earlier that Wednesday.

Picking up the phone, Ben said "Hello" and immediately heard stress in his sister's voice.

"Where are you, Ben?"

"I'm home in DC, Sis. Where are you?"

Penny had lived in Kansas City for about twenty-five years, had raised a family there, and had divorced her husband in the mid-90s, but stayed on there in the mid-west even though most of her kids had migrated east.

"I'm in KC, but I've been on the phone with Corinne. I've also been talking to Dad for the past few weeks. Ben, I'm thinking about moving back to DC."

"Cool!"

"Well, yeah I guess you told me so. You've been saying that's where I need to be. And I have felt stranded out here since all the kids left. There's really no reason for me to be out here other than this big old house."

"Sell it and get your ass back home, Sis. You couldn't get anything that big here in DC for the price, but you could still get a nice home."

"No Ben, if I do it, I'd move in with Mom and Dad."

"Really? Are you sure that's a good idea? You're going to be a little girl again. It doesn't matter how old you are or how many kids you have."

"Yeah, I've thought a lot about that. But Dad says mom's been acting funny. He thinks she might be slipping . . . like ClayClay."

Instantly Ben got an image and his mood turned apprehensive. Ben's and Penny's Aunt Claire was Gillian's next older sister. And Aunt Claire, along with Ben's grandma and Gillian were the fine southern cooks from whom Ben had inherited his love of the kitchen. ClayClay, as everyone affectionately had always called her, used to joke, "You know, my secret ingredient's my elbow. My elbow's sweet as sugar. Whatever I'm cooking . . . I just stick my elbow in it several times as it's poppin' and perkin' on the stove."

Once on a summer visit to Selma, Ben had asked his aunt, "Are your toes sweet too ClayClay? What if you stuck your toes in the food? Would that make it even sweeter?"

"Boy, you're crazy," had said Ben's mom jumping in. "You must not have seen ClayClay's dirty feet."

"My feet ain't never dirty!" shouted Aunt Claire. "But I never use my feet child. The sugar in my body flows down and so the sweet in my feet is so potent, the food would come out making everybody fat. Nope, the elbow sweet is just enough."

Ben's mom and Aunt Claire had laughed for the rest of that long-ago afternoon as they prepared the family meal together. Ben had watched every move, but never saw Aunt Claire stick her elbow in anything. As he grew, he figured out the joke, and later as an adult, he remembered it and used it himself. Ben hadn't seen his Aunt Claire in a decade or more until last year.

Now, in his mind's eye, he saw back the previous year. His Aunt Claire, leaning on his cousin Corinne, was barely able to walk as she was guided through the door on a visit from Selma to Richard and Gillian's house in DC. Ben's jaw had dropped. He had had no idea what to expect. Perhaps no amount of description by his cousin could have prepared him for the tiny and fragile woman who had replaced his vibrant and jovial aunt ClayClay. The thirty or so other relatives, who had assembled last Thanksgiving day for the annual family repast, had all gone silent as Corinne and her mom came in. Aunt Nellie rushed to the other side of ClayClay and helped Corinne guide her onto the soft sofa.

With a tortured face sitting on top of a body that couldn't have been more than seventy-five pounds soaking wet; Aunt Claire's body stepped tenuously . . . one foot . . . then after a few seconds, the next foot . . . and was a continuous river of what seemed like violent shaking. But, the tremors were what shook Ben the most. The pained expression on her face, coupled with Corinne's strained face . . . were like a visual gut punch to Ben's naïve and unsuspecting eyes.

Since then, every time he thought of ClayClay he saw her tremors . . . shakes like he'd never witnessed before. It had taken all of Corinne's attention and strength to guide her mom through the front door and into the first seat in the living room. And that's where ClayClay stayed through the entire visit. After grace was said, the family sat at the dining table and various side tables around the dining room and living room; all except for Corinne who pulled up a TV tray next to her mom and fed her little bites, while she ate herself from the same plate. Aunt Claire was ministered to by various members of the family as they finished their meals and came over to the couch.

ClayClay audibilized, but never spoke an intelligible word. She really didn't seem to recognize anyone or anything. Before they had left, Ben remembered Penny disappearing into the bathroom with ClayClay and Corinne following her with what looked like an oversized baby diaper. Ben had kissed his Aunt on the cheek when she was seated on the couch, but there really hadn't been any conversation about her during the dinner. Ben put two and two together in his mind, but never asked about the diaper. He really hadn't wanted to hear details.

At the end of the evening, Corinne, Gillian, Richard, and Aunt Nellie all negotiated ClayClay back out through the door, out to the street, and into Corinne's car. And, they were gone.

***

Ben thought of Addie. Later that same evening back at home, Addie came into the porch area where Ben sat alone; brooding in silence. "What's up, B?"

"I don't know, A . . . are you all right?"

"Yeah, I'm all right. It's you that's acting strange."

Ben started, "What do you mean, I'm acting strange? I'm not acting strange."

101

Addie's volume went up a notch.

"Don't tell me you're not acting strange. You are acting strange, and you've been acting strange ever since you saw your aunt over at Mom and Dad's. Now, if you don't want to talk about it, cool . . . but don't tell me you're not acting strange."

The sound of her voice was like a loud siren going off in his head. He just glared at her. He didn't have any words. He hadn't processed any of his feelings. He didn't know what was going on with him, or why. He just wanted her to leave him alone. He glanced over at her, and then his eyes moved from hers, down to her breasts. She was breathing deeply and evenly, and they swelled under her soft blouse. Suddenly, Ben wanted his wife. He wanted her in the worst sort of way. He looked back up at her and the expression had changed to alarm.

As Ben moved forward, Addie stood up straight. Ben walked toward her and reached under her skirt to stroke her smooth thighs.

"No, Ben" said Addie. Ben didn't stop moving his hands upward under her skirt.

"Benjamin!" said Addie as a warning. He leaned forward to kiss her as he tried to back her up against the wall. Addie slapped him hard across the face.

Stunned, Ben froze, then he snatched his hand back and stood back.

"You won't talk to me, and now you want to fuck me," she shouted.

Her volume was piercing in the crisp night air in their backyard.

Ben went back downstairs into the yard. He fell back into his blue chair as he partially covered his ears and moaned. Then he snapped, "What's wrong with that? Why can't a man just fuck his wife when he needs to? What's wrong with that?"

Ben glared at Addie and Addie glared back.

"You're right," said Ben. "I just want some pussy. I want to fuck. That's all. I could go out somewhere and find it on the street, but I don't want to. I want it from you. You're my wife. What's wrong with that?"

In her biggest voice, Addie screamed, "I'm not just some pussy you selfish bastard. And what was that crack about getting it somewhere on the street? What the fuck is that all about Benjamin?"

The sound reverberated through in the night. Ben imagined neighbors listening behind their windows all down the alley. Then they fell into silence. Finally, after about five minutes of standing and looking at him, Addie went back inside without another word and went upstairs.

***

On the phone talking with Sis, Penny interrupted her brother's reverie, "Do you ever talk to Corinne or your Aunt Nellie?"

Corinne had left Selma after high school for college at Howard University and had never gone back home. Now she was a successful real estate agent in DC and the suburbs of Maryland. Aunt Nellie, divorced from Herman Tyndale who had fought under General Patton in North Africa in WWII, was the youngest of Gillian's sisters, and she still lived in the Michigan Park section of the District, near where Ben grew up.

"Every now and then I get an email from Corinne, and I hit her back. Mainly I see Aunt Nellie when she's over at Mom and Dad's. Why?"

"She says she's bringing ClayClay to DC 'cause her mom just can't take care of herself anymore."

Corinne's dad had died a few years ago, and Corinne had faithfully visited her mom back in Selma, Alabama every couple of months since then. But soon after her husband's passing, Aunt Claire (ClayClay) developed signs of dementia. Back in Selma, Ralphine was another cousin who had kept up with ClayClay and been the bridge between Corinne and her mom in between visits.

"ClayClay is going down fast" said Penny. "Her dementia is full-blown Alzheimer's now. It's progressing rapidly and Corinne feels like she's got to bring her up to DC."

Ben felt out-of-touch . . . and guilty, "Wow! I didn't know."

Then, cycling back in his mind, "What's Dad saying about Mom?"

"Poor Ben," said Penny. "You know, you really ought to talk to your father. And you could maybe talk to him about more things than just baseball."

"Ouch!"

"I know. Sorry!" said Penny quickly.

"Ben, your Father worries about you and your business and all your travel. I guess I do too; a little. I mean, he's proud of you and what you've built, and I am, too. But you're what, fifty-five years old now? You're constantly on the go. You travel to all ends of the world. You're gone fifteen days out of every month. You must make good money, but Dad guesses that you don't have any retirement. I think he's probably right. Are you ever going to stop?"

Now Ben was feeling defensive but didn't want to be distracted. "Penny, what's Dad saying about Mom?"

"Mom's been diagnosed, Ben. She's in early stage dementia."

The news poured over and around Ben like quick sand. He felt himself sinking, and he couldn't catch his breath. The two siblings were silent on the phone for a while.

Then breathing sporadically, Ben's whispered voice asked, "What . . . what do we need to do?"

"Dad and Aunt Nellie are in crisis mode. That's why I need to be in DC. You're gone all the time, Bro. I need to be there to help out."

"So this is just a courtesy call. All this is planned. You're just letting me know, huh?"

"Ben, I'm sorry! I know you have a good heart. But, you're not in a position to help much. I'm not doing anything out here in Kansas City but sitting in a house that's too big for me and teaching piano to a bunch of kids. Frankly I'm getting tired. I've been away from home for over two decades. I want to come home."

"Let me know what I can do, Sis. I'm sorry, I've gotta run."

"Ben!"

"I gotta go, Penny."

"Love you!" said Penny.

"Love you, too," said Ben.

He hung up. Then, after pouring a triple Irish whiskey on ice with no chaser, he went out to the side porch and turned on the TV. That's where he fell asleep that night. The next day, Addie peaked in with a quizzical look as she puttered around the house; cleaning. They didn't talk.

By the weekend, Ben had pulled himself together. He was ready for this month's adventures up at Howard.

Chapter 22
The July (Saturday) Session

More Flashback: Before that July session began, Ben had written some suggested insights on three sheets of newsprint as a way of reviewing the June sessions. He opened the Saturday morning discussion by asking the students to comment on what he'd written.

In June's session, you seemed to agree on the following:

Source documents such as the Bible, the Koran, the Torah, the Communist Manifesto, and the US Constitution are somewhat unclear or mixed about whether they require animosity toward other religions or political/philosophical traditions.

The most strident writings in the various traditions, while initially off-putting, appear after reflection to be legitimately understandable reactions to egregious circumstances that had befallen those believers or citizens.

When cross-cultural misunderstanding is likely, it may be necessary to slow down and check your understanding before plowing ahead with a reaction that might be off-the-mark and unnecessarily damaging over the long-term.

Before turning to the homework readings for that Saturday's session, Ben had allowed for a leisurely commentary on these three bullets. The comment on the third sheet of newsprint predictably caused a collective reliving of Adam and JD's exchange. It had been great theater for most. The observation on the first butcher sheet had caused students to bare down on one of the sentiments that JD had expressed. It was the comment about the criticism of Islam as not being very tolerant. JD Akinamoto, Ahmad Muhammad from

Howard School of Engineering, and Rashid Jillali, a doctoral student in the School of Management at the University of Maryland were subdued in this conversation and obviously felt out of their depth to thoroughly address the questions that folks were raising about certain passages from the Koran.

Ben had encouraged people to not push the three Muslim students, but rather to give their fellow students the benefit of the doubt. He offered that if the issue kept coming up, he would ask one or more Islamic scholars to come and address the class in the August session. During the wrap up on Sunday, he then had asked students if they would like him to make those arrangements. It had seemed that the steam had gone out of the issue for most, and when he asked the question, the decision was that there were intriguing things on the docket that people wanted to experience and that they wanted to stick with the syllabus.

Ben had doubt. He wondered if this was an opportunity that he should have pushed. But he also knew, or rationalized, that this six-day seminar aimed to cover a huge conceptual and emotional territory and that choices had to be made. Then he received an unexpected affirmation.

"Culture general, right, Dr. Ben?"

It was Damien, with a broad smile on his face.

Ben immediately noted the standard dialect.

"For a moment we were becoming quite specific, but you're right, Mr. Brockington. Thank you for your observation."

"You're certainly welcome, sir," came Damien's reply.

Other students, who'd been lost when Damien had spoken back in June, showed surprise in their expressions. Ben again was faced with a choice.

Do I go down the rabbit hole of dialect? Is that the highest value opportunity at the moment? he thought. But because the tone had been so heavy thus far, he decided not to.

For the rest of that Saturday morning, Ben had let them play. He'd remembered that Dr. Prescott had given him permission, even urged him, to be out-of-the-box in leading this seminar. The following fable: reminiscent of something Rico might have written, provided the context for some fun and games:

Dear Earth Person:

We would like to respectfully introduce ourselves. We are visitors from _____. We are neither missionaries nor colonizers. We are, with one small exception, totally peaceful. But a managed crisis of increased population on our planet, which we have been able to contain for the past thirty thousand earth years since we identified the problem, has finally reached a level that is life-threatening. Therefore, we have embarked on a systematic process of population shifting.

In seeking compatible climates across the universe where we can coexist with indigenous populations, we have come across Earth. We are resource sustaining, so that our presence does not add to the resource demand—so as long as our indigenous neighbors are effectively utilizing resource discipline, there is no problem.

We have been observing your planet as a potential relocation site for fifty years. There are many attractive features here, and we have unilaterally decided to join you on Earth. However, we have come to the tough decision that a one-time remedial intervention is required before you can coexist with us and mutual sustainability can be realized.

You are one of a sub-set of something more than one billion in your species who are simultaneously receiving this telepathic message. Because of their commitment to wars and wasteful resource utilization, the remaining inhabitants of your planet are beyond saving. With or without our presence, these other earth inhabitants are on a course for the certain destruction of your planet.

But for the one billion of you, you are respectfully directed to reflect on anything that you can individually do differently to optimize the planet and to coexist with us as peaceful co-inhabitants. Some tangible actions by you are required forthwith—i.e., in the next three earth days. To the extent that you come up with tangible and non-reversible signs of your desire for a sustainable coexistence in the three day period, we will take your actions as a sign of good faith. We realize that the completion of your transition may take more time, but we must be sure of the seriousness of your intentions within the three-day period. Otherwise you will be immediately terminated along with those who, as we said, are beyond hope.

Those who remain . . . and we hope that will be all one-billion of you . . . will have no fear of us. To the extent that you desire our assistance at any point or in any form, we will be willing and friendly neighbors after this initial intervention. Thanks for your attention, and the clock starts now.

"Well Ben, the whole war-of-the-worlds fantasy drama is a little hokey," said Adam Fierstein as he looked up from reading his handout.

Ben, always scanning, had noticed a momentary scowl on the face of Damien Brockington. Ben's only response was, "Busted! Soooo, are there any other tomatoes people want to throw at me before we get back to the point of what you would do."

Nobody else offered. Adam had continued, "But I did have a serious reaction to these aliens' short deadline for doing something tangible. I suspect that a lot of folks will want to figure out a way to negotiate and I don't think these aliens are playing. At the end of the three days, a lot of folks are going to be zapped."

"Well, honey, what would you do to not be zapped?"

It was Margaret Brown. Margaret was in the master's program in Educational Administration over at Trinity University. She and her friend Zenovia Strong sat in the middle of the classroom and were probably in their early forties. They appeared to be the oldest students in the seminar.

"I don't know. Maybe turn my car over to the air pollution police and ride the bus. Or buy a bicycle. Or both" replied Adam. "That would be dramatic for me. Or maybe go find that little kid . . . what was his name . . . anyway, that kid I used to pick on back in grade school. And I'd mow his lawn with a push mower and rake his leaves for a year. I don't know if the aliens would believe me. They want things that are irreversible. I think I'm going to get zapped."

"I think you may be right Adam," said JD laughing. "You're going to get zapped."

"Chile, I'm just going to pray and keep doing most of what I'm doing" said Zenovia. "I figure if you're already doing good, the aliens know that. I think the gas guzzling is probably a big thing and I'd try to ride the Metro mostly. Just keep my car for out-of-town trips. But

I think the aliens know that I'm good to my husband and my neighbors and that people like me and Margaret are serious about teaching children. I think they'd want to keep us around."

It was interesting how the fantasy medium of Rico's choice could still grab students in their twenties and thirties and tease out ideas that were pertinent to such a complex topic as cross-cultural communication and understanding. Ben directed students at various points to look at their textbooks.

With talk of aliens, religious wars, the James Byrd killers the previous year (1998) down in Texas, ethnic cleansing in Bosnia in 1995, the Tawana Brawley false allegations in 1987, the Lockerbie bombing in 1988, the Bernhard Goetz subway shooting incident in 1984, and a ranging number of other examples of things the aliens could be angry about; Ben had let students pose questions, propose solutions, and explore a wide swath of cultural territory across the lunch hour and way into the afternoon on Saturday. With a head of steam still high, they had come back in the afternoon to talk about Hutus and Tutsis in Rwanda; the occupation of Kuwait; the settlements on the East Bank; the 1989 Exxon Valdez oil spill; the insatiable appetite for fossil fuels; homeless Palestinians across the years; the 1968 My Lai massacre incident from back in Ben's army era; Japanese internment and the Nazi concentration camps of World War II; and even back to the Tuskegee syphilis experiments.

They couldn't get enough of talking about the underlying assumption, what specific things the aliens had observed, and most of all how humanity should respond.

"I'm on these aliens' side," said Margaret. "I think they ought to just wipe out a lot of us."

Damien from the back row nodded in agreement.

"Speak for yourself!"

It was Roger Simmons, a master's degree student in the Conflict Management program at George Mason University. Roger was sitting right in the middle in the front row.

"We have a right to exist. People gotta do what they gotta do. We do a lot of good things too."

"Yeah," said Damien. "And those aliens gotta do what they gotta do," he said mockingly.

The class erupted in laughter. Roger had sat back in his chair showing the obvious embarrassment spreading across his face.

Again, Ben had just listened. His basic premise for the seminar from the start had been that the students' understanding and appreciation of other cultures couldn't happen out of a self-righteous blindness to the warts within their own cultural traditions. He liked the idea that threatening aliens could prompt even perhaps some of the most ideological students in the room to start to admit to flaws in their behavior patterns.

Chapter 23
One More Flashback: The Sunday (July) Session

On Sunday, the day started with more concepts from Lustig and Koester. In particular, they talked about the authors' BASIC model. BASIC stood for 'Basic Assessment Scale for Intercultural Competence.' Each of the characteristics were explored in depth with numerous references back to the aliens and whether or not adopting and building these competencies (display of respect, knowledge orientation, empathy, interaction management, task role behavior, relational role behavior, tolerance for ambiguity, and interaction posture) would be enough to save people from being zapped. Then toward the middle of Sunday afternoon, Ben had shifted and taken another big risk.

"There's a cultural grouping that we haven't heard from to this point and we're more than halfway through our seminar. So, I'll ask the question. Does anyone in this classroom identify as gay, lesbian, bisexual, or trans-gendered?"

Dead silence.

Ben had a stool in the front of the classroom and took the opportunity to take a seat. He'd been pacing up and down and back and forth all day intently listening to the conversation, and suddenly he felt extremely tired. He thought, *Was this the right time to raise this time bomb?*

But he kept seated and kept quiet.

Sadie Struthers, a master's student from the school of African

American studies at Howard finally spoke up and asked, "If someone were gay, would he or she answer up to your question, Dr. Parks?"

"I don't know, Ms. Struthers. Say more about your question please."

"You know Ben,"—it was Adam Fierstein—"it's becoming dangerous to respond to any of your open questions or bite on things that come out here. You trapped me last month, and now you're trying to trap poor Sadie."

Adam looked around for some reaction from other students. He appeared to be joking and wanting approval for his wit, but students weren't reacting.

"Well, Adam," said Ben finally. "That's funny. But I'd offer another version of what happened last month. I didn't think of it as a trap. If it was a trap, you trapped yourself. I thought of it as an opportunity and that's how I'm thinking about where we are now."

"I'm just playing, Ben. Thanks for catching the joke," said Adam.

Ben turned to Sadie, just as she spoke.

"I'm just saying, Dr. Parks. Gay people don't generally go around telling people that they're gay."

"First, I know that, Ms. Struthers. But I want to explore it a bit. Will you explore it with me?"

"Sure, I ain't scared."

"So, why is that, Ms. Struthers? Why don't gay people tell others they're gay?"

"Because they'll get ragged or jumped on. There are so many haters around, you know."

"Wait a minute!" It was Roger.

Ben let him in. "You have something to contribute, Mr. Simmons?"

"You've already told us back in June that you're, what'd you call it—progressive. People I know call it LLLLLLLiberal. But so far in this seminar we've only been talking about genuine cultures. So why introduce immorality now? Maybe we don't want to talk about gay people just as much as they don't want to say they're gay."

"Roger, you can really be stupid sometime, you know that?"

It was Trish Coleman from the same George Mason master's program. She was speaking up for the first time.

Mindful of his gate keeper role, Ben was feverishly calculating whether to let another participant into the fray. He looked at the energy behind Trish's eyes, and knew that she had something important.

"Say more, Ms. Coleman."

"What the hell are you talking about, Trish?" asked Roger.

He appeared shocked and seriously caught off guard. He and Trish rode over to campus together from Northern Virginia.

"Here it is: I'm a Lesbian, Roger. We've been in school together for at least three semesters. And if you hadn't been so busy trying get in my panties and hitting on every other woman in the program, maybe I would have told you that before now. I'm a Lesbian, and I resent the inference that I'm immoral. I'll stack my degree of goodness up against all your carousing and womanizing anytime you want Mister."

Trish took a deep breath.

"For God's sake, Roger, we're in a conflict resolution program. What on earth are you doing there? What are you doing in this program? Are you just trolling for chicks or what? You obviously don't care anything about cross-cultural competence. I don't know why you even bother."

Roger's already pale complexion drained of any semblance of blood that it might have possessed.

Sadie Struthers stood and applauded. Then Adam Fierstein stood and joined. Soon, about half the students were standing and clapping.

"Fuck you, Trish. And Bitch, you can have this coon rent-a-professor and his llllliberal, socialist, touchy-feely seminar."

Back pack in hand, Roger was now walking.

"You can also find your own ride back home off this ghetto campus" said Roger, as he reached the class room door and stormed away.

Ben was calm on the outside. He was still seated on the stool. Students were obviously shocked. Many of the male students from Howard were visibly offended by the remark about Howard. Chauncey Davis from Cleveland, Jacque Chenault from Martinique, and Elmore Steward from Jamaica rose as if to go after Roger. Looking toward the door, Damien Brockington was directly in Ben's line of sight and they caught each other's eyes. Damien quickly got up and stood at the door to block Chauncey, Jacque, and Elmore. Romaine Castor, a Howard Divinity student, rose and stood next to Damien. The ruckus inside of the classroom was okay and potentially instructive. To take it outside the classroom would not have been smart. Damien was every bit as big as Adam Fierstein; and the three Howard defenders retreated back to their seats.

"Where you need to go, Trish? I have a car," said Sadie.

"Fairfax."

"I don't know where that is, but you'll show me," said Sadie.

"I know where it is" said Paul Domenici. That's where I live. You've got a ride today and also in August if you want, Trish."

Trish looked at the same time both defiant and relieved.

"Thank you so much Paul. And thank you, too, Sadie. This means a lot to me."

Now Ben stood and walked to his easel. He flipped to a new butcher sheet. He wrote two words there: 'Judgment' was the first. The other was 'tolerance.' He turned to the students who showed in their expressions that they already were locked in with his train of thought.

Pleased with what he saw so far, Ben said, "Now one path for processing what just happened would be to talk about how these two out of the six seminar themes just manifested right before our eyes. I'm seeing in your faces that you're there. So, unless someone needs to give it voice, I think instead I'll take this opportunity to draw from our text. Look at Lustig and Koester. We've spent a lot of time talking about the BASIC competencies. Would you agree that they are relevant to what just happened?"

Nods from the audience.

"Which ones in particular?" asked Ben.

"Display of respect," said Damien from the back row.

"And I'd say interaction posture, Dr. Parks," said Paul. "That takes us right back to your judgment theme. When you are competent in your interaction posture, you're able to talk about and describe what you think without slamming another person. Roger was slamming everybody and particularly you and Trish. But I felt it too. I think of myself as politically progressive, just like you."

"I agree with those two," said Charlotte D'Souza.

Charlotte and Gail Polenski were from American University's master's program in organization development. Ben, as an OD person himself, had frankly expected these two ladies to be in the middle of the fray in the seminar and had been surprised that their comments had mostly been brief and unremarkable; until now.

Gail picked it right up from Charlotte, "Yes, Charlotte and I came here in particular to explore the theme of ambiguity, and we were quite surprised and pleased to find it on your list of six. But we haven't focused there much to this point."

Charlotte tagged teamed with Gail.

"This is an opportunity to really think about how hard it is to be competent in the face of ambiguity. And it probably also brings in your theme on empathy. Sorry, that's not one of your themes. Empathy is from somewhere in the text. Anyway, I think you're right Ben. I think that part of Roger's issue was that he thought he knew what was going on and then ambiguity walked in the door in the form of Trish's unexpected admission."

Now Gail again said, "Roger seems to have had a paradigm that he was comfortable with. I'm thinking that he sees himself as a stud and that he sees women, especially attractive ones like Trish, as fair game."

"And that whole thing blew up in an instant and he just couldn't handle being thrown into ambiguity," said Charlotte.

The two American University students had the room in the palm of their hands. Gail strode to the front of the room, and Ben went back over to his stool.

"Charlotte and I met in our program and hit it off right away. We're both working professionals, and we both seemed to think we knew a lot. And then they started confronting us with this ambiguous situation and that ambiguous situation. The whole program has been blowing our minds."

Charlotte was suddenly beside Gail. "And to our mutual surprise, we love it!" she said. "So we saw it with JD and Adam in June and now again with Roger and Trish this month. People thrown into situations, making snap judgments about what was, and then totally realizing that they didn't understand; and people can't handle not understanding."

With this crescendo, Charlotte had come to her central thesis.

Gail repeated it, "People can't handle not understanding!" She paused.

"Yet, who the hell ever promised us that we'd be able to understand everything? Which one of our source books makes that promise?"

Charlotte said, "We think that humans are just arrogant as a race and the biggest symptom of our arrogance is our seeming belief that we know everything and if we don't know it now, we can learn it and then totally understand it. That's probably one of the biggest things the aliens are pissed off at us about."

Gail said, "Every time we go back to the OD program we're in, they throw another complex situation at us that could be this, and it could be that, and it could be something else."

Charlotte said, "And now we're in this cross culture seminar; and we thought organizational dynamics were complex. This culture stuff is over the top. Some of these eruptions we've seen here so far are beyond anything we've done over at AU."

It was Delia Menendez from Catholic University now. Delia was in the theater arts program, and she and her friend Xia Liang were the only undergraduates in the seminar. Ben had noticed that Delia seemed quite taken with Damien Brockington, and that the feeling might be becoming mutual.

"I'm thinking ,Gail," said Delia, "about your question about which source book promises us that we'd be able to understand. I didn't bring it with me, but there's a passage in the Bible that says something like, "Lean not on your own understanding.""

"Proverbs!" shouted Zenovia; slightly ahead of Romaine, who signaled a thumbs-up sign to the Trinity student across the room.

Gail looked at Delia, then at Zenovia, and then over to Ben.

"We rest our case!"

The classroom erupted again with joy and applause, and Ben found it quite ironic that their joy was in large part a function of a collective realization and seeming acceptance of their inability to understand everything.

What an epiphany, he thought.

Eventually, at the end of the day, Ben came back to tie up what he thought was a loose end.

"I have the view that there is at least one culture, probably more, within the grouping known as GLBTs. It was my view that these several cultures are often invisible, even in a seminar with a label like 'cross-cultural interaction.' And I raised that issue at the outset of our most recent wild and bumpy ride because I didn't want by omission to exclude any members from those cultures, who might have come to this seminar to find their place within the discussion. That was my motivation for asking my question. I didn't know what to expect. I certainly didn't expect what happened to happen. But I'm not sorry that I asked the question."

"I'm not sorry, either, Dr. Parks," said Trish Coleman.

"So," continued Ben "on page . . ."

"Wait a minute, Ben." It was Adam Fierstein again. "You're not going to leave us hanging. Surely, you have something to say as our erudite professor about Roger Simmons."

Slowly Ben regrouped. Ben's first thought was, *And now there are thirty-six.* But he didn't say that.

Ever so willing to call this rent-a- professor to task aren't you, Adam? Well, as you point out, I do it to you so . . . Ben thought, *I also notice that I've gone from a rent-a-professor to erudite in a very short time. That's interesting.*

He physically relaxed himself with a few deep breaths. Then he said, "I guess the first thing I need to say is that I hope no one draws any negative inferences about the conflict management program at George Mason from what you've just witnessed. I know it to be a top class program with many first class professors and graduates who have gone on to do important work."

Ben paused and breathed again. Trish Coleman also exhaled with a look of appreciation.

"Second, I found this ambiguity dialog that we've just heard quite compelling. In my view you've opened up perhaps the toughest nut in the whole cross-cultural communication phenomenon. If we can't wrap our minds around something, it makes us nervous, and once you cross a cultural boundary, the chances of being able to wrap your minds around everything go way down. Those who handle not understanding well do better, and those who can't handle not understanding have bad experiences. Some react benignly, perhaps in the form of just staying away from the other culture, and some become ugly in ways that we've just witnessed. I hope you all will ponder how you personally handle ambiguity and the implications for you when you're confronted with things from another culture. And I'd like for us to thank Gail, and Charlotte, and Delia for bringing us these insights."

Delia said, "Don't forget Zenovia."

"And Zenovia's instant Biblical recall," said Ben.

Everyone applauded.

"So, in the light of ambiguity as a competency, and this may surprise you; it occurs to me that I ought to suggest that you consider cutting Mr. Simmons a break. Or using the language we've been using—give him the benefit of the doubt."

Trish Coleman shot Ben a look of shock.

"Please stay with me, Ms. Coleman," said Ben.

"Here's my point. There are all sorts of narrations that we might give to the events of the last fifteen or twenty minutes. And many of those narrations would cast Mr. Simmons in the most awful of terms. And those narrations may even be true. But I'm not willing to say that I know they're true just yet."

"Here's what I want to say that I know. In response to a can that I opened up, we all just saw Mr. Roger Simmons start down a particular rhetorical path. He had a particular point of view, and we don't really know if he's the only one in this room with that point of view."

Ben scanned the room. Nobody noticeably reacted.

"Then he suddenly got presented with some surprise information; some information that he obviously was not prepared to handle. And he handled it in a particularly ugly way. And we may all agree that he shouldn't have said any of the things that he said. And some of you are already prepared to judge him for it. And I would hope that those of you who are in judgment mode should never catch me when I'm caught off guard, or when I've had too many drinks under my belt, or when I'm feeling particularly lonely, or when I'm feeling particularly angry. Because, while I like to think of myself as a nice guy; I must confess to times in my life when I haven't been especially nice. With more observances, I might eventually come to join you in the harshest judgment of what just happened. But I'm not there yet. That's what I want to say Mr. Fierstein. Is that sufficient?"

118

After a long silence, a broad smile came over his face and Adam said, "Is that what empathy looks like? Well, that's outstanding, Dr. Benjamin Parks."

"Thank you, sir," said Ben.

Then, "So, we've talked about how cultures can be born and maintained within racial groupings, in ethnicities, in nations, in religions, in organizations, and families, but I want us to go back once again to the basic level of definition. Will someone read from Lustig and Koester on page twenty-five, the italicized segment after the first paragraph?"

It was Margaret who spoke up and read, "Culture is a learned set of shared interpretations about beliefs, values, norms, and social practices, which affect the behaviors of a relatively large group of people."

"Thank you, Ms. Brown."

In the few minutes remaining in the day, Ben allowed the students to engage around definitions of culture, and they quickly concluded that many kinds of groupings had cultures, including GLBTs. Ben's last instructions for July were, "So, while your texts are open, for next month's reading you should look at chapter ten, 'Intercultural Competence in Interpersonal Relationships.' Find one passage that you'll be prepared to lead us in exploring during our sessions. Then I also want you to journal. And here's how I want you to journal between now and our last two days in August. Use these three questions: What's standing out for me about the things that have happened this weekend? How do I feel about them? And is there something that I need to explore and how do I put it on the table, or is there something that I need to do based on this experience? Just use those three questions. Remember when you answer that second question that a feeling isn't an analysis. A feeling is mad, sad, glad, or something of that nature. Allow yourself to acknowledge how you were emotionally stirred by that part of the seminar that's standing out."

By 3:00 p.m., everyone was spent. They sat and stood and applauded themselves and each other. All eventually left the classroom.

Chapter 24
The August (Saturday) Session

Now: What a week! The retreat at the J Street Mansion . . . the incident in the alley . . . the night of unexpected and passionate love-making with Addie.

***

That Saturday morning, August 1999: Ben wanted to be ready to make this morning's seminar session even more special than the previous ones in June and July. As always, he also wanted to see if he'd be able to work through whatever was put on the table. He had no confidence that he could anticipate where these bright and opinionated students would take things. And for a while as he locked the lightweight Centurion into the bike rack between the Ira Aldridge Theater and Frederick Douglass Hall, he thought of Dean Prescott.

What a remarkable visionary, was Ben's first thought.

Also Ben just couldn't imagine what Prescott had gone through to recruit and assemble these students and to convince their home Universities to buy-in to the notion of this seminar. He wondered about the dynamics at each of the schools. What he knew back in June, based on the papers they'd written as a pre-requirement to compete for a slot in the seminar, was that this group was special. And in the four sessions prior to today, the students had lived up to Ben's high expectations. Ben thought of the crafty Prescott, how he'd approached Ben in Flagstaff and then pursued him like a terrier until he'd worn Ben down.

Finally, as he walked into Douglass Hall, Ben thought, *I don't know if I'll ever do this again. But I'm going to remember and cherish this summer. This has been quite a ride.*

"Good morning, Dr. Parks," Ben heard as he crested the steps up to the second floor. Delia Menendez and Xia Liang stood at the door as if waiting for him to arrive.

"Good morning, young ladies," he replied. "Isn't the classroom open?"

Ben was distracted by these young ladies and something he'd observed on more than one occasion during the summer. They were both drop-dead gorgeous. Ben fought to keep the lecherous old man thoughts from showing visibly on his face. This effort, he found, was made much easier because Addie had been so exceedingly nice to him the night before. He realized that Delia was speaking.

"It's open," she said. "Xia just wanted to say something to you before we went in."

Ben slowed his walk forward, stopped in front of them, and waited.

Xia spoke hesitantly.

"Dr. Parks, sir. I have made a comment in my journal. I showed it to Delia and told her that I wanted to discuss with you in private. She said no. She said that it should be public so everyone can hear."

Xia looked over to Delia for encouragement. Delia nodded.

Ben asked, "What would help you, Xia?"

"I am an undergrad, Dr. Parks. Everyone else is a grad student. They are all very smart and very confident. They have strong opinions. I want to say something but then I wait my turn. My turn never comes."

Another guilty thought, *I'm obviously not monitoring and doing a great job of gate keeping. I should have seen that Xia wanted to say something. I should have let her in.*

Ben was having a hard time staying focused this morning. Ben hoped that didn't continue because he knew that the most important skill required in facilitating a seminar like this was the ability to stay present and in the moment as the process twisted and turned in unexpected directions.

Xia continued, "Dr. Parks, I want to practice. I want to share with the students. But I am a little shy. Will you help me?"

"Of course, I will. How shall I help you, Xia?"

"Call on me, Dr. Parks. Just call on me. Okay?"

How elegantly simple was this request.

"I will, Xia. And thank you for asking."

Ben held the door as the young ladies went into the classroom. Five minutes before time to start and just about everybody had arrived. Some students were reading from the text. Some were making notes in their journals. There was very little conversation, but the atmosphere was palpable with sensations of intense reflection and anticipation.

Ben scanned and immediately took note—no Roger Simmons. He hadn't signed a withdrawal slip. In due course he'd deal with whether his grade would be a W or an F. But Trish, Paul, and Sadie were sitting together, three abreast right in the middle of the front row.

"Good morning, Ben." It was Adam from the back of the classroom.

"Good morning to all," said Ben, placing his beat up brown leather satchel on the desk in the front of the room and striding to the easel. With a broad tipped blue marker he wrote in large script, "Our journal questions and insights," and punctuated the five words with a large question mark.

"Ben, we thought you'd never ask," said Adam. "My journal insight actually comes from the text." Adam strode to the front of the room, text in hand.

Ben took up his position on the stool to the side by the large window.

"This is page one hundred and fifty-one. It's five lines up from the bottom," said Adam. Ben suddenly realized that Fierstein had the same first name as his step son. And then he thought, *why hadn't I made that connection before?*

Adam read the passage:

"Prejudiced people ignore evidence that is inconsistent with their biased viewpoint, or they distort the evidence to fit their prejudices."

Adam stopped and looked up at the students.

"We could take almost that same definition and shift the context from cross-cultural relationships to politics and we'd have a perfect fit. Out of Dr. Ben's six themes, the only two we haven't spent much time talking about are belief and ideology—the last two. Now I'm thinking this is the definition for ideology. I was talking to Candace on the phone during our break."

Immediately Adam got heckled. "Oh, you were, were you?" yelled David Anderson. "I didn't know you were talking to Candace. Candace won't give me the time of day."

David and Candace Lane were both students at the GW Law School. David looked over his shoulder at Candace sitting one row behind him, and Candace turned bright red.

"Damn, Adam Fierstein! You old stud you," said David.

Adam retorted, "See, I learned a new word in this seminar Dave. It's called 'hating.' Stop hating."

"Naw playa playa," said Sadie loudly. "You ain't saying it right, Adam." "You cain't be all proper with it—hating. It's 'hatin.' You feel me? Get it right!"

"Stop hatin," mimicked Adam. "Anyway, Candace told me about something in one of her law books. What was that quote you read me?"

He looked out in anticipation, as Candace struggled to regain her composure having been made the unexpected center of attention. Ben wondered whether, if Adam and Candace had been courting, if that would continue after today.

"I told you, Adam, it's not from a law book. It's from a 1990 journal article. It's by Duncan Kennedy from Duke."

Reading underlined sections, Candace went on, "Kennedy defines ideology as 'A set of contested ideas that provide a "partisan" interpretation (descriptive and normative) of a field of social conflict.'"

Candace continued, "So, here's what he says that's similar to the text's definition of prejudice. He starts off, 'the ideologist' and then he puts in some stuff but the important part is: '. . . has chosen his ideas to fit his partisan allegiance and therefore lacks allegiance to the truth.'"

Adam exclaimed, "You see! There's belief. And then there's ideology. All of us come from cultures that have beliefs. But ideology is beyond belief. Ideology, just like prejudice, lacks allegiance to the truth. The ideologist, I believe, or Candace and I believe, is prejudiced. It's someone who will ignore the evidence if it doesn't support what they already think. It's someone who's determined to hang on to a fixed way of thinking in spite of data, or evidence, or anything else."

"Thank you, Adam and Candace," said Ben. "First of all, Adam, I want you to know that I realize that your citation from the text is not from the assigned chapter."

Adam seemed prepared. "Extra credit, Ben! Extra credit," he called back over his shoulder as he returned to his seat in the back row.

Ben noted that Candace swiped at him as he went by her in the third row. Ben laughed.

"You're sharp as ever aren't you. So, what do you all think about their insight?"

Joseph, Paul, Delia, and Sadie were the first to say they agreed.

"That's deep," said Sadie with a sense of discovery in her voice.

Adam took his seat, and for most of the rest of the morning, other students offered journal insights. Some were from the text, and most had clearly limited themselves to drawing from chapter ten. They were struck by things like the similarities and differences between prejudice and racism, ideas about the differences in the way various cultures think about who is a friend and who is a stranger, and the ways that non-verbals have different meanings.

As it got close to lunch, Ben was gazing around and he suddenly noticed Delia erect with her arms folded stiffly across her chest. Was she scowling at him? What was up? He glanced to the side and there was Xia with her head down on the desk.

Then it hit him. There it was again. He'd managed a whole summer in this seminar without an incident but couldn't make it through one more weekend without a serious memory lapse. He'd just had one three days ago with the managers at the city public health agency. Now, he had totally forgotten Xia's request.

"Ms. Liang, please forgive me. I believe you wanted to raise something from your journal. The floor is completely yours."

The young woman raised her head. Delia poked her once. Then she poked her again. Xia visibly collected herself and summoned strength from within. In a quiet voice she began.

"Dr. Parks, I thought a lot this month about how you took the mean names that you were called last month. I wrote in my journal that I would have been very hurt. You didn't seem hurt. You didn't even seem angry. I spoke with my family about it and asked my father if he would have been hurt as a Chinese man if he had been called a racial slur and other mean things. He said it would have been his duty as a Chinese man to be angry and to strike back. He said that he couldn't maintain face without responding. I don't understand why you weren't hurt or angry."

Ben took his time. Actually, he stared at his Sperry Capitola Slide sandals. He stared at a crack in the highly polished floors in Douglass Hall. He stared out the window and could see across the quad to the Library clock tower. Ben had stared up at this clock tower many times since he was a little boy. He remembered walking with Richard Roscoe Parks across campus and his dad would ask, 'What time is it?' Ben would look at the clock tower and proudly answer.

"Dr. Parks!" It was Delia with an agitated voice.

"I'm here, Delia. I'm here, Xia. I haven't lost my place."

"I would have answered more quickly if you hadn't added the issue of face. Without that wrinkle, I think I would have quickly said something like 'what good would it have done for me to get angry.' But the issue of face is important to your dad, and I respect that; although I probably don't feel the same cultural pressure that he feels. As a black man, maybe I should. And certainly when I was a younger man, I was keener on not being disrespected; on not losing face. But when I look back on fights I was in as a young man, and offenses that I took against slights, what good did it do me? I can't honestly say anyone respected me more after a violent reaction. And sometimes I actually paid a price for my response that wasn't worth any temporary satisfaction that might have come from trying to whip someone's butt."

"What kind of price, Dr. Parks?" Rashid Jillali and Elmore Steward had simultaneously asked the question, their voices practically in harmony.

"Well, once I vividly remember that my butt was the one that got kicked."

Ben smiled at the memory.

"Actually, that wasn't so bad. For some reason, I was never really scared of losing a fight as long as I could really hurt the other guy in the process. But once I remember being suspended for three days from school. I didn't think going after someone who'd offended me was worth that."

Now Ben was finding his legs in his explanation.

"You know, since I reached a certain age—maybe forty-five or fifty—I've started to go on alert whenever I hear the phrase, 'I take offense.' I'm becoming very skeptical in my old age, about people's ability to engage seriously and authentically in difficult conversations without pulling out some game. The reaction I have, more often than not, is that it's a ploy to tip the tables in a verbal struggle. The playing field was level in a verbal disagreement, and then someone says, 'I take offense at that.' Suddenly, the offended party has an advantage because, assuming the offender intended no offense, now he or she has to shift attention from the argument to an apology; advantage to the pseudo-offended. It's a trick play. But I'm probably digressing. Let me get back on track."

"I wish I had brought a certain book with me, Ms. Liang. But I'm going to tell a story and I hope I get it close to right. Is that okay?"

Xia nodded.

"It comes from a guy named Bruce Jacobs who wrote a book called 'Race Manners.' Essentially the author says that he and a friend were out on a certain street somewhere and they encountered a woman. Jacobs, I believe, is black and presumably his friend was also black. The woman that they encountered spotted them on the street and did something offensive. I don't remember exactly what it was, but let's say she clutched her purse very tightly in a visible manner that the two black men could see. Jacobs called attention to the woman's act and said that he was offended, and was surprised when his friend said, 'I don't care."

Ben had been looking blankly as he tried to recall the details of the story. Now, he looked back directly at Xia and repeated. "He really didn't care. And because he didn't care, that paranoid woman with whatever stereotypes were in her head didn't have a chance to ruin the friend's day. It's not even that she was trying to ruin his day. But her actions might have had that effect. It doesn't matter. The friend's day was not to be ruined. And this got Jacobs starting to wonder why he cared, and wasn't the friends attitude somehow more beneficial than his."

Xia spoke up.

"I've seen my father become very angry when he sees how people react to him in public places. He doesn't speak very good English but he can curse up a storm in Chinese."

"What's he like an hour later, Xia?" asked Ben. "What's he like two hours later or even a day later?"

"He's still mad," said Xia. "Usually he is."

"You see, Xia" said Ben. "With all due respect to your father, that just doesn't seem like it's worth it to me. I'm not saying that it's easy to not be affected. But what I'm saying is that I don't want other people to be able to highjack how I'm feeling because they say or do something stupid. I've tried to train myself to not care. Sometimes, it works and sometimes it doesn't. That's the only explanation I can give for how I dealt with the name calling last month."

"I can't do that, Dr. Parks," said Elmore.

Rashid said, "That takes a lot of discipline."

"And Allah's grace," said Ahmad.

Romaine said, "Amen."

"Yes, that could be, and I'm sure about the grace part, but I submit, Mr. Jillali, that when it takes discipline, you really do care. What I want is to really not care. Then it takes no discipline at all. And sometimes I'll admit that I have to fake not caring just to deny someone the pleasure of knowing that they got to me. But I want to be like Bruce Jacobs' cousin more often."

Xia asked, "And how does that benefit intercultural communication and understanding, Dr. Parks?"

Ben turned back to the young woman and a smiled slowly spread across his face. Touché, Ms. Liang. I don't really have a good answer to that. Maybe it doesn't. Maybe in this kind of situation, I'm only dealing with my own psychological and emotional well-being. But you've given me something to think about, and if I come up with more of an answer I will come back to that question. Thank you for initiating an important line of dialog."

"You're welcome, Dr. Parks. And thank you for giving me the opportunity. I will be able to go home, and for better or for worse; I will have more to say to my father about his face," said Xia.

Delia was observably delighted. She patted Xia on the back and Xia grinned from ear-to-ear. Delia looked to the back row and Damien held up his hand. They air high-fived each other.

After lunch, Ben shifted the mood in the class. He had them play another of his goofy games. It wasn't really his goofy game. In fact it was an exercise called the 'Opportunity Walk,' and it was pretty standard fare for many diversity trainers, with more than one person suggesting or claiming they invented it, but these students had never seen it.

Ben had asked the students to push all the chairs to the walls before they left for lunch. Then he'd spent his lunch hour using masking tape to make strips on the floor so that the place almost looked like a football field when students started wandering in. Several started playing in the middle of the room with Chauncey and Elmore trying to cajole people into lining up like an offense and defense. After much jabbing, Trish and Sadie were the only takers. Elmore looked over at Damien shouting, "What about you, big man?"

"You don't want to see me on a football field youngins," said Damien, standing by the wall with Delia inched up seductively close by his side.

When he'd counted heads and everyone was back from lunch, Ben put a stop to the shenanigans.

"So I need everyone back here in a tight line by the back wall. You'll have to get friendly to all get back here, but the starting place for this activity imagines that we all start at birth with some sort of equity in terms of our potential success in life."

Students stared at him.

"Let's go! Back against the wall! Hut, hut!" shouted Ben.

Students complied, but of course Adam Fierstein had a crack, "You're really starting to get full of yourself aren't you, Ben? Okay, we're playing along."

Now, standing facing the students about two striped lines away, Ben turned and strode to the opposite end of the large classroom. Once there he turned and yelled across the room, "Where I'm standing now represents the place most Americans are presumed to aspire to, assuming that they or you see yourself as residing in the good old US for the major part of the rest of your lives. Folks who wind up here are in positions of opportunity and privilege in our society. They WILL succeed. That's how they see themselves and that's how they generally are looked at by others. Is that understood?"

"Understood!" came the reply in a chorus from across the room.

"Wonderful!" said Ben.

"Now I submit to you that your chances of reaching this end of the classroom are, not totally, but largely affected by your history, including various group identities that you have or have had. To demonstrate that to you, I'm going to give you a set of instructions, and without talking, I'd like each of you to make the indicated movement. Again I'm going to ask you to respect this as an individual journey each of you will take. Kibitzing, which you all love to do, will not be useful."

And so the activity began. Students strode forward to the next line or in some cases, two or three lines forward, as they identified with certain commands. Sometimes, students identifying with certain commands had to step backward one or more lines. With all these students except for Xia Liang being graduate school participants, Ben knew that the first movements would keep people pretty much together for a while.

"If you graduated from high school, move forward one line," was the first instruction. After two more commands, students were on three lines with Delia and Xia behind, Rashid in front, and everyone else on the same middle line. Then it got more interesting.

"If one of your parents finished college, move forward one line. If both your parents finished college, move forward one more line. If either of your parents has an advanced degree, move forward yet another line."

Now quite a few students were a line or two ahead of Rashid. Xia was up with the rest of the back row students. But the next set of instructions spread the room to the point that people audibly gasped as they moved and looked around.

"If you consider yourself to have been raised in a middle class family, go up three lines. If you consider yourself to have been raised in an upper middle class family, move up another line. If you think of yourself as having been raised in a wealthy family, take another line forward. If you consider yourself to have been raised in a poor family, move two lines back. If you've ever stepped out by yourself and taken a strong position against what you felt was blatant discrimination either of yourself or someone else, move back another line."

Now Delia found herself on the last line along with Elmore and

129

Sadie. They had only advanced a couple of lines from the original starting place. Margaret and Zenovia were ahead of them by one line. In the front of the pack were Gail, JD, and Candace.

Through a series of about ten more commands, the room spread even further, with Adam joining the front group and those four maintaining—and somewhat increasing—their leads over the rest of the field.

When at the end, Ben asked folks to silently look around the room from their final lines and notice whatever they noticed, the room was filled with a sense of profound discovery. Ben asked folks to remain silent and pull out their journals so they could reflect and write using the three journaling questions that they'd all memorized by now (what's standing out for you, how does it make you feel, and what if anything do you want to explore or do about it?).

The next instruction led to quiet conversations over the course of another hour. Students were asked to roam and talk to various students about the experience. They were asked to share how they were feeling as they moved throughout the activity. They were invited to ask their fellow students how they were feeling. They were invited to share from their journals and then add to their journals as they explored the histories that had come out and the ramifications of those histories.

By the end of the day, the students were mostly somber. Ben invited them to stay in the question about what it all meant. There would be time on Sunday, the final day, if someone needed something for closure.

Then Ben said, "I have a request. I'd like to ask everyone to come tomorrow in school colors. It's our last day of what's been an amazing experience for me and hopefully for most of you. And I've been trying to think of a ritualistic way to wind it down that would be a little offbeat and memorable. School tee shirts, jackets, caps, or whatever might be a nice way to do it. What do you think?"

Most seemed to think it would be a good idea.

"And we'll need to talk about grades. If you review your syllabus you'll see that there are three considerations. So I want you tonight to write me a one-page summary of what this seminar has meant to you. If you go past one page, I won't read the extra. No tricks! Twelve point font and standard margins. Those summaries, plus my observations of your participation this summer, plus an activity that we'll do tomorrow where you'll speak to each other from your papers, will be the ingredients for your grades. And I will say just to allay your fears, that I don't see anyone who has remained with us getting less than a B, with most probably in line for an A. But don't slough off on these papers because they are likely to be a difference maker. Do you understand?"

Finally, "And of course you're always encouraged to reflect in your journals. Right?"

Quite a few of them answered, "Right!"

"Have a good evening, Dr. Parks," said Xia.

Ben smiled warmly and nodded to the young woman who'd come out of her shell.

Chapter 25
Chicken Coop

That evening, Ben felt wrung out but wonderfully satisfied with the dialog he'd witnessed that day. After the seminar session, he had taken the short route home on his bike, flying down the 4th Street hill much faster than he should have. But the speed and exhilaration suited his mood. Addie wasn't home when he'd come in, and he knew she had had plans with her girlfriends. He put on some Thelonius Monk: "Misterioso" and then, "'Round Midnight." Then he switched to Mahalia Jackson's rendition of "Come Sunday." Finally, he wanted to hear Brooks and Dunn's "Neon Moon."

But he was also troubled.

What about that memory lapse in the middle of dealing with Xia Liang? he thought. *Delia looked like she wanted to kill me.*

***

Selma, Alabama, Summer 1953: Little Benjamin Parks and all the cousins were sitting on the front part of the wrap around porch on Hayden Street. His granddad, a deacon at the Tabernacle Baptist Church and the first black ever hired at the paper mill outside of town, had just come in tired from work. Granddad didn't ever say a word. He just nodded at the children and went inside. Some jealous folks at church whispered that the only reason granddad got hired at the paper mill was that he was light enough to pass. But they never said such things to him or to anyone else in this proud black family.

Ben and Cousin Ralphine (a tom-boy) had challenged each other to a water melon seed spitting contest. Penny was trying to get into it, but she couldn't get the seeds off the porch when she tried. Cousin Ralphine was actually pretty good for distance, and she and Ben matched each other spit-for-spit.

Aunt ClayClay, from inside the house, called Ben to come inside. Ben's mom, Gillian, and Aunt Nellie were knitting by the old RCA Victor radio. This parlor and this radio had been the neighborhood place for listening to Joe Louis fights back in the 1940s, for listening to president Roosevelt's fireside chats, for listening to the news about the end of the war, and then about President Truman's order to end segregation in the military.

Aunt Nellie, Gillian Stoddard's youngest sister, was the only daughter in the family who was still unmarried. But she was gorgeous and had a lot of suitors. The latest one was known as Mr. Herman. Herman Tyndale sat in the parlor, holding forth about his war exploits as Aunt Nellie, chaperoned by the vigilant Gillian, listened with rapt attention.

But Aunt ClayClay was working, getting ready for the afternoon influx of customers.

"You gotta go gather some eggs."

"Now?"

"Now, young man. You skoot out back and get some of those eggs out that coop. The neighbors will be coming by and we don't have a thing to sell. Take that pail and get to steppin'. There's gotta be three pails worth by now, so go ahead."

Ben had looked at his mom, Gillian, for relief.

"Do as ClayClay says, Ben. Go ahead."

Dejectedly, Ben grabbed the pail and went out back to the chicken coops. He'd done this many times. They always cackled and made all kinds of racket when he came out. This was one of his chores every summer when he visited his grandparents and family for eight weeks in the summer time.

I want to be out-spitting Cousin Ralphine, he thought. *Her last seed landed at least a couple of feet past my best, and if left to stand, she'll never let me live it down.*

He'd put down the pail to open up one of the coops. The chickens screamed. He turned and forgot the pail. Then, he forgot why he was out there. He stopped and tried to concentrate.

What am I doing out here with all these screaming chickens? he thought.

Behind the fence, he spotted the two roosters. He was deathly afraid of one of them. That speckled rooster had chased Ben and cornered him. On that previous occasion, his granddad had thrown a rock, and the rooster retreated after five or six pecks. But though they couldn't get to him now, Ben still froze at the sight of those roosters. What possessed him to be out in this chicken coop? After a time, Aunt ClayClay came to the back step.

"You should 'a brought in at least one bucket by now, Ben. What's taking you so long?"

Ben looked back at her. Gillian stepped out beside her sister on the back porch. Mr. Herman had left and Gillian's duty was over in the parlor. Gillian immediately recognized what was wrong from her son's expression. She walked out to the chicken coop and found the pail. She held it up and Ben suddenly remembered. He started scooping up eggs. One immediately broke.

"Take your time, Ben." Gillian was placing two eggs softly in the pail. "Take your time."

She and Ben collected one pail-full and delivered it . . . then three more. Aunt ClayClay already had customers coming on the side of the house where the makeshift sales operation took place every afternoon.

Chapter 26
Rain

1958: Ben had a hair trigger temper in Junior High School with any student who seemed to offend him. But he wasn't a great fighter, and he often jumped into something with another boy only to get his ass kicked. Once, over taking offense at a swinging door being flung in his face as his class line had passed through the hallway, Ben had charged at the apparent offender who happened to be one of the biggest, baddest boys in the school. As he'd swung wildly at Tracy, the all-around jock had placed the big hand attached to his long arm on Ben's head and just held him out of reach as he laughed.

"Break it up!" The word came from a teacher who was pulling hall duty.

"I'll be waiting for you on the court after school," Ben had shouted after the laughing Tracy's back as the line proceeded to the next class.

Now, after school, Ben stood on the court alone in the rain for almost an hour. Finally, a girl came out with an umbrella. She thrust it over Ben's head, though he protested.

"Ben," said Davita Sheridan softly. "Tracy isn't going to come out and fight you. He's probably already home. He just would 'a beat you up if he'd come out here, and you know it. But, that wouldn't be good for his rep."

Ben was crushed by her words but knew them to be true. But bruises and bumps, nor winning fights had never been the issue with Ben. The point was to never take any shit . . . to never be bullied . . . to never be taken lightly. That was the point . . . Ben felt stupid.

"Come on, and I'll walk you home," said his friend.

Davita wasn't a girlfriend or anything. She was just nice and strangely, she saw something in Ben. He didn't have a clue why she liked him. She might have been his first platonic friendship with a female, although he nearly screwed that up that day. Walking past her house on Monroe Street, Northeast, Ben stopped.

"No, Ben! I said I'd walk you home."

"Nah, you don't have to. I'm good."

"I want to."

Ben was resolute. Davita was making too big a deal out of his embarrassing incident. Davita came back toward him. Then something else stirred in Ben.

Davita said, "Come in for a few minutes, Ben. I'll make you some hot chocolate."

Ben couldn't move now. Davita tugged at him down her walk way. In the living room, she helped him get his coat off, threw some sort of quilt over the couch to shield it from any wet clothes, and then disappeared as he sunk down into the soft cushions.

After a few minutes, Davita reappeared with tray in hand. She'd also changed clothes into something that sort of looked like a pink sweat suit—but form fitting and alluring to the virginal Benjamin Parks. Davita came over and sat next to him. As she handed him the warm mug and began to sip hers, Ben's jumble of confused emotions bounced around like a pinball. He'd gone from rage at Tracy when they'd left school, to embarrassment at Davita's kindness, and now something else.

Suddenly, Ben placed his cup of hot chocolate on the tray and put his arm around Davita. He couldn't say anything. It was just flaring and uncontrolled emotions. Sitting on the left of her, his hand slid immediately to her right breast. Davita tensed and stopped sipping.

Now, Ben was trying to reach up under her sweat shirt, and Davita stood up and put her cup down. She didn't seem angry. But she said, "I'm sorry, Ben. You're a sweet boy. But this isn't what I meant when I asked you to come in."

Stunned, Ben was now over the cliff of his raging emotions. He stood and wrapped his arms around the board-stiff body of Davita and tried to kiss her. She turned her cheek but didn't move or yell. Ben tried to find her lips with his, but she managed to keep her head turned just out of his reach.

"Stop Ben!" "Stop Ben!" "Stop Ben!"

Her voice was so soft . . . so controlled . . . so adult for a fifteen-year-old . . . and yet so kind.

Finally, Ben released her and stepped back. Davita relaxed and said, "Now that hot chocolate is probably cold. Let me warm it up for you."

Ben grabbed his coat and flew out of the house without saying a word. As tears streamed down his face in the rain, he heard Davita at the door.

"Ben, I really care about you."

He couldn't turn. He couldn't say anything. He ran five or six blocks to his home on Brentwood Road, off South Dakota Avenue. The next morning, fifteen-year-old Benjamin Parks awoke to sticky sheets. Later that day in school, Davita smiled warmly at Ben when they passed in the hallway between classes. Ben couldn't look at her.

Chapter 27
First Time

1959: Ben Parks and Davita Sheridan had moved from junior high to high school at Harrison Tech. After their episode the previous year, Ben had withdrawn and Davita had conscientiously worked to keep lines of communication open. Eventually, they resumed walking home together occasionally; though Ben never stopped to come into the Monroe Street house on his way home.

On the first day up to the High School near the Eckington Yards the next year, Davita and Ben boarded the trolley on Rhode Island Avenue together and then met after school to ride back home together. On the ride home, Davita leaned over and whispered, "You're coming home with me."

Suddenly, Ben felt a squeezing in the pit of his stomach. He breathed deeply to relax. Then another part of his anatomy woke up. He looked at Davita as they came to their stop. She took his hand, and they disembarked. Standing on the sidewalk, he tugged his hand free and looked in the direction of Brentwood Road.

Davita grabbed his hand back and said, "Ben, you're the nicest boy I know. I want to have sex for the first time and I want to have it with you."

She was sixteen now, just a few weeks older than Ben, and quite a looker. She'd always been one of the cutest girls wherever she was.

"Okay, said Ben."

An hour later, sitting up on the couch in the Monroe Street house, Ben was beside himself. They had kissed and petted, and then Davita produced a plastic wrapped something that Ben didn't recognize. She opened it and a latex sheath appeared . . . something Ben had never seen. Then she had touched him between his legs. Still clothed, Ben's pants immediately filled with that warm sticky substance. When he'd tried to leave, Davita, also still clothed, moved around on her knees in front of him and rested her hands on her chin in his lap. Looking up at him she said, "My mother told me that some guys need to masturbate the night before they're with someone. She said that some guys even need to do it for two or three nights before. Then they can hold themselves."

"Your mom told you that?"

Ben was flabbergasted on top of his embarrassment. The warmth between his legs felt awful. He didn't know how he was going to walk home. He knew he was going to need to wash out his pants before Gillian got to them in the laundry. Again, with eyes wide in amazement.

"Your parents actually talk to you about sex! They actually tell you stuff?"

"My mom does most of the talking, but my dad was in the room when she was telling me stuff. They weren't telling me to do anything. But they didn't want me to do anything before I had information, and they didn't want me to learn from anyone but them. They said that young people mess up their whole lives because they have sex before they know what they're doing."

"My parents would never do that," said Ben in amazement.

Davita moved up to sit in his lap. They just held each other for a while. The mess in Ben's pants was hardening, but Davita felt so wonderful in his arms, Ben stopped even caring about it.

"You're coming home with me again after school on Thursday. That will give you tomorrow and Wednesday to get ready. Also, I only had the one prophylactic. So, you have to go to a drug store and buy another one. I don't know how much they cost because I got that one from my mom, but you should take this wrapper so you know what to buy. Oh, and mom says that since I'm a virgin, I'll bleed the first time when your penis goes through my hymen. But it won't hurt me bad. It may even feel nice."

"Bleed?" said Ben in horror. "Davita, are you sure you want to do this?"

"Yes! Of course, you're a virgin, too, so this will be a big thing for both of us."

"I'm not a virgin!" protested Ben."

"Chile pleeease!" screamed Davita in impish derision.

139

She laughed and laughed until Ben relented.

"Okay, okay! So we're both virgins. Okay, I can get another one of these prophylactics, I guess."

Ben's visit to the Peoples Drug Store on Rhode Island Avenue was an adventure on Tuesday afternoon. He walked the isles over and over, clutching the little wrapper in his hand. He didn't see anything like what he had in his hand. Finally, after about twenty minutes of pacing back and forth, the elderly lady toward the back at the pharmacy counter waved him over.

"They're back here young man," she said. "They're behind the counter."

"What?" asked Ben?

"The condoms . . . the rubbers . . . they're back here. That is what you're looking for, right? Let me see that wrapper you keep sneaking a peak at. Oh, you don't want these dry things. You want lubricated. That way it goes on you better and it'll feel better for her. What do you want, three or twelve?"

"Can I buy just one?"

"Three or twelve, honey?"

"Three ma'am. Thank you!"

"First though, how old are you, honey?"

"Sixteen."

"Do you have something to show me that says that?"

Ben was suddenly proud. He'd never been carded before. He pulled out from his wallet the almost brand new driver's license he'd been issued just that summer.

A slight smile on the face of the cashier as she carefully read the date and counted.

"And how old is she?"

"Sixteen, ma'am."

She looked at him hard. Then eventually said, "Well, I guess I'll just have to trust you on that one since she's not here for me to see for myself."

For three times fifty cents, plus tax, Ben first dropped the plain bag and kicked it forward as he tried to scoop it up without being observed, but finally walked out of the store with a three pack of Gladiator lubricated condoms. Mission accomplished!

Even more of an adventure was the other part of the assignment

Davita had given him. Foreshadowing the kind of diligence that he would not often demonstrate in high school or college, but that would later emerge for him by his late twenties; Ben wanted to know everything he could about what was going to happen. He proceeded to the Woodridge Library at 18th and Rhode Island Avenue. There he consulted an encyclopedia that Tuesday night. He couldn't think of that word that Davita had used. He looked up 'vagina.' The definition read:

> The membranous canal in females leading from the vulva to the uterus.

That wasn't very enlightening. Ben started to look up vulva but then suddenly remembered Davita's word: 'hymen.' He went to another volume . . . flipped some pages, and there it was:

> The membrane that, when intact, indicates that a female is a virgin. This mucous membrane is folded and stretched so that it partially obstructs the external opening of the vagina.

In a medical journal, Ben found a picture that showed the vagina in detail, with arrows pointing to the hymen, the vulva, the canal, the uterus, and two ovaries.

Ben sat back satisfied. He could picture in his mind going through the hymen, and sitting right there in the library, he started to get erect. Sheepishly, he looked around and closed the volume. Nobody was paying him any attention as he adjusted himself, stood up, returned the volumes to the shelves, and strode out of the library with a new sense of understanding.

I can't believe Davita's parents actually tell her about all this stuff, thought Ben as he walked home to Brentwood Road. Coming in the door, he first saw Penny sitting at the dining room table, counting on her fingers.

"Where you been?" she asked.

"At the library, studying," said Ben.

Gillian was across the room, bending over the sink washing a dish. She smiled.

"I'm studying too," said Penny.

Ben thought, *That's nice little sister.* And he left it alone.

Later that Tuesday night, he tugged and pulled and didn't seem to be getting anywhere. Luckily, his mind wandered back to the sensuous feeling of Davita sitting on his lap. Things perked up, and soon he was successful.

By Wednesday night, he'd gotten the idea of getting a girlie magazine. He knew of a junk yard down on Bladensburg road where piles and piles of old newspapers and magazines were dumped in some sheds. Rummaging around, he had finally found a couple. He smuggled them back home into his room. That night he also developed the innovation of wetting his hands and using some soap. With magazines open side-by-side, some music on the radio, and some periodic re-lathering, Ben really enjoyed himself.

Thursday afternoon, Davita and Ben had sex on the couch, with the quilt thrown over it and then, for good measure, some kind of plastic sheet that Davita had found and placed under her before laying down and motioning Ben onto her. It was awkward . . . sweet . . . tender . . . fumbling . . . and the best thing that had ever happened to Ben. Davita winced at one particular time, and there was a sort of 'pop' sound. She put her hand on his chest, and he stopped moving until she said 'okay.' Then they started again, and Davita started moaning, "that's nice Ben . . . oh, that's nice Ben . . . oh, oh, that's nice."

When they finished and Ben got up, his private parts were covered in blood. Davita washed them clean with some soapy water from a pale that Ben hadn't noticed. Then she busied herself removing the plastic and the quilty thing, disappeared to the bathroom, and then came back to make sure there were no other visible signs as the now clothed Ben sat on a cushy chair, grinning.

When, the following week, he wanted to do it again, Davita said, "Ben, you're my best guy friend, and I adore you. I really had fun, but I don't want to do it again. I'll always remember it, and I'm glad you let my first time be with you. I'm glad your first time was with me. But now I want to focus on high school. I have goals. I'll do anything for you that I can, Ben, but we're not going to do that again. Okay? Please say it's okay. Please don't be angry with me. Okay?"

Ben was deflated. He was really hurt. He now knew what guys were talking about when they said they were 'horny.' He thought that maybe he was in love with Davita. He already wanted some more. But then he remembered that he'd learned a new skill. And he had the magazines hidden away in a very secret place to help him out.

With a straight face, but smiling on the inside, Ben finally had said, "Okay!"

"And just one more thing Ben. We won't ever talk about this to anyone. We won't even talk about it to each other. Is that okay?"

"Sure, Davita! That's okay."

Ben never told anyone about that first week in high school. But he savored it for the rest of his life.

As they went through high school, Davita met many of her goals. By the time they were seniors, she was a cheerleader, honor roll student, and the student body president.

•

Chapter 28
Meanderings

On the other hand, Ben had been a jumble of contradictions in those adolescent years. His grades were never much more than average. He really didn't know how to study. He'd watched his dad, but the focus and determination that his dad showed about almost everything was daunting to Ben, and he didn't try to imitate it. Occasionally, a gift would flash in the midst of his mediocrity.

Once in their senior year, when Ben had totally forgotten about a book report that was due the next day in a class called "Classics of Modern Western Thought." His best male friend, Levi, reminded him on the way home from school. Levi Chance, a brainiac, hadn't realized that Ben had slipped the whole assignment in his mind. Levi was the perfect-pitch, prodigy musician at Tech who made straight As, played organ at church for the youth choir in which Ben sang, and wrote his own music—both gospel and jazz. He'd just turned eighteen, and so he was now legally old enough to start playing a gig on the weekends uptown at the Dance-A-Lot, the club owned by Davita's parents.

Ben had made a quick U-turn and left Levi on the sidewalk. He found a book at the neighborhood library and brought it home after school. Out of the list of acceptable authors Levi had ticked off from memory, Ben had, at random, chosen John Dewey's "'*Morality is Social*" (1922).' It was the first suitable book that he saw on the shelf.

After his dinner, he went up to his room and opened the book to the table of contents. He didn't recognize anything and quickly became afraid that he wouldn't be able to pull this off. But then he thought about the index at the back. He flipped back there and slowly worked his way through every note. His eyes eventually fell upon the words: "*pragmatic knowing.*"

With renewed hope and some curiosity, Ben studied those "pragmatic knowing" sections one by one. Then, he selectively read through them again. Ben flipped back to the table of contents and went through it again. Some of it still didn't register, but other parts that had been Greek to him suddenly sparked understanding.

For the next three hours, looking only at the table of contents and inferring all the rest, Ben made up his summary of the book. Somehow, certain subjects and ways of thinking just made sense to Ben. Not Latin, not algebra, not chemistry—but rather: The book of James; The Preamble to the US Constitution; The Gettysburg Address; anything written or quoted from Martin Luther King, Jr. . . . and now he'd added John Dewey.

A week later, when the graded papers were being handed out by the teacher, Ben didn't receive his paper. After the teacher had handed out all but one, she said, "There is one paper that's probably the best I've ever read in my seven years of teaching. Both in content and in style, this paper just took my breath away, and I want to ask Ben Parks to come up front and read it aloud . . . I've graded this paper with an A++. Please come up now, Ben."

Arthur, sitting next to Ben in the row of classroom chairs, looked at his B- on the paper he'd worked on for weeks, and was stunned. Up front, Levi, who also had an "A" smiled at Ben throughout the recitation. Only he knew the truth, and he was friend enough to keep it between himself and Ben. Davita was smiling broadly and clapping her hands. Tracy, the BMOC in the last row in the classroom, usually got As or Bs and didn't seem that impressed, but was grinning slightly anyway. Clyde, Deana, and Janice . . . all from the neighborhood . . . joined in with Davita in sending up positive vibes. Ben walked to the front of the class, took the paper, and started reading. Every now and then, he paused and interpreted further some thinking that underlay the point he was making in the paper.

At one point, Ben interrupted his reading.

"What Dewey seems to be suggesting is that the pragmatist has the ability to get beyond insoluble problems. The skeptic expected the problems in the first place, and so he never set his goals very high. The idealist encountered the problems and was devastated by them. The pragmatist works on her problems as long as is reasonable. But eventually if they prove intractable, the pragmatist just moves on. At the end of the day, the pragmatist solves insoluble problems by getting past them and focusing instead on things that she or he can do something about."

Gerald Prentiss, who lived right across the street from the Parks home and fancied himself a braniac, was the one class mate who peppered Ben with questions.

"What's the point if you don't solve the problem? What kind of failure syndrome does that set up?"

Ben, searching for his own answer, looked at his friend and neighbor for a moment before his understanding of Dewey set in.

"What might be a problem today might be irrelevant tomorrow. If it wasn't solved when it was relevant, what's the point of spending time working on it after it no longer has any importance for the present you're facing now? Dewey believed that we have better things to do than to solve irrelevant or outdated problems."

"Bouyah!" said Lou Bonefant sitting behind Gerald.

The rest of the class applauded, the teacher smiled, and for the rest of that class period, Ben seemed to hold the class in his spell.

This was probably the biggest academic success of his life up to that point. Though the incident foretold his later career successes in teaching and public speaking; at that point it had been a total lark. In fact, until Ben had been through college, the army, and then started back in graduate school for his master's on the GI bill; he never again showed academic insight in his studies. Except for this incident, born out of forgetting about his assignment, Ben was just average.

***

Sitting in the backyard, Ben got up and went inside for another Irish whiskey. The memories were flowing and he didn't want to stop. The last session was tomorrow, but his reverie was infectious.

Chapter 29
The Lovely Davita

After high school, Davita had gone directly up on the hill, to the Mecca. As a freshman at HU, one day while roaming down by the lower part of the campus, Davita met her husband to be: a senior medical student who'd graduated from Calloway High in DC and from undergrad school in Boston. Now Jackson Ferrier was a renowned cardiologist.

Davita Sheridan had caught his eye that day on the lower campus, and as she liked to say to her close friends: 'He never had a chance.' Apparently, Jackson Ferrier also never had any money and would always be hungry. Davita would let him in through the kitchen up at the Dance-A-Lot, a little uptown bar and lounge in the neighborhood bordering Walter Reed Army Medical Hospital. The bar and lounge had been in her family since the 1950s. She'd put him upstairs in the quiet room where her parents did their book keeping. There, she'd make a space for him to study, and bring him food. And if her parents weren't at work on a particular evening: "Every now and then, I'd give him a little taste of me," she retrospectively joked some years later when Ben was sitting at her bar and Davita was tending behind the counter.

Jackson and Davita waited until after her senior year in 1966. The week after her graduation, they tied the knot and Ben hadn't even attended the wedding . . . not because he wouldn't have. He'd enrolled in summer school to make up a course he'd failed out at Middle State . . . still another semester or two from his own graduation. Once Jackson had got himself through the gauntlet of internship and residency, his practice had started to take off just as he and Davita were settling in. From that point on, Dr. Ferrier got paid handsomely.

Sipping on a dark Guinness draft, perfectly chilled but not cold,

Ben had listened without comment as Davita Sheridan Ferrier continued confiding, "Ben, I really hadn't expected to go through high school with you as my only one."

"I thought we weren't ever going to talk about this," said Ben, breaking out into a broad smile.

"That was then, and this is now wise guy," said Davita. "I got something to say, so don't interrupt me again!"

Ben raised his beer mug for a refill. Davita took it over to the tap and came back to lean on the bar in front of him. *She was really gorgeous*, thought Ben.

Continuing as though the interruption had never occurred, Davita said, "Sometimes, I would see you and think about whether you and I should get together again. But I was so driven to do my thing, and you didn't seem serious enough about the books for me."

Ben feigned a protest, and Davita cut him off, "Don't you even try to deny that you were trifling in high school Benjamin Parks! All you wanted to do was play—whether it was music, or sports, or girls . . . including the choir director you had the crush on . . . I sure did . . . I kept up with you playa! I don't mind saying that I'm the one who broke you in . . . Yes I did . . . and by the way you never thanked me. But . . ." she paused for emphasis, "You're welcome!"

Again, Ben wanted to speak, but they were alone in the bar and Davita, in a raised voice, now seemed to be unloading years of bottled up memories that had been waiting just for this moment to come out.

"And I kept score on you and your little chippies."

Ben hadn't really had a lot of girl friends in high school, although he had a lot of crushes. Actually, he'd only had sex with one other girl during those three years, and that wasn't until the twelfth grade when he fell in love with a junior named Bobbie McKenzie, whose daddy was a Deacon at Ben's church. Bobbie was sweet and devoted, but although she wrote to him for a while at college, she and Ben never got together again after he graduated. He never saw Bobbie again. But Ben didn't disabuse Davita of the idea that he'd been a player during the rest of the high school years.

She went on, "But I didn't think you were going to *be* anything after a while. The shame is that everybody knew you were smart; except for you. When you went away to college, I just hoped you would buckle down. But then I met Jackson and I stopped thinking about you altogether."

Davita didn't need money, and she didn't need to work. She worked up in the Dance-A-Lot because that's what she'd always done. Eventually, she took over running it and changed the name to 'Davita's.' She could have sold it or just closed it up anytime she wanted and would have never been worse for the wear. But out of love and out of honor to her parents and grandparents who started up the Dance-A-Lot with almost no front money, Davita had kept the place open.

"After you came back from the army and walked into my bar one day, I took one look at you, Ben, and knew you'd changed. What was that . . . maybe 1972 or 73? I was so proud of you."

"Yes, I remember coming home and catching up on all the news. It seems like I was gone forever . . . eight or nine years total; between limping my way through college, working some here and there, and then getting drafted and managing to get through the army. When I got back I can't remember who told me you'd married. But I knew I wanted to see you and say hello. I waited for quite a while. But, that's why I finally came in that night."

"I'm glad you did . . . I was already married to the love of my life, but I knew you were back. I'm glad I got my friend back . . . and I'm glad you're quite a man now, Dr. Parks. Not quite as cute as Dr. Ferrier," she said smiling . . . "but quite a catch."

A few years after reuniting with the happily married Davita, Ben had met Yvette and they had started their family. And the rest was history. They produced Anthony Richard Parks and Ricardo Benjamin Parks, and despite irreconcilable differences between them, Yvette and Ben were thought to have had one of the most amicable divorces that many of their friends had ever seen.

Chapter 30
Coming of Age

The army had been a life changer for Ben Parks. In war time, Ben had somehow drawn a long straw and not been sent to Nam. Instead, his overseas assignment was in The Republic of South Korea, where as a First Lieutenant, he commanded a security detachment for an Honest John missile base. Many of his soldiers were medevacs from Nam who'd been patched up but were too short-time to be sent back there. They served out the remainder of their tours pulling security around the perimeters of these strategic cold war sites . . . serious duty, but rarely life threatening.

Ben had had such tender feelings for these medevac'd "Nam" vets. By then, he was in his mid-twenties and many of them were nineteen or barely twenty years old. Yet their injuries were often horrific, and the stories they told let Ben know that any affronts he'd ever experienced in life were really child's play. Ben was a soldier's officer. He never really thought of a military career, but while he was in-country, he did his job and took care of his troops to the best of his ability.

Much later, after getting out of the army and growing up in major ways, Ben had calmed himself down and gained an impressive quality of emotional self-control. Underneath he might occasionally feel the temper flare, but on the surface he could be implacable. He'd learned in the army not to take himself so seriously.

By the mid-1970s all of the guys from the old Michigan Park days were either back from the war . . . or were never coming back. One day Ben learned that Tracy was back . . . Tracy (the BMOC from Junior High School and High School) had always been charmed. In fact Tracy did a total of three combat tours before the war ended. Then there was Lou Bonefant, who'd been medevac'd to Korea, Ben learned. But they hadn't hooked up over there. Lou actually extended for another year, and when he came back to the States, it was with Han, his new bride. Han Bonefant couldn't speak much English. Lou had picked up some Korean. But Han was cool. On the other hand, Clyde and Arthur didn't come back. After "The Wall" had been built on the National Mall, Ben went and paced back and forth between their names every Veteran's Day. Once on Veteran's Day, Ben bumped into Lou, Tracy, and Gerald down at The Wall, and they hugged and wept together for their fallen friends.

Gerald had moved to the west coast after returning from Vietnam. He'd taken the GI bill benefits and attended school in San Francisco where he'd received an M.B.A; after which he spent twenty years in the banking industry. Somewhere along the line, Gerald had become very Republican and very conservative; but he maintained contact with his family and old friends back in DC. Starting in the Ronald Reagan presidency years, by letter and later by email, Gerald and Ben debated the politics of the day. In an odd way, they grew closer than they'd ever been as kids, even as far apart politically as Ben discovered them to be.

And then there was Levi Chance. Levi had also gone to Nam, but was supposed to stay safe behind the scenes. He played music. That was his job. However, something about the Nam had just gotten inside Levi. He was different. Something was wrong with Levi. Once back in the states, he picked up the church gig . . . choir director. He was fabulous at it as long as he was sober. He wrote music and was very successful. But all the gang from the neighborhood, especially Ben, knew Levi was changed.

Chapter 31
Prescott's Inspiration

Ben had finished his second drink. He knew he should go in to be ready for the last session. But one more memory stole into his consciousness.

***

1995: At the Colorado Convention Center in Denver, on the stage at the Conference of Industry Executives, were Dr. Benjamin Parks and Dr. Theodore Freer. Ted was at the podium as the spotlights shone down. His image also appeared around the room on two jumbo screens, for the better viewing of the eight hundred or so executives assembled. Ben was seated to the side of the stage, transfixed as Ted took the room through his simplistic but profound thought experiment.

Audience members had individual finger activated controls that wirelessly fed into some kind of computerized gizmo that instantly displayed their responses with means, median scores, and range. The gist of the thought experiment became self-evident with the aid of the worksheet he used. Paper copies were distributed to the audience, and it was on the jumbo screens so Ted could use the laser pointer in his talk.

"Thanks. If you don't mind, Ben and I plan to introduce our topic by running you through a thought experiment we've been working out for several years. I'll start first with it, and then Ben will do some interpretation after I'm done."

A slide came up on the jumbotron screens. It showed a typical diversity statement from one of the major corporations represented at this conference. It was a very nice statement as far as it went. At the end of the statement, the words were:

. . . without regard to race, religion, gender, or disability.

"Well, that's pretty inclusive, isn't it?" asked Ted. That pretty much does it, doesn't it?"

Ted left the question out there for a while until a Hispanic man in the middle stood and called out, "Well, it leaves out a lot of things including language."

Quite a few people in the room applauded.

"But the man continued, given the title of your talk, I guess you want us to see that it leaves out sexual preference."

"Partially correct! Thank you sir! It does leave out a lot of things including limited English proficiency. And it leaves out attraction orientation. Note, that I didn't say sexual orientation. The first thing I want to propose is the commonly used term 'sexual orientation' hits some people as vulgar and it may, in some cases, block opportunities to enter into serious conversations about the phenomenon. I submit that, just like not all straight people are having sex, similarly not all gay people are having sex. But there's a difference that's more fundamental than whether one is having sex, and that's the issue of attraction. I could say more about that, but I just seized the opportunity to make that comment because you set me up sir. Is that okay?"

The gentleman in the audience waved his hand and nodded. Ted continued, "And I also didn't say sexual preference. That's a marvelous segue into our thought experiment. Sir, you can pick up your check at the door."

Some in the audience picked up on the joke, and laughed. But others looked around puzzled. Ben observed Ted, the extravert in the spotlight. Ted proceeded.

"The framing question I want us to explore is this: 'Is Attraction Orientation a Choice or a Discovery?'"

On cue, the jumbotron showed the question in big bold letters.

"If it's a choice, as my new friend out there suggests, then preference would be the appropriate term. But if one discovers it about oneself, like many other discoveries that happen during our formative years, then preference would be inaccurate. And attraction orientation would be a more appropriate term. Do you follow me so far?"

Many in the audience nodded. Others didn't.

"So, coming up on the screen, you'll see our first continuum and the dimension we'll be looking at is 'workaholism.' The further on the left side you are, the more you believe that workaholism is innate and those who have it can't do anything about it. The more you move to the right, the more you believe that folks have control over workaholism and can stop it anytime they want. Now, please press the left side buttons on your individual controllers if you think workaholism is innate and the right side if you think it's fully controllable. Oh, for those of you who are left-right challenged, let me demonstrate."

As people laughed, Ted stepped away from the podium, turned his back to the audience, and repeated the instructions while pointing left and right. Then he turned back around and the jumbotron lit up with audience responses. Studying these data and using his laser pointer, Ted observed.

"Well, there seems to be a rather even split of opinion on this first one. That's interesting, and I have no idea who's right or wrong, so I won't linger. Is that okay?"

The audience smiled their approval, and Ted proceeded through a series of similar slides for such things as: fear of snakes, being a sports fan, organizational skills, and enjoyment of broccoli. Sometimes, the audience responses showed a clear majority in the choice corner. Other times, most voted in the discovery corner. And still others were more or less in-between just like the first item.

"So now, before showing the next dimension, I want to do a little bit of definition for you. Opposite sex attraction doesn't necessarily lead to overt sexual behavior with the opposite sex. But an author, Eric Markus, says that the key to knowing isn't in your behavior. It's knowing your underlying feelings of attraction, regardless of whether you act upon them. How many in the room are buying in so far."

The overwhelming number in the group raised their hands. The final three slides allowed for a smooth transition. The majority in the room thought that male attraction to females and female attraction to males was a discovery. On the final dimension, which was worded: "same sex attraction," most voted that it was a choice; the first time. But after the data were displayed, spontaneous and loud debate was heard in the room. Ted indicated over the roar that this probably wouldn't be settled right now and somehow regained control of the room. Ted asked if they'd like another chance.

More said yes than no, so the screen reappeared: "same sex attraction."

This time, the results were split almost exactly down the middle. Without further comment, Ted moved to his chair. Then, Ben took the podium. He was holding a silver laser pointer in his left hand as he adjusted the microphone. Then, in switching the pointer back to his right hand, he dropped it on the floor, and it rolled over to where Ted was seated. Ted chuckled as he scooped it up and tossed it over to Ben, who one-handed it . . . to some mild laughter and light applause from the audience. Ben composed himself and started, "Thank you. That was very interesting, and Ted and I often get a rather mixed result when we get to that last dimension: same sex attraction. And we have people say in our sessions, or who come to us afterwards—commenting that it's quite a revelation for them that folks are willing to see opposite sex attraction as a discovery, but not same sex attraction. If the answer is that unclear—and by the way, science seems to come down pretty squarely in the direction of discovery for either orientation—let's look at the implications of viewing same sex attraction as a choice and not an innate orientation."

Ben paused and seemed to lose his way a little. Closing his eyes for a moment, he recovered.

"I'll tell you, I've been sitting here through Ted's talk, and I've changed how I was going to do this multiple times. And if I did what I was going to do, which was to go through a number of slides on culture and diversity with you, we'd go way over the time they have graciously given the two of us. So, what I've decided to do instead is to just talk for a few minutes about the fifteen years I've known Ted Freer and about some of the things I've learned about myself only because I was fortunate enough to have him come into my life."

At this, there was a ruffling and some coughing in the audience as Ted blushed a bit. Ben put the laser pointer that he'd intended to use to highlight data on Ted's screens in his pocket. On the jumbotron screens, people see that the camera has panned to Ted, and then quickly back to Ben.

"Now, let me tell you, I met Ted Freer fifteen years ago . . . and uhm . . . I probably have five minutes to do this . . . (nervous chuckling) and we had a professional relationship and we were friends. And at some point he started doing the work that he needed to do to become a more authentic person, and I gotta tell you (pause), my reaction in those early days to his coming out of the closet was not pretty. This gets back to the point that integrating attraction orientation into the mainstream diversity conversation is hard work."

"This is really hard work. My reaction was not pretty, but luckily I didn't close down completely. I kept in touch with Ted, and I worked on what I was feeling ... and over time, here's what came to me."

"I mean, at some point it dawned on me that what I was feeling and how I was headed in terms of my overt reactions to Ted, fit under a label that I ... I sort of rejected this label for me until I had this discovery. The label was homophobia."

"So, Ben ... doggone, you're a homophobe" said Ben with an inflection of wondering and questioning.

Eight hundred people in the audience laughed out loud ... some probably to ease a welling tension they were starting to feel and some, still not connecting with their own feelings, just because of the bluntness of Ben's statement.

"Um, well yeah you probably are, Ben, and what's that all about?

"I remember Ted and I were at another conference about a year ago, and I'd used the term homophobe. A black mid-forties gentleman came up to me on one of our breaks and said, 'Dr. Parks, I see you're using the term homophobia. I resent that term. Homophobia suggests fear. I don't fear Gay people. I just don't like them.'"

The instantaneous 'woohoo' that swept through the audience took Ben by surprise. On the jumbotron, a few faces from the audience came up ... then back to Ted who seemed alarmed ... then back again to Ben who held his hand up and the audience eventually quieted.

Ben noted that he'd already used five minutes or more.

"But right on the heels of my first realization, came another that was horrific to my sensibility as a moral and fair person ... even more scary to me ... um ... This new realization for me was that the outcome of my continued homophobia would contribute significantly to Ted's oppression."

Utter silence. Ted's eyes were down toward the table in front of him. Ben panned the audience and a few of their mixed expressions were shown on the jumbotron. Now, Ted looked back up at Ben, and Ben continued. Ben's head was spinning with thoughts as he flashed back to vivid memories that were surfacing. Suddenly, Ben looked back up with concern. He'd forgotten his place in this talk. In an instant, Ted saw the recognizable panic and stood. But before he could take his second step over to the podium, Ben recovered and smiled at Ted. Ted sat back down.

"The big realization for me was, I couldn't deal with that. I couldn't deal with the idea that I was contributing to the oppression of another human being."

"My father and mother grew up in the Deep South, and my dad was in the military before President Truman integrated it. I remember, personally, sitting in the crowded balcony of a movie theater in Selma, Alabama and wanting to get one of the many seats I saw below us on the first floor . . . only to be shushed by my maternal grandmother without any explanation."

"I remember, as a boy, bending over a colored only drinking fountain as a passing white man spit directly into the basin . . . feeling the flash of anger . . . and having my mother rush over to pull me back and cover my mouth before I said anything."

"Oh no!" screamed a black woman at the back of the auditorium.

Quickly, one of the camera men found her, and she appeared on the screen in tears. But, Ben couldn't wait any longer.

"Now, I'm getting a time cue here so let me try to hurry through."

"Take your time, Doctor!" yelled a senior looking white man in the front. He obviously had stature, because the time cues stopped.

"Someday, I may write a book called: 'Confessions of a Recovering Homophobe.' After years of moving toward some sort of enlightenment about choice versus discovery, I find that I continue to have to work on myself and my responses to the GLBT community even today . . . it's hard work."

"To the straights in the audience, even if you're of open mind . . . straight but not narrow as they say . . . let me explain to you about the association phenomenon."

He let this term sink in.

"Here's how it goes. Ted and Ben show up somewhere to do some work with some group around sexual orientation as a legitimate diversity issue—just as much as race, just as much as gender, just as much as limited language proficiency, just as much as disability, just as much as any other."

"Sometime later, a person who took part in that process recognizes me on the street somewhere or at another meeting. 'Dr. Parks,' they'll say. I'll turn and acknowledge them, probably not recognizing them."

"'It's good to see you,' they'll continue," said Ben. "Then they'll mention, 'You know, I was walking through the train station, or I was catching a flight out to the west coast recently, and I saw your lover . . . what's his name? . . . oh yeah, Dr. Freer.'"

An Asian woman and white male sitting together in the audience came up on the jumbotron. One's head nodded and the other's was shaking . . . back-and-forth.

"That's the association phenomenon, straight folks. And some would say this person, having seen Ted and I at a conference doing our thing, would be coming to a very logical conclusion."

"By the way, just in case anyone is wondering, my lover's name is Addie Sherrie Parks."

"But, for folks who are proudly straight, what I want you to understand is that, when you decide on the courageous path of speaking out for the rights of our GLBT brothers and sisters, the association phenomenon will happen to you. And there is nothing you can do to prevent it. Your resolve will be short lived if you can't deal with that. It can put an immediate and iron clad clamp on any openness you intended to have. If you didn't expect it and it blind-sided you . . . you might not ever try to be open again."

"But, straight people, if you don't work on it; if you aren't committed to overcoming the association phenomenon, you're going to revert right back to being part of the tide of oppression that Ted Freer and maybe 3 percent, or 5 percent, or more of the people sitting right in this room today have to deal with . . . whether they are still in the closet . . . or courageous like my good friend, Dr. Ted Freer."

"Don't segregate people in workplaces or in movie theaters. Don't spit in people's drinking fountains. Don't oppress any human being in any way . . . even by forgetting them, or being ashamed or afraid to include them in a conversation about diversity! Don't resent anyone who's only motivation is to love someone else; even someone else of the same sex. Don't oppress! Thanks for your attention."

Ben walks away from the mike and is embraced by Ted, to a standing applause. From the back of the room, Dr. Ralph Prescott stood and applauded. He'd been a conferee here, but he'd never heard of either of these speakers before, even though he was a Dean at Howard University and both of them lived in DC. At that moment, he decided on his fateful course of action to rope Ben Parks into teaching the seminar on cross-cultural communication that had been on his mind for many years.

***

Ben realized that he had been dozing. It was pitch black in the backyard at midnight. A dog howled from somewhere down the alley. Groggily, he rose from his chair, went into the house, and up to bed. Addie didn't stir as he slipped in beside her . . . he didn't touch her. She'd be gone to breakfast; and then Sunday School and church when he awoke for his final day at Howard.

Chapter 32
Grand Finale

An August 1999 Sunday Morning: Ben locked the Centurion in the bike rack, retrieved his satchel, and rushed into the building; bounding up the steps to his classroom.

Ben had stopped off at Starbucks and ordered two pots of coffee, and at the bakery next door he ordered bagels, cream cheese, croissants, and juices. The Takeout Taxi delivery person appeared about fifteen minutes after Ben had arrived. After tipping the driver, Ben busied himself setting up the back table with goodies.

As the students filed in that final morning of the Seminar on Cross Cultural Communication sponsored by the Consortium of Washington Area Universities and hosted by Howard University, Ben couldn't help being tickled at their embrace of his request. There were Bisons, Eagles, Hoyas, Colonials, Terrapins and more.

"Good morning," said Ben.

Some nodded, but most said good morning. Ben was a stickler for people speaking back to him when he spoke to them. Somewhere he had somehow gotten the idea that going forward without this ritual of cordiality was bad luck for whatever was to follow. Ben was a man of patterns and rituals. They were important to him.

"Please don't leave me hanging like that ladies and gentlemen. You know how I am."

A few smiles broke out. The next 'Good morning,' received a hearty response. Ben was pretty systematic about setting up these seminars. Many years ago, one of his teachers had told him, "Look! Your audience doesn't want to sit through a dry boring talk. If you need certain things to help you feel comfortable, go for it. Except for the occasional monster crowd—you can't do much with them anyway—most groups want the facilitator to succeed. They want him to be great. Relax, take your time, and be natural."

All sorts of lessons like this guided Ben's approach to working with groups.

He was, as usual, dressed in a rather wrinkled linen suit (gray yesterday and tan today) with comfortable brown sandals . . . highly polished. The pant legs were, as usual, extra wrinkled from the bands that Ben wore when riding the Centurion, to keep from getting caught in the bike gears. Ben also wore a beige short sleeved sweater shirt, as was his habit, instead of shirt and tie. This one was open necked as a modest style variation from the crew necked one from yesterday. As the debaters got into the flow of things that had triggered them, or bothered them, or reinforced them, or whatever, Ben would almost certainly take off the suit coat to be more comfortable.

A large cup of ice chunks for periodic sucking was on the table beside him . . . a habit he'd developed to help him counter the habitual dry mouth that would occasionally come over him when he was lecturing. But he wasn't going to be lecturing today. Mostly this required intense listening. Ben knew that the less said by him today, meant the more engaged and stimulated they would be by wherever their one-page summaries had taken their fertile minds.

The process he had outlined for today's proceedings was very active and participatory. Six wooden chairs had been placed in the middle of the room. All the rest of the chairs, except for Ben's which was at one mouth of the row of threes, were back around the walls of the room. At the other mouth of the row of threes was a wooden stool with a five-minute egg timer on it.

In a moment, Ben would say 'go,' and whoever started first would be off. Ben warned them that their comments from their papers should be short . . . thirty to sixty seconds or less was the standard he'd set for the day. So, part of their preparation had been to compose their insights from the summer with clarity and precision. The egg timer would be flipped at the word 'go' from Ben. When the sand ran out, someone from the initial six who had already taken one or two turns would be tapped on the shoulder by someone from the outside ring who wanted to take their place. The person leaving would flip the egg timer and retire to an open wall seat.

Nobody seemed to need Ben to go over the process further. As a matter of fact, several eager students had anticipated what was going to happen and sprang for the middle seats as soon as Ben had arranged them there. They were ready to go.

At 10:45 a.m., Ben called a fifteen minute biology break. As was his custom, the ground rules were always that students self-regulate if they needed to use the facilities and it wasn't a break time. A few had been doing so, but at this formal break, there was a rush to the doors. When they trickled back in, the last one entering right as fifteen minutes elapsed, Ben had replaced the five-minute timer with a ten-minute timer. Now, he felt, after the crush of people wanting to get something on the table, he'd give them more time for back-and-forth before being replaced in the fishbowl.

The students' didn't miss a beat. At the lunch hour, they didn't want to stop. Someone suggested a lunch run, and a list and money were quickly passed around. Ben was too amped up on adrenaline to eat. He sipped water and fiddled as they self-organized these logistics. Though he wasn't one of the food runners, Damien Brockington had slipped out and when he came back, Ben noticed a small black and silver gadget in his hand. Ben started to ask what it was, but then the three volunteer runners came back in, food was distributed, and students called for the egg timer to be flipped. Ben forgot about Damien as the conversation started back up . . . some of the earlier participants were getting their second turns in the fishbowl.

By 3:00 p.m., everyone was spent. They sat and stood and applauded themselves and each other. Then they wanted to hear Ben's summary.

"Dr. Ben, Dr. Ben, Dr. Ben," they chanted.

Ben hadn't intended to give a summary. The day's exchange contained little mini-summations as a topic was raised, explored, and in a number of instances—put to bed. During the day, students had sometimes turned to their faith to enrich the dialog and deepen the meaning for themselves. They weren't proselytizing. If someone from another race or faith said something differently, they just listened intently and either nodded understanding or asked for clarification. Cross-cultural understanding had become their strong value and a way of interacting for them.

Ben thought about what he might say. He sat still on his stool for all of two minutes. Nobody said a word. Finally, Ben looked up at them and started, "Here's what I think. The idea of this seminar was to stimulate your reflection about yourselves, your cultures, and the culture of others; and to promote authentic dialog that would contribute to connections across your differences. I offered six themes that would serve as landmarks in our journey. At the time I listed them, I wasn't sure how they would hold up; but I think that tolerance, judgment, knowing, ambiguity, belief, and ideology have worked well for us. They've given us touch stones to go back to whenever we spiraled off the mark, or whenever we needed to be reminded of what we were here to talk about. So that's one thing I think."

Ben paused and went back inside his introverted head for more inspiration.

"More than I expected, you've been extremely interested in moving out beyond yourselves and others singularly; to exploring issues of our society. That's been a good thing. Our society, nested inside of our Nation but distinct from our Nation, is in trouble. It needs caring people like you to pay attention to it and rescue it as it spirals closer and closer to sociological anomie. The fact of our society is that we are not all the same. Anybody who imagines that we are is out of touch with reality or just silly. We aren't even equal. But there ought to be more equity."

He paused and looked around.

"You sometimes hear people say, 'I know what you're going through.' Well, maybe! But here's what blacks and other people of color for instance, can never know or feel about being white. We can never really get how hurtful it is to be totally innocent of malice against a black person, and yet to be viewed with suspicion and even outright attacked as bigoted or part of a racist system. We may say we understand, but we can never really fathom the depth of the hurt that white person feels."

"And what whites can never feel as I, a black man, do, is the need to be so constantly vigilant every time I come into new encounters with whites. Even if we've been in great relationships across the color line for months or years, some us can't get free from our long history in which it's been drummed into us to be watchful, careful, and even on guard . . . because the next encounter might just be the one that puts us into a kind of danger that we might not recover

163

from. And parallels exist if you substitute many other identity groups that we've learned about this summer."

They just listened. He imagined that earlier in the summer he might have gotten push-back. But he saw heads nod.

Now this is a complication for some who think about our society and have some sort of utopian wish for Kum Ba Yah . . . a wish for a society in which everybody gets their forty acres and a mule and goes off happily together. Inequality is inevitable for a variety of reasons, including the fact that God didn't give us all the same gifts. I wish I could defy gravity like Michael Jordan, or sing like Michael McDonald, or play guitar like Jimi Hendricks, or govern like Franklin Roosevelt, or innovate like Steve Jobs, or elocute like Maya Angelou. But I can't. Even if people should be equally valued; their skills, talents, and the tasks they are able to perform are valued differently . . . they will always be valued differently . . . and so I can't expect to get whatever it is that society gives these gifted ones because of how what they are able to do is valued."

"One of my hopes for you is that you leave here this summer with an open question about what equity could look like—not equality—in a world of unequally gifted human beings. Answers won't come easy for you on that one. But I hope you'll stay in the question. Be patient with yourself and with others who want to join you in pursuit of some answers to that question."

"For me, as I have thought about that question for much of my adult life, there have been at least two sources of inspiration for figuring out an answer; not necessarily the answer."

First, there's my faith. My faith teaches me to judge not, that ye be not judged."

"Matthew!" shouted Zenovia Strong.

"And it teaches me that he who is without sin . . ."

"Should cast the first stone . . . that's John" exclaimed Zenovia.

"You go, girl" screamed Margaret Brown; the two of them high fived.

"I don't know what other faith texts would say in a similar vein, but if someone of my faith were looking for guidance about cross-cultural tolerance, I don't know what could be clearer."

"See!" said Sadie Struthers, who was standing on the side of the room next to Trish Coleman. The two of them hugged. Then Trish blew a kiss to Paul Domenici, still seated but clapping his hands with approval. Paul looked to the next chair and Romaine Castor looked back. The two young men nodded in agreement.

Smiling at the scene, Ben continued, "It's not about any of us looking out at this crazy complex and diverse world from the inside of our little heads. Instead it's about: Did you support someone today? Did you make things better for someone besides yourself?"

He paused. All eyes were riveted. Some were becoming noticeably moist.

"There's a saying. I can't quote it exactly, but it's something like: 'If you did it for you, it's gone when you're gone,'" continued Ben. "But if you did it for somebody else, there's a chance it will be remembered."

People looked over at Zenovia expectantly. She just shrugged her shoulders.

"Don't know that one," she said sheepishly.

Ben was again deep in thought. By now, many more students had left their chairs and were standing along the walls of the class room like Sadie and Trish. Some were shifting their feet back and forth. Some were embracing others or holding hands.

"Sometimes, I think of myself as a Christian. I think I told you that early in our first session. But I was admonished many years ago to be careful in making that claim."

Silence again in the room.

"I had a pastor once many years ago. And he said something during one of his sermons that has been unmatched in its profoundness in my whole life's spiritual experience. He asked the congregation that Sunday morning: 'If you were picked up by the police, and charged with the crime of being a Christian, would the prosecution be able to find enough evidence to convict you?'

"I was absolutely stunned when I heard it the first time, and it brings me up short after these many years every time I think of it. I think for me the answer is unclear if they'd find enough evidence in my behaviors toward others to convict me. I know I do a lot for myself. That doesn't count."

Ben stood up now and said, "I'm going to move on. But we can't just pray about stuff or find the answers to everything in whatever Word we use. If that were the case, this elegant human design wouldn't have needed to include a brain. My daddy could figure out just about anything because he was never too lazy to use his brain."

"The second source of clues for me about how to coexist in a multi-cultural society and world—and to care about and facilitate equity—is the Constitution of the United States. You know, our Constitution is shamefully misrepresented in many parts of today's public discourse . . . it's misrepresented by all sorts of ideologues as providing easy answers to very complex problems. I really want to thank Candace and Adam who put us in touch yesterday with the lack of any relationship between ideology and truth. Folks talk about 'strict constructionism.' Well, you can have strict constructionism if the Constitution is clear. But it often isn't clear."

"How so, Dr. Ben?"

It was Damien from the back wall; with Delia Menendez leaning back on him and the black and silver thing at his side.

"There are folks in our society who either believe, or want us to believe, that the Constitution was written to establish individual freedoms. That's not so!"

Adam Fierstein spoke up. "Ben, I think you're about to start up a whole new seminar."

"That certainly is not my intent Adam. I'm rambling. I didn't know all of this was on my heart until I started talking. And I know I'm straying from bringing closure to the cross-cultural understanding thing. Please bear with me, a couple more minutes and I'm done."

The doors to the classroom suddenly opened and students from other classes, who had been listening from the hallways, crowded into the back of the classroom. Ben was surprised to see several professors among the new members of the audience. Taken off-guard, Ben poured himself a glass of water and drunk deep to regain his composure.

Finally, beginning again, Ben spoke, "Our founders: How was it that those brilliant minds all somehow managed to land on this planet, and on this continent, at the same moment in time in our history? Destiny is part of the legacy of this cross-cultural puzzle that we call the United States of America. But constructionism? These founders didn't have the hubris to believe they could answer all the important questions for all time. They wanted to do something very specific. And it wasn't about individual freedom initially. It was about liberty in a collective sense; liberty from tyranny of a monarchy across the waters.

"More specifically, they wanted to establish a government that could provide structure for a new nation as well as lay the foundation for a new kind of society. Make sure you hear what I said: their intent was to establish A GOVERNMENT . . . A GOVERNMENT! That's not a bad word. They understood that we needed a GOVERNMENT. And contrary to the opinions of many in today's society, we still need A GOVERNMENT!"

"You're so deep, Dr. Ben. How can you stand yourself?" said Chauncey Davis.

Rashid Jillali, JK Akinimoto, and Gail Polenski all high fived Chauncey.

"The truth is Chauncey that I get up many a morning and look in the mirror and can't stand what I see. Let me be perfectly clear. You don't ever want to get me in a confessional about my stuff. And if you put me on the witness stand, I'd probably either plead the Fifth or lie."

David Anderson, the GW law student said, "With all due respect, Dr. Parks, the founders wanted to design a government that would preserve freedom."

"Yes and no, David," replied Ben.

"A government that would do a number of things—as a matter of fact—I'll give you the exact number: it's six things. And liberty is the sixth; it's not the only thing. And there's nothing in the written history to suggest that they meant for the sixth thing to trump any of the other five. As a matter of fact, later history suggests that both the first President and the sixteenth President held the first thing as more important than the sixth thing. That first thing was 'union' and that gets us into longer stories than I have time for right now. If you want to do some more homework after this seminar, read up on Lincoln and the Civil War or Washington and the Whiskey Rebellion."

"Where's all of this in the Constitution, Dr. Ben?" asked Chauncey. "All I ever hear people talking about is the First Amendment or the Second Amendment, or the Fifth Amendment and so on. People talk about the right to this and the right to that."

"Yes they do Chauncey. But those places in the Constitution are the teasing out of higher level concepts . . . higher level values . . . and

167

sometimes they're the result of compromises to preserve "union." Actually, the Founders had considerable disagreement about whether to even include those first ten amendments. Many felt that the original document was sufficient for guidance. But even though they eventually were added to; basically in order to get the cooperation of slave holders in the Southern states, you're not excused from going back to the mission statement to put them in context."

"The Constitution doesn't have a mission statement," protested David.

"Oh yes it does, Counselor" said Ben. "They called it 'the preamble."

Ben paused and looked around very slowly.

"They called it a 'preamble.' That's where they articulated why they wrote all the rest of the Constitution. And if you go back and study it, it's simple, brilliant, and timeless. It doesn't have to be interpreted for you. All the words and meanings are understandable by the time a student is somewhere around the sixth or seventh grade. It puts everything else in context.

"We the people, etc . . . Our founders wanted to establish a government that would legitimize a nation, and allow for a society based on six core values: union, justice, domestic tranquility, common defense, general welfare, and liberty. At the highest level of framing, they didn't beat around the bush. They didn't leave their intent to interpretation for those who came later. They didn't want you to have to have a law degree to know what they were after. They probably even anticipated that later pontificators would try to spin their intent. That's probably why they were very explicit.

"The problem for those strict constructionists is that if you have only one value to adhere to, it's easy. As soon as you add another one, you introduce conflict. Add still another and the conflicts jump from one collision to three collisions. And by the time you get to six, there are fifteen collisions between the things the founders wanted our government to do. And the strict constructionists can't open up the Constitution and point to the single solution anywhere when two or more values collide, because the founders didn't provide that kind of neat and tidy solution."

Ben paused and then said, "Ladies and gentlemen, we have to think! We are expected to think. That's what we have to do. We have to use our brains. We can't look up the answers to today's complex problems. We have to think! Isn't that terrible?"

Everybody in the classroom was laughing uproariously. Many were hunched over holding their sides. Even a number of the newcomers in the back were clapping.

Ben wanted to wrap up, "Now Madison, and Jefferson, and Washington, Hamilton, Laurence, Mason, Hancock, Franklin, the Adams' . . . I'm talking about both Abigail and her husband . . . and even that guy Patrick Henry who really didn't buy into all this 'union' stuff . . . but by career end he'd realized that he'd lost that argument—none could have imagined the diversity of the society that would eventually materialize in this new nation . . . and the degree of complexity that would evolve because of all that diversity.

"But their gifts were their collective inspiration about an organizing framework that would be malleable; and that they hoped would therefore be relevant over time. The one thing you have to give them, that we seem to have lost today, is that these folks were students of history. Many nations and many societies had been tried and failed, and they knew from their studies that the ideal answers to issues of governance hadn't been found yet. What their studies did provide was answers about what not to do; and they didn't want to redo all the crazy solutions that had been proven not to work.

"I need to stop. Adam, I certainly am not trying to open up a whole new seminar. But what landed on my heart when I thought about how to wrap up our summer together was our faith teachings—I don't think it matters much which faith you come from. There's probably something in your faith teachings as well as in our original political teachings . . . something that tells us that we can all get along if we treat each other equitably and without jealousy, selfishness, or judgment. We're not promised that it will be easy. We're not promised that solutions will be clear. But we've been given the gifts of reason and each other . . . and we're challenged to use those gifts to work things out.

"Many of the so called Protestants, and Catholics, and Muslims, and Jews, and Republicans, and Democrats, and young people, and old people, and gays, and straights, and women, and men, and yellows, and browns, and blacks, and whites, and reds, and all the others of today . . . we all seem to want to act like Pharisees. They or we don't want to be shepherds. They or we want to be Pharisees. When they or we disagree with someone, they or we don't want to understand and keep the whole flock of humankind on our planet together and safe. They or we want to demonize the other guys. It's our jealousies, our judgments of others, our selfishness, our behavior, and our blindness to the man in the mirror that have caused us to become more and more like the Pharisees in the Bible rather than like the blessed shepherds: those are the things that get us into trouble with each other. I love Dr. King's notion that to survive together we have to become more ecumenical. That's a great summary for how to move toward greater cross-cultural understanding."

"When you go home at night and look in the mirror before you turn in for bed, just ask yourself if you've mostly done for yourself that day. Ask yourself what evidence the prosecution would be able to find to convict you of doing for others . . . of taking care of the flock even when it means putting our treasure, ourselves, and our loved ones in harm's way. If you do that every night I think things will start to get better in your families, in your communities, within and across faiths, and in the world in general. Thanks to all of you for this summer. This has truly been an honor and one of the most rewarding experiences of my career. Thank you! Thank you! And travel safely."

Ben sat back down on his stool. The room erupted with applause. Many students hugged each other. Most came to the front to shake Ben's hand. Some of the spectators in the back of the room joined in while others left without comment. Gradually, students got their things and started to leave in ones, and twos, and threes, or more.

No sooner had the room emptied out that Dr. Ralph Prescott wandered in with a wry smile on this face.

"Were you aware, Dr. Parks," he asked, "that the hallways outside this room have been full of professors, students, and God knows who else—myself included—practically all day?"

Prescott continued, "It came to my attention around 11:00 a.m., when several professors came into the office complaining that they couldn't keep their students in the classroom. By the afternoon, at least three or four of those professors were outside your door right along with the students. I'm the one that suggested they come in for your wrap. I didn't come in myself, because I thought that might throw you off too badly."

"Damien had a wireless microphone?"

"Very perceptive, Dr. Parks."

"Not really. I just figured it out."

Ben hadn't left the room in, what was it now . . . about seven hours. He became aware that his bladder was overfull.

"That's cool, Dr. Prescott" said Ben as—coat across the arm and bag in hand—he rushed out to the facilities. Janitorial folks were coming in to clean.

"Good job, Ben" shouted the Dean after the receding figure ducking into the men's room.

Part Two:
The Middle

Chapter 33
Klutz

Tanya Potter, the book keeper at Parks Freer Associates (PFA), had her farewell party the Friday following the last two days of the August Consortium seminar at Howard. Ben was out on client assignments in the morning that day, but the afternoon was a relaxed celebration of a person who'd been with the firm for more than ten years and would be missed. She was moving to the west coast to follow her husband, who had been given a promotion and transfer on his job.

Years ago, when PFA was just getting off the ground, Ted and Ben had flipped a coin to see who'd do the book keeping and Ben had lost. So he knew how to do the end-of-the-month reconciliations, pay the bills, and get out the payroll. That Monday, after Tanya's retirement, Ben was working from home. He'd taken that morning to do his admin tasks; and he hoped that by the next month, Amanda Joseph, the office manager, would find a replacement for Tanya.

Ben's bronchitis had been acting up, so for the past few days he'd nixed his usual decaf coffee in the morning in favor of hot tea. He nuked a hot cup of water and dropped in the bag of Yogi Brand, Lemon Ginger tea. Then he poured in several drizzles of Sue Bee honey and topped off the brew with some Safeway brand lemon juice from concentrate. He took his concoction downstairs to the office to continue steeping and turned on the computer to warm up. As he did so, he realized that an arm on his prized office chair from the Strong Back store in Rockville, MD was loose. From the closet under the steps, he retrieved a Phillips head screw driver and returned to find that the screw required an Allen wrench.

Back to the closet, he pulled out the whole roller bag full of tools, pulled it over to his work area, and promptly jostled the small table where he'd placed his tea to steep. Tea spilled over the table and the floor, and now his cup of tea was only half full.

"Damn!"

He went back upstairs to the kitchen and was disappointed to find they were out of paper towels. He wrote that down on the list attached to the refrigerator so he wouldn't forget. Then he scratched his head, disoriented for a moment. Sub-vocalizing, he said to himself, "Spilt tea."

He retrieved two sponges from below the sink, soaked one and slightly wet the other. Back downstairs, he cleaned the table and the floor, and for good measure, sprayed the area with a generous dose of Lemon Power Antibacterial cleaning product that he got from the shelf in the basement bathroom. Satisfied, he picked up his half-full cup of tea, drank it, and was disappointed. Back upstairs in the kitchen, he remade a fresh cup and took it back downstairs to steep. There, he noticed again the loose arm on the Strong Back chair and the roller bag of tools.

Allen wrench, he remembered.

After finding the right one, he finally had the chair repaired, and Ben returned the tools to the closet below the steps. Now sitting at the computer, he opened up his email and quickly responded to a few, before reading the next one which reminded him of a response that he owed to Marta Crossman, a museum client in New York.

He wrote:

Dear Marta,

Thanks for your email this morning and for your notes on the two courses we've been discussing. I think I can accommodate the facilitation course for your HR staff and select managers in either one of the two early November dates. The teaming course for your public programs staff and docents could happen in a two-day version in mid-November or in a three-day version in early December.

I hope you will be at the meeting at 4:00 p.m. when I come up next Thursday. I'll have my calendar and we can lock in the schedule then.

Looking forward to seeing you.

Ben

With a satisfied flourish, Ben pushed the send button. Then he sat back and wondered what he'd do next.

***

Around 5:00 p.m., Ben remembered Tanya was gone and that there were bills to pay.

Chapter 34
Church

After the summer seminar wound up, Ben had planned to take off for a few days. He realized that he was exhausted after focusing on the seminar all summer, while maintaining a full load of real paying clients. The Wednesday evening two days after his little mind freeze with paying the PFA bills, he and Addie had choir rehearsal at church. He was a part-time singer in the choir because of his heavy travel schedule, but when he didn't have a conflict he liked to participate. Addie was very conscientious about the choir.

That next morning, Ben boarded the train at Union station and rode up to NYC. That afternoon, he would meet with Marta Crossman, his Museum administration client re: two requested courses—one on facilitation skills and one on basic skills for team members.

He hadn't been in the apartment on Hamilton Terrace for a while and hadn't hung out in the city for even longer. His trips here in the past year or so had all been for business. That Thursday evening after the meeting, he wanted to play. For the next two days, his plan was to see at least one play and hear a lot of music. The Jazz Standard, Jazz at Lincoln Center, and the Vanguard in the Village were his favorites. Friday night he caught Pancho Sanchez at the Vanguard. He boarded the train again on Saturday morning for the trip back to DC feeling refreshed.

Puttering around the house that Saturday afternoon, Addie warned him that there was some mess stirring at church. She didn't quite know what was going to happen, but there might be a special call meeting after the service.

Addie was an alto and Ben a tenor. Choir was one of the few things they've tried to continue to do together. They enjoyed it . . . until the church imploded. The anthem that next Sunday had been Gilbert Martin's serene arrangement of the well-known Hymn

'When I Survey the Wondrous Cross.' Then service had ended and the choir was in the back. After the benediction, Levi Chance, from the front, gave the signal. They started in softly singing Shelton Becton's *a capella* "Alleluia." The church members were transfixed in their seats.

Then everything fell apart. After this particular service, a call-meeting started up. Although Ben had been clueless, the rumblings in the church had been brewing for months. This was going to be the show down. At the end of the meeting, Pastor Ralph Creed had been voted out. Ben was disheartened. He had grown up in this church. He and Addie had been married in this church and by Pastor Creed.

"A church isn't supposed to come apart like this," said Ben with noticeable agony.

"These wanna be Saints are all sinners. Heaven knows, I'm a sinner. Pastor is a sinner. That's what a church is supposed to be for. There ain't no saints in churches. Hell, there aren't very many saints in the history of the whole world. These know-it-alls think they know how to run a church. Well, they don't know what the hell they're doing."

Addie was silent, but held Ben's hand as they sat together in the car outside the church.

"What do you want to do, B?" she asked.

"I'm not coming back here," said Ben.

"Then, I'm not coming back here, either . . . after a while, she said, "we'll find another church, B."

Eventually, she did. But Ben didn't. Though he briefly tried Addie's new church and several others, he would never again trust a church to be the seat of his faith.

Chapter 35
The Mistake

Ben had been writing that morning. He worked downstairs in the office from about 8:30 to 11:00 a.m. Then he got stir crazy. He pulled his powder blue Ford Thunderbird out of the garage and drove up to Malaguena, a favorite chill-out spot uptown by Walter Reed Army Medical Center. Davita's Bar and Restaurant was just a few blocks away, but he didn't stop there.

Big, open, relatively undecorated, but with a super-speed WiFi hook up that was free and unsecured, Malaguena was a favorite spot for students and professionals alike. People arrived there early in the morning to get seats near the outlets so they could plug in their laptops. They ordered regular and specialty coffees and worked on whatever projects—work or school—they'd brought with them.

Some people broke for lunch, and if they didn't eat lunch from the limited fare there, they negotiated with some stranger at the next table to watch their stuff. Then they'd walk down a block to Crisfield's, the hole-in-the-wall seafood place. The Crisfield family from the Eastern Shore of Maryland had operated this little place in the District of Columbia for decades. And the shell fish and other seafood were to die for . . . hard seats and large crowds notwithstanding.

Then, people would slip back into Malaguena and work until 7:00 p.m. or later. Ben found a place and ordered his favorite, decaf mocha with soy and just a dot of whipped cream. He surfed the web for a while and played a couple of games of spider solitaire. He couldn't get his mind back to the client report he was supposed to be working on.

Finally, on the spur of the moment, he drove over to Addie's school. The principal knew him and didn't say anything when he walked directly past the front office. He slipped into the back of Addie's classroom. He'd been there for a few minutes before she even recognized his presence. It never occurred to Ben that the kids might have been off-the-chain for most of the day and that Addie might have just gotten them settled down.

After five minutes or so, Addie wandered back to the back. "Sup, B?"

"Nothing. Just in the area."

"Just in the area and you found yourself wandering into my classroom, disturbing my kids." Now, whispering Addie intoned, "I don't appreciate this Benjamin."

Ben looked over, and the kids, who should have been working on their assignments, were all looking back to the back of the room watching Ms. Parks and that man.

"Sorry, B. I just wanted to see you. I guess this wasn't a good idea."

"I guess not, Benjamin."

Addie walked back to the front and said, "Say hello to Dr. Parks, kids."

They all said, "Hello, Dr. Parks."

Then Addie said, "Now you can get back to work, kids. Dr. Parks is leaving."

Later that night, Ben eased into bed around 10:30pm. Addie was propped up by three or four pillows, checking papers. The TV was on, but she wasn't watching it. The TV was almost always on, as were all the lights in the bedroom. The bedroom was Addie's sanctuary.

Finally, she was done and shut down the TV and turned off the lights. Ben moved close. Addie moved away. He placed his arm across her. She sucked her teeth and pushed the hand off. "Stop Ben!" was all she said. That was the sum total of interaction between Addie and Ben that evening.

***

Aunt ClayClay died in October of 2000.

Chapter 36
Rage

Addie whimpered in another of her sleeps. This horrific dream again . . . that man again . . . that paragon of the Little Western Pennsylvania Black community: whose face had appeared over and over through the years whenever she thought she was past it. He was touching her again. He was breathing on her again. Little innocent fourth grade Addie Sherrie Isles: who sang like an angel at church and got straight As in school—Addie was never bad in school. But she felt like she was bad.

Why was the teacher . . . this Deacon in his church . . . this man whose wife was important in the town and knew her parents . . . this man with the horrible breath . . . why was he so mean to her? He was her father's age. Why wasn't he more like daddy?

But she must be wrong . . . all the other kids seem to love him . . . one of her girlfriends was upset with Addie because she never got the "extra credit." The other girls teased her on the playground.

"Addie is the teacher's pet. Addie is the teacher's pet."

She wondered if they had any idea what "extra credit" was like. But she thought, *They must know. They're smart. It's me. I don't like it. They can have it, but he won't ask them, and they don't like me for it.*

Why did he wink at her in class when he knew the other kids weren't looking? Why had he singled her out for "extra credit" after school? She thought her grades were good enough to get her A in class. Why did he tell her she needed "extra credit" to keep her A? Sometimes, she thought she didn't need the A. But she knew her parents were so proud of her . . . that she never got Bs . . . only As.

He can feed the fishies himself. Little Addie learned to bottle her resentment and never let anyone know . . . especially that man. But he always wanted Addie to earn her "extra credit." Maybe she was ungrateful. After all, he was concerned about her keeping her A. He was helping her. But when she got up on her tippy toes to sprinkle the fishie food, why did he have to stand close behind her; breathing on her, "teaching" her as he called it. She knew what to do. But every time, he needed to "teach" her. Maybe she wasn't smart enough to keep her A without the "extra credit." She really wanted to keep her A.

And what was it about her that made him want her to write the lessons for tomorrow on the chalk board? He said she had "beautiful handwriting." But other kids had very nice handwriting. She knew that. She saw other kids' papers. And why couldn't he write his own lessons? He was the teacher. She was just nine years old. Why did he look at her like that? She couldn't even reach the top part of the chalkboard without standing on that three-step stool. She hated that three-step stool. The chalkboard was almost the whole length of the front of the room.

She tried to come down and move it over to write the next part of the lesson that the teacher had written on several pieces of paper for her to copy.

"No, my dear Addie! That will take too long for you to go up and down and up and down. Just stay where you are."

That teacher would have her turn toward him and wrap her arms around his neck. Then he'd pick up the stool and edge over and sit it back down for her to write the next section. This had to happen four or five times for her to cover the whole chalk board. And he'd move up close to her and tell her.

"Keep holding on! I won't drop you. I'd never drop you."

Why couldn't she tell someone? Why was she so ashamed? She was her father's little baby. He would stop it if he only knew. Couldn't he? But maybe not . . . and if she really needed the "extra credit" to get the A, wasn't that important to daddy? He told everybody in town how smart his little girl was. So did her mom. Her big brother David Isles would stop it. Why couldn't she tell them how it felt to have this man's hands on her? But maybe David couldn't stop it. He was still a boy and teacher was a man. What happened to boys after they weren't boys anymore? Daddy was daddy. That was different. But teacher was scary; men were scary.

Addie whimpered again and startled herself awake. She looked at the illuminated clock on her dresser across their dark bedroom. It was 2:14 a.m. Then she heard the soft snore and was startled again. She sat up and looked over at Ben who was sleeping on his side; facing her. He had drifted toward the center of their queen-sized bed. She could feel his breath. She didn't smell it; so much as feel it. She didn't like feeling it. He was sleeping too close. This man was sleeping too close. Addie pushed Ben hard against the raised shoulder. She was pushing her teacher. She was pushing Ben. She was pushing men.

Ben was groggy, but his eyes were opening.

"So you have to take up the whole bed?" Addie was screaming.

More alert, Ben retreated to the edge of the bed where he usually camped out.

"Sorry, Addie. Sorry. Go back to sleep, A. Sorry."

Chapter 37
The Family's
Thanksgiving Ritual

November 2002: Ben had stuck to his guns and refused to do the Summer Seminar in 2000 and 2001 . . . but by the summer of 2002, Dr. Prescott had prevailed again: More students, more fireworks, more learning, much, much more.

***

Rico, Tony, and AR had already started the assembly line process at the family car wash . . . it really wasn't a car wash in the commercial sense . . . it was the large driveway in front of Ben's parents' house on 19th Street in the Carter Baron section of Northwest Washington. The red brick, two-story house, with finished attic and basements, sat amidst a large, well-manicured lawn. The driveway ran up into a garage, but there was room outside on the driveway for three rows of two cars abreast off the street.

Of course, Rico and Tony had washed their own cars first. Rico, home from Columbia College of Arts in Chicago, was pushing Tony's hand-me-down Cressida. Tony's shiny new black 2002 Toyota Prius stood clean on one side of the wide driveway. Ben's dad's dark blue Volvo sedan also gleamed as Rico backed it slowly into the garage. The finishing touches were being placed on Aunt Penny's silver Buick, when Ben eased Addie's white-on-white Lexus sports car (a Christmas morning surprise that Ben had orchestrated for her last year . . . after he'd seen those TV commercials) up behind it.

Penelope Parks Tompkins (Ben's sister) was an organizer and planner down to her toes. She couldn't help herself . . . and she was good at it. As an example, she'd persuaded her ex (Jermaine

Tompkins) to buy a house at the birth of each of their five kids. When Jerrie (the eldest) reached college-age, Penny and Jermaine sold a house. When Jernelle, the next in line, reached college-age, they sold another house. When Jeralyn reached college-age, they didn't need to sell a house because brainiac Jeralyn got full-ride offers from all over the country. When the first boy, Jermaine Jr., reached college-age, guess what . . . another house financed his tuition. Finally, they did the same thing for Jerome, Penny's baby boy.

Jerrie had matched her mom in brood size. She'd been ensconced down in Charlotte, North Carolina since meeting her future husband in college and settling there. Jerrie taught music, just like her mom. Jernelle, the business-woman, and husband Neal were in Pittsburg. Jeralyn (the medical doctor) married to Igor (a dentist), had gone out to Phoenix, and Jermaine Jr. lived in Teaneck, New Jersey. The only unmarried one of Penny's offspring was Jerome, who resided in L.A. (not lower Alabama), but traveled the world for months at a time.

This year, all of Penny's kids were here at their grand parents' house in the Carter Baron section of DC, except for Jerome. Thankfully, he'd recently left Afghanistan, but now he was in South Africa filming a documentary on a girls' school. Jeralyn and Kristin (Jermaine's wife) were both with child. This would be Jeralyn's second and Kristin's first. And Jernelle's precocious daughter was AR's age. Jermaine was one of the most sought-after rave deejays around; and he worked from Philly, to Manhattan, to Boston.

Addie jumped out from the passenger seat of her new Lexus, hurried up the seven flag stone steps from the sidewalk, and then cut right off the front walk and across the lawn to the back of the house, where she knew the kitchen back door would be open. She clutched her dish of lovingly seasoned and prepared fresh green beans (the sister could burn . . . she just didn't choose to very often). Inside, she joined the Parks clan women preparing the annual family Thanksgiving dinner. Ben piled out of the car smiling at his sons' handiwork. "Nice job," he observed. "We're next, right?"

"You ain't said nottin butta word, Pop," croaked Rico as he opened up the hose on the Lexus, making sure he got some, but not too much, on his dad. Tony was backing Aunt Penny's car into the garage next to his grandfather's Volvo.

The horn blew from the street behind, and Adam (the accountant) with wife Asia and Addie's two grandkids (Shawnda and Little Adam, AKA Deuce) pulled up in his gray Chrysler van, complete with DVD player and wall-to-wall sound system blaring "Pass the Courvoisier" from the Busta Rhymes CD. Ben jumped back into the Lexus and pulled forward so the van could be behind it in the driveway. Adam's family piled out and went back behind the house. Now, four Parks males: Ben, Tony, Rico, and AR, plus Addie's son Adam and grandson Deuce, were taking all comers.

Cousin Corinne, in her silver Mercedes, pulled up in the street behind the driveway and called out, "Have you got time to do mine, too?"

Rico was the first to answer. "If u family and u pull up to dis house, u gone get washed. Find a spot on the street Auntie Corinne 'til we get room, and leave us dah key. We take care of it."

They all high-fived as they flung more suds in the direction of the Lexus and the Van. Ben silently shook his head at his son's hipster English. Rico knew how to speak Standard English. He just didn't usually choose to; except when within earshot of his grandfather, Richard Parks. Then the King's English flowed so naturally, you wouldn't know Rico could speak any other way.

When Rico had been in high school, Ben took him to task one day when Rico cursed at home, "This fuckin' jon. It's like that."

Ben didn't know how this slang-word, jon, was spelled. He knew that "it's like that" meant that it's really good . . . it's fabulous . . . it's like that. But Rico and all his buddies talked about jons. Jon, however it was spelled, seemed to refer to anything . . . it could be a rap song, it could be an automobile, it could have been one of Tony's heavy punches in the ring . . . it could be anything. But jon wasn't what Ben responded to on this particular occasion.

"I get to curse in my house because it's my house. I don't get to curse at your grandfather's house. Out of respect for my father and mother, I don't curse around him. Out of respect for my clients I don't curse around them. Out of respect for my wife . . . unless she really pisses me off . . . I don't curse around her. Out of respect for me, you don't get to curse around me. Whatever you do on the street Rico is your business. Not at this house. Is that clear?"

Rico had always been his well-behaved kid. Tony pushed the envelope wherever he could. But, Rico held himself in check.

"Okay, Pop" he said simply. And that was the end of that incident.

Back in the Carter Baron driveway, Erica Badu and Common's *"Love of My Life"* was playing from the boom box inside the garage. Then Ben's mom, eighty-seven-year old Gillian, wandered out from the side door onto a raised patio on the left front of the house, stood at the top of another set of flagstone steps that came down into the driveway outside the garage, and looked over the scene with a slight smile masking confusion. From below in the driveway, everyone greeted her and she smiled back in the absent recognition that had become her signature in the past year or so. She didn't seem to know anyone. AR ran up the five steps and hugged his great grandmother.

"Nice to meet you young man," said Gillian. "A, a, a, i, o."

Nobody commented, and the nonplussed AR went back to working on the wheels of Adam's van. Then, Gillian stepped carefully down the five steps using a railing on the right side. Picking up a scrub brush from one of the many pails lined up in a row, Ben's mom started toward Tony's Prius, and before anyone could stop her she started applying soap.

"Wait, Mom," said Ben with a quiet voice that belayed underlying desperation. "Those are the cars we've already finished."

Gillian looked at him blankly, and then confusion and anger crossed her face. Nobody else spoke, and Ben waited for the explosion that might happen if his mom felt threatened. Just then, Penny appeared, walking fast across the patio and down the steps to her mom's side.

"Mama!"

There was no recognition from her mom. Then Penny re-loaded, "Gillian! There you are, out here with the men."

Ben silently thanked his sister for the rescue. Gillian dropped the scrub brush, threw up her hands, and smiled sheepishly toward her daughter. The two women went, arm in arm, around the right side of the house, across the lawn, toward the kitchen door in the back.

The dinner was grand, as it was every year. This year, more than fifty family members showed up . . . from East Coast and West Coast they came. Zach was there (Jerrie's husband) with all the Carolina kids. He and Jernelle's Neal performed their usual slapstick, improvised comedy routine that always had family members rolling across the rugs.

Jeralyn and Kristin patted each other's stomachs and conspired together with Ben's cousin Ralphine plus aunt Nellie, who offered them that special brand of older-woman advice.

Eighty-eight-year-old Doctor Richard roamed the house, refilling drinks every time he got a chance, whether the person wanted more or not—while at the same time keeping an eye peeled for his younger (i.e., eighty-three-year-old) brother, Roderick Parks, who had a habit of tripping as he followed his big brother around.

Ben stuffed himself, though he remembered a time as a youngster when stuffing himself required a lot more food that it did now. After dinner, Adam's wife Asia and Shawnda took charge of clearing and restoring order to the house. They cleared away dishes, loaded the dish washer several times, brought out the desserts, and generally did whatever they could do to make sure the place wasn't a total wreck when everyone left later in the evening.

Meanwhile Ben, AR, Deuce, Adam, and Igor, with several of Penny's grandkids looking on, retreated to Dr. Richard's oversized study to play twelve-spot dominos. Ben usually played with a six spot set. Twelve spot dominos were really over his head.

Deuce, Adam, and Igor were the best at it. Ben was just frankly trying to keep up with the calculations. Also, Ben realized he didn't know most of the younger kids' names.

Tony left right after dinner, and forty-five minutes later returned with his girlfriend, Portia. Pulling up from the other direction at the same time, Rico's squeeze (Rayann) jumped out of her black Chevy 4X4. Ben really liked these gorgeous two young ladies, but he knew well enough to hold back because, as he privately had said to Addie, "you never know where things are headed with these young folks."

Having finished up their dinners with their respective families, Portia and Rayann, in their liquid black jeans that looked like they'd come off the same rack, had accessorized differently . . . reflecting their individualized stylish tastes. Portia was cloaked in tight black, both above and below the belt. She'd completed her ensemble with an African tie around her head and silver jewelry. Rayann wore a full print throwback 1960s-styled dashiki that was cut short so as to not interfere with the look and the lines of her jeans. Her accessories were amber.

Both young women attracted oohs and ahs from all the old folks as they smoothly joined into the after-dinner board game that Addie had started up: Cranium, The Turbo Edition. Jerrie, Jeralyn, and Jernelle seemed to be able to match Addie answer for answer. The double-forte noise volume in the dining room where all the women were playing reached into the study, and the men yelled for them to quiet down ... to no avail of course.

Of Ben's sons, Tony was the life of the party, smoothly moving from cluster to cluster making his own special brand of suave small talk. Rico was out in the backyard with Jermaine spitting his new lyrics. Levi popped in, just to say hi, but wound up getting pulled out into the backyard. Rico had become bored with the sound recording program he had enrolled in at school—having forsaken the visual arts. He'd mastered Pro Tools, the mixing and recording software that had largely replaced a lot of the older recording technology, while hanging out at "uncle" Levi's house during summer vacation before he'd shipped out to Chicago for college. Ben didn't know it, but Rico had bused over to New York once since school started in September to hook up with Jermaine and pickup whatever Deejay techniques he could. He thought he knew more about mixing than a lot of the students and several instructors at college. Two years later, at the end of his junior year, Rico would announce, "They holding me back, Pop!"

Speaking from his cell phone while lying in the dorm room, "I gotta git on wid my career."

On and off, through the afternoon and evening, Ben flashed back to his mom. Maybe it had been a while since she stopped recognizing him, but he'd not realized it before the episode outside at the car wash. He'd watched her off and on through the rest of the dinner. She was gone. She was really gone. At the end of the evening, before anyone could get away, the cameras came out. Everybody gathered in the big living room. Cousin Charles, married for thirty years to Ben's cousin Ralphine, took all comers as folks handed him Nikons, cell phones, and throw-aways. He didn't like to have his picture taken, so Ralphine had brought her customary sign, "Me and Charles" and was holding it in front of her. In the position of honor, seated in the front of the pack were Ben's mom and dad; his Uncle Roderick (dad's brother); and his aunt Nellie, the younger sister to mom ... the family matriarchs and patriarchs.

Chapter 38
Folding

"Mama, Oh, my sweet Mama," said Penny in a slightly raised voice.

Despite all of the on-the-spot help, it took several days to get Richard and Gillian's house back in order after the annual Thanksgiving ritual. Penny had a load of laundry going and was running the vacuum cleaner in the basement, but she'd heard footsteps which told her that Gillian was on the move from her usual chair in the den. Coming up the stairs, she turned left into the dining room and spotted her mother about twenty feet away, looking lost.

"Mama, Mommy, Mom, what are you doing just standing there?"

After a moment, "G, a, g, a, e, e, o, o, o" was Gillian's response. Then she looked around and raised both hands out to her sides in a gesture of "I don't know."

"Well that's all right, Mommy," said Penny moving toward her mom. "You don't have to know. Did you finish your tea? Are you wet?"

Before any response, Penny had already determined that the Depends diaper needed to be changed. She'd devised a scheme for getting her mom to follow, which she'd taught to Richard and Ben and a few others. She stepped in front and took Gillian's hands from behind and placed them on her shoulders. Thus, in a choo-choo train fashion, Gillian followed as Penny led her back to the master bathroom.

"Hi, ho! Hi ho" It's off to work we go," sang Penny.

Gillian hummed with her and was fairly cooperative in the course of the diaper changing procedure. But Richard Parks was adamant about keeping Gillian hydrated, so as soon as the liquid came out, he and Penny endeavored to get some back in.

"Now let's get back to the den and get you some more tea, Mama. Okay?"

"Pen, Pen!" said Gillian with some sort of a smile. She patted her daughter on the shoulder as they choo-choo trained back through the house to the den. "Pen, Pen, Pen. Ha, ha!"

Now settled into the reddish leather chair that was her favorite, and with one of the never ending cooking shows on the TV, Gillian seemed to be settled just as the buzzer sounded from the basement that the drying cycle was complete. Penny left her mom, gathered some clothes from the dryer, and brought up one basket and placed it at the top of the steps . . . returning to the basement for the next basket. As she came back up with the second basket, she noticed the first one had been moved. Turning the corner to the right and looking into the den, she saw Gillian seated in her reddish leather chair, with the basket of dried clothes to her right on the floor. Gillian had a table napkin in her lap and was folding it very carefully and precisely.

Penny put the second basket down and took a seat on the couch opposite her mom's chair and watched.

Gillian folded and unfolded several times to get the edges to match just right. It might have been two full minutes just on that one cloth table napkin. But when it was done, she patted the napkin and nodded her head. She put the completed napkin over to her left on a table and reached into the basket for another napkin.

Penny smiled and reminisced about her mom's roots in Selma in her big family, and about her training in home economics, and about her fastidiousness as a home maker for many decades. This was peaceful for Gillian Parks. Penny reached into the second basket and took out five or six small pieces, mostly table napkins and washcloths. She replaced some of the larger pieces in the first basket with these more manageable pieces and Gillian looked down but didn't protest.

Gillian dutifully folded about eighteen pieces from the basket in about forty minutes as Penny went about continuing to get the house back in order. When the basket was empty and the pieces were folded and stacked on the table, Penny took them and kissed her mom on the forehead. Then, around the corner, she unfolded all of those pieces and put them in a new basket.

"Mom, would you like to do some more? You did such a good job."

"O, o, o, i, i, a, g, a" said Gillian with a slight smile and a noticeable nod."

Placing the basket by Gillian's right side, Penny sat on the couch to watch. Gillian reached into the basket and took out a hand towel and began to fold on her lap.

Richard Parks pulled into the driveway with a car loaded with groceries . . . a restocking from the Thanksgiving dinner. Penny went out to help him carry bags in and told her father of her discovery.

"That's wonderful," said Richard, as he placed a grocery bag on the kitchen counter. Then, standing in the door watching his wife calmly fold a table napkin, "That's wonderful!"

Chapter 39
The Doctor

Ben had gone to Dr. Popovich, his primary care physician, to ask about a whole suite of ailments. He wasn't sleeping well. That had been going on for months. Now he was experiencing vertigo. He had gotten out of bed yesterday morning with the world swimming before his eyes. As he swung himself out, he fell before realizing what was happening. He had just laid there for a while as his vision spun out of control. Then there was his sleeping and the increasing severity of the tremor in his right hand.

The doctor first dealt with the vertigo. As he lay back on the examination room table, the crystalline grains that had gotten in the wrong part of ear canal were magically shifted back where they were supposed to be with a series of expert snaps of Ben's head.

"What the hell just happened, Doc?"

"Dr. Parks, if I told you then I'd have to kill you," deadpanned Dr. Popovich. "I'll give you something to read when you leave, but you've got quite a list so let's move on. Hold out your hand."

She observed the shaking right hand; then reached over to a table, picked up a pad, and drew a circle.

"Trace that, Dr. Parks!"

Without thinking, Ben traced it counter clockwise. He'd learned all kinds of compensations since the condition began.

"Okay, trace it the other way."

Be smiled. "Caught me huh, Doc."

Ben placed the pencil down and shakily tried to keep the pencil as close as possible to the original lines. The result looked like one of the EKG lines that sometimes showed up with very sick patients in emergency rooms.

"Nope! That's not that bad. It's an intention tremor. It's no worse than the last time you told me about it, and I told you that you could see a neurologist if you were really concerned."

"Aw come on, Doc. You've got magic moves for vertigo. Where's the presto-chango for this?"

"Sorry! Only one miracle per visit, Dr. Parks. What's next?"

"I might need help with sleeping. I don't feel like I ever get to deep sleep, and I wake up tired."

After some conversation and hesitation, Dr. Popovich prescribed Ambien.

"I really don't like to do this except in extreme conditions. But I know you'll monitor yourself and stop using them if you start to slip into dependency. You will stop, right Dr. Parks?"

"Yes I will stop. Thanks Dr. Popovich."

The prescription was for twenty tablets.

"Try to take it only in emergencies . . . no refills. Try to exercise more . . . cut out alcohol late in the evening . . . don't eat protein that the body has to work hard to digest after about 6:00 p.m. Okay?"

"Yep!"

"Is there anything else?"

Ben thought about his memory problems. That scared him the most.

"No Doc; fit as a fiddle now. Thanks!"

As Ben left, he knew he'd missed an opportunity. These were not all the ailments he worried about. Others were just harder to talk about.

***

That night, standing in the door to her study, Ben told Addie about his doctor visit. He joked about Dr. Popovich's miracle touch.

"Sounds like you want her."

"What? Are you kidding me?"

"I'm joking, Ben. Relax!"

"Relax! How the hell can I relax? How the hell am I supposed to know you're just kidding? You don't kid. You don't even smile when you're around me."

Silence.

"I didn't tell Doc about my memory thing."

"What memory thing, Ben? That's your mom, Benjamin. It's not you. Don't put it out that you're going to follow her and you won't. Pray Benjamin. Just pray. God doesn't mean that for you. Pray to God and you'll be all right."

"What about you, A? Will you pray for me?"

"I pray for you every Sunday, B. You don't come to church anymore. So, I pray for Adam, and I pray for Tony, and I pray for Rico, and I pray for Victoria, and I pray for my kids at school and their parents, and I pray for your mom and dad and Penny, and I pray for my family, and I pray for me, and I pray for you."

Addie turned back to the computer screen. Ben stood at the door of the small study for a moment, trying to think what to say.

Then he went back downstairs.

Chapter 40
If I don't work, I don't eat

February 2003: Ben's meeting was near the corner of Greenwich and Murray Streets, on the border between the Battery Park City and Tribeca sections of lower Manhattan. The office was in a twenty-story glass building where bankers, brokers, lawyers, and other financial sector professionals had their offices. This was very near Wall Street, so these types of businesses were mixed in on virtually every block, along with hotels, churches, and all manner of shopping venues—large and small.

The area was slowly coming back to some semblance of order and sanity after the horrific events of September 2001. The previous year, Ben had worked with other consultants and facilitators to support a five thousand-person citizen participation and planning session at the Jacob Javits Center on West 34th Street. That day had contributed significantly to the community's healing and ability to look forward to a restored lower Manhattan that would honor and memorialize those who had lost their lives that dreadful day.

Ben had been here for the past four days, coaching his client, the sharp dressing brother who headed up the mid-sized, but wanna-be-bigger, bank's loan division. He was also doing team building with a startup group within the bank that had landed the responsibility of leading a total IT overhaul.

In the evenings, Ben loved to catch Jazz wherever he could find it in the city. But he couldn't walk the streets and go to the Blue Note every night. His work was mentally and emotionally draining, and his feet always hurt in the evenings. Besides, he was still Dr. Richard Roscoe Park's son and had over-prepared for these types of assignments for his entire career. So, whether it was something like Fred Jandt's *"Win-Win Negotiation"* or the wonderfully refreshing, *"Emotions: Transforming Anger, Fear, and Pain"* by Marilyn Barrick, he always read to prep for client work.

Sometimes, Ben even went back to *"Morality is Social"* by Dewey (the source of his first academic success in high school, when he'd invented his A++ paper). In so doing, Ben recharged himself and prepped for whatever was thrown at him the next day in his adventurous profession.

This had been one of the toughest days of Ben's professional career. It had started a few months ago back in DC, when his old friend Lou had come to him and shared that he was moving on up. Lou had landed a lucrative contract for a large scaled construction project.

"No more small potato home renovations for me . . . except for my homeys, of course," had said Lou.

Then, Lou and Han had found a house in Potomac, Maryland . . . the upscale DC suburb of mansions in the five to twenty million dollar price range.

"Are you nuts, Lou," Ben had reacted.

Addie had congratulated Han. She knew that Han had heard shots a few times at night in the neighborhood and was really afraid to go outside at night. She'd been unhappy for quite a while.

But then, Lou had showed Ben his paperwork. Ben was no real estate or banking or loan expert. He and his dad had acquired a few places over the years that they rented out for a little extra income. But Dr. Richard had trained Ben and indelibly imprinted in him a commitment to fixed-term mortgages. So, when Ben saw the loan terms his friend had signed, he pleaded with Lou. There was a thirty-day rescission provision.

"Bail on this deal, Lou! Please, homey."

Lou had been un-persuadable. Ben had asked Lou for a copy of the paperwork and redacted all the personal information. He'd realized that the lender was the mid-size bank that was his client up in New York City.

Ben placed a piece of paper on the desk by the sharp, well-dressed brother who was his coaching client. They'd clashed before. Sometimes, Ben realized that clients hired consultants to check off some sort of expectation of due diligence. But these clients really didn't want advice. They wanted affirmation. Speaking truth to power was one of the occupational hazards of being an organization development consultant. Ben thought that this brother tolerated him because of his reputation and credentials. But he wasn't serious. Nonetheless, this was a half a million dollar gig. PFA had received half of that amount up-front. The rest would be paid upon conclusion. That wasn't bad money.

The client looked at the single sheet of paper Ben had slid onto the desk. They'd finished the business that he had wanted to discuss with Ben. He'd expected his consultant to leave the office so he could go on about the rest of his day.

"What's this?' he asked.

"Would you just indulge me here and educate me a little about the banking business. You know I really don't know about banking, but I saw something in the newspaper back in DC recently, and it got me thinking. This is just a made up set of figures. Take a look at the calculations here and tell me what you think."

After he'd looked over the figures, he'd looked up at Ben and said, "Bad deal for the shlump who signed on the dotted line, but good deal for the bankers, even if the shlump ultimately can't pay."

"Why's it such a good deal for the bankers?" asked Ben. He really couldn't figure that out.

"Commissions, Dr. Parks. It's all about the size of the commissions."

"What do you mean?"

"The commission is paid up front on the loan amount. Maybe the borrower can pay for a while. Maybe, when the balloon hits, the borrower can't pay anymore. It doesn't matter. Then we foreclose and get another shot at another shlump. In the meantime, the commission . . . somebody gets paid."

Stunned at this asshole's candor, Ben sat back for a minute. The figures on the desk were drawn from Lou's paperwork, without attribution. Ben stood up.

"Sorry, sir, I can't do business with you anymore."

"What the fuck are you talking about?"

"That's somebody's life on that piece of paper, and you're fucking it up."

"Dr. Parks, haven't we only paid you one-half of your fee? There's an old saying in business: 'you never walk away and leave money on the table.'"

"Sorry, but I'm not a good business person. Anyway, I've already figured out what I'm going to tell my wife. She wanted our roof replaced. But I'll tell her that another treatment of tape where it's leaking . . . that'll do us for another year or two at least. She won't buy it, but . . ."

Ben was out in the hall by the time he finished and the banker didn't hear whatever he said to finish his sentence. Ben never looked back.

***

Lou and Han backed out of the new house deal in Potomac, Maryland.

Chapter 41
Harlem

Ben rode the 1 train up to 145th Street and transferred to a west cross-town bus that let him off at the corner of 145th and Convent Avenue. He always admired the stately Convent Avenue Baptist Church on the corner as he crossed the busy intersection. Sometimes, when he spent multiple weeks in the city, and when his heart and soul were particularly heavy, he sat on the back pew on Sunday mornings and listened to the marvelous gospel choir. He hadn't yet found a new church in DC, but in New York he could be anonymous when he was badly in need of being ministered to. Maybe this would eventually become his new church for life.

Now he walked over a block to 144th where he swung left, arriving just before 8:00 p.m. back on Hamilton Terrace at the six-story walk-up condo owned by PFA. The next morning's team building session for Marta Crossman was scheduled to start at the museum down near Lincoln Square at 8:30, and he wanted to arrive for set-up at least an hour early. As he turned on the landing of the walk-up, Beverly, the ballerina who occupied the apartment one level down from Ben's opened her door. He thought she'd maybe been down there for two years . . . maybe three. Ben stopped and smiled at her, then started back up the last flight.

"I haven't heard Addie up there this week."

Ben hadn't known that Beverly tracked their comings and goings from DC, nor did he know that Addie and Beverly had any kind of speaking relationship. Addie rarely made it up to the city with Ben during the school year. Beverly was a sultry, well-toned specimen from the tips of her leathery feet, up her athletic body, past the ass that was a little bit flatter than Ben liked, all the way to her kind of stringy blond hair that she always seemed to tie tightly behind her head in a ponytail.

"I'll tell you what," said Beverly. "I've made too much salad. Go wash up from the day, and meet me down here for some supper. Ben had planned to order a pizza. They never kept much food at the walk-up because their comings and goings were so off-and-on. He thought briefly, and then said, "cool!" Immediately, Beverly beamed and closed the door without another word.

About twenty minutes later, Beverly was performing slow ballet moves before Ben. Some soft Russian or Turkish sounding music was playing from her system—it was pulsating and sensual. Beverly had already eaten, so Ben sat alone at her small nook, eating the delicious salad with lettuce, avocados, tomatoes, grilled red and yellow peppers, and small chicken breast pieces. Beverly had made sure to remove all the skin before flash frying them and throwing them into the salad. She served him a drink . . . his hostess called it a Kir. It had a fruity sweet taste that Ben had never had. But he immediately couldn't imagine him ordering something like this at Davita's place.

After Ben had eaten, Beverly cleared his plate away, topped off his drink, and asked, "So what is your pleasure tonight, Dr. Parks?"

Without hesitation, she leaned forward and kissed Ben. The canine in him responded as if on automatic pilot. With moves like a cat, Beverly was on his lap, and they necked long, deep kisses as she adjusted herself to straddle him on the chair. Beverly smiled as she felt the movement of the instrument below her.

"Hmm, I see someone has joined us," she purred.

Pushing her back, Ben said with alarm, "Yes, that's a problem, Beverly. Thanks for the dinner, but I see I'd better go."

As if she hadn't heard him, Beverly plunged her tongue deep into Ben's mouth, and he responded like an animal having been thrown some fresh meat.

Ben stood in a way that Beverly would slide off of him. On second thought, he realized that she was nimble enough that she might have wrapped her legs some sort of way and stayed connected to him in his maneuver. Her weight was light as a feather. But she stood and stepped back.

"Did I mistake the sign that's trying to bulge out of your pants, Dr. Parks?

"No Beverly!" said Ben. "Johnson is standing at attention. He and

I don't get it very often, and you're quite a beautiful and sensuous woman. You're also young enough to be my daughter."

"I bet you've never kissed your daughter like you just kissed me, Dr. Parks" said the woman in front of him, whom he suddenly thought might be of Slavic decent.

"I don't have a daughter," admitted Ben.

"So, now we come to the end of this gambit, Dr. Parks. Both you and Johnson down there would like to fuck this woman who is young enough to be your daughter. Your wife isn't upstairs on this trip, and you and she apparently aren't getting it on very frequently anyway."

"Actually," said Ben, "Johnson doesn't wake up very often anymore without medicinal assistance. Even if the mind's willing, the body just won't firm up like it used to. This is quite unusual for him."

"Well, Johnson obviously has good taste, Dr. Parks. I think he and I could be good friends, and I don't think he'd have any problem waking up when I wanted him to. My men don't ever have to wait. My men get sucked and fucked every day," said Beverly, "and they get sucked and fucked very, very well."

The thought of multiple men bedding Beverly broke the spell and was a clincher for Ben, though he didn't say that to her. It wasn't virtue or morals kicking in. It was John Dewey and that damn pragmatism. Straightening to fix himself in front, he had found his resolve. He backed away toward Beverly's door. She spread her legs on the floor. Then she slowly pulled her right leg up, balancing herself on the left. Up and up it went until she held it almost directly over her head, with her smiling eyes and face still riveted on Ben.

That was it. Without another word, Ben was out in the hall and bounding up the steps, reaching for his keys and dropping them at his front door. As he fumbled to retrieve the keys and find the right one, the dog in him reappeared and he started back down a few steps. He hadn't heard her click the lock. But about halfway down the flight of steps, Ben heard a low moan coming from behind Beverly's door. Below the moan was an unmistakable electric reverberating sound. As Beverly's moans grew louder, Ben made it back through his door. This time he didn't drop his keys. He crawled into the bed without taking off his clothes. He took an Ambien with a whole glass of water, but just lay in bed staring. Then he disrobed from the waist down. He didn't have anything mechanical and he didn't flip on the satellite TV. Every time he closed his eyes, first it was Addie . . . then it was Beverly . . . then it was both of them above him.

The right hand worked below on Johnson. Ben had become quite practiced, and finally exploded in silence. No emotion, but welcome physical release. He wiped himself off with tissues from the nightstand, and the next minute, he was dead to the world.

Chapter 42
Aftermath

Groggy, Ben didn't like this left-over Ambien feeling. This was only the third one he'd taken since he got the prescription from Dr. Popovich. He'd carried them as an emergency, but now he vowed to leave them at home. He might even flush them. Ben doused his face with water and looked in the mirror. Now came the vertigo. Ben stumbled back to bed. After lying down for a while, the spinning subsided. Ben turned over and tried to do his exercises: on his back, head to the right—quick flip to the left—reverse—repeat—repeat. When he finally sat up again, the spinning didn't return.

Walking down the steps the next morning, Beverly's door opened and she stood behind the slit in a thin negligee. "Good morning, Dr. Parks," she said lowly.

"Good morning Beverly" responded Ben.

"What did you do last night after dinner, Dr. Parks?" said the vixen with the hard but supple rubber body.

"Watched the news and then fell asleep," lied Ben.

"Oh, I see," she said. "Anytime you want me to come up and watch the news with you, just let me know."

Ben walked out of the building relieved but smiling. At that moment, he didn't know if he'd ever watch the news with Beverly. But the thought of it was kind of cool. *Especially,* he thought, *for an over-the-hill guy like myself.*

Work with his team building clients in Midtown Manhattan wrapped up around 3:00 p.m. and Ben made the 4:00 p.m. Acela back to DC. He settled back into his seat on the club car, as two sportscasters entered from the front (one white and one black . . . both well known to national TV audiences) on what was probably their daily commute from the Apple back to their homes somewhere in the DC suburbs. The white one knew Ben.

More than a decade ago, Ben had tried to run with a middle-aged group of guys at the YMCA at 17th and Rhode Island Avenue in northwest Washington, DC. Probably ten years younger than Ben, this white guy had a really decent game. But people tended to remember Ben, not because he was really good, but because of his unusual use of the backboard for all of his shots. He didn't dribble well, couldn't leap very high; and when defending he couldn't run with the speedy guys. But back then Ben Parks could spot up almost anywhere and hit that funny-looking jump shot off the backboard.

"What's up, Dr. Parks?" he asked, turning around in his chair with a smile. "Don't you just love New York?"

"Sure do," said Ben nodding back toward both smiling sportscasters.

Chapter 43
Back to Normal

They rolled into Union Station from New York around 7:30 p.m. that night. It had been a full day. He found his car in the Union Station lot, and headed up North Capital Street towards LeDroit Park. He didn't roll up to Davita's because, what he wanted more than anything else was to snuggle with Addie. So, the sex had become minimal, but he still liked the feel of her. Also, he needed to shed the memories of his near miss with the neighbor last night up in Harlem.

He was home by 8:30. All the lights were off downstairs. He went to the kitchen and fixed himself an Irish whiskey with a generous dose of ginger ale. He stepped into the backyard and sat to listen to the sounds of his urban neighborhood and stare at the stars. After thirty minutes and two drinks, he ventured back in.

When he walked upstairs, he saw the light on and heard the TV in the master bedroom. Peaking around the corner, he saw Addie there sleeping soundly. Checked papers were in a large folder on the other side of the bed. Her glasses were still on and a pen was on the pillow next to her head. We watched her for a long time. Then, he stepped into the room, clicked off the TV, tidied up a little bit, but was careful not to disturb her. He mouthed a little prayer over her. Then, Ben turned off the lamp and slipped in on his side of the bed. He lay awake again that night in the semiconscious stupor that had become his routine.

"No Ambien tonight. No Ambien tonight. No Ambien tonight. No Ambien tonight. No Ambien tonight. No Ambien tonight. No Ambien tonight. No Ambien tonight. No Ambien . . ."

Somewhere in the middle of the night, mercifully, sleep finally came.

Chapter 44
Life in the City

Ben awoke the next morning in a panic. Addie had gone to work. It was full daylight . . . nearly 8:00 a.m. Addie would already be in her classroom prepping for her kids to come in at 8:30. "What? What? What?"

He couldn't fix on his schedule for the day. As he sat up, he expected the vertigo. But the spinning didn't come. In a panic, he got to his pocket calendar on his dresser. As he started to open it, it slipped from his hand. Ben groaned a little as he bent over to retrieve it from the floor; then came the bout of coughing.

"Argh, argh, argh, argh, argh." Ben was now stooped over. "Argh, argh, argh, argh, argh, argh" . . . again with the nasty looking bronchial phlegm. On the bedside table, Ben fumbled for the Albuterol . . . exhale, squeeze, and inhale . . . two quick puffs of mist. "Argh, argh, argh, argh, argh, argh."

Not enough, thought Ben: *Exhale, squeeze, inhale, exhale, squeeze, and inhale.*

Ben lay back on the bed, shut his eyes, and tried to calm down. After several minutes, all of his myriad frailties began to subside . . . just a bit. Then he sat up and fumbled to find today's page in the pocket calendar. Relieved, he saw his first meeting was at 11:00 a.m., not far from the Parks Freer Associates (PFA) office in Dupont Circle.

After parking the car in the below ground garage, Ben walked upstairs to the Safeway on the first floor of his office building. Coffee with cream, some grits with butter, one fat smoked sausage, and a dollop of soft scrambled eggs in a Styrofoam container was his breakfast. As he ate at his desk up on the fifth floor of this office building, Ben read and rehearsed in his head. The 11:00 a.m. client was none other than Adam Fierstein, who'd graduated from his MBA program at GW and was now a mid-thirties nonprofit deputy executive director. Adam had been one of the standout students in Ben's first Seminar on Cross-Cultural Communication. The evening before, Adam had faxed him a list of issues to be discussed in regard to the strategic direction for his non-profit organization, whose mission addressed development issues in the Middle East.

Dupont Circle was one of Washington, DC's most diverse sections of town with headquarters for National research organizations; think tanks and labor unions; all kinds of cuisine served in eclectic restaurants; a thriving small business community; and spacious renovated apartments, condos, and town houses that residents of all shades, colors, ages, and attraction orientations called home. The Circle itself—sitting at the intersections of Connecticut Avenue, 19th Street, Massachusetts Avenue, and P Street—was a hub for park sitters, speed chess players, skate-boarders, guitar players, messengers and their bikes on break from their rounds, and business people taking their lunch.

Ben crossed the street from his S Street office and reached the intersection of Connecticut and R, going south toward the Circle. Across the intersection he noticed three young men in their twenties eying him. He didn't stare, but kept them in sight with his peripheral vision. As he reached the opposite corner, one of the men smiled and said, "Hey, sir, can I use your pen for a moment?"

Ben realized that his engraved Montblanc was in the breast pocket of his shirt and his jacket was open. The smiling young man was pointing at it.

Without hesitation, Ben reached in the front compartment of his canvas briefcase, took out a blue Bic pen and handed it to the surprised young man.

"Keep it, bro," said Ben, smiling and not missing a step.

Halfway down the block, the young man caught up with Ben and fell into step beside him. Warily, Ben looked over and stopped.

"That was slick what you did back there old man."

"Slick?"

"Yeah, you the first one today that spotted the hustle."

"What hustle?"

The young man held out his hand to show an assortment of

expensive pens including several Montblancs, an Aurora, a Bexley, and a Faber-Castell.

"We ask to borrow them, and the chumps just hand them over. Then they actually expect us to give them back. But that ain't happening. We sell 'em!" The young man was smiling proudly. "But I give you props."

Ben was unsmiling now.

"Young man, I need to get to my gig. And I'm not interested in your props. As a matter of fact, I'm mad at you."

The expression changed on the young man's face.

"I was lucky, but I don't like you ripping people off in this neighborhood. That ain't right. Back on the corner I called you brother when I gave you the pen. But you ain't no bro. You're what gives brothers a bad name."

Tempers flared.

"The next time I see ya mother fucker, Ima take yo damn pen. As a matter fact, I should take it now."

Imperceptibly, Ben had already flexed his knees slightly and shifted his weight to the balls of his feet.

After a long pause and a lot of glaring, there was an intention flicker in the man's eyes. Easily, Ben lifted his right heel and pivoted on his toes just a few inches to his right as the young hustler faked with a violent head-shrug. The man yelled just to amp up the effect. In the off angle from the man, Ben's face was expressionless and a passerby looked over at the two.

Finally, the young man looked around and noticed the people staring. He retreated down the block in the direction he'd come from.

"Punk-ass old man" he yelled back over his shoulder. "Remember, Ima fuck you up. Punk-ass old man."

Now, Ben was in Adam Fierstein's office near the Farragut North Metro station, about ten blocks south of where the confrontation occurred. Adam's boss was a globetrotting political wonk with visions of bringing peace to areas of the Middle East by tapping into the mutual need of warring factions for various types of public works projects, the scale of which would be unfeasible for one side or the other alone. Now traveling in Lebanon, Adam's boss had tasked Adam with pulling together a board of luminary advisors and bringing these notables to consensus on a vision for the non-profit's work abroad. Smart as a whip, Adam was highly engaged, but had reached back to Ben to support him in thinking through issues of planning—largely because Ben had made such an impression on him in that seminar at Howard University back in 1999. They met for about two hours and came up with an agenda for the kick-off meeting of the advisory board.

***

Three hours later, Ben was walking back up Connecticut to the office. He veered right up 20th Street and halfway up the block he heard a woman screaming behind him. Turning, he saw a man running his way. He had a woman's handbag open as he ran, and he was taking out a wallet. The screaming woman was about twenty steps behind. Ben saw she had little chance of catching the man. And what would she do if she did?

Five steps away, Ben recognized the hustler from earlier in the day.

Not paying any attention to Ben, the man almost ran past him with the woman in hot pursuit, "Help me! He's got my purse. Help!"

Ben turned slightly, whipped his foot out, and tripped the man.

Off-balance, the man's momentum carried him forward several feet; he fell hard on the sidewalk, lost the purse and wallet, and blood spattered from his nose and busted lip. He was stunned. Ben stood as the woman ran up and retrieved her bag and wallet. She screamed at the man on the ground, who still hadn't recovered from the sudden fall. Then she kicked the sprawled man several times, and Ben pushed her away.

Johnny B. was a homeless man who hung out with his sidekick, Tricky, in front of the Safeway at 20th and S.

"Yo, Doc! That's some sick-ass karate shit!"

Johnny had come down the street to spectate, and now he straddled and sat on the sprawled young man, while yelling back to Tricky to go into the Safeway and get Officer Smith.

Ben was still holding back the woman, who wanted to put a serious hurt on the defenseless purse snatcher. Tricky and Officer Samantha Smith came down the street. The officer was talking on her hand held walkie-talkie, with hand cuffs out.

"Get off him, Johnny B," said Officer Smith.

"Yes ma'am," said the homeless man with a smile on his face. He high-fived Tricky, and the officer cuffed the sprawling man and started saying Miranda. Officer Tommy Davis pulled up in his cruiser and was out in a flash beside Officer Smith.

"Tommy!" Officer Smith looked over and made instant recognition.

Officer Davis said. "Dr. Parks, what's up?"

Ben said. "This fine woman has her stuff back, but I need to let her go. She might kick the shit out of desperado there." Tommy's expression was blank at first. Then he stepped between Officer Smith and the woman Ben was holding.

Ben started to tune out the whole scene. It was 4:15 and he had a conference call in fifteen minutes. He released the woman and walked the rest of the way to his office. He made it back into the office with five minutes to spare before his call.

The follow-up call with Marta and the museum clients in New York went well. They had transcribed all of the newsprint notes from the recent meeting, and people had been assigned to monitor various commitments to share information across functions and between shifts.

About 5:30, Ben wrapped up for the day and went down to the Safeway store where he picked out a fresh set of flowers—lilies and bluebonnets, with some greenery interspersed throughout. Ben thought Addie might like the surprise.

At the cash register, the thirty-something-year-old clerk wore a tight short-waisted top with the word "hot" stenciled on the front and her midriff showing just a little bit of flab. Her tight blue jeans hugged an ample expanse of backside. Ben didn't realize he was salivating.

"You staring at my ass, Doc?"

Out of his reverie, Ben caught sight of the small oval mirror on the side of the cash register where his eyes met the young woman's.

"Busted!" was all he said.

"Nice flowers, Doc. Here's your change. And have a good day."

"Thanks!"

***

At home that night, Ben ate alone. Tony rarely came over

anymore, and Rico was off at school. When he heard Addie's key in the door, he went toward the front to greet her. He'd thought that he might tell her about the adventure that afternoon.

"Hey. A!" He said as she picked up her mail off the table by the door.

"Hey. B," she responded without looking up from the mail.

"How was your day?" he asked.

"Fine, and yours?" was the curt response. Without waiting for an answer, Addie was bounding up the stairs, saying, "Gotta pee . . . Gotta pee," Ben heard her say in the tired routine they'd become so accustomed too. At least Addie seemed to have become accustomed to it.

Ben inwardly fumed. At some point that evening, Addie came back down and grabbed some lean cuisine food from the refrigerator. Humming softly, she microwaved the measured amount of skinless chicken, noodles and broccoli; poured herself a glass of Domaine Pichot Vouvray wine from an already opened bottle on the door of the fridge; and went back upstairs to her bedroom sanctuary.

Ben sat reading on one of the cushy chairs in the living room and observed the ritual. He looked up at her as she emerged from the kitchen. Her eyes met his briefly and then turned to the stairs. They didn't see one another for the rest of the evening. Ben threw the flowers in the trash. Addie never heard about Ben's Dupont Circle adventures.

Chapter 45
The Call

Ben had a prime spot at Malaguena; one of the cushy overstuffed chairs with an ottoman next to the wall and an outlet. He was reading the Washington newspaper, about the trials and tribulations of the Montreal Expos and major league baseball's arduous process of finding new ownership and a new city for the team. Of course, Washington, DC was the logical choice, but major league baseball had always had a love-hate relationship with DC.

Then, there was the matter of that rich class action lawyer up in Baltimore. His team had claimed jurisdiction over the whole mid-Atlantic region, as far as he interpreted that to run. No competing franchise for the area . . . American League . . . National League . . . it didn't matter. It would be unfair competition, and he wasn't having it.

Ben was procrastinating a bit. But this also was his routine. First the paper, then a computer game, then work. He was flying out to San Francisco tomorrow morning to start facilitating a strategic change meeting that would involve hundreds of participants. Electronics executives from all over the world were flying in. for the four day event.

Tomorrow was the travel day. Wednesday would be the staging day. And then, Thursday through Saturday would be show time. The design team had been working for four months, and Ben thought their design was going to be successful. Also this would be one of those rare chances where he and Ted would work together. Outside of the stuff they did on culture together, he and Ted rarely teamed on the same project. Ted had things he did well, and Ben had things he did well. They often didn't overlap. Ted had wanted to learn about how to do the strategic change process with such a large group, and Ben had been happy to have him co-facilitate the design team process.

The cell phone vibrated at his side. The time was 8:50 a.m. And he saw the number. She should be in front of her kids by now he thought. He answered, "Sup, A?"

The voice chilled him to the bone. "Benjamin, I fell."

"What?"

"I fell down the stairs. I fell down a dozen steps at school. The kids were acting up in the hall, and I was trying to get them quiet. I wasn't watching how close I was to the stairwell. And I just fell."

Ben was already powering down, unplugging the computer, and packing up his satchel. He'd turned it on when he came in, but hadn't done any work. He always read the paper first.

"A, what's broken?"

"I don't know. I'm on the stretcher. They're about to put me in the ambulance. Victoria is riding with me to the hospital. They're taking me to Howard."

"I'll be there, A." Ben was outside sprinting to the car. He arrived at the hospital and was shown upstairs. Victoria was on the telephone talking long distance with Sue Ann. Adam had beaten him there and was pacing. Addie was somewhere in surgery.

Later, in her private room, Addie woke up and Ben, Victoria, Adam, Tony, Rico, and Han were surrounding her. Victoria did all of the talking:

"Girl, you got a hard head. The doctors said you don't have any kind of concussion or anything."

Addie tried to move and immediately yelled out.

Victoria continued. "Hold on, hoss! That doesn't mean you can hop out of bed. Your foot is fucked up. When the medics got here, they told the doctors that they could twist it around forty-five degrees. You have all kinds of contusions up and down your body girl. You're not moving for a good little bit."

Addie started to cry, "B! B! B! Where's B?"

Ben had been sitting on the opposite side of the bed from Victoria. She hadn't turned that way, and so she didn't know he was in the room. He leaned over and kissed her on the forehead. She turned toward him and cried louder. It was a long sustained cry, and Adam said, "I'm here, Mom."

Nobody else spoke. Addie fell back asleep.

While she slept this time, the pastor from Addie's new church came and went. Addie's principal came and went. Sue Ann and Dave were already heading to Pittsburg to catch a plane to DC. Emmett, Addie's attorney brother from Boston, would be in after he got a continuance from the judge first thing in the morning.

Addie slept into the evening. Adam and Han had greeted Sue Ann and Dave when they rushed in straight from the airport. They'd sat and talked and cried. Now everyone had gone down to the hospital cafeteria.

The next morning, Ben was alone with Addie just as she woke again, and Ted Freer came in. Ben was distracted now. He saw the concern on Ted's face. Instantly he imagined that Ted was concerned not only about Addie. He was also concerned about their San Francisco assignment. Both had a flight to catch at Noon.

Ted stepped to the bed and bent over and kissed Addie on the forehead. Addie painfully smiled and said, "Thanks for coming here, Ted." Ted stroked her hair. He liked to play with her locks and Ben didn't mind.

Then, Addie's expression changed. She turned back in the direction of her husband.

"B . . . San Francisco?"

Immediately, Ben and Ted's eyes locked. Then Ben turned back to Addie.

"Hold on, Addie, let me speak to Ted in the hallway." The two men started out of the room, when Addie called out.

"Benjamin." They stopped and looked at her. "You're going to San Francisco."

"Ted can take it. I'm going to walk him through it. He'll be fine." Ted nodded. That's what he'd come to offer. He'd never led one of these before, but this was a crisis and Ted was ready to step up.

Addie turned and looked at Ted.

"Dear Ted. My B can't speak six languages. He can't even speak two. He tries to speak hip hop and it's funny to hear it. Tony and Rico laugh at him all the time. Ben can't even speak pig Latin. That's your thing."

Ted's nervous laugh came before his protest, which Addie headed off at the pass.

"But Teddy, you can't do what my B can do. I know you want to try. But you can't. This is what B does. God knows how much money these people have spent flying people in from all over the world. They expect our A-game. And they expect our A-team. And, they expect our star player and that's Benjamin."

Now, Ben started to protest as Sue Ann and Dave walked in.

Addie said, "You and Ted are going to be on that plane at twelve o' clock."

Sue Ann flew into an immediate rage. She pulled Ben out into the hall.

"You asshole. That's my little sister in there, and that's your wife. You're always flying all over the place leaving her at home. She talks about missing you, and you're gone for weeks at a time. She needs you now, and you aren't going anywhere, you bastard." Ben was speechless. Dave came out and pulled Sue Ann away.

"Addie wants to talk to you Sue Ann. She says that Ben and Ted are to leave right now and get packed. Don't go back in the room Ben. Ted is bringing you your coat. Just go."

Sue Ann and Dave stared each other down. Ben was frozen. Dave's insistent tugging eventually prevailed and Sue Ann followed him back into the room and Ted came out with Ben's coat.

***

In San Francisco, Ted was very helpful. Ben called in to Addie several times each day. By the time he returned to DC, Addie was back in LeDroit Park. She cried a lot. She never asked about the meeting in San Francisco.

Ben didn't work for three weeks. Addie eventually was on crutches, which she didn't like because they bruised her under her arms. But nine weeks after the fall, Addie used a cane to return to school.

Chapter 46
Slow Psychological Recovery

2004: The fall had given Addie and Ben a curious benefit. Ben supported her recovery to the extent that he could, and they were forced, because of the time together, to focus on their relationship. As soon as she felt up to it. Ben suggested a date.

This time they went to Arigatou Sushi downtown. The restaurant was located on the first floor of a substantial eight-story red brick building on I Street near Pennsylvania Avenue, The White House, and The George Washington University. Ben thought the chef was the best in town. As was their custom, Ben and Addie asked for edamame while they decided on the rest. The miso soup warmed them at the start, and the piping hot sake kept the chill off for the rest of the meal. Then they'd placed one big order to share: two eel hand rolls, two avocado rolls, two orders of fatty tuna nigiri (four pieces), and two orders of yellow tail nigiri (four pieces).

When they'd gotten back together after the first marriages had ended, Ben had brought Addie here on one of their first dates after Addie moved to DC. She'd never had sushi before, and she loved it. Ever since, especially when they'd hit rocky spots, Ben figured out a way to get her down here.

It was still hard to get her to do anything without the excruciating twenty-questions she'd put him through before she would say "I guess" or "if you want." She rarely said a flat out "yes" to anything Ben wanted. "No" came out real quick. But "yes" just didn't happen. But, he'd finally gotten an "if you want" from her and so here they were.

Sometimes, Arigatou Sushi worked. Tonight, eating from the

common plate was about the only connection they had. Addie was preoccupied and just going through the motions. Though physically fully recovered from her fall, Addie's blues lingered for weeks and weeks. Ben had tried to comfort her and be there for her. The emotional toll on him was heavy. For brief periods, she would come out of it. But then the ice would return.

The next day, he arose wordlessly. Ben fixed breakfast and took it up to Addie, still in bed. He stared at his wife. He felt a mixture of feelings . . . from love to dislike . . . from apprehension to exhilaration . . . from regret to fear . . . from longing to fading hope. His wife was quiet now. After eating she came downstairs and sat on the same sectional sofa as Ben Parks, that is, on the short L section to the right of the long L section Ben was slumped into.

"How's your foot feeling now, Addie?"

"Fine."

"You don't even have a limp."

No response.

"Is there anything I can get for you?"

"I'm fine."

Ben was suddenly overcome with bottled up feelings.

"I'm, uh . . . I'm not happy. That's different than saying I'm unhappy. Sometimes, I'm unhappy, but usually it's more that I'd like to be happy and I'm not. Can we talk about this?"

Addie just looked at him.

"Last year we were having trouble and almost called it quits. You were pretty determined to keep us together. I never will forget one evening during that time. I still hear your words sometimes, 'Ben, we belong together.' It was you that held us together and for a good time after that, things really were different."

Ben thought about that memory. It was crystal clear to him. Addie had looked at him with such despair countered by the determination of a little child. The tears in her eyes as well as the depth of feeling behind her words had instantly penetrated him.

There was the jealous and firm and street-fighter Addie. But at the point of the near breakup, it was the passionate and committed Addie; mixed with her childlike state that broke him down to putty. Addie had gotten through to Ben, and he again felt the parental emotion of caring that was part of the complex mixture of emotions that he felt for her. Addie was his wife. Addie was his lover. And Addie was very much a daughter figure in Ben's mind, and she was his responsibility. Ben didn't have any daughters, but as independent as she claimed to be, Addie needed a lot of taking care of. Ultimately he was put here, he often thought, to take care of Addie ... for better or for worse.

Now, Ben was mostly looking ahead into the fire he'd made, straight ahead in the fireplace. It wasn't chilly. As a matter of fact this late winter day, it felt almost spring-like outside. Last week had been in the teens, with wind chills in single digits. The thing about DC weather that made people catch such nasty colds was that it wasn't cold all the time like Minnesota or upstate New York. It was frigid and then it was balmy and then it was frigid again. You could never get used to anything between December and April, because it was going to change. Today, people were washing cars outside in the alleys.

Out of the corner of his eye, Ben could see Addie intently watching him. Ben kind of wished that he hadn't started this conversation. He wished he was outside, maybe turning over some soil in preparation for lawn re-seeding in another ten to twelve weeks.

Addie was four years his junior, but sometimes looked ten years younger than that. She was short and shapely; with medium length, well-kept locks. Her smallish glasses had a little tint in them, and her face was a little freckled, adding highlights to her smooth medium brown skin.

"Well, then you broke your foot, and since then I've tried to do everything I could to help you recover. I'm proud of you Addie. You're better."

Still no response.

"I'm feeling like we're back to where we were a year ago. We don't talk. We don't interact. We didn't split up last year, and we were better for a while, but now we're back to not having much of a relationship. At least, that's what I'm feeling. I was wondering how you were feeling?"

As he asked the question, Ben turned his gaze toward Addie. She was tearing up. She got up and went up the stairs before Ben could say another word.

Chapter 47
Uncle Roderick

2004: At 9:00 a.m. that September 30th morning, Ben was reading the newspaper. The sport's page story announced that yesterday, Major League Baseball had officially said that the Montreal Expos franchise would be moved to Washington, DC.

Ben was reaching for the telephone to call his dad, Dr. Richard Parks, but the phone rang first. It was his sister, Penny.

"The nursing home says that Uncle Roderick is missing. Mom has started screaming at night and Dad can't sleep. When I left home for work, neither of them was up yet, but he won't be able to leave her, even if he did feel well enough. Are you in town? Can you look for him?"

"Yes, I am, and I'm on it."

"Love you, bro!"

The phones were simultaneously hung up. Rushing out of the house, Ben jumped in the car. Suddenly, Levi appeared and slid in on the passenger side. He reeked of alcohol. Saying buckle up, Ben pulled out. They found uncle roaming in the shopping center near the Silver Spring, MD nursing home. As they pulled up, uncle became alarmed and started to run. Levi giggled, and Ben shot him a nasty look.

"Sir, can I speak with you?" said Ben getting in front of his uncle. Roderick stopped and looked carefully. He was totally disoriented and didn't know where he was; although he was only about five blocks away from the nursing home.

"You're my uncle. Can we talk a bit?"

Roderick seemed to relax a bit.

"I'm not your uncle, am I?"

"Yes you are. I'm Richard's son."

"Dr. Richard Parks" said Roderick loudly. "My big brother, is Richard here?"

"No, he asked me to come and help you back home."

Then Roderick giggled. After they talked some more, standing in the shopping center parking lot, Ben finally convinced Uncle Roderick to calm down and get in the car. From the back seat, Uncle Roderick looked at Levi in the passenger seat. Finally, he said, "You're drunk as a skunk ain't yah?" Levi didn't answer.

Ben dropped off Uncle Roderick back at the nursing home. The attendant came out to greet him on the front stoop. This would become a pattern over the next few months, and folks would grow used to this routine. Whether it was Richard, or Penny, or Ben; or whether it was the five or six local police men and women who all had come to recognize Uncle Roderick by sight, this was the life of the eighty-something year-old little brother to Ben's dad.

Chapter 48
Levi

Driving back to the LeDroit Park neighborhood, Ben wondered where Levi had come from on the sidewalk outside his house. Levi lived in Bloomingdale, just South of LeDroit Park. He wouldn't normally be walking the streets this far from home. Ben wouldn't look over at Levi.

"Sup, Ben," slurred Levi.

"You're a damn drunk, Levi." whispered Ben.

"What'd you say?" shouted his childhood friend.

Ben didn't respond right away. Then, "Levi, you got God-given gifts. You're the most talented man I've ever known. What the fuck is wrong with you?"

Punching his fist into the dashboard of Ben's car, Levi convulsed. Ben immediately swerved the car and pulled over. He got out and quickly went around to open the passenger door and haul Levi out. Levi fell to the side and immediately spilled his guts. Ben leaned on the car, watching in dismay and disgust. When Levi finally stood and looked back at Ben, he immediately saw the expression. Levi flew into a rage.

"I'm Levi Chance. I'm Levi Chance. I've got mad skills. They play my music on every radio station in the country. Fuck you, Ben Parks!"

Levi began to weep, but continued to shout.

"Me and you used to be family Ben. My house was yours and yours was mine when we were kids. I schooled your kid, and he's going to be a star one day. Your name has always been on any backstage pass list at my gigs. I cried with you and stood for you when your Aunt Claire died. I've lied for you to back you up when you needed to get out of trouble with Yvette and now with Addie."

Hitting an even higher gear, another memory flashed for Levi.

"When you came back from Korea, I told you about Davita and her Doctor. You were sad and wouldn't go see her for a while. So I introduced you to that great piece of ass . . . what was her name . . . Regina. You and me shared everything, bro."

Suddenly, quiet, Levi said, "Now you look at me with those eyes. Fuck you! Fuck you! I never judged you. I never ratted you out with some of the shit that you know, I know you pulled."

Ben continued to stare. Levi continued, "You ain't shit, Dr. Benjamin Parks. I always got better grades than you. You name the game and I beat you . . . I take your money in cards, horse, whatever. My chops have always been better than yours. All the way back in gym class when we used to measure, you know my dick is bigger than yours and I've had tons more pussy in my life than you'll ever have."

"You can't tell me not to take a drink. I take a little drink when I want to because I'm Levi Chance. I'm Levi Chance."

Finally, spent, Levi slumped. "Get in the car," said Ben quietly.

"Fuck the car. And fuck you. I'm through with you, Ben Parks. You're probably going to wind up like that damn Uncle we just picked up. Fuck you and your nutty-assed people." Ben watched as Levi stumbled away. Ben didn't go after him. He just watched his friend and didn't try to help anymore.

Ben knew that Levi would make it home . . . it was maybe fifteen blocks away. He knew that by the next day, Levi would have a headache. He knew that, if Levi remembered the incident at all, he'd be sorry. He knew that his friend would want to take it all back. But he also knew that Levi would start drinking again as soon as he could find a bottle. He'd go down to his studio and play that beautiful music, and he'd drink. At some point, somebody would clean him up so he could be presentable for church. But that somebody couldn't be Ben anymore. He couldn't handle it. Ben had his own demons, and carrying Levi's as well was just too much to bear.

Chapter 49
Some

January 2005: Addie had fully recovered from last year's accident.

Ben had recently admitted to Dr. Popovich that he wasn't responding to Addie the way he used to. He'd reluctantly filled the prescription she wrote for him, feeling old and just plain embarrassed about the whole notion of needing medicine to get it up. But then the blue diamonds just sat in the drawer by the night stand. A few times, he'd thought the signals were there, and he prepared by taking a tablet. Then, nothing had happened. Ben had usually taken things in hand later on those nights.

Addie had eventually asked him about the missing blue diamonds. He didn't know that she went into the drawer and counted them from time to time. After another big fight, she'd made a decision. "I'll just keep these. Then I'll give you one when the time is right. There won't be any confusion. You won't have to take any pills unnecessarily. Is that satisfactory with you Benjamin?"

What could he say? "Fine!"

***

The St. Petersburg House occupied the ground and second floors of a five-story building at the corner of Connecticut and Florida Avenues. Patrons would ascend about fifteen carpeted steps up to the second floor and enter a vestibule of dark mahogany with oil paintings covering tapestried walls. The thickly accented waitress ushered Addie and Ben back down a set of inside steps, descending into the small ground floor dining area. They took seats by the window looking diagonally across the Connecticut Avenue to a set of three commercial row houses.

There was a great steakhouse on the southeast corner, which

225

happened to be S Street, several doors over from the office building where Ben and Ted Freer had their offices. Next to the steakhouse was an eclectic newsstand. The business that had caught Addie's attention was on the northeast corner, which was Florida Avenue. A tan colored paint covered the brick façade of a funky three story building. Addie read the sign aloud, "Fancy Panties Nightclub. What's that, Benjamin?"

"I think you know what that is, A. It's a strip club."

"Oh really, have you ever been there?"

"Not so to speak," was his answer.

"And?"

"Here we go again with the 'and,'" said Ben. Do you want to pick a fight Addie? I thought we were out for a nice dinner. You said you wanted to try the genuine Russian Vodka and some good caviar."

"I don't. We are. And I do" said Addie. "And I want to know if you've been in the strip club."

"Tony used to be a doorman over there, maybe for about five months. And as you know, my office is right around the corner. I used to see him there during the day and I stopped at the door a couple of times to talk."

"You just talked to him at the door. You never went inside."

Actually, Ben knew that he had always stayed away from the door and had never gone inside, but she was pissing him off.

"I can't remember, A."

"Yeah, I bet you can't, you old dog. See, I told you what I was going to do. You think I'm playing with you. But if I ever think you're dogging me, I'm going to try to find out for sure. Not because I'm going to leave you. And I'm not ever going to let you leave me. But that will hurt me Ben, and I'm going to do something bad to you in your sleep."

The waiter had come up and was standing by the table with a deadpan expression. Ben looked up at him.

"Well, that's a nice reminder at the start of our meal. Thanks for the image, A."

"You're welcome, B."

"They skipped the dinner and went straight for the sampler vodka shots. They split six, Addie ordering a combination of fruits and non-fruits. When the waiter brought out the sampler, he said, "Wait a few minutes for them to chill before you start."

Addie said, "I know the drill."

In another minute, the waiter brought out the Beluga.

"That's what I'm talking 'bout," said Ben.

"And you accuse me of spending too much money. By the way, are you wearing white socks," said Addie.

For a second he thought he might not respond to the socks jab. He'd just let it go. Addie liked to needle him about his choice of colors. Actually he was slightly color blind and it was just easier to wear gray with gray, black with black, brown with brown, etc. But, for instance, if he had on brown slacks and tan socks, Addie didn't like the socks being lighter than the pants. So, she'd call them white socks just to get his goat. He was kind of proud of himself for hanging in with her rapid fire thrust and parry tonight and felt fine about letting this one go past him.

Ben waited for Addie to taste the caviar. She took an ever-so-slight spoonful and placed it carefully on the cracker looking thing, and then . . . "Umm," she said letting it slide down her throat and chasing it with one of the non-fruity vodka samples. Ben moved the small dish toward him to get some. Addie reached out and pulled the dish back toward the center of the table. They'd also done this routine many times before at dinner.

"Sorry!" said Ben.

"No you're not," was Addie's retort.

From the dish in the exact center of the table, Ben spooned a somewhat more generous portion than Addie's. He tried the Raspberry Vodka for his chaser and the whole feel of the mixture was exquisite. Suddenly, he felt good enough to share his most recent story.

"Uncle Roderick got lost again."

"I won't say 'and' anymore if you don't ask those 'you're going to do such-and-such, aren't you' questions."

"Deal! So, I picked him up and took him back to the home. Levi drove with me."

"Was Levi drunk?"

"I'm getting to that, A."

"B, it's a conversation not a lecture. I can ask questions."

"Yep he was drunk! Even Uncle Roderick knew it."

Benjamin spilled the rest of the story without many interruptions from Addie. When he got to the end, she was in a different frame of mind. They were nearing the end of the Vodka sampler and the Beluga was long gone. The waiter had asked if they wanted another serving.

"Is it on the house?" asked Addie. The waiter smiled and left them alone.

"Ben, you need your friends. Levi is one of your oldest friends. You can't just give up on him."

"I can't handle him, A."

"Don't try to handle him, B. Just be his friend. Say what you think and be his friend. If you need to tell him he's messing up, tell him that. If he gets angry with you, so be it. That's what me and Victoria do. Victoria is my friend and I'm there for her and she's there for me."

"You have some really good friends, A."

"Yeah, I do, B. And you don't. At least you don't keep your friends."

"Yes I do. Tracy is my friend. Davita is my friend."

"And Levi is your friend."

"I have my family."

"Yes you do, and you're blessed for that. But you need Levi, too, and he really needs you."

"I have my family, and I have you. At least I usually want to have you . . . most of the time."

"You have me, Ben. You may not have me like you want me or when you want me or every time you want me. But you have me. And I have you. I know you have trust issues with me, and I have them with you going way back to college and you leaving me. But if God ever intends for you to lose your memory . . . if God wants it to happen . . . and I don't think he does . . . but if it happens, so be it. You don't think I'll take care of you, but I will. God wants you and me to be together, B . . . for better or for worse. So what if A comes before B? Deal with it bucko! (This was the first time she smiled at her own joke). If you do lose it by the time you're eighty, I'll get you a nice young live-in attendant with a big ass. And you can just look at that nice ass and in your fading mind; you can pretend that you're tapping that ass. And you won't be able to get it up anymore. But you can just look at that ass anytime you want. I'll do that for you, Ben."

The spell was broken with Addie's last few lines. From serious to funny and now both of them were smiling across the table.

I know I don't tell you that I love you, B. I don't know why I don't tell you. It's probably because I'm angry with you all the time . . . or most of the time. I'm working on that. So, just this once, I do love you, B. You got that!"

Now, Ben cracked up.

"But you still need your friends, B. Levi has problems. That's what friends are for."

As Ben drove back to LeDroit Park that night, Addie rested her hand in a very nice place across the car. And when they got home, A brought B a blue diamond and some water. Then, she went to get into something from her wardrobe that he hadn't seen before.

And A gave B some. Ben didn't know it then. Addie probably didn't, either. But this would be the last time.

Chapter 50
Strangers in the Same House

Winter 2005: For the next few weeks after the St. Petersburg House date, Ben and Addie interacted almost as friends. By now it was March Madness, and Addie joined Ben several times on the porch to pretend to watch games with him; though she always brought along something to read or some school papers to grade. But she'd bring him another beer, or he'd make her one of her favorite Vodka and tonics. What they couldn't seem to master was talking about anything. As soon as a conversation would start it would devolve into a debate.

Then gradually, they fell back into being strangers living together. He came and went. She came and went. After work he'd usually get home before her and he started intentionally trying to be back out on the prowl before she came home from school.

Ben had started riding up to New York on the train once per week to work with Jason Queen. Sometimes, he stayed overnight in Harlem, and sometimes he came straight home after a two or three hour meeting. Jason was a senior executive whose civil engineering firm, a privately held billion dollar corporation, touched transportation issues around the country and around the world. He was a smart black man, about ten years Ben's junior, and Ben admired him for his smarts and his toughness.

Ben had answered the phone at the office one day, and heard the voice on the other end, "Dr. Parks, please!"

"This is Ben Parks. How may I help you?"

"Dr. Doris Smith says you're unique . . . a no-bullshit brother who can help me think."

Ben flashed on Doris, the Chief Medical Officer at the DC Public Health Agency, and was immediately intrigued.

"What do you want to think about, sir? No, before that, can I have your name?"

"I'm Jason Queen, and I'm in Midtown Manhattan. I need to think every day, and about many different things. I understand you're in the City quite a bit. When will you be here next?"

"Nothing scheduled at the moment."

"The seven a.m. train would get you here around eleven. Can you be at my office at noon tomorrow?"

"Whoa! Slow down. There's the matter of a contract . . . my fee. We haven't . . ."

"Dr. Parks, I know you work for Doris at her agency in DC, so I know that what I'll pay you will be at least double what you're used to . . . Tomorrow at noon?"

"Let me have the address and your number," said Ben.

Jason and Ben took care of those particulars, and suddenly Ben had a new client. Gradually, in working with Jason in a coaching capacity, this dynamic new client let his guard down with Ben. Now Ben got surprise emails at the office at odd hours of the night. Jason needed to talk. Jason needed to think about something. Could Ben find time tomorrow? Usually, when he wanted Ben, he wanted him tomorrow . . . whenever that was. Ben always tried to find time. He really wanted the brother to succeed. Lately they'd settled into a pattern of one visit per week—on Tuesday.

Addie was always gone in the morning before Ben got up, except for those mornings when Ben went to NYC. One day after she left, Ben moved every clothes item from his assigned dresser in the master bedroom to an oversized chest in the guest bedroom where his hanging clothes were already. He made up the bed there, and that night Addie and Ben slept apart. Ben wanted a reaction. Addie never said a word about it. The next night he was back in the master bedroom.

Ben kept himself out of a funk by working hard and by going out at night. He was heavily engaged in an assignment to facilitate a series of community meetings for Sonja Clement, who was still the Director at the District of Columbia Public Health Agency where Doris Smith worked. One night he was working in the basement office, prepping for the next meeting which would be in the northeast DC section known as Trinidad. He heard Addie come in from work and heard her footsteps as she went up to the second floor bedroom. Thirty minutes later, he heard her pad downstairs and straight to the front door. The door opened and shut quickly.

Ben had planned to go out, but now he had the house to himself for a rare evening. But he'd just gotten into the habit. Thinking about where he wanted to go, he quickly realized that he wasn't in a book store kind of mood; nor was he interested in going to the Soldiers Legion Post, over near Capitol Hill. He came out to the street and jumped into his powder blue Thunderbird. Addie's Lexus was right in front. She'd obviously been picked up by one of her girlfriends who drove something bigger.

Ben hopped in the powder blue Thunderbird and steered over a few blocks until he swung up Georgia Avenue, headed for Davita's. Davita's was where he usually wound up, one way or another. This is where Ben came when he just wanted to kick it. Davita and Ben had a lot of history. They'd gone to junior high and high school together in the DC public schools many years ago. Davita had started running the Dance-a-Lot for her parents after college, and at some point after their passing she had renamed it for herself. Davita was one connection Ben had to this place.

But more than his life-long friend, there were the Vets. Specifically, there were the battlefield injured Vets who walked, hobbled, or wheeled themselves over the couple of blocks from Walter Reed Army Medical Center to Davita's. They came to watch sports together, play cards or dominos, dance to the jukebox or (on certain nights) the live deejay, and to just hang out away from the medicinal reminders of war and death that came back to them when they returned to the hospital.

At the Soldiers Legion Post on Capitol Hill, there were a few real old-timers left from WWII. But most of the regulars were in Ben's age range and had served during the Vietnam era. Ben had been in the army many years ago, and though he had never fired a weapon in anger during his time of service, he loved the notion of service to the country. He had a kinship to these warriors that was fond, and deeply respectful, and he just liked being around them.

Walter Reed was a great place for Gulf War and Afghanistan vets. It probably provided the best critical warrior care in the world to soldiers of this sort—notwithstanding the legitimate but over-sensationalized attention that had descended on the facility. Problems of poor upkeep in a few of the aftercare facilities on the base, as well as in some of the long-term care dorms that were mostly in the neighborhood surrounding the base, had surfaced in the media.

But sometimes, these vets needed to get off base to connect with and retrieve some semblance of the rest of the world . . . the world that they hoped one day to rejoin. Davita's was where many of them went for their unstructured transition therapy.

"Sup, Heavy? It's good to see you," said Ben upon entering and seeing the large red-headed double amputee that he'd, on a previous visit, found out was from Aniston Alabama.

That had given them an instant topic to talk about, since Ben's maternal family was from Selma. Ben had spent many summers in Selma with his grandparents, aunts, and uncles as a boy; before the civil rights shit hit the fan in the late 1960s, and mom and dad wouldn't send him south anymore. Grinning up from his wheel chair the crew cut, barrel-chested young man of about thirty answered back with a raised Rolling Rock in his hand.

"Sup, Bee Bop? How they hanging? It's mighty good to be seen."

Friend, General, Sarge, Dahlin', Youngin', Soldier, Heavy, Buddy, Player, My Dawg, Honey, Homey, Homes, Shawty, Sugah . . . these were the names people called each other at Davita's. Here, off the base, if folks knew or thought a soldier was an officer, the name was 'General.' Assumed enlisted soldiers were 'Sarge.' These names were applied without regard to rank, race, ethnicity, or age . . . and many times without regard to gender. For instance, a female soldier was just as likely to be referred to as 'My Dawg' as her male counterpart. And a male soldier was just as likely to be 'Sugah' as a female. It just didn't matter. They were all equal opportunity nick names. Nobody really seemed to know anybody's real names . . . except for Davita's.

Also there was the genuine article: Brigadier General Tracy Brown, who never wore a uniform when he stopped into Davita's, but everybody knew the highly decorated DC favored son. Tracy had been another classmate of Davita and Ben's back at Tech in the late 1950s and early 1960s. He'd been a straight A student, triple letter man, and second string high school all American forward in basketball. Folks usually stood and saluted when General Brown tried to surreptitiously slide into Davita's.

And people knew the deejay that was there on Thursday through Saturday evenings and Sunday afternoon. They didn't necessarily know his real name, but everybody called him 'Old School.' And, for the last year or so, people had grown to recognize Ben—or Bee Bop.

'Chief'—who knew what the real name was of this Native American soldier, also a scholar athlete when he was in college, who was trying to operate his recently acquired left hand prosthetic to hoist his beer—was holding forth at the other end of the bar from Heavy. Ben moved to an open seat as Chief was just getting started.

"Here's a question," said Chief. "I'm looking to name a professional sports team. Which of these sounds the least offensive: Honkies, Niggas, Gays, Bitches, Kykes, Japs, Towel Heads, Chinks, or Redskins? Or as they used to say back in my great grandfather's day: 'You dirty Redskin?'"

"Hold it, Chief! Be nice, said Youngin', who occupied the seat next to where Ben had slid in. "Where ya going with this? You probably insulted everybody in here."

Chief replied, "I'ma tell you where I'm going. I come here to town, and what do I find? There's this Washington Football team owned by a cat of a certain origin. 'Scuse my French. I mean, owned by this wealthy local businessman of a certain extraction."

Folks nodded that this seemed to be duly respectful and let Chief proceed. Ben thought about the Soldiers Legion Post.

"Was there any bar where the dominant conversation wasn't about politics or sports; or both at the same time?" he mused.

Noting permission to proceed, Chief said, "I bet if that upstanding gentleman had bought a team named something derogatory to his people, he'd have changed that name quick, fast, and in a hurry."

Triumphantly Chief took the high fives with his good hand that were offered from up and down the bar.

Tracy, the general, spoke: "The truth is, Chief. None of those are any more or any less offensive than any others. They're all racial slurs. Anyone of the owners in that franchise could have changed the name anytime they wanted. Not one of them has the soul of Abe Polin. Abe changed the name of his team."

Ben chimed in, "But Abe had been wounded in his soul when his dear Israeli Prime Minister friend was assassinated with a gun. Our Washington Football team owner hasn't been forced to think about names in a deeply personal way like that."

Tracy replied, "At least bullets don't mind being called bullets. Native people mind that stupid football team name. Right, Chief?"

"You got it, General," said Chief. "But I gotta say this isn't the only place. I can't stand to watch baseball when the Atlanta team is playing. But the truth is, we Indians call ourselves Braves; and it's actually a term of pride. So we really can't complain too much about that one. I just can't stand it when they start up that phony war chant and chopping their paws in the air."

More mindless but tension-relieving talk was what Ben needed. . . and that's what he got that evening at Davita's.

***

Late that night, Ben arrived home to a dark house. He went down to his basement office and sat at the computer. A sealed envelope with his name written in Addie's hand rested against the monitor. With trepidation, Ben opened the envelope and pulled out two red and white tickets. The note read, "For you and your dad. Enjoy!"

Ben stared at the tickets. The printed date was April 14, 2005. The tickets were to RFK Stadium: Washington Nationals versus the Arizona Diamondbacks. It would be the first home game for the new DC sports team. Ben just stared and stared.

Chapter 51
Dominos

There had been another incident with his mom. ClayClay was already gone. His mom's dementia signs were advancing more rapidly . . . not nearly as bad yet as ClayClay at the end . . . but she couldn't figure out stuff, and her speech was increasingly garbled, interspersed with occasional lucid sentences. He'd been sitting with her while dad and Penny ran errands one Sunday afternoon, and he'd tried to play dominos with her . . . finally he'd turned over her tiles and walked her through every one of her moves . . . when he'd placed a tile for her, she'd say, "Wonful Pen, ger gee gee gone beat you."

Ben had gotten past trying to tell his mom that he was Ben and not Penny.

When Dad returned, he smiled at them both huddling over the table in the large kitchen nook of the house in Carter Baron, DC. Dr. Richard spoke to his son on his way back out to Ben's car, parked in the driveway where the annual Thanksgiving car wash took place.

"How was it with the game?" Richard asked.

Ben was sad.

"Dad, she couldn't add five and five."

Dad had nodded in recognition and then walked back up the driveway steps and across the patio. Ben drove back to LeDroit Park in silence . . . no radio or CD to occupy himself. He'd been experiencing more of those repetitive thoughts:

Going to beat you . . . going to beat you . . . going to beat you . . . going to beat you . . . going to beat you . . . going to beat you . . . going to beat you . . . going to beat you . . . going to beat you . . . going to beat you . . . going to beat you . . . going to beat you . . . going to beat you . . . going to beat you . . .

It lasted for the entire twenty-five minute drive back home.

Ben prided himself on being able to pull things together. He did!

***

On April 14th, Ben and Richard Parks came out of the Stadium-Amory exit of the Washington Metro. Dr. Richard had a red curly-W baseball cap on and smiled as he slowly used his cane to walk alongside his son. The walk was farther than Ben had remembered and he started to worry about his dad. But Dr. Richard was in good spirits, and they eventually got into their seats on the third row of the third base side, right across from where Vinnie Castio, who almost hit for the cycle that day, played the hot corner. Livan Hernandez was the winner of the five to three contest. The walk back to the Metro station was slow and Dr. Richard was in obvious pain, but smiled the whole way.

Chapter 52
The Dance

In the summer of 2005, Ben again did the seminar up at Howard University. He loved it.

***

One Thursday evening in February 2006 at Davita's, Ben watched from the bar as a uniformed female doctor, a major, known to be a trauma surgeon at Walter Reed, finished her steak meal over at one of the tables. She downed her apple juice and then jumped up alone on the dance floor to a classic Temptations song that Old School had just started playing . . . "The Way You Do the Things You Do."

On a total spur of the moment thing, Ben had joined her on the dance floor, and at some point Old School blended the Temps down and went right into Chuck Brown's "It Don't Mean a Thing if it Ain't Got that Swing" (the funky go-go remake of the classic Duke Ellington tune). Old school to new school funk . . . Ben and the major didn't miss a beat on the dance floor. The two of them swung across the floor as if they'd been dancing together for years. Theirs was the locally grown DC version of swing dancing known as hand dancing.

In Chicago it was 'stepping.' In Philly, it was 'the bop.' In Dallas, they called it 'swing out.' There was the 'west coast swing' in California and there was the 'shag' in the Carolina's. Of course, Big Apple dancers had to distinguish themselves. They called their version 'the hustle.' Here in DC, it was simply 'hand dancing' i.e., the partner in the male role connected to the one in the female role, and communicating through that hand-to-hand touch . . . more accurately fingertip to fingertip touch . . . about what step or move was coming next. The partner in the female role executed the spins, turns, wraps, crosses, or other moves without any anticipation and totally by feel.

Within the first four to six bars of dancing with a new partner, a skilled male hand dancer should know, totally by feel, whether the partner in the female role had grown up with this dance or learned it more recently in the schools that had revitalized DC's old school art form. And that partner in the male role would dial down the complexity if this new partner needed simple moves, or totally cut loose if the new partner proved to be up to the challenge of double- or triple-spins, spaghetti-styled double-handed turns, whirls, or complicated footwork.

Assholes were guys who wouldn't dial down the complexity when dancing with an inexperienced female . . . or who, unasked and under conditions of social dancing, would launch into an impromptu lesson upon finding a flaw in the gal's technique. Hijackers were gals who didn't care what the lead was from the guy. They wanted to dance their steps and do their own thing regardless. Ben had grown up with this dance, and though he'd never laid eyes on the major before, Ben immediately knew that she'd obviously grown up in this city (probably from Calloway High) . . . and she'd grown up hand dancing.

Everyone in the bar had stopped to watch, and after they had stopped, Homey lumbered onto the dance floor on his new prosthetic left leg.

"Show me some of those moves, Bee Bop," said Homey.

Without hesitating, Ben had transferred the female doctor's hand into that of Homey. She stepped to him with a wide smile, and Old School didn't miss a cue. The Deejay faded the music and came back up with the moderate tempo number by Luther Vandross, "I'm Only Human," very suitable for a beginning dancer. Ben coached Homey, who had already mimicked the six step count he'd seen Ben using. Homey was more than game on his one good leg and one new one.

"One and two, three, four, five and six; between the two and three you can take her to your right/her left by moving your hand by her left ear palm down. She'll do the rest. One and two, three, four, five and six. Good, do it again: one and two, three, four, five and six."

The major smiled at Homey as he executed the turn and she smoothly came back around to face him in step.

"Now you can take her to your left/her right. This time between the two and three you bring her hand up on the other side. Now your palm will be up. She'll do the rest."

"One and two, three, four, five and six—try it now. One and two, three, four, five and six. Do it again Homey. One and two, three, four, five and six."

This time, the major showed Homey how she would maintain the hand connection if he just held his hand the same way as she executed the turn. Now, other soldiers—men and women plus some woman/woman combinations—had joined them on the dance floor and were following Ben's instructions.

Just then, the major's pager went off at her side. She glanced once, turned a silent excuse to Ben, and was out the door in a flash. The two-block sprint back to the Walter Reed front gate probably was covered in world record time as Ben and others came out on the sidewalk to watch. She could already hear the chopper landing on the lawn. Waving her badge, the guards gave her a wide berth and she never broke step as she sprinted across the lawn into the hospital. Three stretchers from the chopper followed her in close succession.

Clapping their hands, Ben and the others came back inside and Davita came out from behind the bar.

Chapter 53
Class

Having witnessed the major's quick exit, Davita took the major's place as Ben's instructional partner. Old School had started back up his music after he'd come back in with the watchers on the side walk. While dancing, Davita said, "I hope those new boys or girls get over here in a few months. That'll mean that Doc did okay tonight."

Ben nodded.

Still dancing. "By the way, tell Addie that somebody beat her score on the machine."

After they'd married, Ben had brought Addie up to Davita's one weekend and introduced her to Davita as one of his oldest and dearest friends. He hadn't told her all of their history, but one of his motives was to let her know one of the places he went at night . . . and that it was innocent fun. Davita was pleased to meet Addie, and Addie in a reserved way, seemed to accept Davita as Ben's platonic friend. Ben didn't know when Addie came here alone to sip her vodka and tonic drinks and play the machines.

Now Ben smiled as he led Davita between the two lines he'd formed with the Major's help. The people dancing the male role were on Ben's left, and those dancing the female role on the right.

"So, we've already done the left stationary turn and the right overhead turn. Now are you ready for something a little trickier?"

"Bring it!" Shouted Molly Moo, the big breasted woman dancing across from her diminutive female partner, known as Little Bits.

Back to Davita, *That'll get her in here before the weekend is over*, thought Ben. Aloud, he asked, "Which game?"

As they demonstrated a more complicated dance move: a left-side pass and tuck turn, Davita continued, "She's not the top player anymore on Wheel of Fortune. Somebody using the tag 'Wizard' posted a 282,250 sometime this week. I wasn't in here then, so I have no idea who Wizard is. It might have been some freckle-faced twenty-one- or twenty-two-year old soldier from Iowa for all I know."

Now counting as he brought Davita forward on his left-side.

"One and two, three" . . . Ben's left hand was raised and suddenly on three was applying pressure to Davita's right hand such that she had to reverse her steps back to her right completing the six-count move in the exact reverse position from where they'd started.

"Now let me see you try it," Ben said to the dozen watchers. "Make sure to count, and leaders make sure that your hand is clear and firm on the three, so your partner doesn't have to guess what you want her to do."

Old School was in total sync with the teaching; lowering the volume when Ben was giving instructions, and then boosting it again without being told once the students started back to practice.

Back in the conversation with Davita, Ben knew that Addie would be bothered by not being top dog on Wheel of Fortune. But that wasn't her favorite.

"What about the Quiz Whiz?"

Davita said, "Nope! Addie (who played under the tag 'Sweet Cheeks') still reigns supreme on that one. What's her score? I think it's over one hundred and thirty thousand. Nobody's even close."

Addie liked to win. She had gotten nothing but As in school. This had always been one of their fundamental differences. As a kid, Ben, probably intimidated by the example of his dad, had never expected to be more than average. But as he had grown into adulthood, Ben came to like to excel, and he was methodical about trying to get better at almost anything he tried: cooking, dancing, sex, bowling, dominos, or anything related to his work or his academics.

But Ben didn't mind people being better than him. In fact, he admired the artistry of excellence, whether it was from him or somebody else. He liked being around the best, but he didn't have to be the best as long as he kept getting better.

On the other hand, Addie was a stone-cold competitor. If she couldn't eventually win, she got mad or lost interest. Things tended to come easier to Addie than they did to Ben. Ben could imagine her coming in here without him, and sitting at the bar working the old

Mega Touch Infinity Multigame Arcade machine that sat on the countertop at the bar. She would probably sit there for hours, sipping Vodka, until Sweet Cheeks had overtaken Wizard on the list of high scores for Wheel of Fortune. Then, before giving up the machine to someone else, she'd probably check the Quiz Whiz to make sure she was still way out in front. But then, when she got back home, she wouldn't mention anything to Ben. Ben would hear the new news from Davita, or would overhear a conversation on the telephone between Addie and Victoria. But Addie and Ben would never talk about it. That was just one of the many quirks of their relationship.

As the dance lesson continued, Ben was suddenly reminded of how smooth Davita had been as a dance partner back in high school. As a matter of fact, Davita had been one of the best dancers at Harrison Tech, where they both went to high school. Ben had been sort of average, but he'd actually gotten better as an adult. For the rest of the night, the impromptu dance class, led by Davita and Ben, took over the joint.

For a few months after that evening, whenever Ben (or Bee Bop as he was called here) came into Davita's, he would be asked by soldiers with two legs, one-leg, or no legs—it didn't matter—to show them some moves. If these soldiers wanted to move on the dance floor, Ben found a way to start an impromptu session so he could teach them something that they could do, and something that made them feel connected and alive. One wheelchair warrior, aka "Baby Carriage" left instructions at the bar; that anytime Ben showed up, to call him over at Walter Reed. He'd come over, and with one hand on a wheel and the other leading his partner, he became one of the smoothest student dancers Ben had had the honor to teach.

Chapter 54
Couples Retreat

June 2005: Ben had thanked Addie profusely after the surprise of the baseball tickets. He brought her some more flowers and set them in a vase on the dining room table, so she'd see them when she came home. He'd done the same thing on the day after he and his dad went to the game on April 14th.

"You're welcome, Benjamin. Did Dad enjoy the game?"

"He couldn't stop smiling. He ducked a couple of times when foul balls came anywhere in our direction. But other than that, he cheered, drank two beers, and ate half the bag of shelled peanuts that I bought. He had a hard time walking, but Penny took us back and forth to the Petworth Metro station so at least that part of the trip wasn't so hard on him. I don't think he'll go again, but it was a good memory for him to have."

"That's nice."

Now Ben asked "I was thinking, A, could we go to a Friday – Saturday couples workshop in Boston the weekend after you get out of school?"

"I think we should get counseling from my pastor. I'd feel more comfortable with a spiritual person. Who's in Boston? Do you have some writing on this workshop?"

"Yes, I'll leave it for you. I think we need some skills. I'm not feeling like I need to be prayed over. I can pray for myself. I'd like us to learn some skills together, A."

"I'll read your literature, Benjamin."

***

After more back-and-forth Addie had agreed, and Ben made the arrangements. School let out for the summer after the third week in June.

Ben thought this workshop would really be good for them. He hoped that the conversational form they would learn would come in handy for helping them work through arguments and misunderstandings.

The instructors' names were Carla and Ron: two Gestalt therapists. The essence of the workshop was a lot of practice with a conversational form based on taking turns: make a statement and keep it short; ask a question . . . a real question . . . not just one designed to set up the next statement you want to make . . . really listen to the answer . . . keep that going . . . keep it going . . . keep it going . . . back-and-forth towards mutual understanding.

At one point on the second day, Addie broke in when she and Ben were in the middle of the fishbowl trying to talk about an incident with a cab driver that had tried to overcharge them the evening before. Ben had wanted Addie out of the cab and back in the hotel so he could focus on the driver. Addie had hung around, concerned that there might be some sort of physical confrontation. The police had come to the scene and resolved the matter in favor of Ben and Addie. But later that night they had words over why Addie wouldn't leave it to Ben to take care of.

Now in this skills practice session, Addie was clearly frustrated with the slow and deliberate pace. She stopped and turned to Carla and Ron as the other couples looked on.

"I can't do this."

Yesterday, the instructors had opened the workshop with introductions and some ice breaking. Then they did a demonstration of their conversational form that was based on intense listening and affirmation, confirmation, and clarification along the way. It was slow and quiet.

Addie had interrupted them, "Does anybody really talk this way?" She had her mouth open and was obviously incredulous.

"Where's the emotion? Where's the passion?"

Ben had silently wondered if Carla and Ron always evoked this kind of response from their couples when they presented the first demonstration of this form.

Carla said, "Yes, we really talk that way. We have to."

Ron picked it up, but Addie tensed imperceptibly as the voice shifted from Carla's to Ron's.

"You see this is precisely when we want to keep the emotion and the passion out. The emotion and the passion were in control up to this point, and if they stay in control, our spiral of upset would just continue. I'm really upset with Carla. The trick is to have a switch or button to push that tones it down so she can receive me and not re-trigger her upset. In brain research language, we want to avoid what's called an 'amygdala battle' where we're both threatened and are being high-jacked by basic survival impulses. When that happens, the rest of the brain just shuts off."

Tag teaming, it was Carla's turn again.

"I'm feeling you, Addie. This must feel painfully slow and unrealistically calm. It's even more deliberate because we're starting and stopping to answer questions. We're not finished. But we want to work the process in the group this morning, and then this afternoon and tomorrow, you couples will each get in the fishbowl and we'll have some intense laboratory practice. We hope, you'll start to see how in decreasing the emotional edge you actually get to some shared understanding. Are you willing Addie, to let this play out?"

"Yes," said Addie.

"What about others? Is this making enough sense so that we can go with our plan?"

The nine couples, including Ben and Addie, all nodded and some verbally said, "Yes."

Carla and Ron finished the morning of teaching and orientation. Then three couples worked the process on the afternoon of the first day. One of these couples kept stalling and getting lost as they tried to use the form, and Ron stopped them.

"Is this real for you two? Or are you role playing?"

They had been going back and forth about sharing the load in housework and cooking. At first they said "yes" and then the wife looked at her husband.

"We agreed to not talk about the money situation and pick something safe. It's not working honey. We don't really have issues about housework."

The husband flushed.

"We won't learn anything by just going through the motions. I'm willing to put things on the table if you are."

The husband acquiesced, and the couple worked for more than an hour at the end of the day, with Carla and Ron coaching, and the other couples observing.

At the end of the day, Carla thanked everyone and said, "So we have six couples to do tomorrow. "We'll shoot for three in the morning and three in the afternoon. Have a good evening."

Ben and Addie had gone down to Faneuil Hall for a great seafood dinner, and it was on the way back to their hotel that the incident with the cab driver occurred.

That next morning was a Saturday. Carla again opened up, "Yesterday, we dealt with a real issue between me and Ronnie to show you the conversational form that we believe can open up lines of communication between you that you might not otherwise have. Let's hear it for the couples that have already gone."

The room erupted with applause.

"Now, who wants to go first today?"

Ben and Addie had looked at each other and kept their hands down.

So did the other five couples who hadn't gone yet. Ron picked it up, "Remember that the trick is to go very slow; so you can breathe. As we're forcing ourselves . . . our bodies . . . to take it slow . . . our minds are following and our voices are lowering. And guess what? You're really hearing what your partner is saying."

All the couples in the room nodded. The room was silent for an extended period. Then, a young engaged couple, who clearly were having second thoughts, volunteered and that got the day started.

Addie and Ben didn't go until the next to last slot in the afternoon. And they were stalled.

Ron and Carla had waited for Addie to breathe and compose herself. Finally, Ron asked, "Addie, what would help at this point?"

Addie was sitting stiff. She was facing Ben, but not looking at him.

Carla, asked, "Are you able to continue, Addie?"

After another long pause, Addie said, "I don't think I can right now. I get caught up in the topic, and I've got more to say that this form allows. When it's my turn, I need to get it out. I was trying to back up my husband last night. I didn't know if that guy had a gun or what."

Ben exploded, "That punk didn't have a gun. But what if he did? What the hell would you have done?" Ben was trying not to sneer. "So maybe he shoots both of us. That's real smart."

Ron interrupted, "Let's stop! Everyone quiet!"

Carla rose and put on some quiet music. Nobody talked.

Finally, after about five minutes, Carla turned down the music, "Ben, Addie says she was trying to back you up. She was trying to support you. Can you receive that?"

Ben didn't believe it. He didn't see Addie as supporting him. He'd felt he could handle the situation and Addie sticking around just distracted him. He actually had felt diminished by Addie sticking around . . . like he couldn't handle things.

"I don't know, Carla. But I'm trying to relax. I really believe in this form and I was into it before Addie stopped us. You're right, I'm triggered right now. I'm upset. Maybe after another couple goes, you can come back to us."

Ben, sitting to Addie's left in the circle of chairs, had been intently staring at Addie during this whole exchange. Addie's focus was straight ahead on the instructors. Now, she sat back but didn't look over to Ben. After nodding and surveying the room to make sure they had maximized this teachable moment, Carla and Ron asked the last couple to go. At the end of the day they came back to Addie and Ben. Ron looked at the two of them, Ben sensed Addie tensing again.

"What about it, Ben and Addie? We'd love it if you give it another try."

Ben had in fact calmed down and was ready to go again. Addie said nothing but looked over. He reached out, and Addie stiffened some more. Ben looked at her silently for a long time. Then to the instructors and the rest of the class, "Hey, guys, I think we're going to pass."

He looked at Addie for a reaction. She said nothing. Finally, Ben turned back to Carla and Ron and said, "Yep! That's it for us. Sorry! But maybe we'll try again when we get back home; maybe not. Thanks for everything."

The flight back to DC was quiet. They retrieved the car at National Airport's fringe parking area and rode back across the 14th Street Bridge.

"Would you like to stop and get something to eat before we go home?" asked Ben.

"No, I'm tired and I have to sing for church in the morning," said Addie.

They arrived back on Elm Street, and the next morning, they awoke in two different worlds.

Chapter 55
The Book

The rest of 2005 was Antarctica in the little house on Elm Street in Washington, DC.

Addie was sound asleep when Ben came in one evening in April 2006, and he had awoken after she had left in the morning. She was a teacher's teacher. Almost always at school at the crack of dawn, Addie was one of those teachers whose students remembered her five, ten, and twenty years later as the best they'd ever had.

He'd been home when she came in last evening.

"Hey, A, how was your day?"

Expressionless, "fine, and yours?" Addie's robotic retort was always the same as she passed by with no eye contact and headed up the stairs.

"Not even, B . . . Now just, fine and yours," Ben called after her, looking up from the bottom of the stairs—he was instantly angry. He went out. Suddenly, he wanted to dance. Specifically he'd thought about doing the bop (the DC bop, not the Philly bop). He wanted to bop nasty. He drove over to the club on Bladensburg Road, but he didn't dance. He ordered a double Irish whiskey with ginger ale on the side. Twenty minutes later, he ordered another. For another hour, he nursed this one.

When a slow record came on, he stared out at the dancers and their various interpretations of the DC Bop. Suddenly, he was thinking about Davita. That made him smile as he immediately knew that if Addie had suspected he was thinking about his old friend, there'd be no fury like her fury. So, in his mind he wallowed in thoughts of holding Davita on the dance floor up at Davita's place.

Once when they were in the thirties, Davita had said to him, "You know, Ben, you can bop respectable, and you can bop nasty.

And if you're in the mood to bop nasty, it's the next best thing to sex. You can do it to good music. You can do it standing up without taking off your clothes. And when the record is over, you're done and you can go back to whatever you were doing."

Later, in their forties, Ben had come into this club, and Davita was on the floor bopping respectable with some dude that Ben didn't know. The next record coming up was also a slow record, and she grabbed Ben's hand and pulled him onto the floor. Davita had proceeded to bop semi-nasty with Ben, all the while running her mouth. It was only after that record was over that Ben turned and saw Dr. Jackson Ferrier watching them.

At the end of the dance, Davita had said, "See you next time you're up at the club, Ben."

Then she walked over to Dr. Ferrier and pulled him onto the floor. She'd proceeded to bop super-nasty with her husband. All through the record, neither one of them said a word to each other.

Ben had watched with amusement.

Tonight, on Bladensburg Road, Ben finished his drink and drove home. He slid into bed but stayed on the very edge of his side; quietly he went to work on himself . . . as per usual lately. He didn't need magazines or porn on TV that night. His mind was full of groping dancers on the floor over on Bladensburg Road. He also thought of Jackson and Davita . . . Ben and Davita . . . Jackson and Davita . . . success!

Awake and sipping on a cup of coffee to get the grog out of his head from last night, Ben's thoughts now were back to Addie, probably already at school and prepping her classroom. A flash from undergrad philosophy started scratching up, just below the surface of Ben's consciousness. *What was it? Who was it? Maybe Fromm,* thought Ben. Something about the idea of falling in love being a myth. Something about love being an art and a thing you had to practice, and that true love was a verb rather than a noun.

He went down into the basement, where he kept most of his books. After about ten minutes of trying to locate the volume, Ben cursed under his breath. He had a vague memory of lending someone Fromm's *The Art of Loving* years ago and never getting it back.

Now at the desk, Ben popped open his laptop hoping for some sort of divine intervention. Opening up the file, he easily found his favorite Book in the Bible. He mouthed as he read from James 1, verses 2–4. In the Living Bible rendition, it read,

"Dear brothers, is your life full of difficulties and temptations? Then be happy, for when the way is rough, your patience has a chance to grow. So let it grow and don't try to squirm out of your problems. For when your patience is finally in full bloom, then you will be ready for anything, strong in character, full and complete."

Shit! he thought to himself. Then he closed up the file and turned off the laptop. Ben thought back to his time with Addie in Boston and teared up. Accurately or not, he'd felt for a long time that he was patiently offering Addie acts of love—monetary support, vacations, flowers, and expressions of interest in her job and feelings—without much expectation of receiving back in kind. The attitude he'd taken was to soldier on; even though her response would predictably be some non-disclosing and terse remark like: "Fine, and yours?" He couldn't see how he was getting stronger for the effort.

Gradually, an understanding was coming to him. It was the understanding that once, he'd made the decision to love Addie through repeated actions. His hope had been that this would eventually overcome whatever demons prevented her from opening up to him. But he now felt that Addie's love was limited to a feeling-based love. Her love was dependent on her feelings. And so her love bounced back and forth based on the feeling of the day . . . or sometimes the feeling of the minute. He sat back and thought again of the James quote: *"When your way is rough, your patience has a chance to grow. So, let it grow and don't try to squirm out of your problems."*

What am I doing? thought Ben. *Addie's not a bad person. Am I trying to squirm out of my problems? Am I trying to find justification for my own views and reasons to blame Addie for our problems?*

Then his mind took him back to Boston. Addie was saying, "Where's the emotion? Where's the passion?"

Ben understood that with Addie, the emotions . . . the feelings were in charge. No discipline, no skill, no art . . . nothing could overcome what Addie felt. He didn't understand why she felt so deeply; and why she was unwilling to either open up or release feelings that got in the way. But he did understand that the workshop had missed the mark. He now understood his own motivations;

which had been to seek some form of skill, discipline, or practice that would provide them a common basis for relearning how to love each other.

And Ben understood that Addie couldn't do it his way . . . and that he couldn't do it her way. Just as Addie was driven by feelings, Ben had trained himself not to be driven by his. He remembered one of his father's aphorisms: "When feelings kick in, the brain shuts down."

Ben remembered himself with Levi, and how he'd stopped attending the more Levi screamed at him. He'd said to Addie once, "You can scream at me, or you can have me hear you; one or the other. But you can't have both. So you choose!"

He remembered her advice about Levi. "Don't try to handle him, B. Just be his friend."

He remembered Levi screaming at him, and him putting Levi out of the car. He couldn't handle it. He needed to get Levi out of his face. He thought of Levi's drinking. He couldn't stand it. He couldn't deal with the addiction that no amount of reasoning could conquer.

Addie has some kind of demon. Ben thought. *But maybe I do, too. When I'm mediating or team building with clients, I'm paid to remain calm while the parties are railing at one another. If I get sucked into the emotionalism, I'm no longer useful to them. When I allow my emotions to come to play with Addie, it's all nice and good until she pivots and lashes out at me; or even worse, when she withdraws completely. Then I get furious. I don't like myself when I'm furious.*

Ben remembered the bad decisions he'd made as a boy out of anger. He remembered standing in the rain on the playground outside his junior high school, waiting to fight Tracy, who'd become his good friend as an adult. Tracy was the biggest, toughest boy in school, and Ben had wanted to fight him over a perceived slight. Davita had pulled him away from standing in the rain on the playground that day. Many years later, he and Tracy had joked about it.

Tracy had said, "By the time you got home that day, I was probably up in somebody's daughter's house, hittin' some pussy."

Tracy didn't know that Ben had tried, that very day, to score with Davita . . . to disastrous results.

Ben remembered other ass-kickings he'd received because of his flash temper.

And then he thought of his mom, and another realization hit him like a ton of bricks. Penny, his sister was so calm and loving with Gillian Parks. His cousin Corinne had been so wonderful in the final days before ClayClay's death. Even Richard Parks, the paragon of wisdom and rationality, was tender and supportive both with his brother, Roderick, and with his dear wife, Gillian. And Ben had retreated for weeks from even going near his parents' house; just because Gillian couldn't pay dominos with him. Her dementia terrified Ben. He relived his own memory lapses over the years— from the chicken coop, to the team building retreat at the J Street Mansion; to forgetting his place in talking on stage with Ted, to the incident with the office chair, the spilt tea, and trying to pay the PFA bills—all of these memories flooded over him, and terrified him.

And now the emotions rolled over Ben Parks to the point where he couldn't hold them back anymore. He sobbed. He went to the bathroom and splashed water on his face. He took deep, deep breaths. Momentarily he calmed and back in the office he called in to Parks Freer Associates (PFA). Amanda, the office manager, answered, "Parks Freer Associates; this is Amanda. May I help you?"

"Good morning, Amanda! I'm not feeling well," said Ben. "Is there anything on the calendar that I absolutely have to do?"

"Oh, Ben, it's the first of the month, and I'm working on the billings. Wait a minute; let me get to the master calendar."

The phone went on hold and then she was back. "I don't see anything. Why don't you take the day off?"

"Deal!" said Ben. "When does Ted get back from Lesotho?"

"He's gone all month, Ben."

"Right! Right!" said Ben. "Well, I'll be at home if you need me. Bye, Amanda."

Ben hung up without hearing Amanda's goodbye. Tears returned to the edge. He went upstairs and brought the single malt Irish whiskey bottle and some ginger ale down to the office. It was a Thursday morning and there'd be a day baseball game at RFK Stadium today on TV starting around 4:00 p.m. The Nationals were also breaking ground on their new stadium, down in Southeast DC, that day. They were hoping to be out of the old Robert Kennedy Stadium the next season. He turned on the TV to the Mid-Atlantic Sports Network station and turned the volume down. The game wouldn't be on for another several hours. He didn't even know who the Nats were playing. It didn't matter. He stared, and poured, and drank, and stared, and poured, and drank that day.

Ben never saw the game that day. He didn't see Jose Guillen and Ryan Zimmerman get the only Nationals hits off Josh Johnson, as Livan Hernandez lost his fourth game of the season, eleven to three to the Florida Marlins.

Chapter 56
Someone Else?

Ben came out of the basement. It was a Saturday morning. He'd been down there for two days. He tried to focus but he couldn't. He'd been thinking about the close-call separation he and Addie had experienced in early 2003. In fact, he'd told Addie that he was leaving. Instantly, she was angry and suspicious. Certainly, his leaving her back at Middle State must have flashed through her mind. She'd cried and screamed, and he'd relented. As he crested the basement steps, he heard her sounds on the second floor. She was home for a weekend, but any minute she might fly out to church or to some fun with Victoria. Ben rushed up the next set of steps to the second floor and burst into the bedroom.

"There was an incident with mom. She can't even count."

Now Addie was looking at him. "When?"

"Oh, I don't know . . . months ago."

"And you're just telling me now?"

"You know my genetics. I feel like I'm . . ."

"Don't put that out there, Benjamin. Don't put out anything like that."

Frustrated, Ben's tempered flared; and he retreated.

With a rising voice Addie said, "I've been spraying Lysol on the first floor for two days to kill the liquor smell coming up from the basement. You're losing it, Benjamin Parks."

Ben stood in the door, taking deep breaths.

"Benjamin, are you seeing someone else?" The accusation in her voice dripped all over Ben's consciousness.

In as calm a voice as he could muster. "No," he replied.

"Is there someone else you want?"

Again, the answer was *no,* Ben thought; and then he said, "I wish there was."

By now, Ben had honestly felt that he and Addie had irreparably drifted apart, and that there were too many frictions that they just never would get past. He wished he could talk about his worst fears. But, more than anything, he just wanted peace . . . even if he had to be alone.

"Ben, you have to be honest with me. If we can't be honest with each other, we really don't have much."

Ben pushed back.

"Addie, you're not being honest right now. You know just as well as I do that you have secrets. There are things I've asked you about your childhood. Something happened to you, but I don't know what. Whatever it is; it's all over our relationship, and I can't do anything about it; because you won't talk to me."

Now it was Addie's turn to retreat.

Continuing with an agitated tone that was starting to creep up in volume, Ben said, "There are money things I've asked you about. Where's the money Addie? You make a decent salary. I know you shop. You're a champion shopper; but what else?"

Now Ben felt himself shaking with anger. "I pay the mortgage. I pay the gas, and the electric, and the water. Okay, you volunteered a couple of years ago to pay the satellite TV bill. I think you did that just because you wanted to be able to look at the bills every month to keep track of how much porn I'm watching. Well, I'm probably watching more than I'd like to watch. But it comes in handy . . . I think you know what I mean."

Addie started to deny. Then she laughed. Her husband, the serious Benjamin Parks, had actually made a joke.

"And last month, I asked you to take over the payment on the Lex. I told you that Ted and I had lost our biggest contract and that the firm would probably need to let some folks go . . . that I'd probably have to cut my own salary."

Despite himself, Ben was starting to speed up with adrenalin.

"That's my deal, Addie. That's my deal. That's my deal!" Ben was in full voice.

Then getting back under control.

"What about you? What else are you doing with your money? Is there a Swiss bank account somewhere that I don't know about? For all the information you give me, you might be keeping a man on the side."

Addie objected vociferously, "You know me, Benjamin Parks. You know that I'm not keeping no man on no side."

"Maybe you are, and maybe you're not."

"Nobody holds me, B. Nobody touches me other than the little six-year-olds I teach."

"And I can say the same, A. But it's your choice. You recoil when I try to touch you. And that pisses me off. So I don't touch you."

He switched back to money.

"I know you think you're better with money; you want to manage what I bring into this household. But, you don't want me in your business. You don't want me to know what you bring in. You say we need to be honest, and I agree. Let's open up the books at the dining room table. Let's look at everything side-by-side. Let's figure out how we can save and do what we need to do together. Addie, you'll never agree to that. You think what's mine is yours and what's yours is yours."

Addie shouted, "Benjamin!"

"Don't Benjamin me. And don't scream at me, Addie."

"I'm not screaming at you, B. I'm raising my voice maybe a little, but that's the passion. I'm not screaming at you!" screamed Addie.

Ben couldn't believe it.

"Look, Addie. I'm just talking to you. Nobody in my life screams at me but you. What's that all about? You know I'm right. You don't want me to know those things, and you keep them to yourself. And if you told me, I might not like what you had to say, and neither of us knows where that would lead."

Addie was relenting. Inwardly she was acknowledging.

Ben said, "Well, there's an old saying, 'if you can't say something good, don't say nothing at all.' I've got skeletons in my closet and secrets just like you do. You want to know if I'm involved with someone else. Even if I were involved with someone else, it wouldn't do either of us any good for you to know it . . . especially if it were a meaningless someone. You say you want us to be honest, and I do, too. But, there's honesty and there's stupidity. I'm stupid sometimes. But I'm not stupid all the time."

Addie knew that there was only so far she could peek into her husband's dark side. And, she knew that she didn't want him peeking into hers. That's where she left it. She walked into the master bathroom and closed the door.

Ben grabbed a set of jeans, underwear, socks, and a Howard Sweatshirt and went to the basement. He turned on the shower, and the hot water was a therapy that was sorely needed. After fifteen minutes, he dried, dressed, and went out of the house for the first time in three days. By now, it was a beautiful Saturday afternoon in the nation's capital.

Chapter 57
Ben's Turn

May 2006: Ben found himself in Rock Creek Park. He parked in Lot 6, which was a short distance on Beach Drive from the right-turn at the base of a steep hill running down from the Carter Baron Theater and Tennis Center. Ben pulled in and walked over to a wood bench. As he sat and watched the bikers going up and down, he thought about his Centurion. Ben hadn't been riding lately.

Why not? he asked himself.

A gaggle of club riders whizzed by, mostly drafting on the leaders. One competitive rider was obviously trying to move up in the peloton. There were maybe thirty in all. Ben's senses were coming back alive. As the bikers vanished from sight, his next rumination was of his life in and around music. Ben sighed as he thought of his love of jazz; his tinkering with various instruments over a life time: from the piano, to the violin, to the double bass, to the electric bass, to the trombone, to percussions, and the harmonica.

Jack-of-many; master of none, he thought.

Returning to his reflections on his distress at unbridled emotions like fear, anger, hate, jealousy, envy, and self-pity, Ben suddenly had the insight that music had always been able to unleash positive feelings in him: his eustress. Music was uplifting to him; and he literally liked all types of music from classical, to Gospel, to R&B, to Reggae, to Blues, to Latin (especially Afro-Cuban), to some Country, some World Music, and some Hip Hop and Rap. That put another idea in his head.

Ben stood and re-crossed from the rustic wooden bench, walked several steps over freshly mowed park grass and a few more steps over the concrete of the parking lot where he'd parked his blue Thunderbird. He pressed the automatic door opener on his key and then popped open the glove box where he retrieved a certain CD by an artist using the handle 'R².'

As he did so, Ben felt a pang of regret about his estrangement from his lifelong friend Levi. The connection here was that R², who was Ben's son Rico, and Levi had continued through it all to share their mutual love and commitment to each other's musical careers. Lately, in addition to his fledgling studio engineering work, Rico was now experimenting behind the microphone as a rap artist.

For a fee, fans were downloading several R² cuts off the internet. The most popular ones were a funky up-tempo cut called 'Having Things' with over thirteen thousand five hundred downloads, and with just over seven thousand downloads, was another cut called 'Tomorrow.' Ben thought of this one as being about hopelessness; but he was drawn to it because of R²'s plaintive sing-song delivery, the funky track; and also Ben's grandson, AR's voice could be heard in duet with Rico on the chorus. For Ben's taste, Rico's music was dark, moody, and too much in the streets. Many experiences in Rico's youth—not the least of which was the gunning down in the streets of his friend Sniff—had made Ben's younger son hard; and Ben knew he only had surface-level insight into their psychological impacts. But now he wanted to hear one lesser R² cut with a hook-line that had come into his head as he sat on the bench. He popped in the CD and pressed the forward button to track seventeen. Immediately came Rico's sing-song rap:

I'm lost, and I'm looking for a way to go, a way to turn, to get out this maze.

The song was of a youngster pulled by competing forces and trying to find his way to something more stable and fulfilling. There was much cursing and street vernacular through the verses but R² always came back to the same repeating chorus line:

I'm lost, and I'm looking for a way to go, a way to turn, to get out this maze.

At the end of this final cut on the CD, Ben pushed the repeat function, and Rico's voice started up again:

I'm lost, and I'm looking for a way to go, a way to turn, to get out this maze.

Just then, Ben's cell phone rang, and he answered on the third ring.

The familiar voice came, "Where are you?"

It was Penelope Parks Tompkins, Ben's sister. "Are you in town?"

"Hi, Sis! Not only am I in town. I'm right down the street from you; in the park. What's up?" answered Ben.

"Can you sit with Mom? Dad needs a break, and I'm trying to go to my kids' houses on the weekends to prep them for my spring recital; rather than having them come here and never knowing what Mom will do."

Penny always had a lot of piano students, but her load had ballooned to nearly thirty this past year with the word getting around that her young teenage students, almost without exception, were being successful in getting into Washington High School for the Arts.

"When do you need me?"

"Can you come now? Dad wants to hear a 1:00 p.m. organ recital at Washington Christian Church. Then I think he wants to be out of the house for a while; probably to do some shopping."

There was nothing like a family responsibility to wipe away Ben's self-pity with his own state.

"I'll be there in ten minutes. See you!"

As Ben punched out of the call, he heard Penny's, "Luv yah!"

Chapter 58
Gibberish

Seven minutes later, Ben pulled to the curb in front of Richard and Gillian's house. Most of the early spring lilac blooms were gone by now, but their sweet scent had been replaced by the visual impact of scores of azaleas that were in full bloom all around. Ben sat in the car for a moment admiring the spectacle. Then he caught sight of his favorite, a dwarf red maple tree that stood on the left front lawn at the top of steps that led up from the driveway. Getting out of the car, he walked up to this terrace area and just stood there admiring the dainty red leaves swaying in the gentle breeze.

The garage door suddenly started opening and Dr. Richard Parks began backing out of the driveway. He slowed and the driver side window came down. "Two out of three wins against the Pirates this week. Not bad, huh?"

Ben smiled. "Right; that's not bad!"

Ben thought to himself, *Even if the Pirates are awful, it's okay to celebrate any win the Nats get.*

He said, "Enjoy the organ, Dad."

"Thanks." Richard Parks backed out and was gone down the street.

"I gotta go, Ben," came Penny's voice standing three steps out of the side door.

"Coming," said Ben as he hurried over. Penny followed him back in, and Ben saw his mom, seated at the round table in the kitchen, staring at the TV. Gillian wore brown house slacks and a blue pull over top. Her thin white hair stuck straight up over her head in no particular style.

"Hey, Mom," said Ben, walking over to kiss her on the forehead.

"Slurousger ger ger ghee ghee; ger ghee," came some sort of answer from Gillian.

"She must be glad to see you 'cause she hasn't been very talkative today," said Penny.

Suddenly, Ben was painfully aware of the load that his dad and sister had been carrying without much help from him. Penny's finely tuned antenna picked something up and she preempted his apology.

"You know, Bro, you're the family entrepreneur. Dad and I know you can't be tied down like us. You have to travel and run your business. Dad's retired, and if I have to cancel a student's lesson one day, I just double them up the next week. We know you'll help whenever you can; just like today," she said as she came over and gave him a big hug.

"Now, what's your time for the rest of the day?"

"Take as much as you want. I don't have anywhere to be."

Penny stopped in her tracks and stared at her brother. An expression of knowing was on her face, but she didn't say anything. Then she nodded and turned to Gillian, saying, "Mama, Ben's going to think I don't take care of you. Look at your hair sticking up all over your head and I just brushed it down thirty minutes ago."

Penny was about to go reach in her bag for a brush when Gillian flared, pointing a bony finger roughly in her daughter's direction.

"Pen, I told you . . . I told you. Pen Pen, I told you . . . told you . . . didn't I . . . didn't I . . . didn't I."

Penny stopped, and she and Ben exchanged amused glances. She said, "Well, Mom, I now realize you're making a new fashion statement, and I guess I'll just leave you alone." Then, turning to Ben, "Bye, bro! Luv yah! She hasn't eaten anything. Try to get her to eat some soup."

And with that, Penny was down in the garage and backing out of the driveway, on to her waiting piano students.

Chapter 59
Mama Sitting

Ben stood in the middle of the kitchen floor for a long while. Gillian was sitting forward on the blonde wooden café chair. Her hands were clasped between her knees, and she just stared at the cooking show that was playing from the TV against the opposite wall. There was a box of Kleenex tissue near Gillian on the round table. Richard Park's laptop computer was sitting on the opposite side from Gillian of the round kitchen table. He'd probably been sitting here with his wife before leaving for the organ concert.

Ben's mom couldn't be left alone because she would walk away and get lost; just like Uncle Roderick. The outside doors at his parents' house were always dead bolt locked because Gillian had been known to turn the thumb lock, go outside, and be down the street in the neighborhood before Richard or Penny knew anything about it.

"Idonknowwhyhow R ger ger ghee," said Gillian, suddenly looking up at Ben.

Ben was surprised by the semblance of words.

"You don't huh, Mom. I don't, either," said Ben smiling and going over to kiss her on the forehead again.

"I have no idea why or how the ger ger ghee happened. Do you think it's some kind of conspiracy?"

Gillian stared at him for a few seconds. Then, she raised her hands and shrugged her shoulders in a resigned expression of not knowing. The next moment she was staring at the TV again.

Thinking what to do next, Ben realized that his dad and sister were very used to carrying on with household routines in the face of having limited interactions with the shell of this woman, who'd been so vibrant in her day. Ben also realized that he was lost as to what to do. Spontaneously he started singing the first thing that popped into his mind. It was that soulful Gospel song that ended with God delivering what was needed in the nick of time.

He barely made it through this first verse before he broke out into violent coughing.

"Argh, argh, argh, argh, argh, argh, argh," There was that damn bronchitis again.

When he recovered, Ben looked up at Gillian. She was staring transfixed at him, with a slight smile on her face.

"Oh, you think I'm funny huh mom?" said Ben. Then, "Argh, argh, argh, argh, argh, argh, argh."

From his mom came another one of those shrugs.

"You see; that's why I stopped singing. I can't get through a whole song without coughing. But I've got something else for you. Just wait here."

Instead of going out the side door where he wouldn't be able to monitor if Gillian followed, Ben went to the front of the house and ran out to his car. Again rummaging through the glove box, he found a C-major harmonica—a Hohner CX-12. Quickly he retreated to the house, and Gillian was still there at the kitchen table.

He reached in his pocket and took two quick puffs of Albuterol. When the effect took hold, he said, "Check this out, Mom."

He noodled up and down the harmonica for a while, and Gillian perked up noticeably. Then he remembered one of her favorites: "His Eye Is on the Sparrow." Ben played and Gillian just stared. The expression was dreamy. Who knows where the melody had taken her? But she seemed to really enjoy it more than just hearing it. Ben was pleased. Then Ben's cell phone rang.

Answering, he heard his sister.

"Did she eat anything?"

"Shit," said Ben before he could stop himself.

Then, "Sorry, Mom! Sorry, Sis, I forgot. I'll get right on it and call you back."

"Don't call me back, Bro, I'm teaching. She either will or she won't. But you looked a little lost when I left, and I just wanted to remind you. Luv yah!"

The phone went dead.

Ben went over and started opening cabinets until he found what he was looking for. There were probably twenty cans of Campbell's Chicken Noodle soup. On the shelf below was the familiar box of Nabisco Saltine Crackers. Lately, whenever he'd seen his mom eat—this was the menu.

"I've got something for you, Mom" said Ben as he popped the tab on the self-opening can and dumped it into a bowl.

He hit the microwave for two minutes, but then stopped it with about fifteen seconds still to go because he didn't want it to be too hot. Now he carried the bowl and a spoon, along with the box of Saltines over to the table and took a seat on the café chair next to her.

"This is your favorite isn't it, Mom?"

"Pen, I'm eatin' now; eatin' now," said Gillian.

Surprised again at the actual words, Ben responded, "I'm Ben, Mom, not Pen. But that's right! You're about to eat your favorite. Can you use the spoon?"

Gillian's nose was running and she reached for a Kleenex tissue from the box that was close by on the table. Then she placed the mucousie tissue on the table. Ben took out another tissue, used it to scoop up hers, and deposited it in the trash across the room. When he returned to the table, Gillian had a spoonful of soup in her hand, but her hand was trembling, and she looked scared. Ben realized that she could feel the heat from the liquid in the spoon.

"Blow on it, Mom."

She looked at him for a moment and then said, "Pen, Pen, slurousger ger ger ghee ghee."

With a look of self-satisfaction, Gillian blew twice on the spoon and then sipped. Ben cracked up.

"Mom, you are hilarious! You are a funny, funny lady. Do you know that?"

Gillian just scooped up another spoonful, blew on it, and took it into her mouth.

"I love you, Mom" was all Ben could say.

Ben sat with his mom at the kitchen table, singing and playing the harmonica until Richard Parks came back in around 4:30 p.m. and ushered his wife into the den to a more comfortable chair.

"RichaPaks!" said Gillian when he walked into the room. "RichaPaks!" Gillian was clapping her hands.

Richard said, "Gillian, my dear. It's so good to see you. You're looking very lovely today. Did you miss me?"

As he kissed her on the check and settled into his favorite seat by the desk and across from his wife, Gillian responded with animation in her eyes, "RichaPaks . . . O, E, I, O, R, O, O!!! R, R, O, I, A, A!!!"

Father and son talked baseball, politics, history, and business that evening. Penny joined them around 8:00 p.m. and after sitting on the couch next to Ben, and asking all the questions expected from a supervising younger sister, she collected Gillian from her leather armchair.

"It's time for bed, Mom."

Startled awake, Gillian stood silently with Penny's help.

"Ooh Pen; Ger, ger, ghee, ghee, ghee," was all she said as she shuffled with her daughter in the choo choo train formation back to the bedroom.

Ben didn't go home to LeDroit Park that evening. Richard and Ben Parks drank Belvedere Vodka together in the den (Richard's with orange juice and Ben's with tomato juice, lime juice, soy sauce, garlic powder, vinegar, ground horseradish, and Texas Pete hot sauce); while Penny sipped on Miller Lights and checked on the sleeping Gillian every twenty or thirty minutes. No more baseball chit chat.

Richard told story after story about the lovely Gillian Stoddard, whom he'd met and instantly fallen in love with in college. He talked about a pale blue gown she'd worn on a date to an ROTC ball, and how all the cadets' eyes were on her all evening. He talked about their travels all over the world, and about Gillian's willingness to go to and see anything . . . about her sense of wonder at places like the Taj Mahal, Great Wall of China, the Pyramids, St. Peter's Basilica in Rome, the Louvre in Paris, the Grand Canyon, and the Serengeti desert.

Penny chimed in with stories from her childhood . . . many of the stories she told, Ben didn't remember. But she told of Gillian Stoddard Parks teaching her daughter and son to cook; making Penny practice the piano for an hour every night; sitting at her treasured Singer sewing machine for hours at a time; and taking care of her and big brother Ben.

At about 2:00 a.m., Ben awoke on the leather couch startled and realized that Richard and Penny had gone back to bed sometime before. He thought of Addie. He wondered if she wondered where he was. He didn't know. And he didn't care. He was with family and he was strangely peaceful for once.

***

On Elm Street in LeDroit Park, Addie Sherrie Parks awoke suddenly about 2:00 a.m. and noticed that her husband wasn't next to her. In the dark, she listened intently, but there were no sounds in the house—not even from the basement where Ben had been holding up for the past few days. For a moment, she wondered where he was. Then, just before falling back asleep, she realized that she didn't care.

***

Thus began a period of Ben becoming more and more engaged with Penny Parks Tompkins and Richard Parks in the care of Gillian Parks. For instance, one day in late May, Gillian had been dropped off at Ben's house in LeDroit Park.

Ben sat on the enclosed porch with his mom as she sipped lemonade from a straw. Richard had needed a few hours of watching help, and Ben had started regularly pulling shifts over at his parents' house.

The fifty-inch Samsung TV on Ben's porch was turned to "The Iron Chef" program. Gillian, who'd been the master of so many wonderful Southern recipes in her heyday, stared, and Ben got up to refresh her lemonade. Suddenly, from the porch, he heard his ninety-one-year-old mom's voice, "E, I, C;" then, "A, C, I;" then: "I, A, G, I, C, E."

There it is again, thought Ben. Then, with sudden trepidation he heard himself in one of his repetitive soliloquies, "Going to beat you . . . going to beat you . . . going to beat you . . . going to beat you . . . " Or, "No Ambien tonight. No Ambien tonight. No Ambien tonight. No Ambien tonight."

The similarity hit Ben hard. He thought, *I still have words and she doesn't. That's the only difference.*

Penny had shared the folding trick with him, so Ben had

prepared about a dozen bandanas and five or six wash cloths—suitably clean and suitably ruffled. He placed them in a basket beside his mom on the side porch and didn't say anything. He opened up his laptop, went to email, and double-digit messages popped up. Only three required an answer, but in the midst of answering one of those he realized that Gillian had taken the bait. She was calmly folding a bandana that Ben wore under his biking helmet. He smiled and went back to his message. Gillian folded for about one hour until she fell asleep. Richard Parks came to retrieve her about 4:00 p.m. that afternoon.

Chapter 60
Confession

At work, Ben and Ted were dealing with laying off a proposal writer and a program coordinator. With the recent loss of a federal contract that had brought in $1.6 million each year, PFA was in serious belt tightening mode. Twenty-six associates who worked on an as-needed basis had been told that there wouldn't be any more work for them through the firm. Though none of them subcontracted exclusively through PFA, for several of them this loss represented more than 50 percent of their income. Ted was back in the country for two weeks before leaving again for Africa. His side of the business was barely affected by the loss of a domestic stream of income, since he worked mostly solo on international projects. But he was good to have in the office for a while, strictly as moral support for Ben and Amanda Joseph, who were making very tough decisions.

Ben's mom was now deteriorating fast. He had started trying to spell Penny and Richard as often as he could; usually at least two or three times per week, for anywhere from several hours to half-a-day. Richard had tried taking Gillian to a senior care program during the day, but after only a few days he realized that it wasn't right for her. Ben's mom had been a tigress at home on her own turf. But at the program, she took a seat in the corner, and when Richard would come back for her in the afternoon, Gillian was seated right where he'd left her five or six hours before. The staff conducted senior aerobics exercises, had board and table games, and there was karaoke anytime someone wanted. TVs were all around, and the seniors could lie down and nap at midday if they wanted.

The first day, Gillian's Depends diaper was soaking when Richard returned, and he fussed with the program staff. They agreed that there'd been a miscommunication and promised to check to see if she needed changing every couple of hours. At least that problem didn't recur. But in the end, Gillian's shyness around strangers prevented her from joining into the activities. Both Penny and Ben tried to prevail on Richard to leave her at the center anyway, just so he could get time during the day to do what he wanted. But he wouldn't hear of it. After the fifth day, Gillian Parks never returned to the senior center.

At home, Ben had reached a point of no return. He had to get it all out to Addie and let the chips fall where they may. He needed her to hear what was going on with him, and he needed her to thaw the icy wall between them. Ben remembered the conversational form they'd tried to learn in the Boston couples' workshop. He'd state the real issue in the form of a short and clear statement . . . then he'd ask a question and listen. He'd been lost as to where to go, but now it was clear what he needed to say to Addie. As a matter of fact, this was the main thought, and he should have gotten to it sooner. This was why he'd been brooding.

It wasn't so much about all the little things between them . . . or not between them. He certainly wished they had more things between them . . . more shared things in their lives together. But they didn't. They had grown so apart in Ben's estimation. He worried about making a comment that would cause Addie to interrupt his flow with some disagreement. That would take them down another side trail that wasn't what he needed to unload. This was about the thing he most feared; his kryptonite. He had to get it on the table and he needed her to hear it and not cut him off.

It was a Wednesday evening in June, and Montgomery County Public Schools would be letting out for summer vacation at the end of the week. Ben came home that day, and Addie was already there; upstairs in the master bed room. Standing at the bottom of the steps, he could hear her on the telephone. She laughed. She talked. She laughed some more. It was one of those rapid-fire talks: reports of the day, explorations of news events, complaints against the system; and brainstorms about what color paint her friend Victoria was going to use in her condo, who did what on the soaps, on, and on, and on.

Ben busied himself on the first floor by frying up some Tilapia, which he ate with buttered rice and some sweet peas. It was delicious, and he left two pieces covered in foil on the stove for

Addie. Meanwhile upstairs, Victoria and Addie passed the forty-five-minute mark and showed no signs of slowing down. Ben knew because they were directly above him and sound traveled in the house. At 7:00 p.m., he went to the porch and turned on the ballgame, but he wanted to speak to Addie. That night his miserable Nats would lose to the Colorado Rockies, fourteen to eight.

After the first hour with Victoria and Addie on the telephone, he'd gone upstairs and appeared at the door as a signal to Addie that he wanted to talk. She was lounged on the big bed with a huge smile on her face when he appeared. Sensing him at the door she'd turned, and instantly her expression was ice.

He'd gone back downstairs to the game, but resolved to check in every fifteen minutes just to remind her that he existed. He'd done this twice, and Addie didn't turn to even look at him these times. Somewhere after the second hour of the marathon telephone call, Addie and Victoria had said goodbye. Addie said, "Luv yah!" and hung up.

Ben thought she might come downstairs to see about him. When she hadn't appeared after about thirty minutes, he went back upstairs. She was in the small study on the computer.

"Sup, B?"

"I . . ." For the moment that was the only word that came out. Falteringly, but with determination he continued, "I'm really afraid of this memory thing."

There, he had said it. He glanced over at Addie. She was actually waiting. She was listening.

"I'm afraid," said Ben, "that I can't remember things, and I'm afraid of what's going to happen. And, it frustrates me that right now as I raise the issue, you won't want to deal with it."

Addie knew she had to listen.

"What do you mean?" asked Addie. Her voice had elevated.

"See!" said Ben. "Even now, you don't want to deal with it."

The Boston conversational form never got a foothold that night. Ben continued, "A, I double-booked myself and had to choose between one client and another at the last minute last week. I'd just forgotten about the first appointment, but the second client's problems were more urgent. The client I didn't choose . . . who really had me booked first . . . is really pissed."

Addie kept her eyes on the computer screen.

"And?" was her only response.

In his mind Ben instantly flared. He thought to himself, *And? And? What the hell is and? Where is the turn away from the computer and look me in the eye? Where's the 'oh B, what are you going to do? Where is all that conversational skill you've been using with Victoria on the telephone? And? That's all I'm going to get?*

He fought back the urge.

"A, what if I'm slipping? What if I'm next in the family to totally lose it all? Uncle Roderick has the same problems as mom . . . different, but the same."

She didn't say anything. Addie shifted her seat. Ben could see her refocus. She nodded for him to continue.

"Maybe you've seen it too. You might even be afraid of it."

Ben was finding his legs in the unfolding narrative.

"You'll say, 'Don't bring that up' . . . or 'don't put that out there. I mean, I think about this every day, and I see my mom going through it. I think about ClayClay and how frail and lost she was at the end. Uncle Roderick is pretty much locked down in the nursing home. I feel like I'll be next. I feel like I need to talk about it. I feel like it's in me. I can see me slipping into being totally needy, and it scares me that you won't want to deal with it. What does that mean for me when it happens?"

That little expression was back on Addie's face. But she didn't counter. She asked, "What do you think it means?"

Inside, Ben shouted. This was the climax. This was the bottom of the fear. This is what he wanted to get out, even as he feared it. Even as he worried that it would infuriate Addie. Even as he worried that it wouldn't infuriate her enough.

"You'll be in charge of me . . . and you won't want to take care of me . . . you might scream at me . . . you might be mean to me, and I'll be helpless."

They stood in silence . . . for a long time.

Finally, with one more turn to see if Addie had anything to say, Ben left her office and went back downstairs. He and Addie were now in open warfare. Later he went back upstairs. Since the last time he was up there, Addie had moved back to the master bedroom, turned on the TV, but she was out cold. He was so jealous of her. She could fall asleep at the bat of an eye. He turned off the TV, slipped the glasses off her nose ever so carefully, turned off her lamp, and went back down to the TV room on the porch. Sportscasters were analyzing the horrible Nats loss in which Jamie Carroll, traded by the Nats General Manager, was the player of the game for the Rockies.

Tired of listening to the autopsy, he scrolled through the channels until he found a porn station. Then he sat back, zipped down his pants, and vigorously, he worked on himself as he stared glassy-eyed at the two women (one black and one Latin) acrobatically servicing the dark brother across a pool table. Ben finished. Then sat back . . . completely disgusted with himself. He wept until he fell asleep.

Chapter 61
Out of the Bedroom

Ben woke up the next morning back downstairs, in the same chair on the porch. Addie was gone to school. Ben walked down to his basement office. Then, he flipped on his computer and quickly found the file he wanted. He stared at the passage:

Proverbs: 10-14: "A wise man holds his tongue. Only a fool blurts out everything he knows; that only leads to sorrow and trouble." Ben's sorrow welled up. Then, quickly he found another:

Proverbs: 18-1 through 2: "The selfish man quarrels against every sound principle of conduct by demanding his own way. A rebel doesn't care about the facts. All he wants to do is yell."

"Oh my God," moaned Ben. Then, after a while, he turned to his favorite book . . . the one wherein he most often found comfort . . . or at least some direction. There, he quickly found the passage. As he read slowly, he sub-vocalized the words:

James 3-5 through 10: "So also the tongue is a small thing, but what enormous damage it can do. A great forest can be set on fire by one tiny spark. And the tongue is a flame of fire. It is full of wickedness, and poisons every part of the body. And the tongue is set on fire by hell itself, and can turn our whole lives into a blazing flame of destruction and disaster. Men have trained, or can train, every kind of animal or bird that lives and every kind of reptile and fish, but no human being can tame the tongue. It is always ready to pour out its deadly poison. Sometimes, it praises our heavenly Father, and sometimes it breaks out into curses against men who are made like God. And so blessing and cursing come pouring out of the same mouth."

Maybe that's it, thought Ben. "When things are this polarized, does it even do any good to talk across the Venus and Mars divide? Is it even worth it? Maybe the more the tongue wags, the worse it gets." He was despondent. He clicked out of the file to the desktop background screen. There, he stared at the picture of Addie sitting at the piano upstairs. He reached out, touched the screen, and closed his eyes. Quite a while later, Ben rose with some small clarity of purpose. He went up to the kitchen and put on a pot of coffee.

Then he moved upstairs to the second floor and silently made up the guest bedroom for himself. He went to the linen closet, took out a set of sheets and pillow cases, and went to the spare bedroom where his clothes closet was. He had long since moved his clothes into this room to dress and undress. This was where he polished his sandals and prepped for work. But tonight and from now on, this would be where he slept.

After making the bed, he went back down to the kitchen, poured out the cup of black coffee, picked up a honey flavored Flax bar, and wolfed them both down. Finally, Ben went back downstairs to the office where he worked for the rest of the day. Addie came home that evening and went straight to the master bedroom. In their occasional passing, neither of them spoke that evening, and they slept alone in separate rooms.

Ben lay awake in the guest bedroom which was to be his new place. Repetitive thoughts rolled around his head: He couldn't turn them off:

Strike three and it's over . . . strike three and it's over . . . strike three and it's over . . . strike three and it's over . . . strike three and it's over . . . strike three and it's over . . . strike three and it's over . . . strike three and it's over . . . strike three and it's over . . . strike three and it's over . . . strike three and it's over . . . strike three and it's over . . . strike three and it's over . . . strike three and it's over . . . strike three and it's over . . . strike three and it's over . . .

And I pray . . . and I pray . . . and I pray . . . and I pray.

"*Strike three and it's over . . . strike three and it's over . . . strike three and it's over . . . strike three and it's over . . .*

And I pray . . . and I pray . . . and I pray . . . and I pray.

Then it was morning and Addie was gone to school.

Chapter 62
Getting Help

Ben sat in one of the medical waiting rooms, and a sense of ultimate doom enveloped him. After a while, Dr. Popovich came in, bubbly and effusive as she usually was.

"Well, hello, Mr. Parks. It's good to see you," she said.

Ben really liked Dr. Popovich, and felt a little relaxation come over him as she smiled and walked directly to the sink to wash her hands.

Ben started in on a few things from previous visits. Doc listened and made notes into the computer . . . she smiled when she realized he's lost six pounds. But then said, "Those aren't the things you really want to talk about . . . are they, Dr. Parks?"

"No," said Ben. He couldn't get started though.

She prompted him, "In your email note, you said you were concerned about your memory. Start there, Mr. Parks."

For some reason, Ben couldn't speak.

"In your note, you referred to repetitive thoughts. I'm not an expert, but maybe we should do a referral to the psychologist. It may be that you're just under stress, but the psychologists should advise you on that. I'll make a referral okay?"

Ben happily agreed.

"The psychologist may also help you with your memory issues. They may be connected. The short version is that we know age and family genetics are factors that influence the tendency toward dementia. We know that people who've had serious head injuries, concussions and the like, can have elevated risk for dementia. We know that blood flow irregularities between your heart and your head can be a dementia risk factor. And now we even have genetics tests that look for something called apolipoprotein or APOE-e4 which may increase the risk of Alzheimer's. This kind of testing might be indicated at some point.

But before we go down the road toward testing and looking for trouble, can we just do something simple? I want to administer a quick memory test. It won't be a big deal. And, it's not terribly scientific. But it will give us a baseline of information and we can track things over time to see if any changes are occurring that might require us to do more serious analysis. Okay?"

A memory test, thought Ben. *Just what I need when I'm already stressed out.* Bravely he said, "Okay by me."

"What month is this?"

"September. September 2006"

"What's the date?"

Ben had to think for a minute and said, "The twelfth." Dr. Popovich smiled and wrote his answer into her notes.

"And what day of the week is this?"

"Monday," said Ben.

Dr. Popovich turned away and started to note his answer.

"No, that's not right," said Ben with some embarrassment. "It's Tuesday."

Dr. Popovich smiled.

"Yes it is," she said. "Now, we're going to get into it a little deeper. Are you ready?"

Ben nodded.

"I'm going to show you some pictures, and I'll want you to tell me what they are. Later, I'll ask you some questions about them, so it's not just about recognition. Okay?"

"Okay," said Ben, and he was immediately relieved to see the first four pictures as the Doc flipped her page.

"That's a chair . . . that's a school bus . . . that's a carton of milk . . . and that's an owl."

"Right," said the doctor as she flipped another page.

"That's a stop light . . . that's a stapler . . . that's a . . . Oh, what do you call those hats . . ."

A little panic started to set in, but then quickly subsided as the name came to him.

"That's a sombrero. And those are sunny-side-up eggs."

Continuing in silence, Dr. Popovich flipped another page. Ben immediately said, "Well, that one is a laptop computer . . . that's a mailbox . . . that's a pair of boxing gloves . . . and that's a snow shovel."

"Last ones," said the doctor flipping her pad once more.

"Okay," said Ben. "That's a rainbow . . . that's slot machine . . . that's a boom box . . . uh, oh a portable radio . . . and that's a trombone."

"All right," said Dr. Popovich. "Now, I'm going to give you about two minutes, and I want you to call out all the ladies' first names that you can."

She paused a minute to let Ben digest the instructions.

"Are you ready?"

Ben felt his anxiety rise a little, but nodded.

"Go!" said the Doctor.

"Mary, Margaret, Maude, Mandy, Myra, Mariah," yelled out Ben in rapid fire.

Then he stopped. He was momentarily stumped. Then he felt sheepish.

What the hell am I doing? he thought. *Women have names that don't just start with M . . . and why the hell did I start with M anyway?* he thought.

"Addie" was the next one that came to him and he smiled at himself. Seeing his wife in his mind's eye; he thought she might like that. But now he was on a role.

"Ann, Andrea, Betty, Barbara, Bonnie, Carla, Corinne, Davita, Donna, Debra, Ethel, Faye, Gillian, Francis, Harriett, Inez, Iris, Joan, Janice, Judy."

He stopped and lifted his left index finger to his lips, thinking. Then he went back in his mind.

"I forgot about "Grace."

Continuing, Ben said "Kristin, Laura, Mandy . . . (briefly he thought 'shoot, I didn't need another M did I?), Nancy, Ophelia, Patty, Penny, Queenie, Rachel."

He stopped again and reflected on the last name. It was one that he really liked, although he didn't think he'd ever known a Rachel. If he'd have had a daughter, he would have liked to call her Rachel.

"Sally, Susan . . ."

Dr. Popovich looked pleased holding up her hand.

"Two minutes! Not bad Mr. Parks" she beamed. "You named about thirty or so. There are people who can name forty-five or fifty in that space of time. But there are others who start out with 'Mary, Susan, and Joan' and then they freeze and can't think of any others. What you did was really pretty good."

"Now," said Dr. Popovich with a sort of devilish gleam in her eye.

Ben squirmed.

"You remember all those pictures."

Oh no, thought Ben, but he remained silent.

"So, there was a bird in those pictures. What kind was it?"

Relieved, Ben said, "An owl."

Damn that felt good, he thought. His spirit picked up, just to be dashed in the next instant.

The doctor asked, "There was a picture of sports equipment. What was that?"

Sports equipment, thought Ben. *I didn't see any sports equipment.*

He ticked things off in his mind: *Baseball bat, glove, tennis racket, football, and basketball hoop . . . horseshoes.* Then he took a deep breath. That relaxed him, and then there it was. "Boxing gloves," he said.

Dr. Popovich smiled. "There was a weather sign."

Ben looked perplexed.

"If you looked outside and saw it, you'd probably smile."

"A rainbow," said Ben.

"What was the piece of furniture?"

"A chair."

"What was the hand tool you'd probably use in your office?"

"A stapler."

"And there was another office related picture . . ."

"The laptop," said Ben cutting her off.

Dr. Popovich smiled and made a check on her list.

"There were two things that made musical sounds," said the doctor.

"The trombone," answered Ben immediately. Then he blanked.

"The other one can play music, but it can play other sounds, too."

Ben had no idea. Dr. Popovich waited.

"It can sit on a table in the house, but the young folks also like to walk around with it on their shoulders . . . you remember, 'Fight the power!'"

Suddenly, the image came back to Ben. He smiled his biggest smile yet at the Doc.

"Dr. P., what do you know about Public Enemy?'

She winked at him and threw up her right fist.

"A boom box," said Ben.

Without pausing further, Doctor Popovich asked, "What was the food picture?"

Ben had been waiting for this one.

"The eggs," said Ben through his smile.

"And what was the vehicle?"

"A school bus," answered Ben.

"Yes, just a couple more Dr. Parks. What was something you'd find in your refrigerator?"

"A carton of milk," said Ben. "And you haven't asked me about the slot machine yet," he joked.

"That was my next question, but I see you're way ahead of me. Now, all you'd need is the article of clothing."

Oh! thought Ben. "There wasn't any article of clothing," he said aloud.

"Yes, there was, Mr. Parks," said Dr. Popovich. You're close to a perfect score. You're not going to let me down right here at the end are . . ."

"The sombrero!" interrupted Ben. "Boo Yah! What a finish!"

Dr. Popovich made a few more checks on her pad and then turned toward Ben Parks.

"That was very nice, Mr. Parks. And in my opinion, at the present time you're not showing signs of early dementia. That's my opinion and I'm pretty sure. The psychologists will be the last word, but that's my educated guess. You're not even close to Alzheimer's at the present time. You have a lot of anxiety . . . understandably so due to your family history . . . but I'm sure you're nowhere close to the kind of dementia you've described with your mom, or aunt, or uncle."

Ben let her voice just wash over him. At that moment, he wasn't sure anyone had ever said anything sweeter to him.

Chapter 63
Two Simple Declarative Statements

Benjamin Parks hadn't realized how down he had become over his largely unspoken fears. But now he knew because a weight had come off. Dr. Popovich hadn't promised that the dreaded disease would never grip him. But he was disabused of his feeling of being in the midst of a long, slow, and certain slippage into an ultimate end that would manifest with symptoms like Aunt ClayClay, Uncle Roderick, and Gillian Parks. Visits with the medical plan's psychologist supported that there was no evidence of early dementia.

And so, with that weight lifted, Ben realized that he was reassessing. The business was first. Ben was sixty-three years old. PFA had lost its major client recently due to the low-ball bid of a competitor. Ted was unaffected, because his business line had its own life abroad. In fact, Ted's remaining involvement with PFA in the last ten years was an occasional collaboration with Ben when the work involved diversity or some large-systems change intervention. Other than that, Ted was mainly involved as a trusted friend and advisor for Ben, who ran the domestic operation.

Ben realized he didn't want to run a domestic operation anymore. He didn't want to be a rain maker for associates to get work; and he didn't want to think about rent, and payrolls, and unemployment compensation, and liability insurance, and business licenses, copy machine maintenance, and all the other administrative matters involved in the business that was PFA. He liked the kind of direct service work that he did with the District Department of Human Services managers, with Adam Fierstein, with Jason Queen, and with Marta Crossman, the Director of the Technology Museum in New York, as well as a list of similar clients. He also had become very fond of the summer seminar on cross-cultural communication that now was running every other summer at Howard University. The realization was that the things that he liked to do didn't require the infrastructure of PFA.

Next, Ben reflected on his marriage to Addie Sherrie Parks.

What am I holding on to? he asked himself.

The thoughts came rushing at him: *After the breakup with Yvette, I just didn't want to fail again.*

Ben had recognized early in their marriage that there were demons holding sway with Addie's emotional life. He didn't know what or who they were . . . whether they were real or imagined . . . but he was certain of their presence. He was certain that Addie's religious fervor was, in part, a shield against these demons. Addie seemed to think that if she prayed enough, and sang enough, and read the Bible enough, that eventually she would be delivered from whatever ghosts followed her. But Ben admitted to himself that all this was conjecture on his part, because Addie had never opened not even the slightest crack to Ben about these parts of her inner being.

And then the blast of insight hit him. "PFA's time has passed. And . . . I want a different life than the life than I'm able to have with Addie."

There: two simple declarative statements. How did that feel? thought Ben.

Amanda, the lone remaining full-time staff person other than Ben, handled many shut down tasks with efficiency and grace. The next few weeks were full of action. The PFA lease was up at the end of the year, and Ben notified the landlords that they would not be renewing. Signs were put up in various office buildings around Dupont Circle, and every day someone came in to look at and buy some piece of office furniture, equipment, or office art.

"Ted, how much do you use the walk-up in Harlem?" asked Ben.

"Once last year for New Years; that was for pleasure. I haven't done work with the United Nations in at least four years, so I don't have much use for it for business. Do you want to sell it?"

"No, I'm thinking about moving in up there."

Ted blinked and asked, "What about Addie?"

"Addie will be on Elm Street. If she doesn't like that, we can sell it and she can get whatever she wants with her half."

"Slow down, cowboy! That's some major decision making there. Don't you want to take a breath and maybe calm down a little?"

"Ted, I feel like I've been too calm and walking in slow motion for years. I think I've felt like there was a certain future that I was marching towards. And that even though I didn't like that future, there wasn't much I could do to change it."

"And now?"

"And now, I don't feel that way anymore. I want to get back into the driver's seat in my life."

There was a long pause between these two friends. Finally, Ted said, "Good for you!"

***

The next evening, Ben went to the master bedroom door and said, "Addie, I'm going to move up to New York."

Reclining on the bed, Addie Parks looked up from her book. Then she smiled. Then she said, "When?"

Chapter 64
Gillian Screams

Yet another year was coming to an end, and the Parks family was preparing for its annual gathering for Thanksgiving. Ben awoke that morning to the task of heading up to the gourmet food store in Bethesda, MD to pick up side dishes. Ben's sister, Penny had prepared a list.

Richard Parks looked terrible. At ninety-three, he was a little frail as it was, but the haggard expression on his face as he waved when Ben came into the parlor that day just before Thanksgiving 2006 stopped Ben in his tracks. Penny came upstairs from the basement and gathered up her things rushing to a music lesson. Seeing Ben's expression, she gave the report, "Dad hasn't had a good night's sleep in weeks. Mama screams, and the doctors don't seem to be able to get the medication right to keep her calm without her being knocked out all the time."

"Oh, it's not that bad," protested Richard.

"What do you mean; it's not that bad, Daddy? I've got two ninety-year old parents, and I don't know which one to worry about the most. Mom's not mom anymore, and you're going to drive yourself into the grave trying to take care of her. I've gotta go. The list is on the kitchen counter, Bro."

Penny grabbed her car keys and flew out of the house in an obvious state of controlled upset.

Equally upset, Richard Parks screamed at her, "Your mother is your mother. She's still here and I'm going to take care of her!"

Suddenly, there was a scream from the back.

"RichPak! RichPak! Oh ma Ger Ghee. Oh ba Ger Ghee. Oh! Oh! Oh! RichPak!"

Richard was grabbing for his cane which had slipped down on the floor. Ben said, "Dad, please sit. I'll go back and see about Mom."

"I need to . . ."

"Maybe you do, Dad, but I'll call you if it's something I don't know how to handle. Please just sit and rest."

The screams came.

"Pen, Pen, PenPak! A, A, A, I, Ger, Ghee, Ghee, Ghee. I told you! I told you! No! No! Noooooooooooooooo!"

By then, Ben was at his mom's bed side. She was in one of the two four-post twin beds in the master bedroom. Richard had given away their queen-sized bed four years ago and replaced it with these two so that he could sleep in the same room with Gillian, yet avoid being injured by her unconscious thrashing in the night. Gillian was sitting up in the bed looking around but obviously not recognizing anything. Her look was one of terror.

Ben spoke softly, "Mom, Mom. Hi Mom. It's Ben, Mom."

"No, no, no I told you!" screamed Ben's mom.

Her arm swung around, and Ben just barely stepped back in time to miss the punch. Now Richard was at the door with a glass of water in his hand. He placed it by the side table and handed Ben a pill and a spoon.

"Mash this up in the water."

"What is it?" asked Ben.

"It's called haloperidol."

"Will it calm her down?"

"Yes, it's an anti-psychotic that the doctors have prescribed for her. It works pretty quickly."

Gillian swung again and caught Ben on the arm. The punch didn't hurt, but it shocked him.

Richard said, "She fights me, and sometimes I can't handle her. Penny handles her better than me sometimes. But she's confused and she gets real strong sometimes."

Ben was in data-overload. "Anti-psychotic!" He heard the word and recoiled. *Mom isn't psychotic,* he thought.

"The pill, Ben" said Richard in an agitated voice.

Richard was standing back from the bed. It dawned on Ben that he'd probably been punched many times. Emotions rolled in on him in waves.

"RichPak you don't golla golla, fer, ger, fer, ger, ferghee."

His trance broken, Ben used the spoon in the glass to mash the pill until he could stir the dust through the lukewarm water.

"Here, add some sugar to mask the taste. Then use this straw. Even when she's agitated, she'll suck if she feels the straw."

With the glass on the side table, Ben used both hands to take his mom by the shoulder and used pressure to get her to lie back on the two pillows at the head of the bed. She resisted for a while.

"No, no, no, I told you, I told you Pen, Pen, Pen, Pen. No, no, no, I told you, I told you Pen, Pen, Pen, Pen. RichPak, Pen, RichPak, Pen, Ger, J, A, J, A, J, Ooooh, Aaaaah, Aaaaah, Aaaaah, Aaaaah."

From about five steps away was Richard.

"Gillian, my dear. My dear Gillian. Relax, Gillian. Please relax."

Eventually, she was spent and let Ben ease her back. Then he got the glass and moved the straw to her lips. Instantly she began to suck. As she sucked, she looked around the room, and then her eyes stopped moving so fast. Then she smiled a little smile. She nodded.

"Pen, Pen."

And her eyes closed.

Ben left his dad sitting on a wooden chair by the side of Gillian's bed. Ben looked back as Richard dabbed her forehead with a cool wet towel and spoke soft words at her. Ben didn't hear . . . or maybe didn't try to hear the words.

He found Penny's list on the kitchen counter. Rolls, gravy, dressing, cranberry sauce, squash, sweet potato pie, blueberry pie, apple cider, and the raspberry tasting Belgian beer that they had become fond of drinking together for the holidays.

Ben went about the day's chores in a daze. He thought about checking in at the office, but Amanda Joseph, the last staff person had already left with as generous of a severance package and Ben and Ted could manage. Ben knew he was procrastinating and eventually would have to go home. He didn't feel like going to Davita's.

Ben spent that night on Elm Street in the basement office. After storing all the goods from his shopping trip in the extra refrigerator, he sat behind the desk. He didn't work. He listened to jazz music and stared. About 1:00 a.m., he went up to the guest bedroom and fell asleep immediately.

Chapter 65
Beginning of the End

Gillian Stoddard Parks had to be taken to the hospital with severe congestion problems. Richard had ridden in the ambulance with her, and Penny had relieved the exhausted Richard at the hospital around noon that day. Richard had been up with Gillian that entire night at home, and when Penny came to the hospital, he caught a cab home and slept for the rest of the day.

Gillian had suffered from asthma for many decades; the onset of Alzheimer's disease in recent years had made it more difficult for her to self-monitor and control her symptoms.

Ben was conducting a team building session for a new high tech firm client out in Reston, Virginia that day. He got a text from his sister:

"Mom in the hospital . . . I'm sitting . . . cancelled lessons for today . . . Dad's home sleeping . . . Check in after your session."

When Ben called Penny's cell phone around 5:00 p.m., she didn't waste time.

"Can you come now? I need to go home and check on Dad."

Ben, back from Reston, had just walked into the Elm Street house and was locking his door to walk around to Howard Hospital when Penny's call came on his cell.

"Be there in less than ten minutes."

"Okay, I'm leaving now then bro," said Penny. "She's sleeping as usual, but her breathing has been rough off and on the whole time I've been here."

When Ben walked into the ward at the Howard University Hospital, he immediately noticed a gaggle of staff at Gillian's private room door. With apprehension he approached the room and looked over to see his mom in an extreme state of labored breathing. Two nurses were on either side holding her relatively still so that a third nurse could apply the suctioning tube—first to one nostril and then to the next . . . and then back again.

When Ben tried to move through the onlookers, an attendant stopped him, saying, "You'll need to put on a gown and gloves before you go in, Dr. Parks."

Ben was at first irritated at the holdup but then thought of stories about the prevalence of MRSA infection in hospitals. He quickly put his jacket on a hook and donned the appropriate covering.

As Ben took up a position on the left side of Gillian's bed, the nurse on the other side was bringing out another tube of suctioned mucous and depositing it in a tray. Gillian's heaving was beginning to subside as her nasal passages became clearer, and her breathing brought precious air into her lungs. The nurse covered her nose and mouth with a respirator and turned up the oxygen flow. Ben stroked his mom's forehead and she gradually relaxed. But she didn't open her eyes.

The crisis averted, Ben called Penny, "Hey, Sis!"

"How's mom's breathing?"

"When I came in, they were suctioning her. She was laboring really bad."

After a pause, Penny said, "Hey, Ben, you know the combination of mom's asthma and Alzheimer's isn't good."

"What are you saying?"

"I just got off the phone with Jeralyn in Phoenix. She described a pattern with Alzheimer's patients that looks an awful lot like what's happening with Mom."

"What's the pattern?"

"Where are you now, Ben?"

"I'm in the hallway outside Mom's room."

"Why don't you take your time and say goodbye to Mom tonight? But don't stay too long. She probably won't be conscious tonight. Then come over before you go home."

Ben started to buck at the treatment from his kid sister. He breathed a deep breath.

"Ben, just come over after you leave the hospital. Mom is in good care."

Chapter 66
Family Meeting

Penny had been busy. When Ben pulled in front of his parents' house around 9:00 p.m. that evening, the street was full of familiar local cars and cars from out of town.

But Thanksgiving isn't until tomorrow. Strange all these folks are here the day before, thought Ben.

He walked up the steps and started around to the side. Jernelle, Penny's daughter from Pittsburg opened the front door.

"Come this way, Uncle Ben!"

"Pop!" came a shout from the street.

Ben's sons, Tony and Rico, were pulling up in Tony's Prius and parking. They rushed up beside their dad, and the three went in together. Jernelle hugged both her cousins. She had tears in her eyes. The living room was full of people.

Jermaine Jr., Jerome, Tony, and Rico were man-hugging and pounding each other.

"Is that Ben?" came Penny's voice from upstairs.

"Yes, he's here, Mom," answered Jernelle.

Suddenly, Ben had another flash, "Where are all the kids?"

Jernelle answered, "Downstairs in the home theater. They're having a movie marathon. Aunt Ralphine and Jerrie are in charge."

Simultaneously, Penny came padding down the stairs, and Richard Parks, Cousin Corinne, and Aunt Nellie came in from the kitchen. Younger family members sprang to their feet to relinquish their seats. Penny was carrying a long corded telephone. She brought it to the middle of the room and hit the speaker button.

"Can you hear me Sweetie," she said toward the phone.

The voice was the missing daughter: Jeralyn, the medical doctor in Phoenix—with child again in the last weeks before delivery.

"Yeah, Mom! Hi everybody! Sorry I couldn't travel to be with y'all this year. Is Grandpa in the room?"

"Hello, Jeralyn," responded Richard Parks from his seat on one of the large couches. When is that baby due?"

"December second, Grandpa."

Penny spoke up, "Jeralyn, we'll catch up with you and talk more tomorrow. Right now you need to say some of the things you've been saying me today. Everyone I could find is here. We all will hear it together."

There was instant silence on the telephone and in the room; Ben found his heart pounding. Slowly his niece began, "Wow! Where to start?"

"Take your time," said Richard Parks.

"Dementia progresses differently with different patients. Alzheimer's is one of the more serious forms of dementia, and post-diagnosis patients live sometimes one or two years and sometimes seven or eight years or more. Eventually, though Alzheimer's is usually the underlying cause for their passing, there's often some immediate cause, such as stroke or pneumonia."

Jeralyn had a large commanding voice, and even halfway across the country, she had the house in Carter Baron, DC mortified and mesmerized.

"Grandma's problem is that, way before her dementia began, she's suffered from chronic asthma. That condition exacerbates the dementia or the dementia exacerbates the asthma—it's really hard to know which. But it's not surprising that the two together are causing grandma to progress more rapidly than usual into late-stage."

"Jeralyn, don't prolong it," said Penny.

"Mom!" said her flustered daughter.

"Go on, Jeralyn," said Penny.

The assembled Parks clan could hear their kin breathing deeply on the telephone speaker. Then: "Given what Mom and Grandpa have said on three or four phone calls today, there's a strong chance that grandma will not regain consciousness."

Aunt Nellie let out a wail and Cousin Corinne reached out to hold her as she began to sob.

"I'm not trying to lay out a time table, but grandpa thought you all should know what to expect going forward."

"That's right, my dear. Go on," said Richard Parks.

More audible breaths from the speaker phone . . .

"I don't know how long they'll keep grandma at Howard. The likelihood is, after they've stabilized the asthma and respiratory problems, they'll want to discharge her. Assuming that I'm correct and she doesn't regain consciousness, I recommend that she goes from the hospital into hospice rather than coming home."

Nobody spoke. Softly Jeralyn asked, "Did you hear that?"

Ben spoke up, "Yeah, baby, we heard you. Continue please, Doctor."

"She won't be able to feed herself and will require a kind of care that you all just can't give her at home. And here's the hard part: she'll need a tube for feeding probably for whatever the rest of her time is. The feeding tube won't help her regain consciousness. It won't prevent recurrence of respiratory problems. It won't even put weight back on her. It will just maintain her for as long as you decide to maintain her. That's all it will do. If I'm right, there will be no quality of life."

Practically every eye in the room was wet. There was an eruption of laughter that came up from the kids in the basement. Jerome rushed to the top of the steps and said, "Shhhh! Please keep it down."

Penny and Richard Parks were the only composed people in the room. After a bit, Penny said, "Thank you, Daughter. I love you so much. Thank you. I'm going to hang up now and we'll call you tomorrow for Thanksgiving. Bye!"

"Bye, Mom and everybody. I'm sorry!" came the voice on the phone as Penny picked up the receiver and placed it gently back into the cradle.

Chapter 67
Closure

As the funeral director and her assistant solemnly folded the cloths and began to crank the bronze casket lid slowly down, Ben sitting on the front row of the sanctuary next to Penny and Richard, was the only one of the three to break. He'd seen Penny tear up briefly a few times in those weeks before Christmas 2006. He hadn't seen his father cry even once.

But for Ben, the loss was nearly unbearable. The confluence of events in his life at this time, the breakup with Addie coinciding with Gillian Parks' death, brought emotions that shook him to his core. Later he would hear, from Penny, of Richard sobbing in the privacy of his bedroom at night. Penny was truly the family rock and had already assumed the role of family matriarch-in-waiting . . . in deference to Aunt Nellie as the most senior remaining woman of the family.

Now Penny was moving to the altar to speak on behalf of the family. Perhaps two hundred and fifty people sat in anticipation. Ben looked up in admiration for his sister. She unfolded her notes and began with a clear and resolute voice. "Memories of Mom—dancing in the kitchen, mixing spoon in one hand, pot holder in the other. Singing while she cooked. Singing while she ironed. Fresh white sheets on the bed every Monday and Thursday nights. What a life my momma lived for ninety-one years. But her longevity is not just measured on time living. My father, Richard Parks, called my mama wife for over sixty-five years. Who accomplishes that these days? Not many, that's for sure."

"My aunt Nellie knew her as sister for eighty-plus years. Wow!"

"Mama had a number of roles in our family. In addition to being wife, mother, grandmother, great grandmother, homemaker, disciplinarian, comforter, and inspirer—after so many of her generation went to God—she remained steady as our family griot. You could ask Gillian Parks about anybody in the Stoddard or Parks family, and she'd just start telling stories."

"Gillian was actually shy around strangers. But get her inside the walls of her own home or in familiar settings such as her church, and she could be in charge . . . or lead from the pack in a sweet, steady, understanding, firm, and principled way that never quite lost that little tinge of Selma, Alabama. Selma was the city that the media made infamous during the civil rights movement, but was also the city that, to mama and our family, was the tap root for us all."

"Just a few short stories, and then I'll sit down.

"I don't know if it's a lost art, but I don't see people pinching anymore. Mama could pinch. Just grab your skin somewhere, maybe on your wrist, with your thumb and forefinger and squeeze a little. Mama could bring you to your knees with a pinch. But the beauty of a pinch is that it's a stealth form of punishment. Sitting one person away on a pew in Tabernacle Baptist Church in Selma, Alabama, a parishioner would never know that Gillian was keeping her fidgety daughter in check so she didn't disrupt the service.

"The second story happened on a gray and rainy day when Ben and I were little. Dad had left for work. Mom was making pancakes, and she made up a game. One of us would tap out the rhythm of a song on the table, and the other two had to guess the song. Ben vividly remembers us sitting around in our pj's (which was a rare thing), eating pancakes, tapping out, and guessing songs and laughing all morning.

"There are a bunch of stories to pick from. I don't remember this one, but Ben told it to me. It's about Mom walking probably fifteen blocks down to Polk Junior high to find a particular crossing guard who had stopped her son walking without being able to get his coat over his arm because he'd broken his collar bone in gym class. The school folks had released Ben to walk home in the snow and cold with his coat draped loosely over his back. Ah, the gratitude of a mother at the guard . . . and the anger at the school."

"But let me tell mine. I had to recite my multiplication tables every morning while Mom combed my hair getting me ready for school. As a fourth grader, I had multiplication tests on Fridays. We had to write down all of our tables inside of four minutes, and grades were based on how quickly they finished. I always did well.

"I've said mom was shy, but this final story conveys the Lioness that was Gillian Parks. Ben had come home from college after graduating in 1967. In 1968, all heck broke loose in the cities and on the campuses. Ben had not yet been drafted and was living a cool bachelor life with an apartment at the Rhode Island Plaza. And then the students at Howard University took over the administration building in a protest that made all the local news."

"Well, Ben's phone rang, and all mama said was 'go see about your cousin!' Corinne, was maybe a freshman or sophomore at Howard, and the Lioness of the family was in protect mode for her sister's baby girl. So, Ben went up to Howard, walked through all the agitated students standing on guard in the A building, and eventually found Corinne sitting on the floor amongst a group of her fellow students. They talked for a couple of minutes, and my brother's assessment was that Corinne and her friends were having just a grand old time. So, Ben said 'cool!' And he went back to the Rhode Island Plaza.

"Well, Ben tells me that the phone was ringing when he came into the apartment, and Gillian Stoddard Parks asked, 'Do you have Corinne?'"

Ben said, 'No, Mom, she's cool.'

"What do you mean, she's cool. I told you to go get your cousin."

Ben says the phone went "Click!"

"Well, Corinne can tell the rest of the story better than me, but just imagine little five foot, three inch Gillian Parks parting the waters of students, collecting the protesting Corinne, and marching her back out of the A building so she could call her sister and say, it's taken care of. That was Mama. Shy little Gillian could be fierce if she thought anybody or anything was threatening her family.

"Mama taught so much wisdom in so many memorable ways . . . here's a final Gillian Parks take-away. Mama said, 'Watch what you get angry over, because you can't fight about everything. Only fight about important things. Otherwise, hold your peace. And even if you get angry and argue, forgive quickly.' That was my mama; my dad's wife; my brother's mom; my Aunt Nellie's sister; the griot of our family now looking down on us from heaven: Gillian Stoddard Parks."

Penny returned to the front pew amid applause and amens. Ben squeezed his sisters left arm and said, "Thank you!"

After a brief eulogy, Jerome, Jermaine, Tony, Rico, and two Church Deacons assembled at the casket, and these pall bearers began the solemn march down the center isle with the casket of Gillian Parks. Richard Parks had said there would be a surprise. As the onlookers observed the moving of the casket, Levi Chance slipped behind the piano from an unseen hiding place in the back and struck some oddly familiar chords. Suddenly, he began to sing, and the sad scene was immediately transformed to wonder. The song he sang, secretly chosen by Richard Parks, was familiar to a few older folks who were fans of Guy Lombard, Bob Dylan, Louis Armstrong, or Nancy Wilson. But the words and Levi's soulful delivery were unbelievably beautiful. It was that ballad about the Angel that had left heaven. The obvious inference was that Gillian Parks had been one of God's Angels that was now home in heaven after a ninety-one year absence. Ben was totally caught off guard; and then a big smile came over his face as he thought about his dad, Richard, picking this particular tune and tasking Levi with winding up the service this way.

Ben rushed forward to his friend Levi. They embraced. Closure!

Epilogue
The End Is Not Yet at Hand

January 2007: Ben Parks walked up the steps in the brownstone condominium on Hamilton Terrace. As he approached the second landing, the door opened, and he prepared to greet Beverly, the ballerina dancer. Instead, a young girl in corn rows with a bat and ball came running past him giggling and vanished out the front door. He stood on the landing as a black man with an attaché case rushed after his daughter.

"Wait, Aisha! I told you not to run on the steps."

"Hurry up, Daddy, we'll be late," said the girl, poking her head back inside.

Passing Ben with his two rather large bags, the man asked, "Do you need help, sir?"

"No, you need to catch your daughter. I'm your neighbor upstairs. But we'll have time to meet. Enjoy your day!"

***

Peace!

June 2007: Ben's cell phone rang as he was about to put a forkful of fluffy pancake in his mouth. He was at Amy Ruth's on 116th off Malcolm X Boulevard in Harlem. Ben didn't cook a whole lot anymore, especially since the move to New York. At least one meal per day was always out of the house, and Amy Ruth's was great for any meal, but especially for breakfast because the cook knew how not to mash down the pancakes with his spatula. So they were just as light and fluffy as the ones that Ben used to fix back in DC when he was doing Saturday breakfast for his boys and all the neighborhood kids who showed up.

"This is Ben."

"Hey, Cuz! It's Corinne."

Ben's real estate broker cousin was closer than ever to Ben's sister, Penny now.

"Hey, this is a surprise. How you doing? What's up?"

"Penny tells me you're teaching that seminar again this summer at Howard. That's going to be hard to do from up there isn't it Benjamin."

"Naw, Cuz! I commuted up here when I lived in DC. This is just the reverse."

"Where will you stay when you're down here? You won't want to be cooped up with Uncle Richard and Penny will you?"

Ben started to get suspicious. "What's up, Corinne?"

"Well, someone asked me to find a nice condo in the U Street area, and I found just the one. As a matter of fact, this person put down 30 percent in your name. That was a really big check. It's just one block off U Street, N.W. You like that area don't you?"

"Yes I like that area. But I live in New York now. What the hell are you talking about? And nobody puts up that kind of money as a surprise . . . or a joke. This isn't funny, Corinne."

"Well, I'm not allowed to say who. But, if you get down here on Friday, you can see it and move in. That's the day before your seminar starts, right?"

"Right."

"See you then, Cuz. I love you!" The telephone line went dead.

END

CPSIA information can be obtained at www.ICGtesting.com
Printed in the USA
LVOW12s1128221213

366430LV00001B/327/P